Malas

Malas

Marcela Fuentes

VIKING

VIKING
An imprint of Penguin Random House LLC
penguinrandomhouse.com

LIBRARY OF CONGRESS CATALOGING-IN-PUBLICATION DATA
Names: Fuentes, Marcela (Fiction writer), author.
Title: Malas : a novel / Marcela Fuentes.
Description: New York : Viking, 2024. |
Identifiers: LCCN 2023029868 | ISBN 9780593655788 (hardcover) |
ISBN 9780593655795 (ebook)
Subjects: LCGFT: Novels.
Classification: LCC PS3606.U38 M35 2023 | DDC 813/.6—dc23/eng/20231003
LC record available at https://lccn.loc.gov/2023029868

Printed in the United States of America
1st Printing

Set in Adobe Jenson Pro
Designed by Cassandra Garruzzo Mueller

For Roberto and Lety
and
For my grandmothers

Malas

el paso de la muerte

A fter children, you can never be whole again. Después de dar a luz, your body comes back incomplete. You're alone inside yourself, like you never were before your man took you, made you a mother.

Once there was a girl, just fifteen. A girl at a charreada, a rodeo in another place and time. A girl standing on a metal staircase, a glass of lemonade sweating in her hand. She lost her heart to a young charro. Oh, he made the dust fly for her.

Invisible girl, snatching at her father's affection. She was a quince, but a secret, pecadillo de Papá, her birthday this clandestine weekend away. *You know you're my favorite,* Papá said, bought her a slew of pretty dresses, a dawn mariachi serenade, tickets for the two of them to the charreada. Let her wander among the vendors and peddlers in the stockyard, said, *Buy anything you want.*

La quince was buying the lemonade when the charro crossed her path.

The charro was not like her papá. Not of the landed class. Young and swarthy, he was a horseman, a vaquero, born and raised on the range, campfires in his blood, his whole life the lariat and saddle, wind and open sky. He wore no charro short jacket, just a white shirt with modest stitching. His leather chaps were oiled but scarred. He was bareheaded and the afternoon light made his black hair glow.

She felt him beside her, quiet as the warm sun. He wanted her to look at him. She kept her eyes down; she was a good girl. When the vendor turned away to make change, the charro leaned in and whispered, "The next suerte is for you."

La quince pulled away, but he was gone, already weaving his way through the crowd.

She stopped at the top of the staircase on her way back to her seat. There was the charro, standing in the arena, the reins of an unsaddled bay in his hand. She could not see his face beneath his sombrero, only the brief glint of his teeth. She didn't smile back. She was a good girl. But she stayed. She watched. His ride was for her.

The charro held up his hand, three fingers spread, at the spectators in the grandstand, at the other competitors sitting on the chutes. Three broncs charged through the stock gate, into the arena.

The young charro sprang onto his horse from the ground. It was a light movement, as though someone had tossed him up. His thighs against the horse's hide were lean and hard. The girl stood, rooted to the landing, the glass of lemonade cold in her hand.

He pulled his mount alongside the broncs, setting his horse at pace with the lead mare. The other charros drove the animals hard, round and round the arena, lifting thunderheads of dust. Hooves rumbled against the earth, riatas hissed, the charros called low and fierce, driving them faster. The young charro rode past, one leg cocked beneath him, ready to spring.

2

She felt the rush of air as he galloped by. His horse's harsh breath flecked the hem of her new dress with spittle. Her heart flew away quick as quick, a golondrina startled from its nest, never to return.

The young charro leaped bare back to bare back, body half-curled, shadowy in the dusty air. And then he was across, fists full of sorrel mane, fighting to keep his seat as the wild horse twisted beneath him. His sombrero tumbled off, swept away beneath the onslaught of hooves. He rode the bronco the circuit twice through.

His teammates lifted their voices in triumphant gritos—"A-ha-haaaaayyy! José Alfredo!"

He was a proud one. But she was prouder. Didn't they see what he'd done for her? Didn't they know?

Looking for that girl is like looking backward through a telescope. She's far away and so tiny I can cover her with the tip of my finger, like blotting out the sun. I can still feel her radiating. But I don't know where she has gone.

Chapter One

----- ◇ -----

A Happy Time

PILAR AGUIRRE, 1951

Swollen feet, Pilar decided as she set hers into the bucket of cool water, were the most ridiculous indignity of pregnancy. Worse than acid reflux or the spasmodic belly twitches of a baby hiccuping in the womb. Worse than a flare of acne or even sudden flatulence attacks, which at least she could repress through sheer force of will. Fat feet and fat ankles. They were the worst.

La de la mala suerte siempre soy yo, she thought. Of course this would happen now. José Alfredo had invited her to the quinceañera of Dulce Ramirez. He was not given to socializing and the girl was not a relation. As such, the invitation was a great concession. An overture, really. He had asked Pilar as a peace offering after months of her unspoken grievances. That suited her very well. Everyone in the Caimanes neighborhood would see that, though Pilar was eight months pregnant with their second child, her husband yet treated her as a lover.

Only, the quince was the third Saturday in August. Pilar woke the morning of the dance with feet gone puffy as fresh biscuits.

Now, she sat on the front steps of her comadre Romi Muñoz's house, pouring Epsom salt into the bucket while her five-year-old son Joselito zinged pecans into the street. Half the neighborhood was probably watching her, but what could she do? Romi was cooking beans for the evening festivities, so the house was like a sauna.

"Leave them in for at least thirty minutes," Romi said from behind the kitchen screen door. "If it doesn't work, I'll lend you a pair of mine."

"All right," Pilar agreed, a little queasy from the heavy pork fat scent of the simmering beans. "But get out of the kitchen or I'll have to do your hair all over again."

"Ya mero." Romi disappeared into the kitchen again.

Pilar rolled her eyes. It wouldn't be a minute, she knew. She'd arranged Romi's hair in pin curls, carefully wrapped the hairdo in a kerchief, but it would be flat by the time the party started. Romi, so clever at organizing and problem-solving, siempre era descuidada about her appearance. Romi simply didn't care about how she looked. True, she was forty-seven, two decades older than Pilar. Maybe you stopped caring in middle age. Maybe it happened along with a thickening waist and canas. Still, Pilar couldn't imagine not caring about her looks at *any* age.

Pilar flexed her toes in the water, willing them back to normal size. Romi's shoes were likely serviceable rather than elegant, but what else was there? None of Pilar's own shoes fit, except her battered old guaraches. The idea of wearing them to the dance appalled her. She'd put together a smart outfit for tonight: a dark blouse patterned with tiny yellow daisies and an oversized gold collar bow. A pair of trim black cotton trousers. She'd sewn an elastic panel into the waist just for this party. She'd wear her hair loose, parted in the middle, with rosette curls at each side of her forehead, just like María Félix.

Joselito darted her way, plunging a handful of pecans between her puffy feet. Water splashed them both in the face. He chortled, hair plastered to his forehead, a damp stain across the front of his shirt like a bib.

"No, no, mijo," she scolded, but without conviction. Her head was tender in the oppressive heat, and her own voice sharpened the pain. Joselito grabbed a fold of her cotton dress and punched the water again.

"Joselito," she murmured, trying to pull his fingers loose. "Be good for Mami."

She should stay home tonight. She was that tired already. Why would anyone want to have a celebration in the full zenith of la canícula, the scorched-earth misery of the hottest weeks of the year? Every day so wretched that the neighborhood dogs crept beneath houses to pant out their misery. The sky so eye-wateringly brilliant it wasn't even blue, but a fierce yellow white. No, she must go or José Alfredo would not invite her again. He would say, *I asked. You said no.*

Hay que contentarme, she thought, though she was far from contented. She grabbed at Joselito's wrists, trying to push him away. Joselito didn't budge. He knew she could not defeat him. He was quick and she was so slow, so heavy. So hot.

It was to be an outdoor gathering, but the night would not make it bearable. After sundown the ground emitted its collected heat, so that it clung to the air, even at midnight. There was no relief.

If it had only been the heat, she could have told José Alfredo. He would have, well, not understood—what man could understand pregnancy?—but he would have sympathized with her, sympathized precisely because it was some feminine mystery beyond him. And, because her suffering was a compliment for himself. After all, she bore this discomfort because of him. Yes, she thought, he was proud of it. Probably proud of her, her love for him, bearing these things for his sake.

Yes, he would have been sympathetic. He would have. Except that José Alfredo had bought a house on Loma Negra, the hill at the end of Romi's street. Pilar hated the house.

The new house, Pilar's silently blooming resentment. She missed the apartment they had rented in Barrio Caimanes. It was small, but clean and well maintained by their landlords, Chuy and Romi Muñoz. She had liked that it was set behind the Muñoz home, away from the street. She had liked living near Romi.

When she'd told José Alfredo about the new baby, he said he was tired of renting. The family was growing. They must have their own home. A few weeks later, he purchased a small house on a parcel of uncultivated land at the edge of the neighborhood. Loma Negra was a very low hill, a knoll really, overlooking Barrio Caimanes. Pilar herself had been enthusiastic, until she saw the house.

There was no way around the fact that their new home was distinctly something more like the shacks in las colonias—the shantytowns outside the city limits. It was a wood-slatted shotgun house, narrow as the path of a bullet. If you stood in the front doorway, you could see out the back door. Two bedrooms, true, and José Alfredo liked the wraparound porch and the big pecan trees in the yard. Pilar pointed out that it had no running water. There was a well and a pump, and an outhouse.

"But it's ours," José Alfredo had said. "I'll put in the plumbing. I'll be done before the baby comes."

Pilar could not argue that this was unreasonable, and he had finished most of the plumbing, but still. It was a fifteen-minute walk down to the neighborhood. Not far, but far enough. In Caimanes, there were real streets with streetlights. Playmates for Joselito. Other wives with whom she exchanged news, lent and borrowed. Had her own share in the collective vigilance of the Caimanes mothers over their children as they wandered the neighborhood.

There was no one near this lonesome spot. There was not even a good road, other than the one José Alfredo had cleared for his truck. Many nights she would awaken to the wailing of coyotes in the dark. José Alfredo, used to ranch life, hardly stirred. For him, the new home was a respite from el hormiguero, he called it. The ant colony of the neighborhood. While he slept, Pilar would sit at the bedroom window and peer out at the darkness, listening to the rustle of the uncleared brush, not knowing whether it was the wind or something else. The moonlight, spectral and remote. The low whistles of hunting owls frightened her most.

She could not say this to him. He had purchased a home for her. He would finish it. He would make it comfortable. And he was doing that—working in the evenings and every weekend on the house. He was working all the time, she reminded herself. It had not gone well when she had asked him to put up a fence in front of the house to keep Joselito from straying out of the yard.

"I'm afraid of the coyotes," she had said. "Joselito always wants to be outside."

She didn't mention owls. José Alfredo thought her fear of them absurd. He'd been a vaquero all his life, spent nights sleeping in the open during the corridas when they drove the cattle down from the sierra. Owls were just birds.

"Coyotes won't come during the day," José Alfredo scoffed. "I'll get a fence up, be patient. I'm doing it by myself."

"I do what I can too," she had said. She had not said, *Maybe you should have waited to buy a house. Maybe you should have chosen a different one.*

She had not said those things. Her words lingered, hot and still as the summer air, unsaid in her mouth. No, she had not said anything to him. But her silence was enough.

Finishing the house was taking longer than he'd thought it would. He knew he had made a wrong decision. He had not said he was sorry. But a week ago, he had come home with their mail, still delivered at their post office box on Main Street, with the invitation in his hand. Would she like to go to the quinceañera? He would like to take her. This was his apology. He knew very well what would bend her to forgiveness.

Pilar relished neighborhood celebrations with the avidity of one denied the flourishes of debutante and bride. Six years before, the train had fetched her north, from the clustered ranchitos of San Carlos in the Mexican state of Coahuila to the town of La Cienega, just across the border in Texas.

She had carried José Alfredo's engagement gift, a pair of gold filigree arracada earrings, sewn into the lining of her rosary pouch, in her lap all the way to the border. Her train had arrived on a Friday, at three in the afternoon. By quarter to four she had married José Alfredo Aguirre, married him in her traveling dress, but with the earrings brushing her neck. She'd been all of nineteen years old.

They had spent the wedding night on the Mexican side of the border, in Ciudad Bravo, at the Hotel Paradiso. They ate dinner in the fancy dining room, waited upon by servers in trim jackets, danced to the in-house band, boleros and American standards. Pilar felt the earrings, the weight of them, swaying with her movements. She had felt beautiful. But it had not been a celebration. It had not been a gala.

I'll wear the arracadas tonight, Pilar thought as she shifted on the front steps, trying to stay shaded under the wide green leaves of the banana tree. Behind that thought was another, one she certainly would not have owned, though it was an annoyance that crept traitorously to vanity: the quinceañera could have waited for October. Everyone said so. Pilar herself would have been over her confinement, her body her own again, and she, ready to dance.

Behind the house, she could hear Yolanda, Romi's daughter, singing as she shelled pecans on the back porch. She had a sweet voice. She sang unabashedly, in the manner of small children who believe they are alone when they cannot see anyone around them. Pilar sighed. She wished Joselito would help Yolanda with the pecan shelling, but he would not settle to the task. Oh well, when Romi finished with the beans, maybe they would take the children for a walk, swollen feet or no.

"Is this the home of José Alfredo Aguirre?"

An old woman stood in the middle of the street in front of the house. She wore a dark high-collared dress and a black lace mantilla over her hair, which was white and pinned in a low bun. She carried a tattered pocketbook tucked in the crook of her arm. She was small, brittle in the way of slight women in their twilight years. Pilar guessed her to be in her seventies.

"Excuse me," Pilar said, tugging down her dress. Joselito laughed and clutched her knee.

"Is this the home of José Alfredo Aguirre?" the woman repeated. She spoke with the strong lilt of a ranch peasant. In spite of her age, she stood erect, considering Pilar and, more lingeringly, Joselito.

"No," said Pilar, not liking the woman's tone. There was something peculiar here, despite her neat appearance.

The woman cocked her head at Pilar. "You are lying."

"I'm not," said Pilar. "This is not his house." More than ever, Pilar was glad that she had made the trek down the hillside to Romi's house this morning. She would not have wanted to face this woman so far away from other people.

"You know him," persisted the old woman. "Don't deny it. You know him."

"I don't deny it," said Pilar. "Who are you?"

The woman snapped her left arm up like an artillery salute. There was a gold cigar label on her ring finger. "I am his wife."

Pilar almost laughed, but the woman was clearly furious. Her face was vinegary as a puckered apple.

"I'm sorry, my husband—" Pilar stopped herself from saying *is only thirty*. "My husband isn't here, but believe me, you're mistaken."

"No," said the woman. Her lips trembled as though she might cry. She aimed a crooked finger at Joselito. "I see his face right there."

The old woman sprang in tiny quick steps, right up to the edge of the lawn, still pointing her gnarled old finger. Pilar thrust herself to her feet, knocking over the tub and drenching Joselito. He coughed and began to wail.

"Don't point at my son!" She felt Joselito sobbing against the back of her calf. "Get away from here!"

There was a brief ripple in her belly, low and deep. The small of her back seized in little fingerlets of agony, but she set herself between Joselito and the old woman. She held her ground. There was a beat of silence. Yolanda had stopped singing.

"Señora Aguirre," the old woman scoffed. "This is everything that belongs to you."

The woman crouched and swept her fingers through the dust at her feet. With one easy twist, she flung the handful of dirt at Pilar. The spray hit Pilar full in the face. She wiped frantically at her eyes, felt them burn. Felt dirt inside her dress.

The old woman's grace was terrifying. In the next instant, she would charge across the lawn and snatch Joselito up in those horrible, strong fingers. She would snatch him up and she would run. Pilar tried to grip Joselito more firmly, but he was slippery in her hands. The small of her back seized again. *If she takes him, I won't catch her. Oh, I won't catch her!*

The screen door banged open and Romi came out on the steps, a broom in her hands. "What's happening out here?"

The neighborhood twitched awake at the sound of Romi's voice: Two teenage boys walking a bicycle through the intersection turned to look. Across the street one of the Zunigas peered out of the living room window.

"Tell me who this house belongs to," the old woman said.

"Jesús Muñoz," Romi said. She was tall and broad, and in possession of an unflappable confidence. There were not many in the neighborhood who could stand her down. "I am Señora Muñoz. What do you want?"

The old woman smoothed down the front of her dress with a prim, girlish gesture. Little particles of dirt slipped off her fingers. Her paper ring scratched against the dark material. She smiled at Pilar. The teeth she exposed were badly discolored. "This is not the place I am looking for."

The old woman walked toward the intersection, the edge of her lace mantilla fluttering at her narrow shoulders. Pilar watched the old woman cross the street and turn west. There were only three or so more residential streets in that direction. Beyond those streets, five miles of dirt road to the ferries on the Rio Grande. The old woman, Pilar thought, was entirely capable of making such a trek.

"Who was that?" asked Romi.

"I—I don't know." Her dress was wet and her lower back throbbed steadily. Joselito's wails had become a full-blown tantrum.

Romi scooped up Joselito, cradling him and patting his back with one large, capable hand. "Ya, ya, mijo. It's okay."

"She said José Alfredo is her husband."

Romi snorted. "That vieja could be his grandmother."

"She must know him," said Pilar, rubbing her eyes with the side of her hand. They still burned, but not as much. "She recognized Joselito."

"Ay, Pili. She probably saw him somewhere and asked around for who he was. It's not that hard to find out."

"Why would anyone do that?"

"Who knows? Those viejitos. They can't remember their own names, but something flies into their heads and nothing will pry it loose." Romi sighed. "Well, we're all going that way."

Pilar gave her a pointed look. It was different for those from el otro lado. Men came from Mexico in whatever way they could: smuggled in or swimming the river, the most fortunate with the government guest worker program. Sometimes these men left their families back home and started fresh new lives. And sometimes wives came looking for lost husbands. What would Romi know about it? She and her husband were both Tejanos, born and raised in Texas, in this very town, their family lines neatly mapped out, transparent.

José Alfredo had come to Texas as a bracero in the government program that took so many young men. He had been in the United States three full years before he sent for her. Pilar did not know how he had managed it. *I made my own luck*, he'd said. Now she wondered how he'd made that luck.

This was all absurd, she told herself. The woman was so old. Besides, she and José Alfredo had been married and living in Texas for years. Why would a woman wait so long to find a wayward husband?

"He doesn't have a secret wife," Romi said, reading Pilar's thoughts. "We knew him a year before he brought you."

Joselito pressed the top of his head beneath Romi's chin, but he fixed his eyes on Pilar. He had resented for some time Pilar's inability to pick him up. Guilt flashed through her. She could not even comfort him properly.

"Oh, I'm a mess," she said, glancing away from her son.

"Never mind, it's all right now," said Romi. But she frowned, looking at Pilar's feet. "I don't think the swelling is going to come down. Come inside."

Pilar followed Romi into the kitchen. Inside, the air was moist with the steam of boiling beans. Pilar went straight to the sink, scrubbed her face and hair, her arms all the way to her elbows. Little Yolanda was sitting at the table eating a cookie, eyes round and solemn, taking in Pilar's drenched body.

"Who was that, Mami?" Yolanda asked.

"Nobody," said Romi. "Go dust the living room and your bedroom."

"Yes, Mami," Yolanda said. She left and Pilar sat down in the vacant chair, at the narrow table beside the icebox.

The room was small, but neat, and decorated with artificial fruit: yellow-painted wood carvings of lemons, plastic purple grapes, a ceramic watermelon half-moon in the middle of the table. Even the beige table-cloth was printed with dim clusters of cherries. Romi shifted Joselito to one hip and took a napkin out of the drawer beneath the countertop. She handed it to Joselito and set him on the chair next to Pilar.

"Okay," she said. Romi put her fingers into the seed indentations in the watermelon's lid and lifted it. It was full of Nilla wafers. "Let me hear you count three."

Joselito counted three wafers out of the cookie jar with the seriousness of a banker tallying a withdrawal. Pilar helped him spread his napkin flat. He liked to put his cookies in a row before he ate them.

"Sure you don't want any?" asked Romi. "There's lemonade too."

Pilar shook her head. She could still taste dust. "I need to go home and bathe."

"Wait a minute. Try the shoes my sister sent me. Son muy chachas, but too small for me." Romi shook her head. "And not my style."

Pilar nodded. The hallway floorboards creaked as Romi retreated to her bedroom. She watched Joselito bite into his second cookie.

"Mami, can I go play with Yoli?" Small beads of sweat sprouted on the end of his nose. He had forgotten his fright, but she had not.

"Yes, go on." He scrambled out of his chair, cookies clutched in his hand. She shut her eyes and pressed her fingers against her eyelids. She could still smell the dirt on herself.

Pilar said, loud, so that Romi would hear her, "You think I should tell José Alfredo?"

"It's up to you," Romi called back. "But what is there to tell? She was wearing a cigar band as a wedding ring. She was crazy."

"That's true," Pilar said, but it was not a comforting thought. Next time, the woman might find Pilar alone at the house on Loma Negra.

Romi returned with a light-blue shoe box in her hands. She sat down at the table and put the shoe box in front of Pilar, gesturing for her to open it, but Pilar did not. Romi gripped her folded hands with one of her own.

"Your husband comes home to you every day. He has given you this boy and another child is coming. It's easy to feel bad right now—when you're so tired and nothing fits—but remember, it's a happy time too."

Romi's hand was large and firm. The ring on her middle finger was fitted with two paste stones, the birthstones of each of her children. The opal was for Miguel, her oldest, who had been killed in the Philippines during the war. It happened a few years before Pilar came to Texas. *It's easy to talk with you*, Romi had remarked, early in their friendship. *You never knew him*. She meant Pilar didn't ask questions about him. Pilar had taken to

Romi for much the same reasons—she never pressed Pilar about family back in Mexico. Their histories were their own business.

"Yes, of course, I'm very fortunate," said Pilar, ashamed. Miguel had been Romi's only son.

"Ándale." Romi drummed her fingers on the box. "Open it."

Pilar caught her breath, dark thoughts receding like shadows before the sun. Nestled in white tissue paper were a pair of gold peep-toe sandals. She lifted the right shoe out of the tissue. Three wide bands of satiny fabric, each cunningly knotted at the top of the foot. An elegant, arched sole. The ankle strap was set with a gauzy golden ribbon that flared at the clasp. The heel was sturdy and square, probably four inches.

"I didn't remember they were so high," Romi said. "Maybe I have something else."

"No, it's fine," Pilar said. She slipped on the sandal. For the first time that day, something felt right. The sandal was a half size larger than she normally wore, and that, or perhaps the banded style, meant it had more give to it. Whatever the reason, her foot looked normal. Almost.

"Are you going to be able to buckle it?" Romi demanded. "You can't even see your own feet."

"Claro," Pilar sniffed. She twisted her leg up behind her and deftly buckled the strap. She stuck her foot out. She'd been right about the ribbon. It distracted from her thick ankle.

Pilar put on the other sandal and stood up. She hadn't worn any kind of heel since she'd started to show. She walked around the kitchen. The clack-clack-clack of the heavy heel made her feel bold, desirable. More herself.

"I can't believe your sister gave you these."

"She gives me things she knows I don't wear just so I can tell her to keep them." Romi smacked her lips. "Not this time!"

Pilar clacked across the kitchen once more. "What do you think?"

"Only you could wear tacones with a baby a month away," Romi said, but she was grinning.

⌐——·•·——⌐

José Alfredo arrived home at five thirty. Pilar heard his truck rumble up to the house, and then his voice in the yard. He was singing some foolish, romantic thing. He was always singing something. He had a good voice but was too shy to sing in public.

"Hello," she said, coming out to the porch.

"And if I live one hundred years, one hundred years I'll think of you," he sang at her. He cut across the yard toward the water pump. He would bathe fully before the quinceañera, but he never entered the house, never touched her, without washing his whole head and torso after work.

He peeled off both his shirt and undershirt and dropped his suspenders to his waist. He primed the hand pump with hard fast strokes. She'd done the same when she'd gotten home, plunged her face into the stream of water, scrubbed the dirt off her skin. She would not bring the old woman's evil into the house.

Pilar watched the water sluice across the flare of his shoulders, down his bare arms and back. Felt, as she nearly always did, a secret tremble at the casual play of muscle beneath his skin's brown glow. She had never seen another man unclothed but could not imagine other husbands looked

like José Alfredo: narrow hipped and lean, with the coiled energy of a panther in repose. Her eyes were full of him.

She would never, never speak her adoration. It seemed too vivid, too
urgent, and somehow dangerous. Even more secret, her utter satisfaction
that this man was hers. No matter what anyone else said. He was hers.

Maybe she would not tell him about the woman. Maybe not. After all,
why spoil the evening? And right before the party too. She went out onto
the porch to meet him.

José Alfredo kissed her lightly, a hand on her belly. She smelled Lava
soap and beneath it, the faint coppery scent of his sunburned skin. It could
not be true, what the old woman had said. It could not. But after Romi
had driven Pilar and Joselito back home, once they were alone on the hill,
the thought crept back. Who had that old woman been? She had recognized Joselito.

"You had a good time at Romi's?" He liked her friendship with Romi,
imagining that she was a steadying influence, someone who could give
Pilar matronly consejos.

"She had a pair of shoes for me, thank goodness. All my nice ones are
too tight."

"Just one more month." He put on the clean shirt she had hung from a
wire hook on the back of the kitchen door. Damp patches bloomed in the
cotton. "Where's mijo?"

"He's asleep on the sofa."

Pilar set out his dinner: a plate of fideo and beans, six corn tortillas
folded inside a hot dishcloth. A glass of iced tea. He sat down, his trousers
scattering bits of chaff on the linoleum. He would collect them after dinner, she knew, pinching them between his fingers one by one, to discard
them in the yard when he went out to smoke. He tore a strip from his

tortilla, rolled it into a thin maize cylinder, and began to eat with it. "You're not eating?"

"No." Pilar shook her head. The fideo was thin and pale and seeing it, resting in its thick reddish juice, made her vaguely ill. "I don't feel like it."

"Sit with me," he said. He reached out and took her hand, rubbing his thumb inside her palm. "Just a few bites."

Pilar relented against the tug of his hand. She was not hungry, but she sat down beside him and ate what he offered her. She shut her eyes as the tortilla touched her lips. In her mind's eye, she saw the old woman in one of the little two-cent rowboats that ferried people back and forth across the Rio Grande.

The old woman had set out that morning, tucking the skirt carefully beneath her, mindful of the rough plank seat while the boat dipped and swayed across the water. She had come in the morning when the dust on the road into town would be lightest. She had come in her very best dress. But she had not known about the new house. If she had, perhaps she would have climbed the hill to find Pilar alone. And what would have happened then?

She wondered again how José Alfredo had managed to bring her to the United States when so many others were trapped in long-distance romances. Amor de lejos, amor de pendejos, the saying went, but so many women lived that way, spent their lives waiting for a man to return to them from whatever American farmland he was working. Maybe the man would, but often, he did not. She had waited two years for José Alfredo, but he *had* brought her.

She ran her fingers through his damp hair. She had a secret of her own. José Alfredo thought she'd run away from home to marry him. She'd been ashamed to tell the truth. Her father had sent her, unchaperoned, all the way to the border by herself. Papá had been relieved for her sake, for his own, that she'd had a place to go.

"Someone was looking for you today," she said, though she had nearly decided outright that she would not tell him. "A woman."

"Oh?" José Alfredo said, smiling. He missed her seriousness. "Was she pretty?"

"No. She was old," Pilar said, trying not to sound impatient. Of course this was his response. Of course. Because it was nothing, wasn't it? Though now that she'd started telling it she might as well say it all. "I don't know who she was, but she told me she was your wife. She said she was your wife. She was looking for you."

José Alfredo dropped the scrap of tortilla in his fideo. In his face she saw nothing that registered as guilt, not one flicker. "What are you saying? What happened?"

"It was earlier today. At Romi's house. I guess she knew we used to live there." She paused, willing the bitterness out of her voice. If only they still lived in Caimanes. Perhaps someone would have known the old woman. Certainly Pilar would have felt safer in the barrio than here, isolated on the hillside.

"She seemed to know you," Pilar said as evenly as she could, gazing straight into his eyes. Though again, all she found was bewilderment. "She said how much Joselito resembles you."

"Well, so what," he said, stung. "How can you believe her?"

"I didn't accuse you," Pilar said quickly. "I'm telling you what happened. I told her you were my husband."

"Good," José Alfredo said, shaking his head. "Set her straight."

"Yes, and she got very angry," Pilar said. She looked down at her hand, at the gold band. Remembered the old woman's twisted cigar label. "She . . . she threw dirt at me."

"Why didn't you tell me this earlier?" José Alfredo demanded. "Were you hurt?"

"No, no. Nothing like that. Romi said she was probably senile. Or mistaken." Romi had not said mistaken. But maybe it had been a mistake.

"That's very strange," José Alfredo said, swallowing a mouthful of fideo. "What about you? Do you feel well enough to go to the dance?"

"Yes, I'm fine," she said. She wasn't going to be cheated out of a party.

By eight o'clock the heat had softened to an evening humidity that was bearable if Pilar ignored the halo of perspiration that threatened to escape her hairline. They drove down to Barrio Caimanes in the truck, parking at the bottom of the hill near the Muñoz home. Pilar smothered a sigh as José Alfredo straightened Joselito's white guayabera. José Alfredo was particular. If the starched lines at the shoulders did not fall correctly, he would want to change Joselito's shirt, even if it meant going back home and ironing another one.

"So handsome, both of you," she said. They had the same thick black hair. In spite of the fresh pomade, their curls broke in glossy, black waves. They were very alike. She thought again of the woman knowing her husband by Joselito's face. But she pushed it away—anyone could have seen them together, anywhere. That didn't mean anything. Pilar slipped out of the truck to stand beside them, slamming the door.

"Be careful," said José Alfredo. He reached out to her. "Those heels are kind of high, no?"

"Not at all. They're good." She set her foot out, turned it so the ankle ribbon showed. "And they're so pretty."

"Ay, Pili. Diosito nos libre de tu vanidad," he said, mouth twitching.

22

Amused, but also, she could tell, admiring her. He tugged at her oversized collar bow. "You look like a little Christmas kitten."

Before she could answer, Joselito shouted, "Look! Here they come!"

Around the bend in the road came the quinceañera procession. At its head, a fat, gray burro with curly pink ribbons tied around its ears pulled a rustic wagon. The wagon, driven by the girl's escort, was flanked on one side by the girl's parents, Hipólito and Carmen Ramirez, and on the other by the neighborhood band, Conjunto Vega, playing "Las Mañanitas" in honor of the girl's birthday.

Pilar craned her neck to see, relishing, as she always did, the presentation of the honored girl. The quinceañera, Dulce Ramirez, sat in the rear of the wagon in a pink dress, a homemade corona of pale baby roses in her hair. The tulle and satin of her skirts took up the entirety of the wagon seat. At every house on the block, neighbors stood on the sidewalk, waiting. They called their congratulations to Dulce as she passed, and then fell in behind the quinceañera court: young girls in vivid party dresses and their respective escorts.

In spite of the noise the quinceañera sat with her hands clasped in her lap, smiling at their greetings with ladylike detachment. Dulce's mother huffed alongside the wagon, out of breath, her brown face shining with sweat. She flashed a broad, gap-toothed smile at everyone. Dulce's father Hipólito moved more soberly. He squinted against the streaks of dying sunlight, one hand resting lightly on the wagon.

José Alfredo lifted Joselito on his shoulders. He set Pilar's hand in the crook of his arm. He loves me, she thought. That's the truth.

She watched as, with one swift gesture, Hipólito motioned to the wagon driver to avoid a pothole. The man's posture was like her father's, sedate and melancholic, his same air of fatigued sentimentality. Her father had not given her a quinceañera, had not given her much beyond the envelope full of American money and a train ticket. *Does he love you?* her father had asked. *Then go. Go.*

Before she could smother it, the old bitterness surfaced. Her husband loved her with more sincerity than Papá ever had. Papá had paid her school fees and bought her pretty dresses, told her she was his favorite. Of all his children, only Pilar had his mother's hazel eyes. Yet, he would not acknowledge her the few times she'd seen him in public with his family. For her fifteenth, there had been a weekend trip to Saltillo, for the national charrería championship exhibition. That had been his choice, not hers. She'd been overjoyed anyway, just to walk beside him in public.

Now she reminded herself not to be angry. Of course Papá only acknowledged her among strangers. Besides, that long-ago charreada had given her José Alfredo. She pressed closer to her husband, grateful, amid the happy crush of partygoers, for his steadying presence.

"Felicidades!" José Alfredo shouted above a wheezy accordion trill. Dulce waved at them as the wagon rolled by.

Pilar's eyes were drawn to Dulce's puffed sleeves, the sleek dark hair pinned up in complicated coils. Texas was not like home, Pilar thought, feeling the heavy thrum of the bass vibrate in the pit of her belly. Here, any daughter could have this fiesta of roses. No wonder Doña Carmen smiled so fiercely. Pilar pressed her palm against her belly. Her daughter would have this too.

Pilar picked her way up the rutted street, not minding the noise or her jostling neighbors. As they arrived in front of the church, the musicians took a spot away from the open doors, in front of the small rose garden, where the new grotto of the Virgin stood. They continued to play as people filed into the building, but more softly.

As usual, José Alfredo chose a pew at the rear of the church, so that if

Joselito began to fuss he could be taken outside with minimal distraction. Pilar heard Joselito whisper to his father his intention to be good. Pilar smothered a sigh. She wished just once they could sit up front. Maybe if they were closer to the pulpit, under the eye of the priest, Joselito would keep his promise.

"You better," José Alfredo murmured, his mouth close to Joselito's ear, "because if not, we don't go to the party."

Ten minutes into the service, Joselito began to squirm. Pilar opened the stained-glass casement window as far as it would go, hoping the air would circulate. The sky had darkened. In the half-light, the storefront across the street looked abandoned. The rose bushes beneath the window bloomed with a heavy sweetness, reminding Pilar of the antiquated talcums favored by little old ladies. Her gaze shifted from the pulpit to the pews nearest the altars. Pilar could see the bowed heads of widows in their mourning veils.

"Mami, I'm hot," Joselito said, too loudly, and Pilar shushed him.

"I'm going to take him out for a few minutes," José Alfredo whispered.

Pilar fanned herself with the missalette, annoyed. She was going to sit through the service alone, as she so often did. She didn't like sitting by herself, as if she'd been abandoned. *It doesn't look right,* she'd told her husband repeatedly. *God sees my heart whether I'm in the pew or not,* he'd insist. There was no use arguing. If he didn't want to do a thing, he would not do it.

Well, and what of it? José Alfredo was not tame. She'd always known this.

Pilar set her fingers lightly on the swell of her belly. It would be different when the baby came. José Alfredo too had had a corazonada that the baby was a girl. Pilar trusted his feeling. She wanted a girl very much. There were so many pretty things for a girl. Lacy infant caps and dainty shoes, tiny gold stud earrings. Later, a First Communion dress. And of course, a quinceañera. Pilar gazed at the cluster of young girls in frothy dresses. Yes, the quince. Her daughter would have one just as lovely as this. Better even.

Pilar heard the snick of a lighter, and the scent of cigar smoke wafted through the window. As she had suspected, José Alfredo was skipping the rest of the service. She wished he would smoke farther off.

"I hope you are a girl," she whispered at her belly. "At the very least, you'll stay with me while the boys play outside."

After mass, the congregation followed Dulce behind the church, to the grotto of the Virgin. Dulce knelt daintily before the grotto. She placed her bouquet of roses at the feet of the Virgin. She bowed her head in prayer, one hand on the rough stone edge of the grotto.

The sight of Dulce's lowered head beneath the gaze of the Virgin felt holy to Pilar. Beneath her pale blue cloak, the Virgin's hands were folded lightly between her breasts. The mild inclination of her head gave the distinct impression of pleasure, as though, perhaps by accident, Dulce had discovered her secret joy.

Dulce stood up and faced them. "Thank you for coming to celebrate with me. I hope you'll all accompany me to the reception at Plaza Estrella."

A scattered applause broke out and people began to mill around, drifting toward the plaza in a disorganized fashion. Pilar saw him then, on the sidewalk near the front of the church, talking with two other men. Joselito was on his shoulders again.

"Come on, Mami," Joselito said when she joined them. "I want cake."

"Yes, I'm coming." Pilar watched as Dulce, her escort, and the entire court of teens set out for the plaza. In spite of the dress Dulce looked quite little. Too little, Pilar thought. The week before she might have been swinging on gates and pinching her sisters during mass.

It was a neighborhood party, so one sat wherever one found a seat, and after dinner, spent the rest of the night table-hopping. Folding tables covered with pink tablecloths, decked with small dishes of polvorones, were arranged in the grass around the concrete slab dance floor, and on either side of the assembly line of food were tubs of iced beer and Coca-Cola. An easel had been set up with Dulce's quinceañera portrait, next to the table with a pink and white cake in the shape of a flying angel and a large curly-haired china doll.

She spotted Romi zigzagging through the throng, two overflowing plates in hand, hairdo already wilting. Romi noted Pilar's heels with an approving nod, but didn't stop. Her husband Chuy was waiting for her to bring him his dinner. Pilar sighed. Their table was full.

Instead, she and José Alfredo sat near Trini Sanchez, who worked with José Alfredo at the livestock port of entry. Pilar liked Trini. He was fifty-ish, had a crooked white mustache, and habitually wore a dented straw cowboy hat. Trini had sangre viva, as Romi put it, lively blood.

"What's the man say?" said Trini, clapping José Alfredo on the shoulder.

"Nothing. Looking for another job." José Alfredo shrugged and bit into his taco.

"You tired of cow shit?"

"Nope, just need another job." José Alfredo worked his jaw faster and swallowed his bite of tortilla. "For after work."

"It must be on your account." Trini nodded at Pilar. "Every time I see you there's more of you."

"José Alfredo's going to add a bedroom to the house before the baby comes."

"Have another boy, that way you have your own workers," Trini said. "Where's the big brother?"

"With them," José Alfredo said, gesturing at the group of children running around the park. "But at least he'll fall asleep fast tonight."

They quieted as Hipólito led Dulce to the dance floor. A moment later Carmen joined the two of them, carrying the china doll. A stitch of pain flared in Pilar's belly, sharp, but brief. She let her breath out through her nose, willing herself not to react. If José Alfredo found out, he'd take her home immediately.

"Felicidades," Carmen said and kissed Dulce's cheek. Hipólito gave the doll to Dulce and wished her many happy returns. It was a ceremonial gesture, his public offering of this final childhood toy. Pilar leaned forward in spite of her discomfort. This was the moment she sought—the father's expression at the instant of his daughter's transformation. His eyes were shining with love. With pride.

Hipólito pressed his hand to Dulce's cheek and then turned toward the guests. "Ladies and gentlemen, my daughter, Señorita Dulce Ramirez."

Pilar clapped along with everyone else. Her father would have looked at her that way, if she'd been properly his daughter. If she'd had his name. Well, so what? José Alfredo would look at their daughter like that when she turned fifteen.

Dulce and her father opened the dance, with the rest of the debutant court joining them after the first waltz. Trini commented on the dancers as they passed. That one danced too quickly, another had a heavy step. One of the damas was a good dancer, and fat too, which, according to Trini, meant she would marry young. Dulce waltzed past with her father. The trees around the dance floor had been strung with electric blue bulbs. Beneath their speckled light, Hipólito's forehead shone with sweat. In spite of the muggy night, he had not, as other men had, removed his suit jacket.

"Poor man. He better watch out for that López kid." Trini pointed at a youth sitting with the escorts. He was the only one at the table not wearing a tuxedo. He wore a cream-colored suit with wide lapels and on the table in front of him was a matching fedora.

"That's Raúl. The one who works at Frausto's tortillería," said Pilar. "He's a good boy."

"Just look at him! He washes off the cornmeal for one night and he thinks he's a dandy," Trini sneered. He shook his head. "Ay, no, I'd hate to have a daughter."

José Alfredo snorted and wiped his mouth with a napkin. "Your daughter lives in Presidio."

"And she's married," said Trini. "That's the only kind to have. Otherwise you spend your money on guns and putting bars on the windows."

"That's not true," said Pilar, laughing, but prickling a little. Did every man want to unload a daughter? "I met Norma when she came last Easter. She's a very nice woman."

"Maybe so." Trini took a long swallow of beer and then set the bottle down with a thud. "But, now, if she isn't it's her husband's problem, not mine."

"You're not eating," said José Alfredo, nudging Pilar's plate toward her. "I haven't seen you eat anything this evening."

"It's too hot to eat." The pain had not returned, but she didn't want to press her luck.

"Do you want to go home?"

"No, no, I feel good." She couldn't leave yet. The dinner was hardly finished. She didn't want to hear how, maybe, they should have stayed home in the first place. She wanted to be at this dance. Though it was certainly hard to see all the pretty young girls, so lovely in their dancing dresses. Meanwhile, she was swollen and ungainly, seemingly *all* belly. If only they'd held off the quince until October.

"Get this poor girl some cake and ice cream, hombre," said Trini. "Go on, they're already serving."

"I'll go with you," Pilar said, rising. "I need to check on Joselito."

Walking was better. Pilar felt her discomfort recede as they joined the cake line. Dulce's mother, Carmen, was setting out rows of thin plates with little pink squares of cake on one of the long tables. Carmen shooed off a young man in a tuxedo. The court had finished their opening dances and two escorts stood around the cake table snatching up sweets.

"What do you have, six weeks left? Let me look at you." Carmen set her hand on Pilar's belly. Her hand was light and sure. "It's a girl. Look how high and pointy she's carrying."

"We think so too! Only the last month takes so long," said Pilar, sighing. "José Alfredo, let's find mijo. He's probably hungry by now."

"I doubt it. He's hanging off the gazebo," said José Alfredo, pointing at the cluster of small children climbing the wooden railing. She turned in time to see Joselito leap off the top of the rail. He popped back to his feet, began to climb again. "Let him be for now."

When they returned to their table they found Trini holding court. Several teenagers had pulled up chairs to hear him. The dandy Raúl López was there as well, slouching on a bench next to Dulce.

"What's this?" laughed Pilar. "Are you telling about the hairy hand?" La mano peluda was one of Trini's favorite tales, always with a different scenario in which the hand attacked someone. José Alfredo always tried to make her jump by grabbing her during the story.

"Not that one," Trini said. "Something else."

"I've already had a fright today," Pilar said, feeling that to speak it would make the thing smaller, less real. The old woman as a story, not a person who hated her.

"Oh?" Trini asked. "What happened?"

30

"It was nothing," José Alfredo said, clearly annoyed with her for bring-ing it up. "Just some crazy lady bothering her."

"You never know about women. Especially the crazy ones," Trini said, twinkling. "I know what I'm talking about."

"I bet you do," Pilar said, pretending not to notice José Alfredo's irrita-tion. She would hear this story. They would both hear this story.

"Not from personal experience!" Trini laughed. "But this really hap-pened. To someone I know."

"Tell it, Trini," said the López boy, settling himself near Dulce.

"Someone bring me a beer," said Trini. Then he began.

"This happened last summer, when I was working at an orange grove in Harlingen." Trini grinned at Pilar and José Alfredo as they sat down. "There was a big group of us, from both sides of the Rio Grande, twenty-ish men, maybe, working in the groves.

"There was one chavo from Sinaloa, named Antonio. Young, maybe seventeen years old. We started noticing that he vomited blood on Thurs-days and Fridays. Not every week, but it was always on those days. I tell you, we'd be all the way up our tree ladders and long about two o'clock in the afternoon he'd start coughing. Bad coughing. He'd climb down as fast as he could, sometimes he made it, but a lot of times he fell.

"Dios mío, it gave me the creeps to see it. He'd lay there at the foot of the tree, just hacking"—Trini bent at the waist, cradling his belly with his hands—"so hard his whole body shook. And then I'd hear a loud, ugly wheeze and I knew he was crying, but he didn't have breath for it. He'd vomit all over himself. And all that came up was blood."

Trini took a swig of his beer. The boys had all gone quiet. A freckly debutante looked at Pilar as if to gauge whether or not she too was afraid. "Did he die?"

"Well, you'd think anybody vomiting blood would be on their deathbed,

31

but no." Trini shrugged. "Every other day he was fine. Even after one of those fits he was fine. That was the strangest part of it. Muy curioso.

"As the summer went on, more men in the camp became aware of the kid's strange problem. Caray, it got to be that by the end of every week there'd be men hanging around waiting to see if it was true."

"How awful," Pilar said, shuddering.

"It is," Trini agreed, "but that's how people are. Anyway, one Thursday a man, Pancho Morales, came out to our section of the grove, and of course, it happened again. The next day he came back and asked Antonio, and the rest of us in that part of the grove, to pray with him. Afterward, he told us what he thought. Antonio was vomiting blood, he said, because he was bewitched by someone in the town in Mexico from which he had come. 'Do you want me to get rid of it?' Pancho asked, and of course Antonio said yes."

"Well, even if you don't believe it," said the López boy, smirking at Dulce, "it's cheaper than the doctor."

"That's right," said Trini, "but if you'd been vomiting blood for weeks, you might have started believing it.

"Pancho went to a nearby ranch the next Friday for some rope. That night he came back out to the grove, where a lot of us were sleeping. He began the ritual by tying twelve knots in the rope and saying a prayer between each knot.

"All the time he was tying the knots, an owl was making noise down at the other end of the row of trees—a big one from the way it sounded. Pancho tied the last knot in the rope, and then he picked up a fallen branch and started walking out to the tree."

Trini paused, looking around at the teens. "This next part is kind of rough for the girls."

"I want to hear it," said Dulce. The other girls nodded, even the nervous freckled one. "C'mon Señor Sanchez. What happened?"

"Well, I couldn't really see that far in the dark. It was all the way down the row and I wasn't about to go down there for a closer look. But he must have gotten the owl out of the tree somehow, because I heard it squabbling, you know, kind of like an angry chicken will, and after a little bit it started screaming. He was beating it with the tree branch.

"This went on for about twenty minutes. I could hear where sometimes Pancho missed and struck a tree instead. The sound was like when you hear a gun crack in the distance." Trini sipped his beer again, as though telling it had left a bad taste in his mouth.

"And all of a sudden it was quiet. Real quiet. And in the quiet I heard a woman sobbing."

An image of her father rose in Pilar's mind: his face flushed, mouth wide with shouting, shouting as he never had, the rest of his face closed over with the effort of his fury. The memory was suddenly there, vivid and whole, as if it had been lying at the bottom of her mind all this time, waiting to trip her. Her father shouting. A woman hurrying away, her low, sneering voice, all shadowed in the dim light just before dawn.

José Alfredo tucked her against his side and squeezed her shoulder, but absently. Now he was invested. He wanted to hear the story. He whispered, "Don't be scared."

Pilar didn't answer him. She had been quite young when Papá chased away the woman. Still living with her old criada Facunda in a tiny adobe house on Papá's family's land.

Trini continued. "Pancho stayed out there awhile, talking to that husky-voiced woman. I couldn't hear what they said, but I could hear their voices. He was talking real calm, but she cried and growled the whole time.

Finally Pancho came back. He was breathing heavy and sweating, I mean, the sweat was just pouring off him. His shirt was bloody and torn and there were scratches all over his forearms."

Pilar felt cold all the way through, despite the humid night. *No se salga de la casa, mi niña,* Facunda would say, her dark face solemn and watchful. *Andan por ahí rondando.* But she had never said what or who might be lurking beyond the door.

"He stood over the rest of us," Trini was saying. "We were laying on our petates too scared to even stand up with him. He bent over Antonio and shook him, kinda rough. 'Do you know—' well, I won't say her name, but Pancho asked Antonio if he knew a certain woman, and Antonio admitted that he did."

Papá had not admitted anything. When she had asked Papá about his fight with the woman, he'd told her she must have dreamed it. Now, listening to Trini, she thought, *Papá lied to me. Of course he had.*

"Pancho told him, 'You have to burn all your clothes,'" Trini continued. "'All of them. Right now—go and get the kerosene.' So Antonio picked up his bedroll and his knapsack and he and Pancho went off a ways from the grove. My God, they burnt up all the kid's clothes, down to his last pair of underpants. He came back buck naked and had to borrow pants and a shirt from one of the other guys. Boy, he wore those the rest of the summer, 'cause he didn't have a lot of money to spend buying up a bunch of new ones."

"And it worked?" asked one of the escorts, a pimply young man with a faint mustache.

"Yep," said Trini, belching into his fist. "He didn't have one fit the rest of the summer.

"But—" Trini looked around at the teens. "You know, that boy had to go all the way back to his home town in Sinaloa and burn the rest of his clothes. Can you imagine having to burn up all your clothes?" He smirked at Raúl López and the boy scowled.

"It's true. The owl was only her spirit; the real woman, a witch, lived back in Sinaloa. When Antonio went back to complete his limpia, he went out with a couple of his uncles looking for her. They caught her and were going to burn her; but the witch started crying, begging them to let her go because she had a baby boy to take care of, and promising that if they let her go, she would never again practice brujería. So they left her alone after all."

Pilar shuddered. Facunda said they whistled for you in the dark. Clicked their talons like scissors opening and closing. Sometimes they mimicked a crying infant or said your name to lure you out. Papá had scolded her for repeating Facunda's nonsense. *Maria del Pilar Corrales*, he'd said severely. *No hables como una india pata rajada.* Soon after, he had sent Pilar to live in town, with the nuns.

Raúl López said, "They shouldn't have let her go. When the boy grows up, he'll probably be into brujería like his mother."

"What a hard heart you have," said José Alfredo, biting off the end of a cigar and spitting it in the grass. "She didn't want to kill Antonio. If she had, he would have been dead."

Pilar wondered if José Alfredo would feel the same if he'd seen the old woman this morning. She watched him light his cigar, noted the little gold paper band. He had denied knowing anything about the unexpected woman too. But no. He was not like Papá. He was not.

"That's the truth. Antonio was the stupid one, pissing off a bruja. Of course, you can never tell what's behind a pretty face." Trini raised his eyebrows and then tugged the flounced edge of Dulce's dress. "Right, Dulce?"

Dulce giggled, but did not reply. What a silly girl, Pilar thought. She doesn't take it seriously. It's just a story to her. What does she know about life?

"My advice to all you enamorados," Trini said, getting to his feet, empty plate in hand. "Watch out."

On the stage, the accordion player burst into a jaunty taquachito-style polka. The teens at Pilar's table took their leave. At other tables, couples rose from their seats, heading to the dance floor. José Alfredo put his arm across the back of her chair. "We'll dance too, when they play a waltz."

"All right." She reached up to rub the hand he had set on her shoulder. José Alfredo wanted to dance because he was ready to go. He always took her for at least one dance before they went home. Even in his consideration he was methodical, and the transparency was comforting. Why had she allowed herself to get so worked up over a story?

"Oye," José Alfredo said, as Joselito ran by with two other boys. "Come eat your dinner."

"I'm not hungry," Joselito yelled, putting on a burst of speed to evade his father. Pilar noted the fresh grass stain on his white shirt, that he had sweated the pomade out of his hair. She sighed. He wouldn't settle down unless José Alfredo dragged him to the table. Then he would refuse to eat. He'd wait until they were home to say he was hungry. He was always that way.

"Don't feed him when we get home," José Alfredo said, watching Joselito climb up the bandstand. "We need to break this habit."

"You tell him no then," she said. "I can't stand for him to be hungry."

"Oh, one night won't hurt him."

Conjunto Vega settled into a vals norteño, the accordion player squeezing out a tender, lovelorn melody. The song was an old favorite, "La Panchita" by Lucha Reyes. For the first time all night, Pilar felt unreserved enthusiasm. It was a good song, and not too fast for her ungainly belly.

José Alfredo led her to a corner of the dance floor. The grass was wet. The Ramirezes had sprayed it down before the party, or perhaps the night dew had already fallen. They slipped into time at the edge of the circle of dancers.

Panchita with the big eyes, the way she looks at me robs me of my calm, José Alfredo sang along, sang to her, as he navigated her through the couples. He made a silly face to show he was teasing, not serenading in earnest. Pilar knew he did mean it, in his way. He teased to hide that he meant it.

"Go sing with Conjunto Vega," she laughed. "You sound better than Ernesto."

"I'm where I want to be," he said, and pulled her into a turn.

"Me too," she said. She reached up, swept a curl from his forehead, allowed her fingers to trace the curve of his face. Brown and smooth, a strong nose and jaw. Heavy dark eyes beneath perfectly straight dark brows. A face that escaped severity only because when he spoke, he revealed a dimple.

Pilar shut her eyes against the blur of the other dancers, reveling in the pleasure of the music, of being in her husband's arms. His breath was feathery and hot against her ear. He had always had a trick of grace that felt, as he swept her through the crowd, as though he were made of wind. It was a little like hurtling through the air, but she was not afraid. José Alfredo knew how to balance her. They had danced all through her first pregnancy.

A bolt of pain seized her lower belly. She opened her eyes. Images whirled past her: Dulce, in the arms of a gangly boy; Hipólito and Carmen on the steps of the gazebo; the china doll beside the cut-up cake, its porcelain skin gleaming in the shadowy light; the dandy Raúl, scowling, standing alone at the edge of the dance floor. The music blared. Her cramp released, but surged again, deep and solidified. Pilar felt a rush of wetness across her thighs.

She collapsed against José Alfredo. "Stop, stop!"

"What's the matter?" He stopped mid-step and the crush of dancers did not. He shrugged them off, tried to shield her. There was pressure, like a wall of iron, across her throat and lungs.

"I can't breathe. I can't breathe."

José Alfredo had hold of her elbow. They staggered through the crowd, the girls in their party dresses standing apart, watching, curious, while the dancing couples knocked against each other in their haste to clear her way. Pilar stumbled as they reached the grass.

"I told you those shoes were bad," said José Alfredo, voice harsh, though he sounded more fearful than angry.

"What is it?" Romi gasped, trotting up to them.

"Can you keep Joselito?" José Alfredo demanded. "We're going for Doctor Mireles."

"Go," Romi said. "Go now."

Pilar moaned in terror and pain. Her legs were slick all the way to her calves. She was like a broken pitcher, everything seeping out the bottom.

Chapter Two

La Muertita

I t wasn't supposed to be this way. Pilar watched the darkened streets flash past the truck window, feeling that she was dreaming. In the more likely version of her life, she was home from the dance. Letting Joselito have a piece of leftover cake before bed, even if José Alfredo grumbled that she spoiled him.

She had not even had time to lay eyes on her son before she and José Alfredo left the party, headed straight for Doctor Mireles's house. There'd been too many people, too much noise. José Alfredo hurrying her along, half carrying her. He'd pulled off her heels as soon as she was settled in, tossed them in the back of the truck. As if that would solve anything.

"Siempre quieres andar de coquetona," José Alfredo snapped, staring straight ahead. "You care more about looking pretty than being safe. It's irresponsible."

"You were the one who wanted to dance," she said, incredulous. "Why didn't you care then? Probably it was you spinning me around so much."

"Stop arguing with me. It's bad for the baby."

Pilar swallowed another remark. The pain left her breathless, at a disadvantage in this argument. Now it was coming at regular intervals. She tried to remember what Romi had told her when Joselito was born. Pick an object and focus. Breathe through the pain. There was the shining chrome hasp of the glove compartment, right in front of her. The night had shattered into a thousand pieces and José Alfredo blamed her for it. She pressed her hands to her belly. Breathe anyway. Breathe. Breathe. For the baby's sake.

"It'll be all right," José Alfredo said, squeezing her arm. He was sorry, but as usual, would not say so. "We're almost there."

But Doctor Mireles was away. He and his family had traveled three hours south to Laredo, to attend a wedding. They would be back Monday morning, probably. So said the Mireleses' housekeeper, who answered José Alfredo's frantic knocking.

"We have to go to el Inmaculado," he said, pulling out of the Mireles driveway. "It's okay. They have everything there."

"All right," Pilar said. "If that's the only choice, we better."

The Immaculate Heart of Mary Medical Center, el Inmaculado, as it was known in the Caimanes barrio, was the only hospital in La Cienega that served Mexicans. On the glass doors of the entrance was a sign, white with black stenciled letters: Latins Welcome. *Latins* was the polite Anglo word for Mexican. Occasionally, someone used the word *Spanish*. That term was for wealthy, light-skinned Mexicanos, however. Not brown mestizos.

When whites didn't want you, the word was Mexican. Irrespective of what side of the border you were from, Mexican was for anyone. Tejanos, Mexicanos, it did not matter. Almost everywhere, signs were posted: *No dogs or Mexicans.* In that order.

But el Inmaculado was a Catholic hospital. As such, there were parochial ties between the hospital and the parishes in each of the city barrios. Pilar had been to el Inmaculado once before, a year ago, when Joselito had had tonsillitis. It was good in its way—if you had a reason to be in a hospital full of white nurses who spoke only English and treated you, and every other Mexican, with a lofty superiority, patronizing in the best case and openly contemptuous in others. *Latins* were welcome, but they should not forget their place.

She's having the baby too early," José Alfredo said in English to the Anglo nurse at the reception desk when they reached the hospital. "Our regular doctor is out of town."

"I assume one of Doctor M.'s patients," the nurse said. She was an older woman with watery blue eyes and a thin face. "Don't worry. Our Doctor Allen is familiar with the very latest procedures."

"Yes, thank you," José Alfredo agreed.

"How far along is she?"

"Eight months."

"So you're pretty close to term," the nurse said, sliding a sheet of paper across the desk. "Please fill out the admission form."

Pilar said nothing. José Alfredo refused to allow her to put the heels back on, even to walk inside the hospital. Here she stood, barefoot at the reception desk, dealing with a nurse who wanted them to fill out paperwork. The floor was ice-cold and probably filthy. She was conscious that her body was still leaking, and while it shamed her, the greater feeling was anxiety. Her baby was all that mattered. Who cared about forms?

José Alfredo squeezed Pilar's hand. She squeezed back, even though she didn't want to. His hand felt strong and warm in hers. The hospital frightened her. The light was overbright and artificial, somehow forbidding. If only she had some shoes, any shoes.

"My feet are cold," she whispered to him.

"I'll get you something. Be patient," he said. The nurse frowned at him.

"Does your wife speak English?" she asked.

"Yes," Pilar answered.

"Then you should speak it."

Pilar kept her lips firmly together. She would not speak to this woman again, in any language, if she could possibly help it. José Alfredo ignored the nurse too, signing his name at the bottom of the admitting form and passing it back to her in complete silence.

"Wait over there," the nurse said, eyes flinty. "You'll be called in shortly."

The waiting area was crowded with a subdued assortment of sick and injured people, and others who were undoubtedly waiting for their relations. A pair of middle-aged women with a frail, elderly mother between them. An old man reading a newspaper. A mother with two small children, boy and girl, sharing a picture book, while she sat with her pocketbook clutched in her hands. Three teenage boys whispering and laughing, even the one with a bloody forehead.

"Let's sit there," José Alfredo said. He pointed at a sofa in the corner of the room. "How do you feel?"

She sat down, tucking her bare feet under the chair. It was humiliating to be seen in a public place barefoot as some neighborhood child playing in the street. "This didn't happen because of those heels. I didn't fall or anything."

"No, of course not," he replied. "I was just so surprised. Sometimes babies come early, you know? It will be fine."

A contraction seized her. She tried to breathe through it. Tried, less successfully, to ignore the resentment that flared at his explanation. He'd blamed her when it wasn't her fault at all. But of course, he was only willing to admit to *being surprised*.

"I'll get your things as soon as they take you in," José Alfredo said. "I won't take long. You know Romi will be at the house, getting Joselito's pajamas. I bet she's packing a bag for you too."

"Thank goodness for her," Pilar agreed, her voice cold. "They better hurry or I'm going to have the baby right here in this chair."

"Exagerada," José Alfredo said. "We just sat down."

"Who has had a baby before? You or me?"

He was silent. There was an assortment of glossies on the coffee table: *Ladies' Home Journal, Better Homes & Gardens, Western Horseman,* and, in spite of the glowering nurse's insistence on English, *Revista Católica.*

Deliberately, Pilar picked up a women's magazine and opened it. The article featured tips on perfecting a poodle hairstyle. She breathed through another contraction. They were coming faster now. To think, some women bought these magazines, left them artfully on coffee tables in their living room. Women who had money to spend, who were used to cold, bright hospitals. She could feel José Alfredo watching her. Let him. She would not look up. She would read the whole absurd column.

José Alfredo grabbed *Western Horseman.* Her mouth twitched, but she held her peace. He would not be able to read the articles. He could not read English well enough for that. *She* could, but of course, he would not ask her to help him any more than he would apologize.

If anything, he was the one to blame, and not just for spinning her around at the dance. Hadn't that woman come this very day, to find him? Even if he were not a wayward husband, and she did not actually believe he was, not really, the woman had meant to curse her. Had meant to because of José Alfredo. Now here they were. And she, without even her shoes.

A prickly feeling washed over her, a tingling sensation, like dirt flecks against her skin. She'd been barefoot this morning when the woman confronted her, too. *Señora Aguirre, this is everything that belongs to you.*

"Mrs. Aguirre, we're ready for you," said a young nurse pushing a wheelchair. "Can you have a seat for me?"

"Yes." Pilar settled into the chair and smoothed back her hair. She was not going to think about strange women or curses, or even this argument with her husband. Not with her baby coming into the world.

José Alfredo said, "You'll be fine."

"I know," she replied, as one did when speaking to a husband. One agreed not to worry, not to be afraid. One agreed, just to stop admonishments for things he would never understand. One agreed because he was infuriating, and she wanted to get away from him.

"Okay, be mad," he said. He bent, kissed her high on the temple, kissed her full on the mouth. Grinned at her. Dared her to resist him, even when he was wrong. "At least if you're mad, you won't be scared."

Another contraction hit. Pilar hissed. He was the one who looked scared, she thought. He wasn't teasing now.

"We should go," said the young nurse. Then she wheeled Pilar past reception into the labyrinth of white hallways.

44

+ + +

This birth was nothing like when Joselito was born.

Joselito had been born at home. Doctor Mireles had brought a nurse-midwife, Azucena Gonzalez, whom Pilar knew a little from church. It had been a painful, but uneventful birth, with Azucena keeping up an encouraging patter the entire time. Afterward, Joselito was washed, swaddled, and given to her. José Alfredo had come in right away, as soon as it was over.

Doctor Mireles had given Pilar a list of foods to avoid while nursing, mainly cabbage and beans if the baby was colicky. Before he left, the doctor shared a whiskicito with José Alfredo to celebrate his firstborn. In the morning, José Alfredo had made Pilar a breakfast of bacon and pan de campo over a fire right in their yard. He had been that proud and giddy to have a son.

Birthing at el Inmaculado was not like that.

Pilar was taken first to a small and austere room with the same sickly green linoleum as the waiting area. She'd been told to change into a hospital gown. She'd shed her party clothes, dark and sodden with the rush of fluids. The nurse, a young Anglo woman with auburn hair pinned in a neat chignon beneath her peaked white cap, had the decency to turn her back while Pilar undressed.

"All right, into bed," the nurse said, patting the narrow mattress. Pilar had never seen anything like it. There were stirrups at the foot and four leather straps affixed to the frame, one at each stirrup and to each side of the metal bed railings.

"No," Pilar said.

"Don't worry," said the nurse. "Those are just for epileptic patients. If someone is having a seizure."

"Go on." The nurse smiled at her. "You'll be okay."

Reluctantly, Pilar lay down. Another nurse came in. This one was older, perhaps Romi's age. She had a syringe.

"What is that?" Pilar demanded. This older nurse ignored her.

"It's medicine," said the young nurse. She was young enough not to have mastered the art of pretending not to hear someone. "Twilight sleep to take away the pain. It's procedure."

The young nurse grasped Pilar's left arm and swiftly, the older nurse plunged the hypodermic needle into it. Almost immediately the world swam before Pilar's eyes.

"No!" Pilar cried. "Let go of me!"

"Hush," the old nurse said. "You need to calm down. Keep a hold of her, Deborah."

Pilar felt limp and floating all at once. They strapped her wrists to the bed. The young nurse, Deborah, was a liar. She was the one Pilar should have been wary of, with those wide, kind eyes. Oh, the treachery. She should not have gotten on this bed. The old nurse meant business, but would not fool you.

Pilar watched them bare each of her legs and cuff them to the stirrups, but as from a distance. Were they her legs? But they must be. She could see the faint marks across the top of her feet, where the straps of the sandals had been.

"Why are you doing this?" Pilar asked. No one answered her. Then she slipped into the darkness.

***

José Alfredo is here. He is with her, he holds her close, he is loving her. He spoons her, one arm across her chest, as he often does in the clutch of their intimacy, in their bedroom, dark but for the plane of moonlight shifting through the window.

She hears the rustling of large birds alighting in the trees outside. Large birds at night, more than likely owls. The sound of their flapping, like the dry whisper of paper, leaves her cold. His forearm is tight across her chest, his hand clamped on her shoulder. She wants to lift his arm away, but somehow, she cannot. He doesn't know he's squeezing too tight. The birds outside are listening. She wants to tell him, but she has no breath. She thinks she hears two voices, but perhaps it is only one, grumbling to itself.

"Espera," she murmurs, unable to speak aloud. She wishes José Alfredo would stop. She does not want the bird listening to the sound of their love-making. *She'll hear us*, Pilar wants to say, but her voice fails her.

The owl chuckles, low and quarrelsome, as though it has been forced from some other roost and has to content itself with the pecan tree in her yard. She grips José Alfredo's forearm. He murmurs her name low and hot against her neck. The muttering grows until she cannot concentrate on their coupling. There is no pleasure at all, only the disapproving agitation of the leaves.

Outside, the bird lets out a piercing screech and bursts from the tree, snapping twigs. José Alfredo slips away, leaving her empty and gasping. She lies still, feeling her own wretchedness, the queer pulsing of her loins. Any moment now, she will break apart, disintegrate into tiny, aching pieces. Maybe she already has. Maybe it was only his arm, heavy as it was, that held her together.

He pads to the window naked. He stands as though he were in the charro arena, feet apart, ready. She lets her eyes trace the curve of his buttocks, the thighs that are thick and sleek. She has touched every inch of his skin, run her palms and her mouth across his body. Marveled that he is hers. He is hers.

José Alfredo puts his hands on the windowsill and cocks his head to see the sky. Terror flashes through her, bright and hot. The owl will see his upturned face in the moonlight. It will swoop down and pluck out his eyes.

"No," she says. Already a huge, dark shape hovers just beyond the window, casting a nimbus of shadows. She tries to rise, but she cannot. "Get away from the window!"

"It won't come now," José Alfredo says.

"What is it?" she asks. Oh, but she knows. *It's her,* she wants to say. *Get away from there, it's her.* But she cannot speak this.

José Alfredo turns back to Pilar. She can see the lines of his brow in the shaft of moonlight. The rest of his face is in shadow.

"It's the owl that is not an owl."

The daughter that came was small and dead. Doctor Allen, the young Anglo physician, told her the baby had died inside her womb. Pilar's body expelled the baby, Doctor Allen said. That was why she'd come so soon.

"It wasn't anything you did. Just happens sometimes. I'm very sorry," Doctor Allen said, in uncertain but perfectly comprehensible Spanish. Perhaps he had not been told about the hospital's language policy.

"No," Pilar said. "No, that's not true."

I haven't had my baby yet, she thought. But there was her belly, flaccid and thick, telling her otherwise. It was midmorning, she guessed, by the quality of the light against the window. That's where the owl was, she thought, but then realized there were no trees visible outside. Had they really been there?

José Alfredo sat beside her bed. He was crying, a thing she had never witnessed in her life. And the doctor, saying this impossible thing.

"It's not true," she repeated. She was very thirsty. Her head felt light, the shadow of a headache, the tail end of one, or perhaps one just beginning.

"Pili," José Alfredo said, he gripped her hand in the two of his, so hard it hurt. "Pili, mi amor, try to understand."

He wept as if he were unaware of it, eyes glossed and heavy, churning out a silent rush of tears. He was still in his party shirt. It was rumpled, as if he'd slept in it. José Alfredo, out in public in a dirty shirt. It was impossible. All of it was.

"I want her," Pilar said. They would see when they brought her baby. They were wrong. "Where is she?"

"No," José Alfredo said softly. "We shouldn't see the baby. It will make you ill."

"I want to see her."

"I can't," he said. "I can't do it."

"What are you saying? She's our daughter."

"Please, Pili, no." She saw, so clearly, that he was not unaware of his tears, he was ashamed of them. "I can't."

The pain in her head bloomed, but it steeled her. She fixed her eyes on the doctor. "Bring me my daughter. I am her mother. I will see her."

"Yes, yes, all right," Doctor Allen said. His eyes were very blue and anxious. "We'll get her."

José Alfredo made an ugly, choked sound and rushed from the room. Pilar was incredulous. How could he be such a coward? But let him go then, she would not call after him.

Doctor Allen spoke briefly with a nurse just outside Pilar's room. The doctor looked young, younger than she herself, though she knew this could not be so. Perhaps it was his fair hair or his awkward manner. No doubt he would have rather she listen to her husband. It didn't matter.

"Try to stay calm," he said when the auburn-haired nurse brought the little bundle.

"Ay," Pilar said. "Ay, preciosa."

The baby was finished even to her tiny fingernails. She was covered in a light down, fine and tender as the velvety inside of rose petals. Pilar brushed her finger along the little narrow red lines above her closed lids, where eyebrows would have grown in. The downy film came away easily against Pilar's finger. Here was her daughter, the only one she would ever have.

The doctor had not made a mistake. The only mistake was that somehow, though she was perfect, the baby was dead.

"I'm very, very sorry," he said, and he too made a swift escape from the room.

Pilar had half an hour with her daughter. After that, the same nurse tried to take the baby, saying she had to be washed.

"No," Pilar said. "There's a basin here. I can do it."

"I'll bring her right back," said the nurse.

"You're lying," Pilar said. She fought her until the nurse brought in two other nurses, including the old one Pilar remembered.

"Settle down," the old nurse said. "Give her back to us, or you're getting strapped in again."

"No. You're not taking my daughter!"

"Let go," said the old nurse. "Let go, or we'll use the cuffs."

There were three of them. She knew they would do it. Pilar hated them all, especially the old nurse. Hated her as she had never hated anything or anyone. It came into her mind with stark clarity that she wanted to kill this woman. She looked at the old nurse's name tag: Susan.

Pilar opened her hands, despising herself. She stared into the old nurse's eyes. Yes, when she got out of this hospital she would come back and kill Susan.

The old nurse took the baby, though not roughly. She said, "It's a real shame."

Pilar had no use for her sympathy. "I felt her moving, even days ago. How can this be?"

The old nurse shook her head at Pilar. "You have to ask the doctor."

When Pilar asked for her daughter later, another nurse told her it was not good for her to see the body anymore.

"Where is she?" Pilar persisted. Even when she spoke to them in their own language, they would not tell her. She felt wretched and weak and feverish. She got out of bed anyway and made it down a sickly-green hallway. Only the nurses found her. They cuffed her to the bed, though Pilar managed to wallop the old nurse across the face and tear out a good-sized chunk of her hair before they restrained her.

They gave her a sedative. This time, she had no dreams. When she woke the second time she was still cuffed to the bed. She thought she heard José Alfredo's voice somewhere in the hallway. It was Romi who walked into the room a few minutes later. She was in a new blue-checked dress, her brown hair swept up in a stiff bun.

"Ay Dios." She fumbled at the cuffs. "Come on. I brought your clothes. Let's get out of here," Romi said in Spanish.

"We can't leave," Pilar cried. "They took my daughter!"

"Pili, you belted that nurse," Romi said. "I don't blame you, but Madre santísima, let's go! I paid her all my egg money not to call the sheriff."

"Oh, Romi."

"Never mind," Romi said, freeing her. She rubbed Pilar's hands. "Are you hurt?"

"No." Pilar broke down, weeping. "I can't believe this happened. Why did it happen?"

"I don't know," Romi said. "Sometimes it happens this way. I'm sorry. Come on, get dressed."

"José Alfredo left me alone." Pilar gestured at the door. "He just went off."

"He's here. Making . . . arrangements."

"He wouldn't see the baby. He ran away."

"Well, he's a man," Romi said. "They aren't like us. We endure."

"We have to get my daughter. We can't leave her here."

"Pili." Romi took a deep breath. "You can't just take her home with you. They won't let you have the body. It's against the law."

Pilar made no response. She did not want to hear her daughter called *the body* even once more. She wanted to argue, even though she knew it too. The dead could not be taken home. But she had no more energy. She felt empty, hollow as a dried bone. Besides, she could not argue with Romi, who was full of a palpable sorrow.

"Joselito?"

"He's fine. He's been asking for you."

Pilar dressed in silence, exhausted. It had been the same when Joselito was born, the deep ache of her insides. The heaviness when she moved.

Outside in the parking lot she saw Joselito in little Yolanda's arms, both of them sitting on the tailgate of Chuy's truck. Chuy, leaning against his truck, looking like an old sad hound. Joselito twisted out of Yolanda's arms and rushed to her.

"No, no, mijo," said Romi. "You must be gentle with Mami right now. Okay?"

Pilar felt fresh pain when Joselito clutched her, but it didn't matter. "I'm fine. I'm fine. Come on, mijo."

She pressed him to her, his sturdy little body. His quick warm breath a balm on her skin. They waited in silence until José Alfredo appeared. He seemed surprised to see them all collected around the entrance to the building. He was not crying anymore.

"Pili's been alone a long while," Romi said.

"Romi," Chuy murmured. "Don't."

"I had to pay the bill," said José Alfredo. After that he had barely enough civility to thank the Muñozes for their assistance. When they had gone, he settled Pilar in the truck gently, very gently, and cradled the base of her neck in his hand. "I am sorry that I left you by yourself. Please forgive me."

Pilar brushed his apology aside. "Where is my daughter? What were these arrangements?"

"I won't discuss it in front of Joselito," he said, withdrawing his hand.

Oh, his familiar implacability. Her rage was immediate, beating inside her like a wild animal. It was unbearable to be this angry and this exhausted at the same time. She leaned her head against the cool glass of the truck window. "Fine."

It was bright outside, nearly noon. They didn't speak on the rest of the drive, nor at home. José Alfredo spent the day in the yard, cleaning his riding tack with an oily sheepskin. She lay in their darkened bedroom, weak with body aches, lulled by the low incessant coo of mourning doves and Joselito, humming and playing with his little plastic soldiers in his bedroom. She slept and slept.

When she woke it was night. Joselito was asleep. José Alfredo was sitting on the porch steps, smoking. She went to him, asked again what had happened to her daughter.

"She died inside," José Alfredo said. "That's what happened. You already know."

"How can that happen?" she demanded. "I felt her inside. Moving. Even yesterday. How can she suddenly die?"

"I don't know," he said. "I'm not the doctor."

"You're not the doctor," she snapped. "Nobody talks to me! What have they done with her?"

He flushed. "I don't know. They didn't say."

"You didn't ask them what they did with your own daughter?"

"The baby is dead, Pili. They did what they have to do with the stillborn ones."

"I held her!" cried Pilar. "She must be somewhere! We have to go back for her!"

"You're going to make yourself sick," José Alfredo said. "Please calm down."

"We have to go back. We have to get our baby."

"No, Pili," said José Alfredo. His lip trembled, but his voice was firm. "No, we can't."

"What did they do?" Pilar demanded, looking at him steadily. "You know."

"I had to pay them a hundred dollars," he said, finally. "They cremate the stillborn ones. It costs a hundred dollars."

"They burned her," Pilar whispered in horror. "You didn't even want to see her, but you paid them to burn her."

"I had to." He would not look at her.

"She won't have a burial. She doesn't even have a name. Don't you care about that?"

"Pili," he said, in a low voice. He stared out into the darkness. "She couldn't have a name on the birth certificate because she wasn't born alive. That is the law with every stillborn baby. To name her, we would have to apply to change the certificate after it is filed. To apply to change the name, we would have to go to the notary. We have to pay the notary. We have to pay to change the certificate. We have to wait two weeks for the new certificate to arrive."

He knuckled his hand in his hair. "We can't get the funeral home to bury her with a name until the certificate is changed. We have to pay for them to hold the body until that happens, for two weeks, to hold the body. This is what they told me. What could I do?"

Good God, how many times would everyone call her daughter *the body*? Was her baby nothing but this bit of cast-off mortal flesh? Pilar wanted to scream.

Under the dingy yellow porch light his hands pulled and pulled at his hair, the rest of him a shadow. She knew even as she had fought for life, for her baby's life, in the birth, he had had to face the white hospital workers and their paperwork. José Alfredo, who was not strongly literate. But still. He had done this and she hated him. She *hated* him.

"How do you even know that?" Pilar sneered. "Did you read that somewhere, all by yourself?"

"No," he said, not even shamed by her insult. "Chuy helped me read everything. That's why I couldn't see her," he admitted. "Oh God, I couldn't see her."

She had never seen her husband like this, so defeated. Undone. But there was no pity for him inside her, only an awful clarity. "It was the price of the two weeks in the funeral home. Wasn't it?"

He was silent.

"We don't have the money," she said. "Because you spent it on this house. That's why."

He still refused to answer her. She knew she was right.

"You had to have your house. You just had to."

"Leave me alone," he said, muffled. "Leave me alone."

"You burned our daughter!"

José Alfredo ran from her. Bolted off the porch and jumped in his truck. She watched him go, bone-weary, aching with grief and the misery of milk surging in her breasts. She didn't have the energy or the desire to call after him. Worst of all he woke Joselito. She heard his anxious little voice in the dark, his padding feet as he ran to her.

Joselito's small hands clutched her nightgown, his head butting against her thigh. "Where is Papi going?"

"To the store," Pilar said, smoothing back his curls. "He'll be right back. You need to go to sleep."

"I'm thirsty."

She lifted him into her arms. He was heavy, but she held him, went into the kitchen and filled a cup with water. He drank only a few sips and then drowsed against her. Pilar carried Joselito to her bedroom, curled up next to him. He fell asleep immediately.

They are not like us, Romi had said. How right she was, Pilar thought. One night after losing her daughter and she was alone, just she and her sleeping firstborn. Husband fled, only God knew to where.

José Alfredo did not come home that night. She lay her hand lightly on Joselito's side, feeling the miraculous soft rise and fall, every sweet breath. The coyotes sent up their thin night wails. Owls whistled and chuckled in the trees. For the first time, Pilar did not fear the darkness outside her door.

Pilar lay awake, filled with a calm that was not serenity. A watchful silence, waiting for him to return. A dull anger that would abide and abide and abide inside her, more fearsome than whatever roamed the brush on Loma Negra.

my name

LULU MUÑOZ, 1994

Mexican dads are stupid about picking names for their daughters. They're old-fashioned. They want something religious like Maria Guadalupe, or super romantic like Isabela. Every other Mexican girl is named Maria Guadalupe and Isabela, but Mexican dads never stop to think about that. Why should they? They're Mexican dads. Whatever they say goes, period.

The worst is if you're a girl and your dad was a Mexican teenager in the late sixties, in the cosmic grip of the Chicano movement. Even if he didn't care about school walkouts or protesting in front of the courthouse, even if all he did for the cause was listen to the Royal Jesters while he hot-boxed in his Nova, he turned *Chicano* forever.

Bad luck. Because instead of religious and romantic, he went political and named his baby girl Crystal for Crystal City, Texas, birthplace of the Raza Unida Party. Or else something idealistic like Esperanza, or he took it back to the roots Aztec-style with Xochitl. He didn't care that you were going to go through life as one of five hundred Crystals. He didn't care that some dumbass was going to call you Esperanto or the fucking worst ever, Xoch-Panoch. He's sentimental.

Bad luck. Because you're a girl and he's a same old same old Mexican, even if he blares Cream and Deep Purple and the Hollies over the stereo while he works in the yard. He won't let you wear Doc Martens, because they're for men and lesbianas. He won't let you go to concerts. What, you think he's a big pendejo? His daughter isn't hanging around with a bunch of devil-worshipping marijuanos who just want to screw her. And let's be clear—those are just the heavy metal Satanists. Every guy is out to screw his daughter.

It sucks being his daughter. Especially if you sort of have a rock band, like me. My bandmates are guys, and if I ever set foot in one of their houses my dad would kill them. I don't tell them that, but they know. He's so Mexican he's Mexicano.

My dad is Don't Tell Me about His Panic, Viva Aztlán, Brown Power militant. That's why I'm the only Lucha in my high school. Lucha, noun and verb. Lucha, the battle cry. Lucha is what my dad named me, *fight*.

Grandma Romi says she never met anybody that liked to get crossways with people as much as my dad does. *Except you, Lulu*, she tells me lately.

I don't mean to. It's just my dad. What he wants. What he says. All the time.

Like this quinceañera. We've been in a deadlock since last summer. He's going to have his quinceañera in February. That's right, it's his party. I don't care if I'm turning fifteen; I don't want to prance around in a frilly dress. I'm not a fucking debutante. Besides, it's all bullshit—they say it's a coming out party for becoming a woman, like getting your Confirmation at church, but really it's just my dad dropping big cash on a circus so he can trot me around like a trained poodle. And afterward, the same curfew, the same rules, but there's a giant glamour portrait of me in a tiara hanging in the living room.

Science says I became a woman when I was eleven. That was three years ago, but do you think I can buy a box of tampons without him flipping out? Nope. It's gross bulky pads for me because plastic applicators scare the shit out of him. Every little thing in the whole world enrages and terrifies him. If he's not watching out, I might become a mala. And for a Mexican man, a mala is the worst. Once his daughter's gone bad, she's bad forever. So it's his job to make sure she never gets that chance. That's my dad's idea of me becoming a woman.

But I can't explain any of this to Grandma because she is old, old, old. If she sits too long, she falls asleep.

It's very sad what's happening, she says. She means my dad and me, our fights. Lately that's all we do, but it wasn't always that way. After my mother died, I couldn't stand to be away from him. I was five years old and, outside of work, my dad took me with him everywhere. I was the whiny kid in the back of the movie theater. I stretched out in restaurant booths and slept beneath his leather jacket. I had to be where I could put out my hand and find him.

I want to tell Grandma that one night I curled up in the back of the Blazer when he and his friend Jesse took a trio of musicians to serenade a girl Jesse liked. That girl, she never even turned on the light to let Jesse know she was listening. *Fuck that bitch,* my dad said, and to cheer Jesse up he drove around for two hours with the musicians crammed in the middle seat. There was a violinist, a guitarist, and a man with an acoustic bass so large he had to roll down the window to play it. My dad wouldn't let them out until he'd gotten the time Jesse'd paid for, plus my requests—*Whatcha wanna hear, Lulu? Y'all better play something for my baby.* They cursed my dad, but they did it.

The guitarist sang in a high sweet voice that warbled when the Blazer hit potholes. My dad sang along too and it was a marvel to me that he knew the words to all those songs. I lay on the floorboard and listened to them sing. The cold breeze snatched their voices out the open window and outside the streetlights loomed and faded, loomed and faded, until I fell asleep.

These days my dad bellows, *Lucha!* And I am readysetgo. I am trapped like those musicians, just holding out for the car ride to be over. Only I won't play for him.

Chapter Three

Witch Luck

My grandma Romi died the first week of October. The night she died, my dad was in his recliner, watching *The Johnny Canales Show* and working his way through a case of Coors Light while I did my Physics homework at the dinner table.

"This chavo's pretty good," he said, all fake casual, like he didn't know I wasn't speaking to him. "That's real conjunto right there."

It was a live performance: a young guy in a cowboy hat and a rhinestone black western shirt crooned mournfully onstage, punctuating his lyrics with sad accordion flourishes. The bottom of the screen said the guy's name, Michael Salgado.

"Uh huh," I said, noncommittal. I didn't want to talk to him. I hadn't forgiven him. No way.

"Who do you think his influences are?" my dad asked. He loved to quiz me on music. His music. "Can you tell?"

He reached into the Igloo cooler he kept beside his recliner and popped the top on a fresh beer. Probably his eighth since he'd parked himself in the recliner. His buzz was making him chatty. I stared at my homework.

Drinking makes him touchy too. He'd take it personal if I went to my room right away.

"I don't know." I doodled on the paper. Since Gonzy died, I said the least I could get away with. But the silence got too uncomfortable. "I guess he sounds like . . . Cornelio Reyna?"

Because of my dad I know about conjunto music. Conjunto is what happened when German immigrants and rural northern Mexicans, norteños, grooved together starting in the late eighteen hundreds. Polkas, waltzes, and cumbias, the signature sound is button accordion. It doesn't matter. I don't like the guessing game anymore.

"That's right, mija. Old Corny." He flashed a grin at me. My best friend Marina says he doesn't seem like a real dad. Maybe not. He's kind of muscly with thick, perfectly straight black hair that he wears a little long. Also, he's the only Mexican dad around who is in his forties and doesn't sport a big Tony Orlando mustache. Tonight, though, he looked haggard. I could tell he hadn't slept for a couple of days. But still, when he twinkles, it's hard not to smile back.

Old Corny was a joke of ours. He loved Cornelio Reyna, a Mexican singer from the sixties. He'd call him Old Corny, and I'd say, *Dad*, all *that music's corny*. Now, I refused to answer, just tilted my face back at my notebook. Too bad for him.

"Anyway, that's why I like this guy," my dad said, a little surly, gesturing at the TV with his beer hand. "Toca más norteño que tejano."

"Michael Salgado's American," I pointed out, just to disagree. "He's Tejano."

"He is, but the music isn't. I told you, it doesn't matter what side it comes from." This is one of my dad's regular rants: Americans stole Texas, but conjunto was born on both sides of the border! On the other side of the river, conjunto is called norteño. On this side, it's Tejano.

"Obviously, it does matter," I snipped. The difference between norteño and Tejano music is just like being Mexican or Mexican American. No, we're not the same. "That's why Tejano sounds more modern."

"Agringado, you mean." Another of his gripes: Tejano music isn't Mexican enough. These days, tejano is full of synthesizer, electric guitar, jazz, blues, pop, and other American stylizing. A lot less accordion. Some groups dress vaquero, but just as many go for flashy sequin outfits and El DeBarge mullets. This is personally offensive to my dad. He thinks stuff that's Mexican should stay Mexican.

I considered baiting him even more by telling him *he* isn't technically Mexican since he was born here, but the phone rang. I grabbed the cordless, figuring it was Marina. It was a good chance to get away to my bedroom.

"Tell your amiguita it's late to be calling and get off the phone," my dad said. I'd gotten on his nerves.

It was a lady asking for Jules. Not for *your dad*, or Mr. Muñoz or even Julio. She asked for Jules. I almost couldn't breathe.

"It's for you," I said, giving him a death glare. It was the same lady; I just knew it.

He must have known it too. He snatched the cordless and walked out to the back patio, shutting the glass sliding door behind him. I went back to the dining room table, but I didn't even try to finish my homework. I strained to hear what he was saying. All I caught was the deep tone of his voice.

"I need to get back to the body shop," he said when he came in. "Have to finish a Suburban by tomorrow morning. Get ready to go to Grandma's."

"Yeah, okay," I said. Unbelievable. Bam, just like that. Lulu, pack a bag, you're spending the night at Grandma's. He's always dumping me at her house. That wasn't the thing, though. It was that fucking lady.

"Hey," he said as I was putting up my Physics book. "Go feed the puppy."

"He's your dog, you do it."

He pulled on one of his black engineer boots. "Lulu, come on. I have to get ready."

"No way!" I ran to my bedroom and slammed the door. Like some new puppy could make up for what happened to my poor old Gonzy.

I heard my dad cussing in the living room, but he didn't follow me. Probably he just wanted to hurry up—it was almost eight o'clock. I dug my black cotton Mary Janes out of the closet, rolled them up with a T-shirt in a pair of clean jeans, and stuffed the whole thing in my backpack.

"You're gonna have to start taking care of him," my dad said when I came back to the living room. "He's your dog too."

I glared at him. "My dog's dead. Somebody murdered him."

My dad was such a jerk he couldn't even look me in the eye. He knew. He just didn't care.

"Hurry up," he said, and stomped outside to his truck.

We didn't speak on the drive. It was a long one because he won't go by the river road if he's with me. We took the La Cienega Avenue Expressway. Six lanes running west of San Antonio all the way to the international bridge at Ciudad Bravo. The river road is faster from our house, but that's where the motorcycle accident happened eight years ago, when my mom got killed.

My dad's totally superstitious. He thinks he's cursed with double-sided luck, witch luck. He's the bad luck charm for everybody else. The accident that killed my mom only broke his wrist. Instead of blaming my mom's death on the drunk driver that hit them, my dad decided it was "the curse." This is why I have no social life.

Grandma's street is off the exit with the bright-green sign **La Cienega Trade Bridge 1 | United States Port of Entry | Cd. Bravo, Coahuila,**

Mex. She doesn't live in Mexico, but almost. Grandma's neighborhood is all stray chickens, tin roofs, and half streets. It's a mile from the international bridge, but all the way across town from us. We live on the north side, where the neighborhood is full of speed bumps and SUV-driving border patrol wives.

Grandma waved at us from behind the screen door as the truck pulled into the gravel driveway. A blue light flickered in the living room window. Grandma's eight o'clock telenovela, the one set in colonial Mexico.

My dad waved back, but didn't get out of the truck. He tried to hug me goodbye, but I jumped out and slammed the truck door on him.

"Have fun *working*," I said, quotation marking with my fingers.

"Get in the goddamn house!"

He gunned the engine, kicking up a spray of gravel against my feet. He pulled out of the drive and I saw his taillights flare at the four-way. He wasn't going to work. He wasn't going back home. He was headed downtown and not even bothering to hide it.

That's when I decided I'd get rid of the puppy. That same night, while he was out doing God knows what. He'd never know it was me. Let him try and ignore another dead dog.

"What was all that?" Grandma asked when I walked up the steps.

She was always at the screen door, watching for when we got there. I don't know, maybe she waited until the commercial break, or maybe she went to the door as soon as she got off the phone.

"Nothing."

"Doesn't look like nothing," she said.

I didn't say anything. She had leftovers warming on the stove: fried potatoes and a couple of flour tortillas. She picked a hot tortilla off the cast-iron comal, something I couldn't do without burning my fingers, and tucked a spoonful of potatoes into the fold.

I slouched into a chair at the kitchen table. "All of a sudden he has to go back to work. Yeah right."

"Mija," said Grandma, sounding tired. "Some people think they can hide the sun with their little finger, but they don't fool anybody. Especially not a smart girl like you."

"I'm sorry."

Grandma took the rest of the tortillas off the comal, covered them, and set the bundle on the table. Her fingers were thin and papery. The heavy ring with all her children's birthstones had slipped sideways. I reached out and pushed it to rights.

"That one's your dad's," she said, tapping the ruby. I knew it, though. My dad bought her this ring, with real stones. I know them all by heart: opal for Miguel, sapphire for Yolanda, ruby for my dad. Tío Miguel got killed in World War II. There's only Yoli and my dad left.

Tía Yoli lives in Houston. I love her, but mostly see her on holidays. Now that her son Carlos is in college she wants Grandma to come live with her, but Grandma keeps saying no. I don't blame her. Yoli is so bossy.

My dad's the baby. Grandma had him when she was nearly fifty. He was a surprise, change of life baby, but Grandma gets a kick out of making up stories about him. She says Grandpa Chuy, who had been a river rider for the government, found my dad by the Rio Grande and brought him home to her, muddy and covered in horsehair because Grandpa had bundled him up in a saddle blanket. Pretty ridiculous stuff, but when I say so, Grandma just laughs. *People believe that yarn ten times easier than the truth.*

Grandma wrapped the taco in a paper towel and gave it to me. "I understand you're upset. That doesn't mean you have to make a spectacle in my yard."

I took a giant bite of the taco so I wouldn't say, *He's a liar, you know he is.* I wouldn't argue with Grandma, not for anything. Besides, he's a holy terror, but my dad is her favorite; her miracle baby and cross to bear, all rolled into one. Grandma says my dad's proof God's got a silver cord for all of us. Only, she says, my dad's is probably made of barbed wire.

"Finish your snack," Grandma said. "I'm going outside to water my plants."

Really, she was going outside to smoke a Lucky Strike. We both knew it. She just didn't want to come out and say it. Grandma smokes a cigarette every day. Just one. I tell her all the time how bad it is for her, but she won't listen. She just says she's eighty-eight years old, so she's allowed.

"I'll wash the dishes, Grandma," I offered. I said it to make myself feel better for fighting with my dad in front of her. I didn't change my mind about my plan though.

Later, I crouched beside my bedroom door, a bunch of peanut butter crackers stuffed in the pocket of my hoodie, waiting for midnight. Grandma had one of those old-fashioned clocks in the living room, the kind that wheezes and grinds when it gears up to mark the hour. At noon and midnight that thing gong-gong-gongs for almost five minutes.

Grandma had been in bed for an hour. I heard her snoring, but still, I needed the cover of that noisy clock. This wasn't like sitting on the back patio at home, talking to Marina on the cordless while my dad was passed out in the living room. Grandma felt the floorboards shift when I padded to the bathroom in the dark. She checked why the lamp was on when I stayed up writing in my diary. She had a radar.

The clock started making its midnight racket and I scurried across the living room. I jerked the front door open like I was ripping off a Band-Aid. The heavy wood creaked once, but that was all. I scooped up the telephone from its nook beside the door and slipped outside.

The night was full of sound. Heavy gusts of wind shook the trees and mating frogs trilled, loud and reedy, from the ditch behind the house. I closed the front door as lightly as I could, leaving a sliver of space just wide enough for the phone cord. I pressed my ear to the crack. Nothing but the clock ticking and, audible from her bedroom, my grandma going like a baby buzz saw.

She was alive at midnight. I heard her.

I hid behind Grandma's bougainvillea bush and paged Ernie, my only friend with a car. He was still at work. He'd been working at the freight yard since midsummer, unloading trucks. Since he'd gotten a job, he didn't have a curfew anymore. As far as I was concerned, that alone was worth lugging boxes around.

I cleared the line and called Phone-In Fairytale, the automated storyteller at the public library. It was one of the first numbers I memorized when I was a kid. The tape would run through about an hour's worth of stories before it cut off. I used to listen to it all the time.

These days I called when I wanted to talk to Ernie. It was a good way to occupy the line so the phone wouldn't ring. The story was the one about the girl with all the swan-brothers. Sometimes I fell asleep before he called, but with the wind cold against my neck, the story didn't lull. I was glad when the call-waiting tone beeped.

"Hey, I'm at my grandma's tonight."

"Well, don't go to sleep," said Ernie. "I'll call you when I get home. I'm off in twenty minutes."

"Wait, don't hang up."

"I'm in Sal's office," Ernie said, impatient. "I have to get out of here before he comes back."

"Wanna go to the lake?"

Ernie got quiet. I thought he wanted to ask why, but he didn't.

"Yeah, okay. Meet me up the block from my house."

"Okay."

"You want anything?"

"No. Like what?"

"I don't know. Never mind." He hung up.

I unplugged the phone and tucked it beneath the bushes. Probably the best thing to do was avoid the street. I could climb the hill at the end of Grandma's street, cut across the front yard of the abandoned Aguirre place, and then come down into the Azteca Courts park. Ernie's house was just two blocks from there. It was a scary walk in the dark, but the shortest route.

I left Grandma's, taking care to keep my hood up and avoid the street-lights. A couple of blocks away the street dead-ended into the foot of the hill, Loma Negra. I hiked up the hill, about ten minutes in actual wilderness: a winding deer trail, clumped over with thorny catclaw bushes that caught at my sleeves. By the time I reached the house, I was amped up by the furtive rustling noises of unseen things moving around in the brush.

The Aguirre place is the only house on Loma Negra. It's creepy for sure. Old, wood framed, just like the houses in Grandma's neighborhood, but empty. There's an ancient shed almost the size of a barn out there, be-yond the house. I didn't stop to look, the house was spooky enough. It even had a rickety wooden wraparound porch, just the kind of thing where you glance over your shoulder, and something is creeping up behind you.

They say the Aguirre place is cursed. Only one family ever lived in it. The mother murdered her son. Legend says if you spend the night out in the yard, you'll see his ghost peeping at you from the windows. The house stays empty because who wants to live in an old, haunted dump? No, I'm not superstitious! Still, I was so unnerved by the scratchy sound of the bare trees in the wind that I flat-out sprinted through the front yard, too chicken to look back.

I jumped the irrigation ditch at the bottom of the hill, the cuffs of my hoodie clenched in my fists. On the other side was a park that was mostly asphalt, just a basketball court and a thin border of grass with a merry-go-round on it.

Four skinny boys were playing hoops in the dark, but they were hitting their layups solid. On the curb next to the court, a guy in a Spurs jersey leaned against the side of a Buick LeSabre, his arm around a girl I knew I'd seen but whose name I couldn't remember. The guy dipped his face to the girl's ear and the girl giggled and fake-punched him, saying, "Whatever, Jaime. Whatever."

I kept walking. Sure enough, I was almost to the next block, passing a yard where a few men, a little older than my father, were sitting around drinking beer in their undershirts and listening to the Mexican station, when the girl let out a high laugh, the kind that rises and carries on the air like a bird's cry.

One of the men bolted out of his aluminum chair and strode into the street with the beer bottle held loosely by the neck. "Bren-da! Get in the house!"

Like that, Brenda dashed inside one of the houses. The man with the beer bottle stood in the street until the boy got in his car. The car moved off, slow and insolent, around the opposite corner.

"And you," the man said, turning his bloodshot eyes on me. "You get your little ass home too!"

I ran away. The men in the yard laughed. Fucking assholes.

I don't know why my dad ever left the neighborhood. He would have been right at home with those guys. A girl could be doing anything. Or nothing. He'd say she was out slutting it around, a huila for sure. In Spanish class, Mr. Ramos says that word means kite. When my dad says it, he means the other word, but I picture girls flying away like little kites, their strings snapped, freewheeling across the skies.

I sprinted the rest of the way to Ernie's street. He lived on the last stretch of road before the neighborhood gave way to the marshes along the Rio Grande. I smelled the water first, mossy and stale, and then saw his '72 Chevelle parked in front of the Dead End sign. He was sitting on the trunk, still in his Yellow Freight uniform, smoking a cigarette.

"We gotta stop at my house first," I told him. "I need to get something."

"Are you nuts? Isn't your dad there?"

"I don't think so, but I left my journal on the patio."

"Then he probably already has it."

"He doesn't. But I have to get it."

"Why? Who'd you write about?"

"None of your business."

"It's me. I know."

"I know you're stupid."

"For real, who'd you write about?"

"Nobody, Ernie! Can we just go?"

"Okay, okay, damn. At least let me change my clothes." He frowned. "You better wait out here. My mom will flip out if she finds you in the house."

Ernie came back with damp hair. He was wearing a black Suicidal Tendencies muscle-shirt. Ever since he had gotten the job as a freight loader most of the shirts he bought were tight or didn't have sleeves. It was kind of hot, but he was such a dumbass, always flexing and saying dorky shit like, *Welcome to the gun show.*

"Check it out," he said. He held up a half-finished bottle of Don Pedro. "Let's go party."

"Sounds good," I said, settling into the seat. "But I'm not gonna drink that. That shit is gross."

"That's why they invented Slurpees. For wusses like you." He dodged my fist and laughed.

The traffic lights on the strip were flashing yellow. It was a Wednesday night and there weren't many cars on the road, just a cluster of trucks at Denny's.

I didn't know what I was going to say to Ernie. Some things could be told. When my dad found my cache of metal tapes and stomped on them, Ernie said, *I'll make you copies*, and he put the phone up to the stereo so I could hear what he was taping for me. Some things could be told, in a way. Instead of telling Ernie that someone had killed Doctor Gonzo, my sweet old shepherd, eight years old and solid gray at the muzzle (he was a birthday present puppy from my mom the year she died), instead of saying that someone had actually gone into the backyard and shot him in the head and hadn't even bothered to close the gate afterward, I said that Gonzy had been hit by a car. Ernie made this awesome pencil portrait of Gonzy (but he signed it *Ernesto Vega* so I sprayed it down with Marina's Aqua Net and hid it in the back of my Trapper Keeper because I'm not going to put Ernie's name anywhere my dad can see), and my best friend Marina said, *Oh my God, Ernie likes you*, and I said, *Shut up*, but it was true.

That's why Ernie took me across town. I knew he would. It was shitty of me, because if he got caught my dad would beat the piss out of him. Ernie knew it too, but that's how much he liked me. I was a fucking dick, because I'd counted on him liking me enough to bring me.

It took thirty minutes to drive to the north side. I live in the new subdivision, where the houses are evenly spaced and identical and behind our street bulldozers are still clearing out the sage. The land behind my house is flat, open desert. That's where I told Ernie to park.

I got out of the car. The rows of tiny lights on the second international bridge, the one over the lake, twinkled at the western horizon. I would take the puppy there. I would drop it off the bridge. I could see it: the plunging white form of the puppy, disappearing. Just a little splash and then the waters smoothing over, like nothing had ever been there at all.

"Okay," I said. "If you see the lights come on, haul ass out of here. Seriously."

"This is fucked up," said Ernie. "What's going on?"

"Just do it, okay?"

He shook his head. "Shit."

I ran to the fence, aware of how easy it was to be seen. The ground was white and dry in the moonlight. I looked back and saw the distinct black shape of the car. But I couldn't see Ernie, and that was something. I hoped he would really go if the lights went on.

The house was dark. I climbed the fence and landed with a thump on my dad's freshly laid Home Depot grass sod. The laundry room was just off the backyard patio. It wasn't a real room, just a small shed with a low wood lattice for walls. The puppy's kennel was in there, next to the dryer.

The puppy was awake. I opened the kennel door and lifted him out. He snuffled my hand as I zipped him inside my hoodie, his little tail whipping hard. I slipped a cracker in his mouth to keep him quiet.

I was about to go back outside when I realized the sliding glass door to the patio was open. I heard my dad say, *Margarita*. A woman's name. Margarita, low and sweet and beckoning. The way I imagined, when I ran my finger lightly across Ernie's signature on the picture he'd drawn for me, it would sound to say, *Ernesto*.

Right then, if my dad had come outside, I wouldn't have backed down. Because I knew for sure now. I knew her name. What would he have done, pretended she didn't exist, just like he pretended nothing bad happened to Gonzy, just like he pretended all the bad things he did weren't real? I wanted them to come out so I could see them. So he'd know I knew.

It was his fault Gonzy died. I told him about the man who called the house that day after school, but he didn't listen. *Your dad's dead meat*, the man had said and hung up. It made me want to vomit the sandwich I'd been eating. A few days later there was Gonzy with the top of his head blown off, pink and gray brains spattered in the yard.

I yelled right in his face, my stupid, stupid dad, who thought I wouldn't understand why Gonzy got shot. *You stupid asshole! You think I don't know why this happened? You think I don't know why some dude is that fucking mad?* Of course I knew. Everybody knew, even Grandma who couldn't stay awake through *Montel*.

My dad was stuffing Gonzy into a black plastic lawn bag, trying to get rid of him. He didn't even have the guts to tell me off for calling him an asshole. He just grabbed up the plastic bag and rushed out of the yard.

My dad didn't come home that night. I talked on the phone all I wanted to Marina, in the middle of the living room even, but I never told her. Not even after.

Because what am I going to say about it? That a couple of days later my dad brought me a new puppy? That he's still fucking some bitch named Margarita, whose husband killed my dog?

The puppy snuggled against my chest, his muzzle in the hollow of my throat. I clutched him, my whole body trembling. I held it in, held it in until that weepy feeling folded up like a hard fist. Ernie was waiting out there.

There were no more voices, just the low sound of music coming from farther inside, probably my dad's bedroom. I walked into the yard with the puppy tucked into the crook of my elbow and did not look back. Climbing the fence was harder with only one free hand. I slipped and tore my sleeve, scratched my forearm from the back of my wrist to the elbow. It burned in the cold air. I gave the dog another couple of crackers. My shirt was probably smeared with peanut butter, but I didn't care.

Ernie was sweating. It was shining all over his face. "Jesus, Lulu! What took you so long?"

"Sorry," I whispered. I was. But I still didn't tell him what we were doing. "Let's get out of here."

The car crept between the bulldozers, quiet and slow, but just when we got back to the street, Ernie got nervous and stomped on the gas pedal.

"Watch out, watch out!" I yelled, but he hit a speed bump dead-on. The car jumped and landed with a hard, horrible scrape on the asphalt. I hit my forehead on the window. The puppy started barking like crazy.

"What the hell is that?"

"It's a dog, duh. Let's go!"

"You swiped your own dog? That's fucking stupid!" Ernie caught a bad fit of giggling and the car stalled out.

"Hurry up, my dad's home!"

"Shit," he gasped, still laughing. He tore down the street, swerving around the speed bumps at breakneck speed. I pressed my cheek to the window, pretending it was his driving making my stomach lurch.

At the fork before the highway, he pulled into a 7-Eleven. He bought two bubblegum-flavor Slurpees. Then he crouched in the crook of the open door with a flashlight, craning his head to see the undercarriage.

"Well," he said finally, "the oil pan's still there."

"Man, I can't believe you choked like that."

"Shut up." He hopped back in the car and smirked at me. "Let's see this dog."

I unzipped my hoodie. The puppy blinked around and then sprang onto the seat, snuffling the stick shift.

"Oh damn. That's a pit bull."

Ernie put his hand over the puppy's face. It tussled with his forearm, mock-growling and gripping Ernie's wrist with its little teeth. He looked at me over the puppy's stout head. "So, what's the deal with this guy?"

"He has to go."

"Why you trying to get rid of your dog?"

"My dad's an asshole. I don't wanna talk about it."

"Whatever." Ernie shrugged. "I bet Sal would buy him. He's been saying he wants a guard dog over at Yellow Freight. Bet we could get two-fifty."

"Sell him?"

"Of course. What were you gonna do, dump him on the side of the highway? He's gonna get hit by a car out here."

"So?"

"God damn, Lulu. Are all the Muñozes bastards like that?"

My plan looked so different with Ernie sitting opposite me and the fluorescent light of the 7-Eleven streaming in through the windshield. I couldn't answer him. So I said, "We should go halfsies on what we get for him."

"Sure," Ernie said. He shook his head. "Hope I never piss you off."

At the lake, Ernie turned down at the end of a caliche road near the railroad bridge. It was an old iron bridge scalloped with low-slung black metal arches, like a row of humpbacks running across the water.

The second international bridge was farther south. I saw the dim yellow lights of the customs port in the distance.

Ernie parked in the brush so the border patrol wouldn't see the car and come hassle us for drinking. He brought the bottle of Don Pedro and the Slurpees. The puppy had crashed out on the drive to the lake, so I left him asleep under my hoodie in the back seat.

"You think anybody else would buy him? Somebody that doesn't know my dad?" I couldn't help it. "What if he runs into Sal or something?"

"Lulu, you just broke into your dad's house while he was home. You wanted to snuff a puppy. Don't puss out on me."

"You're the puss."

We found a big boulder to sit on. Ernie spiked my Slurpee, which made it taste stale. He drank straight from the bottle just to tease me. He was taking little sips though, so I didn't feel that dumb.

The night had a hazy glow. A fingernail moon. Hordes of clear white stars. We were out on the chaparral, which even in late autumn was flush with pale-gray cenizo so that the land above the shoreline seemed covered in low-lying silver clouds. The railroad bridge stretched over the water, its humpbacks studded with blue lights. Only the lake was slick and black.

Ernie kept brushing against me by accident on purpose. Why did it have to be like that? Everybody pretending they weren't when they were.

"What are you doing? Do you want to kiss me or something?"

"No," he said. What a liar.

He slid off the boulder saying he needed some music. A few minutes later, Los Fabulosos Cadillacs cranked out of the stereo. He didn't come back.

Whatever. I didn't need him. I just wanted to be here. No bullshit. Nothing but the water slapping on the rocks.

"I'm going in," I yelled, mostly so I could say I'd told him.

I took off my T-shirt and jeans and waded in. Fuck, it was cold. I kicked away from the shore, scissored my legs hard, arms stretching out and out, pulling myself into the deep black waves.

I was on the swim team all during middle school. Mostly it's my dad's thing. He says his kid needs to know how to handle herself in the water. So, I'm pretty good. Better than my dad. I can outswim him any day of the week. Not that it's hard to beat a forty-year-old whose only exercise is doing beer-curls every night, but still. That's why he won't race me anymore. Now he just brags that I'm going to be the only freshman on the varsity team.

He doesn't know I didn't join. It was easy to just not sign up. Coach left a voicemail on our machine, but I deleted it.

I rolled onto my back and made lazy circles. I had drifted near the middle of the railroad bridge; the blue lights suspended over the water weren't small anymore. The water bumped and swayed. It was good here, outside of everything. No open patio doors. Or girls who drowned dogs. Just the occasional twitchy little splash of leaping bass. Even the music had cut off. I didn't want to go back home. Except the wind was picking up and the waves were getting choppy. I couldn't stay out much longer.

Ernie called my name, his voice far away and distorted. He yelled again, louder—"Lulu! Lulu!"—and a night bird called back to him, a long, warbling cry like a woman moaning and laughing at the same time. The kind of thing that would freak out my superstitious dad.

Michael Boyd drowned out here, I remembered suddenly. Last February. We went on the same mathlete tournament the weekend before he died. He let me borrow his Walkman on the way home. The next weekend was one of those fake-out winter heat waves you get in South Texas sometimes, eighty degrees and sunny out of nowhere. Michael went boating with his little brother and the brother fell out of the boat. Mike jumped in after him, saved his life. Only he got hypothermia because he couldn't get out in time. Horrible thought to have while treading water in the middle of the night, even if I used to be an ace at the 200-meter crawl.

If I drowned, my dad would know I took the dog. He'd know I'd seen him with her. With Margarita. But it wouldn't make him regret anything he'd done. He'd probably just decide it was more of his stupid witch-luck curse. But oh, Grandma. It would break her heart if I died as a thief and a boozer. A crinkly feeling swept over me: I mean, that would be a cursed way to die, right?

"Ernie!" I shouted. "I'm here!"

A spear of light cut across the water, narrow, but bright enough to guide me. Headlights. They seemed very far.

It was a hard swim back. The waves were rough. I fought them and they tossed me and I fought some more. I kept my eyes on the headlight beam. Not far, not far. I'd been stupid to panic instead of pacing myself. I was getting tired. Shit, I was tired. Worse, I was getting cold for real. It hurt to lift my arms and rake them through the water. But I could see Ernie in the spaces between the waves, a black shape running along the beach.

I reached the shallows, lungs burning, barely able to keep my legs moving. There was the rocky shoreline and the car in the acacia bushes, high beams blazing. And Ernie in the water, splashing toward me.

"Jesus! Are you crazy? It's fucking freezing!"

The lake bottom was right under us; he was standing, but I wasn't tall enough to catch my footing. He grabbed my forearms and hauled me up.

"I'm fine," I said, coughing. "For real."

I wasn't though. When he dragged me to the shore, my legs were so rubbery and cold I could hardly walk. Ernie followed me to the car. The puppy started whining as soon as I opened the car door and Ernie scooped him up and set him outside. The puppy ran off into the brush. I sank into the passenger seat, still trying to catch my breath. Ernie leaned across me.

"What are you doing?"

"I'm turning on the fucking heater." He fished a denim jacket out of the back seat. "Here, stupid, get under that."

I curled up beneath it, but it was like trying to warm up under a piece of cardboard. At least the heater worked.

Ernie stalked around the beach, picking up my clothes. He brought them in a wadded-up ball. He turned his face away the whole time he was near me. He perched himself on the hood of the car with his back to me. He said, "Hurry up. I want to go home."

Ernie had to be cold, sitting out there in wet clothes. He wasn't even drinking the booze; the bottle was in the driver's seat next to me, still about half-full. He dropped his pack of cigarettes on the ground, cursing because they were wet.

I didn't know before how easy it was for me to be a grade A asshole. Other people were probably born good. Not me.

"Ernie, I'm sorry. C'mon, man. At least sit with me."

"Whatever."

But after a few minutes he got in the car. He popped the seats back and I put my bare feet on the dashboard, letting the warm air dry them. We sat like that a long time, listening to that Fabulosos tape. Until way after the puppy had come back to the car and fallen asleep again.

"That is the most sleepingest dog ever," I said. "Dog narcoleptic."

"Sal will buy him. Couple hundred bucks, easy," Ernie said. "I'll take him over there tomorrow night."

"Thanks."

"Ready to go?" he asked. He was still mad, but not as mad.

"Can we listen to something else?"

"I guess." He took out the box of tapes he kept stashed under the driver's seat. "What'dya wanna hear?"

I lifted myself across the bucket seats and settled myself in his lap. He tensed a little bit, but he didn't say anything.

"What about this one?"

He shifted beneath me, so that I was leaning into him, cradled, my face against the hollow of his throat, his hand light on my hip. I felt his breath against my forehead.

"Yeah, okay."

It surprised me how, up close, he was so much bigger than me. I fit into the crook of the arm he'd set along the window, between me and the cold glass, and he could still stick the tape in the deck without even jostling me, no problem.

"Lulu," he said, frowning. "The lake's too cold."

"I wasn't in there that long," I said, and kissed him. It was clumsy, a fast peck on the side of his mouth, but that was all the green light Ernie needed.

That feeling when you're warming up, that feeling when you've been so cold your body is half dead, and when it's finally coming back to life, the whole thing is buzzing like a million bees live inside your skin. You're trembling and chattering and it almost hurts to touch anything because you're still frozen stiff, only the inside of you is hot and molten, and that feeling is spreading to the rest of you, that's why everything is tingling, because, little by little, it's killing all the cold. That's the feeling I had when Ernie gathered me up and kissed me.

That feeling's so far away this morning. Eclipsed, something I left in the dark. Because the sun came up and I had to call my dad to tell him Grandma wasn't breathing.

He said it must have happened in her sleep. But I don't believe him. I can still smell the lake in my hair and I know that last night, under that same bit of sky, Grandma woke from a nightmare of me drowning and, quick as quick, bargained her silver cord for mine.

Chapter Four

The Funeral

The way the old folks tell about that mala is always the same: Her parents forbade her to go to the dance, but she still snuck out. There was a handsome stranger, the guy every girl was holding out for, but of course, he only had eyes for her. He held her close through every song. They spun so fast they floated off the dance floor, still marking time. It was all her dreams come true until the dancers started screaming.

She looked down and saw his dead-giveaway feet: the cloven hoof and the rooster claw, the parts the devil can never charm away.

It happened in '75, at El Camaroncito Nite Club. Or it happened at El Koko Loco, across the border in Ciudad Bravo, back in '68. Wherever it happened, it was too late for the girl. He got hold of her, nothing left but the smell of burnt matches and a smoking hoofprint on the floor.

All because (and when they say this part, the old ladies crook a finger and narrow their eyes) she was willful and didn't listen. Era una mala.

I always thought it happened because that girl was stupid. That's what I had told Grandma Romi.

"You'd be smarter, would you?" Grandma had said. "The trickiest devil is the one that lives in your heart. That one comes to us in the light of day just as easy as in the night."

She meant pay attention. Watch out, Lulu. But I didn't listen. Five days ago, that middle of nothing special Wednesday night, I did my sneaking. Why not? My dad does it all the time.

I just wanted to catch him. Say once, *You're lying*, and have the proof. But now it's me full of lies. I was gone, doing my dirt, when God put out His hand and snatched Grandma Romi away. I lied to her. I left her and I'll never see her again. If I think about that, I can't really breathe.

Since she died we live without gravity. Things just float around waiting for us to stumble into them. My dad hasn't even mentioned the stupid quinceañera, except to say he guessed my tía Yoli would order the invitations for me now. Then he started crying because Grandma was supposed to do it and even though I still don't want a quinceañera, I cried too.

He hasn't noticed the puppy is missing. I don't know how you forget a whole dog, but he has, and I'm not bringing it up. It's enough that I got away with it. Only I don't feel like I did, because that's one of those hanging-in-the-air things, just like the quinceañera. And Ernie.

He's the first person I saw when I got out of the funeral limo. He was on the church steps with his uncles, all three of them in black mariachi suits. His uncles have a band, Conjunto Vega, and Ernie's been filling in on bass lately. I knew my dad had hired them. I must have left my brain on the other side of the Grandma's-gone gulf, because somehow I still wasn't expecting to see him.

Ernie came down the steps like he was actually going to talk to me in front of my dad. He must have a death wish! I panicked and bolted for the rose garden behind the church.

I sat down on one of the garden benches, the one in front of the statue of the Virgin Mary. She stood on an outcrop of rock in a shallow pool, like any minute she was going to dip her toes in. There were candles in colored glass jars—red, blue, pink, white—gathered in the water beneath her bare feet.

Nobody was around and I was glad. I don't know what to say to Ernie. He's bugged out that we had sex and I haven't talked to him since. He wants to know why. I don't have an answer. The truth is Ernie's better than me. He has a heart open wide to love me. Me, I'm like my dad. Careless.

I heard Yoli call after me, and my dad tell her to leave me alone, to give me a few minutes. My dad thinks I have susto from finding Grandma's body. He doesn't know Ernie exists.

I pressed my fingers to my temples, hoping Tía Yoli would listen for once, and stay away. Tía Yoli had her own drama going on. She and my cousin Carlos turned up, but no Uncle Charlie. I can't believe he didn't come. He's a white guy, but he should know by now: in a Mexican family, skipping your mother-in-law's funeral is basically treason.

Tía Yoli had arrived the day my grandma died, six hours after we called her—just threw herself in the car and drove from Houston. She showed up, eyes hooded and heartbroken, but also like her normal self: boss-lady generalissima. She was ready to talk to the parish priest to arrange the mass, haggle over the coffin with the funeral home, cater the postservice gathering, and print out the novena cards. What she wouldn't do was tell us why Uncle Charlie hadn't come with her. All Yoli said was she wasn't going to talk about it.

But Yoli's a regular loudmouth, so she's been criticizing everything else. She bitched all the way to church that she didn't pay good money to the funeral home so some tacky Mexican could paint blue eye shadow on her mother.

I hate when she says stuff like that. La Cienega is a dinky little border town where people think it's cool to wear gold lamé sandals with pantyhose and jeans, and if you order at Subway, the guy will probably ask what you want on your *sanguich*, but Yoli acts like she doesn't know that. Even if she lives in Houston now and she has the beige and cream living room set from Bed Bath & Beyond, she's from here too.

Yeah, the eye shadow looked bad, but the truth is Grandma would have liked it. It wasn't her style, but still. She would have said it was *muy chacha* and then gone around blinking a lot so people would notice. I could almost see her doing it. My belly did a slow roll, like I might hurl.

I found Grandma that morning. Her body was lying there in the way she slept—with one arm flung over her head like she was swooning. Her room was too quiet, just the alarm clock ticking on the nightstand.

Thinking about that made me feel prickly all over. What I found in her bed was just . . . something left. Like she took off her Grandma costume and the real her ran off somewhere else. How could she not know about her Debbie Harry eyelids or how we were all fighting and pretending not to, at her funeral? How could she not know what I did that night? Don't you know everything once you get to heaven? What would she say to me when I saw her again? She'd remember it all, even if it was a long time from now. I'd remember.

My moment to myself was short-lived. I heard boots clomp on the sidewalk, just on the other side of the church fence. I couldn't tell who it was at first. There's a row of huge bushes screening the garden, I guess so people can pray without distractions.

"Lulu," Ernie whispered. "It's me."

"You can't be here! My dad's gonna be looking for me in a minute."

"Well, when the hell am I supposed to talk to you? I don't even know what happened."

"Isn't it obvious? My grandma's dead."

"No, I mean what happened after. I mean." He stopped.

"No. Nobody knows anything."

"Oh man, thank God," he said in a rush. "I thought for sure—"

"Don't worry, you're in the clear. You can get over yourself now." It was easy being mad at him. Safer.

"Oh, cut the shit, Lulu. It wasn't my idea." He wasn't even bothering to whisper anymore. "None of it was."

"I can't talk about this right now. I have to do the reading in ten minutes. Just go."

"I'm really sorry about your grandma," he said. He didn't leave. That's Ernie. Now that I knew where to look, I could kind of see his legs. Especially with the twinkling silver that lined his mariachi pants.

"I'll call you when I get to my grandma's house for the rosary," I said. It felt crummy, saying, *My grandma's*, because she wasn't going to be there ever again. I felt my throat get tight and tried to breathe slower. I didn't want to cry in front of him. Why wouldn't he take the hint? "Dude, you're gonna get me in trouble. My dad is right inside."

He still wasn't budging. "What are you reading?"

"Lazarus. In Spanish."

"Oh yeah?"

"Yes, and I need to practice. So can you please go now?"

"Say murciélago."

"What?"

"Say it."

"Murciélago. What's that?"

"A bat, as in vampire. It has all the vowels. Do some tongue warm-ups, Coconut."

He left. I resisted (barely) the urge to yell *fuck you!* after him. His parents don't even speak English, so of course it's not a big deal for him. But if I tell him I'm not a coconut, he just says, *Yeah, you're not really that brown anyway.*

My Spanish isn't all the way bad, that's the problem. It's the most embarrassing bad, the B minus Spanish. If I'm not nervous I can rattle along okay, but if I don't pay attention, my vowels fall flat or I trip over my own tongue and everything goes to hell.

But I didn't have any better ideas, so I opened the little beaded purse my aunt made me carry and took out the passage. I repeated the word murciélago like twenty times. Moor-see-eh-lah-go. Moorseeeehlahgo. Ernie was right, saying it helped.

"Fucking Ernie," I said out loud.

A wink of color—sunburst yellow—flashed on the other side of the bushes as someone walked past. I clapped a hand over my mouth.

It was a woman. She paused, just beside me. I couldn't see her, but she was there. I could smell her perfume, a heavy winter musk. She laughed, low and smoky. Unpleasant. Then she was gone, high heels click-click-clicking down the sidewalk to the church entrance.

One of the little casement windows on the side of the church opened and my dad stuck his head out. He had major luggage under his eyes.

"Mija," he whispered. "Are you okay?"

"I was just looking this over one more time." I clutched my paper. Maybe it looked like I was praying.

"Well, you need to come in now," he said, real gentle. Probably he was relieved I wasn't having a breakdown or something. "Don't worry, you'll do fine."

"Be right there."

"Come through the side door, okay?"

He shut the window. The Virgin just watched me, beatific and serene in her painted blue wrap. I wanted to pray, but I couldn't. Hadn't I just been fighting with Ernie, right outside the church? Bad people shouldn't ask God for anything.

I went inside. There was my poor Grandma's body lying in the coffin. The silver finger curls framing her face gave me this flash-pop: her hair, baby-fine and downy, smelling like rosewater. Oh man, I thought I was going to lose it right there.

"Lulu, come sit by me," Carlos whispered. His voice brought me back from the edge of a total meltdown. He's eighteen and my only cousin, almost like a big brother, except not really, because he's always kind to me. I turned to slide into the front pew next to him.

The woman who'd laughed at me was in the vestibule. A wrinkled old beauty queen with a canary yellow silk scarf wrapped around her throat and shoulders like a cape. She wore big, oval sunglasses too, in church. I couldn't place her.

My dad saw her and so did everyone else. All the old folks started whispering. Yoli looked like somebody had slapped her eyebrows up to her hairline. It was just like in those cheesy telenovelas Grandma had been addicted to, where people glare at each other from across the room and the music is melodramatic.

The woman in the yellow scarf came up the center aisle to the coffin paying no attention to anybody. When she passed us my dad's neck corded up and he clutched my arm above the elbow, hard—wow it hurt—and dragged me past Carlos, who was at the end of the pew.

"Get back," he snapped and shoved me behind him.

The woman set her hands on the edge of the coffin and bowed her head. Her hair was done up in a long braid twisted around her head like a crown,

Frida-style. It was thick and black, that hard shiny black you get from box dye. God knew how old she was. Not as old as Grandma, but old enough to get the discount coffee at Wal-Mart.

After a few minutes she straightened and faced us, her sunglasses still perched on her face. She could have been blind or a movie star. Yoli stood up and blocked the end of our pew with her body. She was like Grandma—built like a Mack truck.

"I'm sorry for your loss," the woman said to her in Spanish.

"How dare you come here?" Yoli hissed. "Get out!"

She didn't seem bothered at all by my tía telling her to get to stepping. In English, she said, "Romi was my best friend. I promised her I would come."

The woman stepped a little closer. She took off her sunglasses, slowly, like she hated to do it. Looked me over, but good. Like she recognized me, only I'd never seen her before in my life. It was creepy and I wished she'd left her shades on. She had eyes like a hungry baby bird, if a baby bird wore dramatic eye makeup and had super-tweezed eyebrows. She probably *loved* blue eye shadow.

"Fine," Tía Yoli said. "You kept your promise. Leave. Now."

"Sí, Yolanda. I'm going." The woman walked out of the church through the side door I'd come through just a little while earlier. She was gone that quick. My grandma's best friend? I'd never laid eyes on her.

"Mom, what's happening?" Carlos asked, sotto voce. He looked at me, but what did I know? I shook my head. Tía Yoli ignored us.

The people in the aisle kept standing there, murmuring, like they were waiting for a voice to come over the intercom and tell them what to do. Father Richard stood at the pulpit looking confused. Not a surprise; that guy needs to get a clue. All he talks about is teenagers going to hell for fornicating, how everyone should vote their conscience, and we all need to pray for a Dallas Cowboys win. One time in confession I told him my dad gets drunk a lot and I don't know what to do. He said since my mom is dead, I need to be the light of the house. Put flowers on the dinner table, that kind of thing. What a dumbass.

Yoli scowled at the windows searching for the woman, but what was she going to see through the stained-glass Stations of the Cross? That lady didn't seem like the skulk-and-hide type anyway.

"Dad," I whispered. "Who was that?"

Yoli had had three screaming matches with my dad since she drove in from Houston, one of them this morning before the service because she got so mad at my dad for calling Uncle Charlie to ask why he wasn't here. But still, Yolanda put her enormous manicured hand on my dad's shoulder. He was her little brother.

"Dad?" I repeated.

Yoli glared at me. "Lulu, will you just drop it?"

Father Richard cleared his throat and said, "Let us pray for our sister Romi Muñoz," and everybody quieted down and found their seats. My dad was sweating. The hairline above his ear was shiny and damp, wisps starting to curl.

"Dios nos libre," Mr. Espinoza, Grandma's neighbor from down the block, whispered somewhere behind me. "Te lo juro, esa malvada es—"

"¡Cállate Rogelio!" his wife hissed.

I stared straight ahead, embarrassed, pretending I couldn't hear them. They were acting like the woman was some apparition, conjured out of gossip and half-truths. The evil fairy in some folktale. Next to me, my dad sank onto the pew, eyes shut, and crossed himself. He never did that. Never prayed. Not since my mom died. I had never seen my father afraid, not of anything, in my whole life. He was scared now. That much was real.

That weird old glamour puss, a long-lost friend of my grandma's? A sworn enemy? A prickly feeling came over me. Grandma Romi had lived nearly a century and, me, I was only a little spark in that span. The whole of her long, long life, just done. So much of it a life I would never know, could never know now.

It should have been beautiful, a reunion serenade for Grandpa and Grandma finally being together again. A whole afternoon of romances and boleros, the old standards Grandpa Chuy had requested to honor Grandma.

Grandpa Chuy died in 1974. We had his instructions from a handwritten note, all the songs he wanted played for her. I'd seen that note all my life, tucked in the bottom drawer of Grandma's jewelry box next to Grandpa Chuy's wedding ring. His notes were all over the house. Specs for the water heater penciled on a wall in the shed, the inventory of wrench sizes taped inside his toolbox, and the little details on the backs of old photographs. My favorite was the baby picture of Yoli dressed in traditional china poblana, his close black cursive: *15 July 1944. Yolanda Muñoz, two years. Pobrecita, she had a fever that day.*

But there were too many things happening. Yoli and my dad started bickering again in the limo, this time because my dad said he'd come to the wake, but not the rosary at Grandma's that night. By the time we got to the cemetery he was ignoring Yoli and she was pretending not to notice, except when other people weren't near us.

"You can't skip Mom's rosary," Yoli said.

The four of us were standing under the tent canopy the funeral home had put up to shade us mourners while Conjunto Vega played. People kept coming up to offer their sympathy.

My dad snorted. "Your husband is skipping Mom's funeral."

"Tío," Carlos said, and I cringed for him. Trying to talk my dad out of anything was a bad idea. "Grandma wouldn't want you to miss it."

"There's a lot of things your grandma wouldn't want," my dad shot back. "Isn't there?"

Carlos flinched. He walked away to find a seat. My tía turned to my dad and said, "That's enough."

They locked glares. I thought they were going to start another yelling match right there at the graveside. An older man came up and offered condolences. I followed Carlos just to get away from Yoli and my dad.

"Hey," I said, sitting down next to him. "What's going on?"

"Nothing," he said. His mouth was a tight line. But then he squeezed my hand, two brief squeezes, like I was still five years old. "Let's just think about Grandma, okay?"

"Yeah," I said, wishing I knew how long he was staying.

Carlos just started college out in California. Before that, he spent half the summer with Grandma every year. He was tight with Grandma and me. He always showed up with cool new music for me, mostly electronica, but it was good. Even when he wasn't around, he was close. He and Grandma watched the same telenovelas. I know, because sometimes I'd be there when he called and they'd rehash whatever happened on the latest episode.

"But are you and my dad okay?" I asked.

"Of course," he said, but he wouldn't look me in the eye.

Another lie. Yeah, they got in a fight over the summer, the last time Carlos was here. They just don't know that I know.

No te metas. My grandma's words rose up inside me. That's what she would have told me, not to get involved. It hurt to feel her, clear and steady, so palpable that she might have been standing beside me. She'd told me so many times that if something was very hard, she would ask her mother for advice and the answer would settle into her mind. I hadn't asked her, but here she was, giving me something I needed. Like always.

"I can't do this," Carlos said. He had Uncle Charlie's complexion, pale and freckled. He was blotchy with weeping, full-on silent tears and mucus flowing out of his face. "Tell my mom I went back to Grandma's. Sorry, Lulu."

I just stared, stunned, while he got up and walked out of the tent canopy and started out of the cemetery. He was actually walking back to Grandma's house right now, in the midst of the burial. He was *worse* than my dad not wanting to go to the rosary.

Right then, my best friend Marina came up to give me condolences. I think my grandma must have sent her. I was so glad. Everyone in my family was being a complete jerk.

"I'm sitting over there with my parents," Marina whispered. "Come find me."

"Let's go now," I said. I wasn't going to sit all by myself at the front. Someone else could tell my tía that Carlos left.

Marina and I didn't go sit with her parents, we went to the opposite side of the tent to find a seat far away from Yoli and my dad. Pretty quick, though, I realized where we were wasn't much better because I had to listen to Conjunto Vega and pretend I didn't know Ernie.

They pleaded Grandpa Chuy's love in passionate croons and half sighs, strumming like their hearts were breaking. *Divine Jewel, you are the gem that God shaped into a woman / When those eyes look at me, my soul trembles with love.* Jesus, I don't know how anybody stands serenades, they're so in-your-face. Ernie stared at me the whole time, until I wanted to jump behind the pile of floral wreaths and hide out for the rest of the funeral.

"Is it just me, or is he being weird?" Marina asked.

"Probably annoyed that we haven't found a new place to practice," I said. This was technically true.

We used to practice in the afternoons during summer school. I was there to take Algebra II in the mornings so I could get ahead and be in Physics when the school year started . . . but I stayed the whole day so I could do my homework in the library. Really, my dad just didn't feel like picking me up at lunchtime, so he just left me there. I didn't mind. After class, I'd head over to the band hall and the guys and I would practice the whole afternoon. The band director let us because Ernie is his favorite. Ernie's the most talented musician in the whole school.

In August, we moved the band to Olmec's garage, since he lives across the street from the high school. It worked for a while. I had a couple of hours every weekday because my dad thought I was at swim practice. I just had to wet my hair before he'd pick me up. But Olmec's mom got sick of our noise and said we had to go somewhere else. We haven't figured out where to meet. I mean, I can't just tell my dad, *Hey, I'm gonna go hang out with three pelados every day for a couple of hours. Don't worry, I'll do my homework.*

For real though, the band practice problem was a totally bogus cover. I just didn't want to tell Marina what happened with Ernie at the lake. Not yet.

It's not that I don't trust her. It's that she's going to say, *See? I told you. Are you guys together now or what?* and then it would be the third degree. *Oh my God, Lulu, why did you do that?* I don't know what she'll find most shocking—that I had sex, that it was with Ernie, or that I don't have a good reason. Eventually she'd figure out that I was with Ernie the night my grandma died. At any rate, what I said wasn't enough to throw her off the scent.

"The band," Marina scoffed. "He's not worried about that. That dude is in love with you. He just won't admit it. Like, ask a girl out already or get over it." Marina paused. "I mean, not *now*, at your grandma's funeral. That would be so tacky."

"Yeah, I don't know," I said. "He's awesome, but I don't really want a boyfriend."

Marina rolled her eyes at me. "Ay, ay. You're too punk for a boyfriend."

Right then, some busybody said something in a low voice to her comadre.

"Imagínate," she said, in Spanish. "That woman showing up after all these years. All the way in the front of the church too!"

"I heard she and Romi were close. Before," the other voice said, also in Spanish.

"Is that really true?" said the first voice. "Romi never said anything about her."

"Well, she wouldn't have, would she?"

"You can bet Yolanda knows."

God bless Marina. Her face went still and deadly as a cobra ready to strike. She flipped her long black hair over one shoulder, swiveled in her chair, put her finger to her lips, and actually shushed them. A loud shush, like an outraged librarian.

"We can hear everything you're saying," Marina said in her snottiest Spanish. "Can you please show some respect?"

I glanced over my shoulder. Sure enough, there were Mrs. Fabela and Mrs. Acevedo, the biggest chismosas ever, sitting right behind us. They looked affronted as only old ladies who've been told off by a teenager can look. I gagged back something, giggles or sobs, I wasn't sure.

To make matters worse, Uncle Zero was sitting next to them. He's not really my uncle, but he's my dad's best friend. His real name is Eliseo. He's a big man with always-sleepy eyes and wild, curly gray hair. My dad says he got the name because zero is how much work he ever does.

"¡Órale!" Zero laughed so hard. "You heard her! Go home if you want to tell stories!"

"Shut up, Eliseo," Mrs. Fabela snapped at Zero, in Spanish. She and Mrs. Acevedo took off, pissed. Zero just kept laughing. Marina and I grinned at each other, trying not to laugh too.

One day Marina and I will be comadres. Your comadre is your ride or die. You share secrets and gossip, know each other so well that even if you don't tell her something, she'll probably guess it anyway and then not say she knows, because you're not ready to say, and she knows that too. And you do the same for her. You're there for her and she's there back. Always. The only reason we're not comadres yet is we're not old enough.

Only grown women can be comadres. The word means *co-mothers*, but you don't have to actually be a mom. Tía Yoli says comadres are the ones who turned into women with you, know your whole bumpy road like you know theirs, and, *You know what mija, the truth is your man is just a man and he does not fucking get it, but your comadres always will.* She's really mad at Uncle Charlie about something. I don't know what. But I am one hundred percent sure her comadres know.

My dad calls it *comadreando* whenever there are women laughing and talking, being loud and taking up space. But he says it where they can't hear him, because if they are real comadres all huddled up together, nobody better tell them anything. Not even Jules Muñoz.

The only reason Marina got away with shushing those old ladies is I'm Romi's granddaughter. They knew they were wrong for gossiping in front of me. Still, I could see them as they left the funeral tent, their heads tipped toward each other, whispering a blue streak, probably about how rude Marina and I were.

"Those total wenches," Marina said, slitting her eyes after them.

I wanted to laugh, but my face kept going trembly. It sounds dumb, because my grandma was almost ninety years old. But still, it seemed impossible that she was actually dead. How could she be gone? How could it really be true? I felt like any minute, someone was going to say, *Just kidding, you dreamed this entire thing. It's time to wake up.* At the same time, I was mad because it was her funeral, and that crazy lady had messed it up. No wonder everyone was talking.

"I mean, probably a lot of people are saying stuff," I said, shaking my head. "That lady in the church made a total scene, right? I just hope she doesn't come back."

"Your tía would so throw her out if she showed her face again." Then, because Marina cannot help saying what's on her mind, she added, "Besides, she can probably see us from her house."

"What?"

"Over there." Marina pointed at the hill just beyond the cemetery. "I heard that house up there is hers. That's what they say."

My insides felt all squirmy. Loma Negra. I'd been there the night my grandma died. I thought of the woman's low, rumbly laughter, aghast. She'd supposedly killed her own little boy. Had she been in the house that night, watched me run across her lawn? "The old Aguirre place. She's *that* Aguirre?"

"That's what my mom says."

"No way. My grandma was not best friends with a murderer."

"Be serious," Marina scoffed. "If she had killed someone she'd be in jail. Those are just stupid rumors."

I slouched in my chair, mentally kicking myself. Marina was right. It was gossip. In La Cienega people couldn't just let things be what they were. They always had to put a lot of salsa on the tacos, like a story isn't good unless it has extra stuff on it.

"Whoever she is, I hate that she made a scene," I said, scanning the tent for my family. "Like there's not enough going on."

"Don't worry about it. There's always drama at a funeral. My dad and my tío Esteban got in a fistfight at the graveside when my grandpa died."

"I remember that," Uncle Zero said, horning in. "He broke your tío's nose."

"Anyway," Marina said.

Uncle Zero took the hint and said he was going to go find my dad. I turned to Marina as soon as he was gone. It was easier to focus on the strange woman instead of my family's squabbles. "There has to be something there."

"Maybe she stole something," Marina said. "Or maybe she was your grandpa's sancha. What else would break up best friends?"

"Gross," I laughed. Maybe it was true. My dad's barrio nickname is Muy Romeo, because women flock. Maybe Grandpa Chuy had been a Romeo too.

"Money or betrayal," Marina said. "It has to be."

"Yoli'll never tell me."

As though I'd magicked her up by speaking her name, Yoli dropped into a chair next to me. She started unloading her business, like Marina wasn't sitting right there. "Your dad says he's not coming to the rosary tonight! I don't know what to do anymore. Go talk to him."

"He never listens, Yoli." I shifted so my back was to Ernie. My tía didn't even notice Carlos was missing. All she was thinking about was making my dad do what she wanted.

"Well, still. He's over there somewhere. Go on." She waved me off.

"I'll save your seat," Marina said. "No worries."

I tried to look around and avoid Ernie at the same time. People gathered in small groups, pretending to listen to the band and whispering, no doubt about the presence of that woman at the church, or maybe even my absent uncle and cousin. Zero, talking to the funeral director. Little old ladies wanted to hug me as I walked by, and I let them. They must all shop at the same stores because every one of them smelled like that fancy talcum powder Grandma had in the drawer of her vanity.

I spotted my dad in the parking lot. His back was to me and he was talking into someone's car window. It was a sporty little Honda CRX. Yellow. He had his arm on the top of the car and I could see, through the little triangle his body made, that the driver had long red hair. I walked faster.

He straightened up abruptly and banged his fist on top of the car. "You can't be here. This is my family."

"And that's why I should be," a woman said. I still couldn't see her face. "It's your mom."

"You're joking, right?" he demanded. Then he glanced over his shoulder and saw me. "Hang on, Lulu."

He held up his hand, like doing that was going to keep me from seeing the car. I just walked faster. Middle-of-the-night Margarita. Married Margarita. That was her, had to be.

"Look," he said to the driver, real cold. "I don't want you here."

The CRX screeched out of the parking lot. I watched it go, memorizing the license plate. There was a Mean People Suck sticker on the back bumper.

"Who was that?" I asked, eyes still on the car.

"I don't know. Somebody who needed directions."

Same old guy; deny til you die. It's only been a week and he's already up to his old tricks again. It didn't matter what happened to my dog Gonzy. It didn't even matter that Grandma was going into the earth right over there under the tent. Here he was, meeting up with that married lady and lying to my face, like always. I choked back the urge to scream, but only because it was Grandma's funeral. How could he do it? How could he?

I didn't ask about Margarita. I didn't tell him I knew her name. Nope. I didn't show my hand. I said something else. It was mean of me, dirt mean. That's why I did it. Because, good. He deserved it. Not respecting my grandma on her day. Not respecting me, ever.

"I meant earlier. At church. Mr. Espinoza said that lady was your dad's girlfriend," I said, making up a story too, just to poke him. "Was that Grandpa Chuy's sancha?"

"What is wrong with you?" he demanded. His face was so close I could see the tiny beads of sweat across his nose. He's never done it, but for a minute I thought he was going to smack me. Instead, he jabbed his finger toward the tent. "Your grandmother is lying in her coffin. How can you disrespect her like this?"

"So, who was that?" I asked.

"A terrible person who doesn't respect family," he said, voice flat. Damn, he always knows how to cut me down to size. He does it easy.

"Speaking of family, your mom's over there, not in the parking lot," I shot back, not flinching. I kept eye contact with him, to show I wasn't scared even though I kind of was. "Yoli sent me to find you."

He walked away without another word. Didn't look back to see if I was coming, and I didn't follow.

I watched him stalk back to the funeral gathering. I could see how mad he was from the way he moved: tight, quick steps, head low. I didn't care. He thought he could get away with saying anything he wanted to me just because I'm a kid. Like I'm supposed to believe him instead of my own eyes.

From where I stood, in the parking lot, everyone was small and indistinct. Just figures shifting under the pale swell of the tent. My dad slipped in among them, and I lost him. Conjunto Vega was playing "Las Golondrinas." The strains of music were somehow the clearest thing about it. One of Ernie's tíos was really belting out the ending, "Adiós, adiós," in an impressive operatic tenor. The sky was open and blue over the dark fir trees.

Sometimes you can know it for yourself, how shitty you are, but still be miles away from sorry. That was me. I was not one bit sorry at all. I was happy. Not happy, really. But I felt like, finally, I got to him. It made me feel strong. It was satisfying.

I should have remembered what Grandma Romi said. The devil that comes to you in the light of day, the one that knocks on your heart. For me, it wasn't a smoking hoofprint. It was the clickety-clack of high heels on the sidewalk that brought the devil into my heart.

That's true. Because my eyes lifted over the tree line of the firs to the hill beyond, drawn by a dark thought to Loma Negra. Whatever the real story, I knew one thing. Nobody makes a stink at someone's funeral like that for nothing. That stranger and Grandma Romi had been comadres. I gazed at the hill, my heart swollen with pride and rage, and knew what my dad would really hate. What would really get him.

————◇————

Chapter Five

La Llorona In Levis

After the funeral my dad left me with Yoli, saying he'd be right back. He was going to gas up the truck. But then he didn't come to the first rosary of Grandma's novena, didn't come back in the morning. Yoli took me to my house to get fresh clothes, and I could tell my dad hadn't been home. Everything was just like we left it the morning of Grandma's service, down to the butter knife I'd left beside the sink. It was spooky.

"Is he ever coming back, or am I an orphan now?" I asked Yoli on the fourth night of Grandma's novena. She and her comadres, Renata and Elida, were sitting around Grandma's kitchen. They'd been over every afternoon since the funeral, helping set up for the evening novena. Afterward, they'd sit up all hours in the kitchen, talking and drinking wine. Las copetonas, my dad called them behind their backs, because of their teased-up bangs. They'd been Yoli's best friends since grade school.

"Don't be so dramatic," Yoli said. Her mascara was a little runny from crying, but her voice was strong. "You're with family."

"I'm with you," I said. Carlos was gone too, back to college. He'd driven off that morning. Now it was just me around the house, on Yoli's periphery, thanks to my jerk dad.

"Lulu, don't pester, okay?" Yoli said, sounding tired. She was a ball of energy all day every day, working her way through list after list of things to do. I saw her little pad of paper, the narrow strikethroughs of tasks—insurance, bank, headstone specs, pay the lawn guy. In the evenings, she'd transform into the perfect hostess. Tall and wideset, just like Grandma Romi, ready in a dark silk dress to console everyone. She only wept when everything was done. At night, with Renata and Elida.

"Your dad will be back," Renata said, lighting a cigarette. She had a droopy smile, which made it seem like she was always laughing at you. "It's just what he does. He took off for a while after your mom died too. What was it? A couple weeks?"

"Think so, yeah," Elida agreed. I liked her the best, even with that bad case of mom hair. She was easier to talk to than Yoli and a lot nicer than Renata.

"This isn't the first time he's abandoned me?" But I remembered, kind of. We stayed with Grandma Romi, my dog Gonzo and me. Grandma told me my dad was on a business trip. I believed her. Besides, when he came back, he was normal. Big swooping hugs and wild gifts for everyone. Grandma got a new mother ring, with real stones for each of her children. I got *Jem and the Holograms* dolls, the *entire* set, including their rivals, the Misfits. Even Gonzo got a bag of liver treats.

Now I knew my dad was just buying off his guilty conscience. Wow. It made me even more determined to go find that woman from the church, my grandma's alleged ex-comadre. If he didn't like it, maybe he should stick around instead of hightailing it whenever he wanted.

"He's not abandoning you." Elida wrapped a piece of foil over a tray of enchilada casserole. There were at least three other full trays of homemade dinners, a bucket of fried chicken, and a box of donuts. People kept bringing piles of food every night. "Everybody grieves their own way, mija. Your tía keeps busy. Your dad—"

"Julio is barely housebroken," Yoli cut in, slapping her hand on the table. Her face was rosy and wet from red wine and grief. "Mom always spoiled him. Well, I'm not her. I'm not coming up with some cover story for him every time he feels like running off."

"Ay, Yoli," Renata said, glancing between the two of us. "Don't tell her that. She's just a kid."

"She's old enough," Yoli retorted. "Heck, she lives with him. She knows how he is."

"He's not like that," I said, stung. But it was true. He left me with Grandma a few times a week, basically whenever he wanted to go out. Yoli shook her head. She knew.

"Lulu, help me put some of this in the outside fridge," Elida said.

I grabbed two of the dishes and followed her outside, to the old garage in my grandma's backyard. It wasn't a real garage, more like a tiny apartment, with a kitchen and bathroom, but Grandma had only ever used it for storage. I set the trays in the fridge next to all the leftovers from previous nights.

"We'll never eat all this," I said. "It'll go bad."

"Oh, tomorrow Yoli and I will sort through it. I'll take some home to my boys," Elida said. Her sons were the De la Garza twins, seniors at my high school. "They'll polish it off, no problem."

"Is it true?" I asked. I couldn't help it. "Did my grandma really love my dad more than Yoli just because he was a son?"

"She didn't," Elida said. "Your tía is just very upset with your dad right now."

"Sounds like she's mad at my grandma."

Elida was silent as we walked out to the yard. It was after eleven o'clock, and the night was cloudless and breezy, just cold enough that I wished I'd worn my hoodie. She stopped when we got close to the house, motioned me to stay with her. I could see clearly into the kitchen window. Yoli and Renata were still sitting together. My tía had her elbows on the table, her face in her hands.

"It's complicated for your tía. Your grandma had another son, Miguel. He was just eighteen when he was killed."

"Yeah," I said. Grandma hardly talked about him, but his photograph was on her bedroom vanity, him in uniform. Taken probably just months before he died, in 1944, a year before the war ended. "I know about him."

"Your grandma was a lot like Yolanda. She showed a strong face to the world, but she carried her pain inside. Yoli, you know she was just a baby when Miguel died, so she never knew him. All she knew was your grandma's sorrow."

"Uh huh," I said, uneasy. It was familiar. I remembered my mother, but my father's gloom was a bigger piece of my life. Sometimes he went dark and broody for weeks. Always around my mother's birthday and the day the accident happened. When he was deep in the drink, he'd tell me, *Shoulda known I'd lose her. I'm bad luck for everybody.*

Not for me, Daddy, I'd insist. *Not me.* And I'd hug him so he wouldn't feel bad. I told him if there was a curse, I'd break it. I'd save him.

"When your dad came along, it was a second chance for your grandparents. Especially for your grandma. She had a son again. Maybe that's why she let him get away with so much. She was just so happy to have him." Elida shifted next to me, but it was too dark to see her expression. "It's been hard for Yoli, being in between Miguel and Julio."

"Who was that woman at the church?" I heard myself and knew I should have cared about Yoli, how tough it was for her. I knew it. But I was on another tack.

"Oh, her." Elida waved her hand, as if a possible child killer was no big deal. "She was a friend of your grandma's a long time ago. I don't know why she came. They had a falling out and never spoke again."

"What happened?"

"I don't know," Elida said, annoyed. She stalked past me to the house. "Don't go asking your tía about it. She has enough to deal with."

It wasn't hard to pay a visit to my grandma's old friend. The next afternoon was Saturday and Yoli said she was going to the mall for a few more "no-vena appropriate" outfits. I guess she didn't want anyone to see her in the same dress twice.

"Do you want to come with me?" she asked. She was standing in Grandma's bathroom making faces at herself in the mirror, tweezing some stray facial hairs. "We can get lunch too."

"No thanks." I felt a little bad, remembering what Elida had told me. But not enough to hang out with Yoli all afternoon. "I might walk down-town to Cheve's. Just to window shop."

"Sure," Yoli said. "Be back in time for the novena."

I actually did check out Cheve's Music & Curios, just to give myself some time to be ready. Now that I was going to do it, really do it, I didn't know exactly what I'd say to Señora Aguirre. Besides, I love browsing Cheve's guitar section.

"Hey man," Cheve said when I walked in. "How's it going?"

"Good," I said. Cheve's an old hippie. He's got a big jiggly belly and is always wearing the kind of T-shirt you get at T-shirt giveaways. He calls everybody *man*. He was probably my favorite adult outside of Grandma. He didn't mind kids hanging out in his shop and if you wanted to talk about obscure rock music, he was the guy.

"Cool, cool," Cheve said, giving me a sleepy grin. I would bet money he was high. "I'm gonna be in the office, so holler if you need me."

I nodded, wandering through the aisles. It was part thrift store, part music shop. The front room was wall-to-wall trinkets and consignment items: vintage purses, records, antique dolls, cowboy hats, costume jewelry, San Marcos blankets, old shoes, you name it.

The back room was all musical instruments. Trumpets and saxes, drums, flutes and piccolos, accordions, even a piano. And guitars. Oh, the guitars. At the very back of the store, a whole wall of guitars.

My dream guitar is the Gibson ES-335, but that's five thousand dollars. Way out of reach, and Cheve doesn't carry anything that expensive anyway. The next best thing is the Epiphone Casino, which looks nearly identical to a Gibson. At four hundred dollars, it's *almost* something I could get. Cheve had the most gorgeous turquoise one hanging on the back wall.

Ernie says to just pick something cheap to learn on, like the Fender Squier, a hundred dollars with a mini amp thrown in, probably even cheaper at the pawn shop. But I'm a sucker for that curvy Gibson shape. I went in to look at that turquoise Epiphone every chance I got.

I ran a finger along the guitar's glossy body. No use asking Cheve to take it down for me. Not yet. But if Ernie had sold the puppy like he said,

I'd have half the money. Enough for a down payment. Though where would I keep it? I couldn't stash it home or at Grandma's.

The idea alighted in my mind, like a bird settling on a branch. There *was* a place nobody would go, someone who might let me rent the shed on her property. That's what I could talk to the woman about. Something transactional. She might say no, but she'd crashed the funeral. She might say yes to me, being Romi's granddaughter. If she did, I might find out the real story with Grandma Romi and her.

Assuming she was still in town. If she wasn't, well, the place was empty anyway. It might be a good spot to stash my stuff, haunted or not. I kissed my fingers and brushed the Epiphone again.

"I'll be back for you," I whispered.

I headed up Loma Negra for the second time in two weeks. It was better in daylight, easier to find the dirt road to the house. Someone had been driving on it recently, I could tell by the fresh tire tracks. Someone had clipped back the thorny gatuño bushes too.

I crested the brow of the hill and the house came into view. In the light, it was just an ordinary home in the middle of a wide clearing, the front yard set with four large pecan trees. Modest and old, just like so many in Grandma's neighborhood. A narrow house with a dingy white wood slat exterior and a pointy roof with real shingles, not tin. There was a large window outlined in a black frame parallel to the front door, which was also wood but had been painted a dark color. Together they made the house look like it had two black eyes. The wraparound porch added heft to the place, made it look bigger. There was an armchair on the porch, red and plush. It looked new. Twenty or so yards away from the house there was a graying building, sort of a cross between a barn and a garage. A small truck was parked near it. Chevy S-10, also bright red.

A large dog suddenly burst out from behind the truck. A big chocolate

Labrador. It charged me, sending up a volley of barks. I stopped dead in my tracks, let my arms dangle loose at my sides. *Be a tree*, my dad had taught me. *Strong roots, soft limbs. No eye contact.*

The Lab didn't mean any harm though. I could tell he was all talk, just sounding the alarm. Gonzy used to do that too. I held still while the dog snuffled my feet, nosed my fingers. In a minute he was wagging hard. I rubbed his jowls and he grunted with happiness.

"Hey boy. Hey good boy," I said. The Lab bumped his whole body against my legs. He was so fat he was shaped like a chicken nugget. There was something in the sweet bulk of this dog, his affectionate largeness, that reminded me of my Gonzo. It hurt me, but it felt like home too.

"Ssssst! Wicho! Ven acá!" A woman's voice, sharp and commanding. The dog looked back at her, but didn't leave my side.

She was on the porch. Small as a sparrow, skin like coffee with a little too much milk. No doubt she was old, but her face had escaped major wrinkles. Or maybe it was her eyes, lashy and hazel, that distracted from the pucker lines around her mouth. A rope of black hair lay in a long braid across one shoulder. I've never seen someone her age with hair that long. She was wearing tight Levis and a plaid work shirt, knotted at the waist. Her feet were tiny in a pair of bright-red high-top Reeboks, nearly the same color as the plushy armchair. She had a roll of wallpaper in her hand.

She didn't smile or show any sign of welcome, but she was giving me the once-over again. My skin went all tingly. I could feel her gaze on my sneakers, my grass-stained jeans. My face.

"You came to my grandma's funeral," I blurted. I didn't know what else to say. Definitely not, *Hey, can I leave a guitar here?*

"I did," she agreed. That was all she gave me. Was this the fearsome legend, the woman everyone whispered about? *The Aguirres were a cursed family. The mother went crazy and killed her little boy. Now his ghost wanders the house at night.* What a letdown. Mostly she seemed like an old lady in the middle of home repairs.

"This guy's pretty great," I said. I rubbed the dog's head again. I walked to the middle of the yard and the dog followed.

"He's spoiled," she said. She snapped her fingers at him. The dog went back to her, reluctantly.

I tried a third time. "My name's Lucha. Everybody calls me Lulu."

"Pilar Aguirre," the woman said. She had a curiously flat affect. That, or she really did not give a crap about meeting Grandma Romi's relatives, even if she'd messed up her funeral.

"Where did you know my grandma from?" I asked, not caring if I sounded rude.

"Just a long time ago." She folded her arms. "Why are you here? You obviously want something. What is it?"

"Nothing," I said. "Who said I wanted anything?"

"You came up here for no reason."

"It's not against the law. Just curiosity."

"Oh, you're curious. To find out if I have horns?"

"Why'd you come to my grandma's funeral if nobody wanted you there? You could have said your goodbyes at the cemetery. When everyone was gone."

"Maybe I was curious," Pilar said. Her mouth twitched like she wanted to smile, but not in a friendly way. "To see Romelia's family."

I narrowed my eyes. She'd wanted us to see her, more like. I said, "I'm Romelia's family."

"Oh," Pilar said, with a strange half smile. "Well, you have her confidence. She was bold. Resolute. I admired that about her."

"She was," I said. It was the truth. Somehow, hearing it from this stranger made it more real. More important. A piece of Grandma Romi I didn't already have. This woman had known her before my dad was born. When she'd been another Romi.

"How old are you?" she asked, again looking me over in that funny way, like she was deciding about me.

"I'm turning fifteen in February."

This was something to her. For the first time, a spark of interest. "Ah, so are you having a quinceañera?"

"Yeah. It's the stupidest thing ever. It doesn't mean anything."

"It means you're a woman," Pilar said. "That's what it's for."

"No. It's just a party for my dad. So he gets to say how much money he spent. Nothing will change for me."

To my surprise, she laughed, that same low chuckle I'd heard behind the bushes at church. Nothing friendly in it. "Of course. He's a man. That's the way they all are."

She set the roll of wallpaper on the steps and came to stand beside me. Her voice was eager, almost like she was telling some secret. "But it's still a party, all for you. Your costumes and music, your escort. In your honor. Don't you want that?"

"I don't care." I shrugged. I felt strange being so close to her, but I didn't move. I didn't want her to know she rattled me. She wasn't a murdering mom, but she was nothing like a regular senior citizen.

"Well," she said, her attention slipping from me to the grass, studded with plump brown pecans. She nudged one with the toe of her sneaker. "I bet Romelia was looking forward to it."

Pilar caught me square. How many times had I put off choosing invitations? I could almost hear my grandma nagging me. *Lulu, ándale. Just pick something.* And me saying, *I will,* but not actually doing it.

"She was," I admitted.

Pilar bent swiftly, picked up a pecan and tossed it across the yard. The dog ran after it, huffing with excitement. He lost sight of the nut, then stood there looking around, confused. I laughed. "What's his name again?"

"Wicho," she said. "He's five years old."

She didn't ask me anything else, just handed me some pecans. "You can throw those to him. He needs the exercise."

Pilar grabbed an orange nut gatherer from beside the house and wandered around the yard, collecting pecans. I spent a while just playing with the dog. Tossing nuts to the edge of the yard for Wicho to chase. He was a total oaf, so foolish he ran full tilt for every pecan, even though he spat them out once he had them.

"You're so dumb," I laughed. "You don't even like the taste."

Wicho gave me his big doggy grin, pranced around in front of me, eager for me to throw another.

"That dog. He'd probably fetch for an hour straight if I let him," Pilar said, in that way that sounds like a complaint but it's really affection.

Gonzo had loved fetch too when he was young, only with frisbees. He'd been wild for catching them, diving into the air, flashing teeth clamping on the spinning disc. I almost told her that. But I didn't know her well enough.

"I have to go. It's my grandma's novena in a little while."

Pilar nodded. "Night five. I'm doing my own, here."

"That's cool." In a couple of hours people would gather at my grandma's house, fill the kitchen with more food. Spend forty minutes praying a full rosary, with responses. Pilar would be up here, praying along with us. Again, more evidence of a Grandma Romi I didn't know, who'd been important to this woman. Money or betrayal, Marina had said. But this woman didn't act like she had a guilty conscience.

"You can come back and play with Wicho if you want," Pilar said. "He likes you."

"Thanks," I said, patting the dog's broad back. "I will."

Chapter Six

———◇———

Amachada

PILAR AGUIRRE, 1951

C huy didn't tell me the baby was cremated," Romi growled. "He'll get an earful for letting your husband do that."

Pilar stifled a sigh as she pinned Joselito's pillowcase to the clothesline. How like Romi. *She'd* have changed things. *She'd* have stopped the baby's cremation. "José Alfredo does whatever he wants. Believe me."

Romi had come to spend the afternoon with her. In an hour, they would go down to the grammar school together in Romi's truck, where they would pick up Joselito and Yolanda from school. Pilar smothered her irritation. Romi had stopped by Pilar's house nearly every day since she'd left the hospital, even if just for a few minutes.

"Don't they all," said Romi. She probably would tell Chuy off, Pilar decided. The way her nostrils flared meant that she was angry.

She watched Romi snap a wet bedsheet onto the line, pin it with quick, efficient fingers. Stout, broad-faced Romi, wooden clothespins in hand and all-purpose apron tied sensibly over her dress. Resentment fluttered inside Pilar again. Imagine being indignant that your husband didn't consult you, just one time.

I'm so much better-looking than she is, Pilar thought and cringed. Snobbery, the refuge of the weak-minded. Besides, it wasn't exactly true. Romi was middle-aged, but she was tall and statuesque, possessed of a kind of forcible attractiveness that had more to do with her personality than her symmetry.

Romi was the only woman in the barrio who knew how to drive the big produce trucks and would, too, if her brother Rufino, the neighborhood grocer, was on another errand. She'd have no qualms whatsoever explaining to her husband that he ought to have consulted her. That was Romi, ever-capable, undaunted by life, buoyed by some mysterious quality Pilar herself did not have.

"He told me how expensive everything would have been," Pilar said. "Because of the way it happened."

"Well, yes," Romi said, clipping the last sheet to the line. "And he was out of his mind with worry. We have to remember that."

"I suppose so," Pilar said.

It had been two months since the stillbirth of her daughter, two months since José Alfredo had stayed out all night. He had told her, first thing upon walking into the house, that he did not want to argue. It was a terrible thing that happened, but what was done was done. He would ask Father Camacho to dedicate a special mass for the baby.

Pilar had been patching a pair of Joselito's pants when José Alfredo returned. She sewed steadily on, as if he wasn't there. It was in her mouth to say, *Oh, and will you sit through the whole service?* But more satisfying not to speak at all.

"I didn't go anywhere last night. I just parked down the hill and walked back up later. I slept in the yard. I didn't really leave you by yourself." He had not apologized, but his rush of words let her know how his conscience pricked him.

Again, she'd said nothing. So he had slept in the yard. Good. Let him feel his guilt. She had not been the one to leave, or to pretend that she'd left. She sewed steadily until he finally walked away.

That was mostly how things had been, a lot of silences.

There had been a mass for the baby, prayers offered for Alondra Belen Aguirre. José Alfredo had given their daughter the name Pilar especially wanted. Alondra could not be baptized, but the blessing itself was something. At least her name was uttered in the church. This had thawed Pilar the slightest bit. Though as she sat next to José Alfredo during the mass, she wondered what he pictured when he thought of their daughter. She was the only one in the church who'd seen Alondra. Who would ever see her.

Meantime, Pilar's body mended itself. The bleeding finally stopped; her insides were tender, but sound. Even the burning in her breasts had dulled as the milk dried out. She supposed that, yes, she had finally come to accept the fact of the law, of court fees and the jurisdiction of life and death. She had yielded to José Alfredo and Romi, it was a terrible thing, a tragic but natural part of life. Not the result of a curse from an old woman no one could find.

Still, the fact of her little daughter, unclaimed and burned, sat like a stone on her heart.

"Shape your mind to forgiveness," Romi said, as if reading her thoughts. "You have your family and your whole life ahead of you, with this man. Nothing can take your daughter's place, but there will be other joys coming to you."

Her daughter. It was a strange shadow grief, mourning her. This daughter, who, despite the evidence, had not existed in any finite way. The dead, it seemed, had their place. The living certainly had theirs. But what about one who had never lived or died, the soul that had simply not arrived within its earthly vessel? There could be no markers for her daughter. No baptism. No stone. Had her daughter lived but ten minutes, she could have had these things.

What terrified Pilar was the imperfection of her memory, the brief moment she had had with her baby. She could remember holding her, but not much more than that. It was knowledge of the memory rather than the memory itself. There had been nothing to mark her existence at all, except Pilar's own body, receding to its former dimensions. Except her own grief.

Her grief was alive. It blotted out so much of her life. Other joys coming to her. Where were they?

"I am trying," Pilar said, though she was not, and knew it. She didn't want to, either. Her anger at José Alfredo was like a caged beast, pacing behind the wall of her silence. "I am. But things are not the same."

"Well, they won't be the same," Romi began.

"*He's* not the same," Pilar said, sitting on the porch steps, the empty laundry basket beside her. The truth came tumbling out of her. "He comes home late so many times. He doesn't tell me where he goes."

Romi sat down next to Pilar. She dug in her apron pocket, shook a cigarette out of her pack of Lucky Strikes. She did not offer Pilar one, simply because she already knew Pilar would say no. José Alfredo thought smoking was unladylike. For that matter, so did Chuy, but either Romi didn't care or he'd never caught her. She smoked exactly one cigarette every day.

"Chuy was the same after Miguel was killed," Romi said, lighting the tip. "He couldn't talk to me. All he did was work and get drunk for six months straight."

"What did you do?" Pilar asked slowly. Romi hardly ever talked about her son and never about his death.

"What could I do? I was destroyed. We both were."

Romi smoked the whole cigarette in silence. Pilar took her other hand, squeezed it hard. "I'm sorry, comadre."

"The grief never leaves you," Romi said, eyes glimmering. She didn't cry. She was too proud for that. "They say it gets better with time, but that's a lie. You just get used to carrying it."

"Yes," Pilar agreed. She felt the truth of that. "But what was Chuy doing? All those nights he stayed away drinking?"

"Carrying on. What else?" Romi pulled out a second cigarette, something Pilar had never seen her do. "But then he settled down. That was fine with me."

"It's been two months already."

"Does José Alfredo seem . . . different with you?" Romi asked. "In the bedroom?"

"We aren't having relations," Pilar said, flushing a little. He had not asked her for that, not since the baby had come. She had given him no encouragement.

Pilar reflected. José Alfredo preferred the small universe of his family, the home set away from the neighbors, his workshop out behind the house. He had grown up as a ranch hand and still had the solitary ways of the vaquero. Could he have strayed? Or worse. Maybe he'd returned to the old woman, left his life with Pilar. She could not speak this dread, to anyone. She would sound insane.

Every time Pilar asked him, he told her he was working. He refused to say anything else about it. *I'm working. I already told you. Stop asking me.* It had gotten to where they didn't greet each other when he walked in the door. Pilar thought again of the old woman spraying dirt on her, the malediction. Of the story Trini had told. Hadn't the man fallen ill, vomiting blood, over a curse? The man had admitted he'd known the witch in question. He'd had history with her. She looked at her hands, at the gold band on her finger. She didn't trust anyone with these thoughts. Not even Romi. But what if it was true and this was why little Alondra had arrived dead?

When Pilar let herself consider these things, her fury was so overwhelming it frightened her. If it was true, José Alfredo had done it. Done something anyway.

"What does he smell like when he gets home?" Romi was all business. "Alcohol?"

"No," Pilar said. "He's sober every time."

They were silent. Romi did not ask the other question, but it was in Pilar's mind. *Can you smell a woman?*

"Do you want me to ask around?"

"No," Pilar said. "I want to find him myself."

"Good idea," Romi said. "That way no one wags tongues about you looking for him."

"Exactly," Pilar said.

Romi smoked silently for a few minutes, thinking. Beside her, Pilar regretted even more those barbed thoughts about her friend. Romi would help. She always did.

"Well," Romi said, exhaling through her nose. "The first thing is you have to learn to drive."

⌐—·•·—⌐

The tricky thing about driving was learning to balance the clutch and the gas pedals when shifting gears. Romi assured her that the knowing would come with practice, just like a foot learned the treadle on a sewing machine, so you hardly thought about it while you worked. It was like that.

"The hardest part for me was remembering all the different shift spots," Romi remarked as they turned onto the downtown thoroughfare. "But you learned those pretty fast."

They were on their way across the border, Pilar at the wheel, Romi next to her, one arm resting on the edge of the open passenger window, a cigarette between her fingers. These days, she smoked her one cigarette while they were out driving around. She said it made her feel glamorous.

"Besides, I'm trying to act natural," Romi remarked. She wore dark glasses, which she'd bought at the Woolworth counter on their last drive. Her black hair was tied up in a blue-and-white polka-dot kerchief. The kerchief fluttered in the breeze.

"Like we don't have a care in the world?"

"Exactly," Romi laughed and exhaled a plume of smoke out the window.

Pilar had been driving for almost three weeks. Lately, whenever they went for practice drives—always during the day, while the children were at school—Romi chose a stranger for Pilar to follow. Follow for twenty minutes without being spotted. A woman in a white Studebaker. The family in a dented Chevy pickup, four teenage boys piled in the bed. The handsome young driver of the Sunshine Dairy milk truck. Once, a police officer in his shiny black-and-white patrol car. He'd been the only one to notice them, and even so, all they got was a quick flicker of his eyes in the rearview mirror.

"Who taught you this?" Pilar had asked. Romi knew when to hang back, and how far away. When to weave behind another car. How to park unobtrusively but still have a clear view of the target.

"I taught myself when Chuy got the job riding the river," Romi said. "He works out of town all week. Of course I check."

"You follow him to the cowboy camp?" Pilar asked, amazed. The camp was almost thirty miles away.

"Every Monday morning for years," Romi said matter-of-factly. "He's never spotted me. I just want to make sure he goes where he says he's going. He's a good man. But you never know."

"No," Pilar agreed. She didn't ask whether or not Chuy was always where he said he'd be. "You never do."

Today, Romi challenged Pilar to follow a baby-blue Buick Skylark convertible. The driver was a young white man with a brushy blond mustache. They followed the car through the customs port and across the bridge to the Mexican side of the border. Pilar had managed not to stall out the truck while paying the toll, navigate into the lane marked Nothing to Declare, and then made her way along the narrow one-way streets of downtown Ciudad Bravo. The young man had not noticed them at all, though why would he? They were two Mexican matrons in an old truck. They were nothing at all.

"Let him go," Romi said, as they pulled onto the main avenue downtown. "I want to get tacos at the placita."

"Oh, good idea," Pilar said. Eating out on a whim. You could do that if you had a vehicle. You could do anything you wanted. José Alfredo did not know where she was, didn't even know she was gone. They'd be home long before he returned from work, or wherever he went afterward. He'd never know she'd left the neighborhood. It was exhilarating.

The young man drove through the next intersection. Pilar turned right. A few blocks down, she parked curbside at the plaza, where the open-air vendors sold chili-powdered fruit, corn in a cup, tacos al pastor. It was fortunate, she thought, that there were not many vehicles around the square. She still wasn't good at parallel parking.

"Perfect," Romi said as Pilar turned the truck off. "I don't think you even bent the side mirror."

They bought tacos al pastor wrapped in foil and hot. Romi added onion, cilantro, salsa. Pilar asked for hers plain. Strong flavors made her stomach queasy. She didn't want to get sick so far from home. It had been happening since Alondra, though Doctor Mireles said there was nothing physically wrong with her. Probably just nerves, he'd suggested, in a gentle way that embarrassed and angered her, and advised her to get more rest.

She and Romi sat down on a plaza bench, unwrapping their tacos. There were roses in large red planters all around the square. Though the blaze of summer was long over, the November day was warm, and the roses were in full bloom. Pilar bit into her taco. Alondra would never see an autumn day. The thought snagged like a dark hook in her mind, as these thoughts did. She chewed steadily, suddenly unable to bear the sight of the bright planters.

"I'm going to buy a dozen to take home since it's Friday," Romi was saying. "Then I don't have to make dinner. Chuy comes home stinking of horse and half-starved every weekend. I don't know what he eats all week long at the cowboy camp."

Pilar forced a smile, trying to push bad thoughts away. Chuy was one of the few Tejanos employed as a tick rider for the US Department of Agriculture. Monday through Thursday he stayed at the sector cowboy camp, patrolling his swatch of the border. There, he was on horseback the whole day, riding the river, searching for errant cattle from the Mexican or Texas side of the border, inspecting the animals for the cattle fever tick.

"You better buy a dozen then," Pilar said, trying to sound light. "Are there any new openings?"

"I don't know," Romi said. "I'll ask Chuy tonight."

"Thank you." Ever since he'd gotten his green card, José Alfredo wanted a job riding the river. Initially, Pilar had objected, not at all liking the idea of her husband working out of town all week long. As things were now, though, maybe it would be better. The widening silence between them would be less noticeable if he was gone. Maybe the job would keep him from whatever he was doing every evening too. After all, the men weren't allowed to leave the camp during the week. If José Alfredo got hired on, she'd even ride with Romi on Monday mornings just to make sure.

"I think," Pilar said slowly, "I think it's time for me to drive on my own."

"I know you can drive," Romi said, dark eyes serious. "But are you ready?"

"Yes."

The plan was simple. One weekday, while Chuy was away at the cowboy camp, Romi would keep Joselito after school. Pilar would borrow Romi's truck. A little before five thirty, she would park outside of the La Cienega stockyard entrance, far enough away that José Alfredo would not notice what he wasn't expecting to see: Pilar behind the wheel, lying in wait. She'd watch him drive out of the gates and she'd follow. She'd know his secret.

"Monday evening," Pilar said. Saying it out loud loosed something within her. For the first time in a long while, appetite seized her. She ate the rest of her taco with genuine zest.

The stockyards were five miles out of town, just off the highway going west toward Sanderson, but there was a bodega and gas station right across the highway. She parked behind a big commercial truck, screened from view, yet able to see the stretch of highway leading back to La Cienega.

She didn't wait long. José Alfredo's black pickup, with its shining chrome grill, flashed past her. She pulled out of the parking lot, but hung back, kept him just within her vision, where she'd see which way he turned.

He drove east, past downtown businesses, past the Caimanes barrio, past the green, manicured Anglo neighborhoods, past the train depot, past the eastern city limit marker. They were back on the open highway, cacti and mesquite lining both sides of the road.

She didn't know anyone who lived out here. This was all ranches, white owned. Manned by Mexican ranch hands, and, maybe, some women. A cook. Some vaquero's daughter. Or an old woman, a housekeeper, an ancient nanny, kept on by the family after years of service. Yes. It might be *the* old woman. They might be together here, far out of Pilar's sight. She gripped the steering wheel, resisted the urge to speed after him.

Up ahead she saw the red flare of brake lights. He turned right. She marked the spot, just past a cluster of mesquite trees. A few moments later she drove past the trees. There was the narrow ranch road threading through the brush. She drove on for another mile before doubling back. It would be good to let him arrive, give him time to settle in. She tried to imagine his face upon seeing her. Would he even look ashamed, caught out? The old woman's face came to her more clearly. Tiny and wizened, like a hungry cat. The eyes that glittered with spite and rage.

Pilar was not afraid. Not anymore. If the old woman was there with José Alfredo, they would both answer for her daughter.

She drove up a winding caliche road for three miles, according to the odometer on Romi's truck, before she reached the cattle gate. The archway over the entrance said Double Spurs Ranch. Two giant wrought iron spurs graced each side of the arch, their spikes radiating into the air. She got out of the truck to open the long cattle gate. It was unlocked, but a thick rush of nerves came over her. She was trespassing, and on an Anglo ranch.

I'm here about a job, she decided. If I don't see him and someone stops me, I came about a job.

Around another curve the road opened suddenly into flat, cleared land. Double Spurs was not a working cattle ranch. It was a horse stable, a small one. Rows and rows of covered horse stalls and tack rooms arranged in a half-moon, a half dozen or so trucks parked at one or other of the stable sections. There were several small corrals adjacent to the stables. An old white man was in one, lunging a young roan. Two horses were tied in a horse walker, unconcernedly nibbling at the ground. In the distance was a modest rodeo arena, complete with aluminum bleachers. There, parked next to the bleachers, was José Alfredo's truck.

Pilar drove toward the arena, no longer anxious about being apprehended. No one would stop her here. All these men would see was another truck, just another person coming to feed or work their horse. What could José Alfredo be doing? At least it was not a woman, old or otherwise. This was something else entirely. She pulled alongside his truck, so close it would have been hard for him to open the driver's side door. She climbed the bleacher stairs.

José Alfredo stood at the far side of the arena talking to a man sitting on the top rail of a bucking chute. She couldn't make out what he was saying. He held a coiled lariat in his left hand. She could see from the tilt of his head, the deliberate way he shook out the lasso with his right hand, the inflection of his voice, that he was giving instruction. It took a moment, but Pilar recognized the man on the bucking chute. Doctor Allen.

She sank onto the first row of bleachers, breath suddenly gone. Why was José Alfredo here, with Doctor Allen? This man who'd no doubt convinced José Alfredo to burn their daughter. Almost, she wished she had found her husband with a lover.

The tiny lasso dipped and rose, unfurling with every twist of José Alfredo's wrist. Left and right, left again. He lifted his right hand above his head, so the lasso made slow revolutions around him. When the lasso was large enough, he sent it up in the air, brought it down so that he stood in the middle of the spinning loop. He was showing Doctor Allen how to florear la soga, how to make the lariat bloom.

He sent the loop up, then away from him. The lasso was nearly six feet in diameter now, so he pivoted, following the lasso to control its revolutions. Then, he saw her. She knew it by the way the lasso twitched out of shape, just a little bit.

José Alfredo righted the lasso and completed his turn. Gave her his back. He said something unintelligible, but Pilar knew he was telling the doctor that he must be *on count*. She sucked her teeth. The arrogance of him. The utter arrogance. She would not make a scene. She would not call to him. He would come to her, even if she had to sit through the entire lesson. He would come to her.

He sent the lasso away, snapped it back. He hopped through the lasso, hopped a second time on its return, a third time. Pass after pass, springing on count, as if he were dancing. Choked with rage as she was, Pilar could not help but admire those deft leaps, the way he commanded the lasso. She had always loved him in the arena—his artistry, his precision. The hot prickly feeling she got watching him move. She was angrier still, at herself, that she felt this way even now.

Her husband shrank the lasso, re-coiled the lariat. Gestured that Doctor Allen should come down off the chute. The doctor made wobbly but competent passes with the lasso. He could make it slide down his arm and back into orbit, but that appeared to be the limit of his abilities. Still, Pilar knew the doctor must have been practicing for weeks if he could do that at all. This was what José Alfredo had been doing. Teaching charro skills to the Anglo doctor. Her eyes burned. She would not cry. She would not.

José Alfredo said something to the doctor, then clambered up the chute and dropped to the other side of the arena wall. Moments later he was standing at the top of the bleacher stairs. She stood up too.

"You need to go home now," he said, voice pitched low. He spoke to her as he might have spoken to Joselito, not at all as though he'd been caught out. "I'm working."

Pilar was seized with an urge to slap him. It was frightening. She had never in her life wanted to hit him. She clutched the folds of her dress in case her hands might leap at his face. "Why are you working for him? *Him* of all people!"

"Keep your voice down," he hissed, taking her by the elbow. His face loomed so close to hers she could feel his hot breath. Smell the arena dust clinging to him. He steered her with him down the staircase. He was not rough, but his grip was unrelenting.

"Why would you do this, after what he did?" Pilar demanded, tears falling swiftly now, in front of him. She hated herself for it. Why couldn't she be like José Alfredo, made of stone?

"Pili, you need to leave," he said as they reached the parking area. He saw Romi's truck. "Where's your comadre?"

Pilar yanked her arm out of his grasp. She climbed into Romi's truck, slamming the door.

"We're going to talk about this tonight. That is a guarantee," she said. She cranked the engine to life, revved it hard. José Alfredo looked utterly astonished, as if she *had* slapped him. A wild exuberance washed over her.

"That's right. The doctor's not the only one learning new things." Her parting shot tasted sweet in her mouth. She pulled away before he could answer.

She glanced in the rearview mirror as she neared the ranch entrance. He was still standing where she'd left him, next to his truck. She snapped on the radio dial and laughed. A sign if there ever was one—Pedro Infante's "La Que Se Fue" came blaring into the cab of the truck.

She turned up the dial as far as it would go. Rolled down her window. Threw back her head and uttered a long, loud grito as she drove away. Yes, indeed. Let him watch her now.

———◇———

Chapter Seven

El Último Hijo

D octor Allen had come from the East. Boston. Almost since his arrival to La Cienega, he had been in love with Celeste Ruiz, daughter of Don Alvaro Ruiz, Mexican cattle exporter and patriarch of the wealthy Ruiz family. For Celeste's skeptical father, the doctor had converted to Catholicism and, because Don Alvaro was the chief patron of Ciudad Bravo's charro team, the doctor had pledged to become a charro.

"That gringo wants to be a Mexican cowboy. What is that to us?" Pilar demanded when José Alfredo recounted this absurd story at breakfast the next morning. "How could you work for him?"

"What can I do?" José Alfredo asked, infuriatingly calm as he spooned salsa verde onto his fried potatoes. "I owed the money. So I bartered with him."

"You paid the bill already." *To burn my baby.* Pilar bit back the words, but it was hard. The thing was done, she reminded herself. It could not be undone. Bitter remonstrances would get her nowhere with him.

"Not all of it," José Alfredo said. He chewed silently for a moment. "It was more money than I had. He offered a trade, so I took it."

"He shouldn't have asked you. It's wrong."

José Alfredo shook his head. "This is why I didn't tell you, Pili. What happened wasn't his fault. There's no one to blame."

"I need to get Joselito up and dressed," Pilar said and abruptly left the kitchen. She could not stand José Alfredo a moment longer. Her own fault he didn't tell her. He was trying to wrong-foot her again.

Last night when he'd come home from that gringo ranch, he told her point-blank that she would end her childish spying *at once*, and further, how could she have gone behind his back about learning to drive when she could have just asked him to teach her? She'd proven herself untrustworthy.

Now, he called after her, "I'm leaving for work. Is there anything you want to say?"

"Like what?" she asked, a hand on Joselito's door. It was partially open. He was still asleep. He'd kicked his blanket on the floor.

"I have no idea," José Alfredo said. "I leave it to your conscience whether there's anything else you think you should tell me."

"What about your conscience?" she demanded, unable to keep her voice low. Joselito stirred, but thank goodness, did not wake.

"Mine tells me to pay my debts," José Alfredo said. He walked out, letting the screen door slam.

⌐——·•·——⌐

"Ay, Pilar," Romi said that evening, when Pilar came to relate the news. "The plan was to follow him. Find out where he was going. That's what we said. Why did you confront him?"

"He went behind my back," Pilar said. She didn't care whether Romi agreed. "He's working with that doctor."

"That is exactly the point," Romi said, sucking her teeth at Pilar. "He wasn't with another woman. He was working a job."

They were on Romi's front lawn. Romi was watering the banana tree near the porch steps. The streetlights had just come on, and several older children were still playing kickball. Joselito and Yolanda had gone inside Romi's house to watch *The Lone Ranger*.

"I can't believe you're taking his side."

"I'm on your side, Pili," Romi said. "I'm always on your side. I'm telling you this for your own sake. He's working. That's all he's doing. So let this go."

"He should find somewhere else to work," Pilar argued. "There have to be other things he can do besides teach that doctor to be a horseman."

Romi folded her arms and gazed at the distant horizon. She was serious and mournful, radiating an aura of muted emotion. "Do you even care that he's going to tell Chuy? Because he will."

"I told him you didn't know about it," Pilar said quickly. "I said I just asked to borrow your truck."

"But Chuy's going to say not to lend you the truck anymore," Romi said. "He'll be mad I taught you to drive without telling your husband. You shouldn't have done it, Pili."

"So what? Are you afraid of your husband?"

"No," Romi said evenly, digging in her apron pocket for her pack of Lucky Strikes. She shook one out and lit it. "But I don't need problems with him because of your tonterías."

"Oh, is that right?" Somehow, hearing this from Romi felt worse than anything José Alfredo had told her.

"Yes," Romi said, the words rushing out. "He's a man. He's not going to tell you everything. He never will. You need to let this go. You're not going to win him back by fighting with him about a *job*."

"I don't need to win him back," Pilar snapped.

"I hope you never have to," Romi retorted. She turned off the water faucet and began coiling the garden hose onto the wall hook. "I'm trying to give you advice."

"Haz lo que te dé la gana." Pilar didn't want advice. Not at all.

"Just let it go," Romi said, looking her squarely in the eye. "He's not with another woman. He's working a job."

Pilar stalked to the screen door and called to Joselito that it was time to go home. Romi's husband told her everything. What was wrong with Pilar expecting the same? It was the man, more than anything else. That man had burned her baby.

"Mami," Joselito said as he came outside, letting the screen door bang behind him. She lifted him, the warm weight of him dampening her anger. "Did you know the Lone Ranger's friend is named Tonto?"

"That's not nice. Why would the Lone Ranger call his friend stupid?" Pili said, knowing she sounded like a spoiled child. Romi had made it possible for her to find out what José Alfredo had been doing. And yes, it was true, José Alfredo would tell Chuy, who would put a stop to Romi lending her the truck.

Romi stood there smoking her cigarette, pretending not to hear Pilar's sulky comments. It was insufferable.

"It's funny though," Joselito said, giggling. "He just goes around and his name is Stupid and he doesn't even know it."

"Come on, I can't carry you all the way home," Pilar said. She set him on the ground and took hold of his hand. "Let's go, papacito."

"Bye, thank you!" Joselito yelled at Romi, who blew him a kiss.

"See you later, angelito," Romi said.

Pilar knew quite well Romi would drive her home if she asked for a ride. If she did not, it would be a twenty-minute walk through the brush, Joselito trying to wriggle out of her grasp the whole way. Romi was not going to offer it though. That was Pilar's own fault, the way she was acting. She knew that.

Pilar stuck out her chin. She did not ask for a ride.

⸝⸺ ·◦· ⸺⸜

"Are you going to tell Chuy?" Pilar asked in the darkness the following Friday night, as she and José Alfredo lay in their bed, each curled away from the other.

Chuy was home tonight, would be home until Monday morning. She had not visited with Romi all week long, dreading, despite her bravado, what would happen. Maybe Chuy would forbid Romi from driving at all. Pilar didn't think Romi would take that, but it might turn into a real fracas. All because of her tonterías, Pilar could admit to herself. She ought to have been more circumspect.

"No. I'm tired of fighting," José Alfredo said bluntly. "I don't want everyone else fighting too. I just want a normal life again."

"Me too," Pilar said in a small voice.

José Alfredo rolled over and pulled her into his arms at once. She pressed her face to his chest, listening to the beat of his heart. How sweet and wonderful it was, how blessedly familiar, being in his embrace.

"I know it's been so hard for you," he said into her hair. Almost she felt

137

him trembling, as she was trembling. "We'll have another baby one day. We will."

"I don't want to talk about that," she said. She felt the dark anger inside of her stir, threaten to rise. It didn't seem to have an expiration, but she suspected, despite his solicitude, that his patience did. She shut her eyes, willing the anger away. "Please. I don't want to talk about another baby."

"All right," he said softly, kissing her, slipping her nightgown up her thighs. "All right. We won't."

It was easy to shut her eyes. To let him love her, to love him back.

By December life seemed perhaps not better, but endurable. Pilar moved through her days careful to keep her voice light, to find her way back to her former self, largely because the world was ready for her sadness to be finished.

Maybe she *was* getting better. At least, now she saw that it might happen, in time. If she tried. If she let it. Though, truly, the thought of overcoming her grief seemed like a betrayal. She kept it a secret now. It was like a bruise she felt all the time, but she could perform an absence of pain. For José Alfredo's sake, Pilar put on good cheer like a garment every day, even feigning that she had forgiven the doctor. Because José Alfredo was still working for him.

José Alfredo had bartered off their hospital debt. The doctor was a competent rider, could perform some of the charro suertes. He could stand atop a saddled horse and florear la soga, even leap through the lasso. He would make a decent charro, José Alfredo told Pilar. Good enough not to embarrass himself in the arena.

Now José Alfredo was training horses for him. A pair of Andalusian mares the doctor had purchased as a gift for his future father-in-law. José Alfredo worked with the doctor's horses on Saturdays and two evenings per week.

"It's good money for us," José Alfredo told Pilar one evening after his regular workday at the stock port. "He didn't even try to haggle with me. That gringo's family must be loaded. He brought those horses all the way from Argentina. I know he couldn't have bought them out of his own pocket, doctor or no."

"I'm surprised he didn't get one of Don Alvaro's men to train them. He has his pick of the whole charro team," Pilar said matter-of-factly. She'd decided to keep a neutral tone anytime they discussed that man.

"No, no." José Alfredo shook his head. "He has to do it on his own or Don Alvaro won't respect him."

"Well, it works out for you," she replied, settling herself on the porch steps to watch José Alfredo lift Joselito onto the lowest branch of the pecan tree. Something happened to boys when they became men. The less she said about her sorrow and suspicions, the more José Alfredo talked to her about everything else. Joselito, though, noticed everything. Sometimes he would hug her knees and say, *Mami, what's the matter?*

What was the matter indeed? The matter was her menses had not come yet and it filled her with terror. To go through it all again, so soon after Alondra. She refused to tell José Alfredo. He would want her to be happy and she could not perform happiness about this.

"They're pretty horses," José Alfredo ventured. "Maybe, after they're broke in, you'd like to see them."

"I would," she said, though it wasn't true. She wanted to say yes because

José Alfredo had asked her. *Be kinder*, Romi had said. *He loves you. He wants you to be happy.*

"And me," Joselito yelled, then tossed himself out of the tree at his father. José Alfredo caught him, kissed Joselito's curls.

"Of course you," he said, and airplaned him back onto the branch.

⌐— •• —⌐

Doctor Allen kept his horses across the border, at Lienzo Charro Los Potrillos on the outskirts of Ciudad Bravo. It was a longish trip, half an hour by truck from their front door to the mercado on the other side of the border, and another fifteen minutes to the city outskirts and the highway that forked south to Monterrey and Saltillo, north to Ojinaga. The lienzo charro, the rodeo grounds for charreadas, coleaderos, and jaripeos, was just past the highway fork.

Lienzos were made for celebrations, Pilar thought as they drove through the wrought iron gates. The enormous white pavilion, set well away from both the stables and the arena, was large enough for a hundred dancers. The courtyard around the stables was green and tidy. At intervals along the footpaths there were wooden benches and flowering bushes with pink and yellow blossoms in marble planters. One could almost forget that not far beyond the arena the ranch terrain resumed its thorny vegetation.

It began to mist as José Alfredo parked the truck, a soft graying that made the air smell like wet clay. He got Joselito out of the truck and jogged around the other side to help her.

"I'm fine," said Pilar. She wrapped her rebozo around her shoulders and squinted at the sky. "I don't know how long the rain will hold off."

"I think it's going to pass us," José Alfredo said. "And if not, we'll come back quick."

"Freddie!" The doctor waved as they approached. His sunburn made him look like a rancher's son. He nodded briefly at Pilar. "Bring that boy over here. Come see these ladies!"

The doctor's new mares were indeed beautiful. He had taken them out of their stalls and let them graze in one of the grassy enclosures adjacent to the stables. They were strongly muscled, like Quarter Horses, but taller, with light gray coats and silvery manes that fell in waves past their shoulders. The doctor held Joselito up to pet one of the mare's necks. The horse grazed, her forelock long enough to flutter past her jaw.

"Look, Mami," Joselito said, pointing a small finger. "They have hair like princesses."

"Yes, they do," said Pilar, smiling. "I've not seen horses like this before."

"Andalusians," said the doctor. "My father-in-law can't find fault with them."

"Well," said José Alfredo, as he clapped his hand along the back of the second mare, "they're too tall for charrería, but he doesn't compete anymore."

"I want to ride, Papi," said Joselito.

"Maybe your wife would like to ride too?" the doctor asked. "In the paddock. It's safer."

"No, no," Pilar said. She would not get on the doctor's horses, lovely though they were. "I prefer to watch."

"Wait," José Alfredo told Joselito. "We're going to warm them up a little first. Go with Mami and see the other horses."

Pilar made her way down the first aisle of stalls, Joselito running along beside her and kicking up dung-smelling dust. Around the corner was another row of stalls. Horses poked their heads out above the half doors as she and Joselito passed them. Beyond the stalls were the tack rooms and two large cement bathing blocks. The barbed wire fence dividing the lienzo proper from the back ranch where the livestock was kept ran a few yards behind the tack rooms. A teenaged groom was scrubbing down a bay horse on one of the blocks; she could see the horse raising its lips as water struck its head.

"Look, Mami," said Joselito giggling. "That one's making faces."

"He's trying to keep the water out of his nose," said Pilar. "Look how he curls his mouth."

"What's that?" Joselito had already found something new. He pointed at the horizon. "Those white things."

At first, she did not know what she was looking at either: small brown and white shapes flitted in the underbrush on the low brown hills in the distance. She walked with her son up the dirt road through the ranch entrance. From there she could make out half a dozen thatched jacalitos scattered unevenly across the hills. Smoke from their cook fires wafted from makeshift chimneys. Seeing the settlement, the little animals made sense: kid goats scampering in the sage.

"Chivitos," she said. "They belong to the rancheritos who live up there."

José Alfredo and the doctor rode the mares around the corner near the bathing blocks. They stopped to chat with the groom, who left his bay gelding to pat the broad shoulder of the doctor's mount. José Alfredo nodded at the groom and trotted up to the ranch gate.

"Climb up on the gate post, mijo," said José Alfredo, riding alongside the fence. "Mami can't lift you."

"I can," said Pilar.

"I can climb by myself," said Joselito gripping the post. Pilar put her hand on his back to steady him as he climbed the gate.

"How far are you going?"

"Just down to the bronc corrals and back. We won't take long."

"I want it to take a long time," said Joselito from the top of the post. He reached out and José Alfredo grabbed one of his arms and swung him onto the front of the saddle. The horse danced a little, but Joselito was not afraid. He reached up and took his father's cowboy hat, set it on his own head.

"Míralo, míralo," said José Alfredo, tipping the hat back so Pilar could see Joselito's face. "C'mon tough guy."

"Go on then," said Pilar, trying not to smile. Joselito held onto the saddle horn, his small face stern as a vaquero surveying the llano. "I'm just going to walk a little while."

"I won't fall," said Joselito, kicking his feet against the heavy leather. "Don't come, Mami."

"Don't talk to Mami that way or you're getting down right now." José Alfredo swatted the side of Joselito's leg. Her son scowled but said nothing.

"Bueno, I'm going ahead," said Pilar before he could get sulky. Joselito was like his father that way; she had to let the moodiness pass without appearing to notice it. "You have to wait for the doctor anyway."

The three of them rode by her a few minutes later, as she walked along the roadside. Near a dip in the road ahead, the prickly pears were crowned with fat red fruit. She would ask José Alfredo to cut some for her on the way back. She watched them crest the next rise. The sky to the west foamed dark blue with thunderheads. Joselito pointed again at the small hills on the horizon and his father turned in the direction of his small hand. In profile, the hatline at the back of his bare head was evident. Then they descended and Pilar could not see them anymore.

It began to drizzle. Pilar quickened her pace, the damp ground changing color before her eyes. The land was so dry that the raindrops did little more than darken the pale road.

Later she would remember things differently. In her memory, the rain meant something; she had known it from the first moment of misting. But as she made her way down the gently sloping trail, it was only light rain, unexpected and brief. She did not mind the feel of it on her face, even with the wind picking up. She caught sight of them again as they rode past an ancient, broken corral. Joselito stuck his foot out and knocked one of the old posts down. She heard José Alfredo's sharp *Stop that.*

The next moment, a space of a few breaths, took root inside her, alive, constant as her beating heart, so that long afterward she remained within those breaths, suspended, unable to relieve herself of the sight before her eyes: How the wasps rose out of the rotted wood in a low black swarm, how the doctor's horse bolted and carried him into the brush. José Alfredo's mare rearing and plunging. How he twisted atop the mare, one arm clamped over Joselito, who was screaming and screaming, his little arms beating the air. José Alfredo hitting a corral post face-first. The mare's hide dark gray in the rain, her princess tresses plastered to her neck, Joselito caught, briefly, in her hooves. She herself running and running, but too slow. The wet brush of wind as the mare bolted past, missed her by inches. Joselito, limp on the ground, his face dark and swollen with wasp stings. The wasps themselves swallowed by the rain.

"No, no, no." Pilar cupped Joselito's face. His skin was hot and bruised. He was still. So still.

"Don't move him!" José Alfredo choked, face a bloody mess. He staggered to his feet, fell again.

Pilar was listening but she was not listening. The sky was closing over them. The rain came down faster.

The doctor stumbled back into the road. It was clear from his clothing that he'd fallen off his horse. His face and neck were covered in red welts. He crouched on the ground beside Pilar, gently pushed her hands away. He touched Joselito's throat and shook his head.

"His neck is broken," he said in a low voice.

"I've never seen that," José Alfredo said, still on the ground where he'd fallen. "I've never seen them come out in the rain."

He kept saying that all the way to the hospital in Ciudad Bravo, as though because he had never seen it, the thing could not be true. Pilar held Joselito against her chest, her fingers laced in his hair. She pressed into the corner of the truck cab, her face against the window. He was still, so still, and the warmth in his body was receding. Only his curls, sweaty at the roots, still felt the way they should.

<hr>

They buried Joselito on a Tuesday, just after the feast day for La Virgen de Guadalupe. The morning of the funeral, Pilar heard José Alfredo make hoarse noises in Joselito's dark bedroom, an approximation of weeping. His sobs sounded painful, like an empty belly convulsing. The sound of it was an outrage. Weakness, from him? After he'd taken everything from her? No, absolutely not.

"I'm not going to sit with you at church," she said, standing in the doorway. He was sitting on the floor next to Joselito's bed. "Not if you're going to cry like a woman."

She could say this to him and look him full in the eye, show that she, a woman, was yet master of herself, while he was not. Her own grief was hardened and mute, like a bone bleached by the sun. Because it was true. Now she knew it was. The old woman had vanished, but her curse had not.

"Don't start," he said. "Not this morning."

"You're a fine horseman," she said. "You are the best. Everyone says so. How could you lose hold of him? It's not possible. It was that woman. She made it happen."

"Stop. Just stop," José Alfredo said. The dark hollows beneath his eyes made them seem larger, like a begging dog's.

She savored that she had almost heard him say please. Please stop. Perhaps she would never hear him say it. But it was there, lying just beneath his pride.

"Pili, you haven't been right since you got sick," he said. He never spoke of the baby girl. Only as some obscure event, like an accident on the side of the road, a glimpse of horror, quickly blurred and gone.

"I wasn't sick. I had a baby."

"Estás mal," he said, in his way of persisting and yet avoiding. "La pura verdad es que estás mal."

"My children are dead because of you. Don't cry about it! You're the one who did it! She came looking for you!"

José Alfredo sprang at her, so swiftly she didn't have time to flinch. He slapped her face. Pilar did not mind the slap; it was out in the open now, she did not have to make pretenses.

"I'm not crazy. You did something," she repeated. She walked away from him, back into the bedroom. He did not follow her.

She heard his voice from the living room. "We're sitting together at church. We're his parents."

Pilar had not had to ask what had been done with the body of her son. It was different for children. The doctors did not make them disappear. Joselito had been taken to the funeral home. She knew this. She had seen his prepared body: eyes gummed shut, the pancake makeup that struck her as obscene though she knew it was there to disguise the tattoo of welts left by the wasp stings.

She had selected the clothing Joselito would wear in his coffin. She had attended with José Alfredo the meeting with the funeral director, who gave them prices for services. The headstone was another matter, but could be purchased at any time, even years later. For now, they had agreed on a small plaque inscribed with Joselito's name and the dates of his life. There had not been much money for Joselito, not so soon after the hospital bills. Her hospital stay, as José Alfredo referred to it.

For Joselito, Pilar had agreed, without comment, to allow José Alfredo to sell her gold arracada earrings. He had not assured her he would buy them back, nor would she have believed him if he had. Moreover, Pilar realized she no longer wanted the earrings. One day perhaps she would buy different ones. With her own money. These thoughts came to her unbidden, but sweetened by her anger. One day things that belonged to her would be only hers. Nothing would be taken away again. One day. But she held her peace about these half fantasies.

José Alfredo also held his peace. Though his own silence was a bitter, stony one. He wanted forgiveness. Wanted it without asking for it. But she would not bend to him now. When she looked his way, she looked through him. He was furious, banging the doors and stomping around the house, entirely loud and pointed in his silence.

It did not matter. She had found something at which she could be stronger, forever. Let him break and rage. Let him beat her. She would last.

Alone in her room, Pilar laid her funeral garments out on the bed. Her slip and hosiery. She would wear paste pearl earrings and a white lace collar. The shirtwaist black dress, simple but elegant, with asymmetrical buttons curving down the length. In a few months it might not fit her, not if she was right about her missing monthly. She had not told José Alfredo, would not tell him. He would find solace in the news. *No hay mal que por bien no venga*, he'd say. She could almost see his face, flushed with relief and gratitude, eager to discard this horror for a new baby. They would all do it, smother her with their persistent demand that she be happy. *How wonderful! You see? Every cloud has a silver lining!*—determined to eclipse Joselito, consign him to the past. He'd become, like lost Alondra, a story no one wanted to hear. No, she could not bear that.

Pilar curled and pinned up her hair, inspecting her work in the mirror. She painted her mouth with a dark lipstick, smacked her lips together. She wasn't going to tell José Alfredo, or anyone. Not until she had to.

The funeral service was mercifully brief. She sat with José Alfredo, who put his hand over hers and then removed it when she stirred not a finger. He wept. She did not. She kept her eyes on the coffin. Afterward, she never remembered what the priest said. What she remembered was kissing her son's cold face.

She would always remember that. Kissing his small cold face. The smell of him, which was no longer Joselito's warm, almost puppy smell, but a mix of some astringent chemical and makeup powder. His stiffness, his inanimateness. Even so, a mad compulsion gripped her: to sweep him up in her arms and run away. His little body! Dead or not, it was Joselito. She wanted to keep him with her, forever.

She did not snatch him up. But it was a near thing.

"Come away, Pili," Romi said. "Come on."

"I want to ride with you and Chuy to the cemetery."

"All right," Romi said. "I'll tell your husband you're coming with me. Can you wait by the truck?"

"Yes," Pilar said. "I'm going now."

José Alfredo was so furious at her leaving the church with the Muñozes that he did not sit with her at the graveside. He stood beside the trio of musicians playing songs for Joselito. When everything was over, Pilar went back with the Muñozes, not to her home on the hill but to Romi's house. Romi told her to go to bed. Pilar went, feeling a kind of serenity at not being near her husband.

"She needs rest," Pilar heard Chuy say outside the house. "Just let her be. We'll bring her home tonight for the novena."

Apparently, José Alfredo made no answer because all she heard was the truck roar away. That evening, the neighbors gathered for the first night of Joselito's novena. Romi set herself as the matron in charge.

"Just go sit in the living room," she told Pilar. "I'll sort it all out."

Her presence was a relief. Someone to marshal the neighbors through their communal mourning. Someone to organize the kitchen, arrange the seating. Pilar was grateful to settle herself in an armchair. All she had to do was accept condolences, but it was draining.

The neighborhood women filled the house. Someone brought pitchers of lemonade and a platter of polvorones. Another brought chiles rellenos, enough for two nights' eating. At six thirty the rest of the neighbors began arriving, combed and pressed, setting their own outdoor chairs in a circle outside the kitchen door. They waited, their drinks at the foot of their chairs, making small talk, until Romi told Pilar that she must come outside. So Pilar did, moving slowly.

At seven o'clock the novena began. Pilar sat with her rosary slack in her hand, watching her neighbors—the Camachos, the Rodriguezes, the

Silvas, three elderly spinster Uribes—pray for her dead son. She sat, mute and still among the petitioners. They called him el último hijo de José Alfredo Aguirre when they asked the Virgin for intercession on his behalf, as though a multitude of sons had been lost.

José Alfredo did not come home. Pilar took it as evidence of his guilt. Of course he must have gone to find the old woman. To punish her for her crimes. Or perhaps to return to her. Pilar resolutely went to bed, refused to cast her eyes toward the windows at all. Let him stay away. All the better.

José Alfredo returned on the third evening, amid their sonorous Hail Marys. She smelled him before she turned around. They all did, she thought, seeing them shift in their seats and pretend not to notice. The air around him was sour with whisky and cigar smoke. He leaned against the corner of the house, shirt rumpled, his eyes bloodshot and rheumy. In spite of the hour he might have just woken from his debauchery. On the next Our Father he began praying too, counting off his Hail Marys with his fingers. His voice sounded scratchy, unused.

After the rosary José Alfredo shoveled cookies into his mouth, handful after handful of polvorones, until Romi told him there were tamales warming in the oven. Pilar sat at the kitchen table, tired and hating him. He crouched over the stove eating his tamales without a plate, powdery brown sugar stuck to his chin, his cheeks.

"You should see the way you look," Pilar said. "Imbécil."

"Leave me alone," he snapped. He wiped his fingers on the front of his shirt and walked past her into the hallway, to Joselito's bedroom.

Romi came back inside so fast Pilar knew she had been listening. She redistributed the cookies on the platter to cover the sections José Alfredo had eaten.

"He's drunk," she whispered. "Don't make it worse. Just ignore him."

Outside the neighbors were relaxed and chatting in low voices. It was right, thought Pilar, with José Alfredo sleeping off his drunk, to sit with them for a while. She went outside and sat beside Romi. Mr. Camacho and Mr. Silva were talking about the new Woolworth downtown. One of the Uribe sisters had gotten a new dog. For once, no one had any stories about children.

It was nine o'clock before the last guests left. Pilar heard José Alfredo snoring in Joselito's room. She looked in on him. He was sleeping on the floor in his undershirt, the rest of his filthy clothing wadded up next to the leg of the small bed. She sighed. This was so like him. He had not wanted to dirty the furniture. Pilar picked up the pile of clothes and took them into the kitchen, mindful of his pocketknife and billfold. She would begin the washing in the morning, but his clothes reeked of smoke and his own heavy unwashed smell. She wanted to air them out on the porch.

Pilar turned out his trouser pockets on the kitchen table: lint, a few pennies, the house key. A scrap of paper caught her fingernail as she pulled the pocket inside out. There was a crumpled gold foil cigar band stuck to the hem of the pocket.

Pilar dropped the piece of foil on the table. She felt her own pulse thumping in her fingertips. She pulled the shirt out of the pile. She smoothed out the wrinkles. All over the back and sleeves were tiny gray hairs and on the collar one long silver strand. She mashed up the roll of dirty clothes, all except the shirt, and went out to throw them in the trash bin outside. She recleaned the kitchen table, scrubbing the formica until she could no longer smell smoke. She washed her hands with Lava soap, though it chafed her palms red.

Pilar picked up the shirt and stalked back into Joselito's room, snapping on the light. She prodded José Alfredo hard with her big toe until she roused him. "Ay, déjame ya," he grunted, voice thick with sleep and drink.

"You went back to her," she said accusingly. "You found her, didn't you?"

"What the hell are you talking about?"

"The old woman who came. Your other wife."

José Alfredo pressed the heel of his hand against his eye. "I don't understand."

"The woman who came. That day I lost our daughter. Admit it. Here is her hair," Pilar said, throwing the shirt at him.

He blinked at the shirt, held it up to the light. "That's horsehair. I stayed in the stables at the livestock port."

"You'll never admit the truth, will you?" Pilar said softly, more to herself than to him. Of course not. He was a man. He didn't have to. Ever.

José Alfredo dropped the shirt and rolled over, giving her his back. "Just leave me alone. I'm tired."

That was the beginning of the end. He began to stay, as a matter of course, in Joselito's little room. His movements were unrelated to Pilar. She might not know when he would arrive home, or from where. He no longer ate what she cooked, and soon, she stopped cooking the meals he preferred. She did not tell him what was growing inside of her, and not just out of spite. It had come to mean something terrible. Perhaps the old woman had set it there, inside her, somehow. Perhaps it would be deformed, show a sign of some inherent wickedness. Her husband's sin.

Her loneliness was a living thing now, beating inside her like a heart, alive and thriving. Though, too, she no longer found it unwelcome. It was better than José Alfredo. It was preferable to his company.

Whatever he had done, whoever the old woman was, a dream or a reality, his true wife or some castoff, he was guilty. He was guilty and she would not find him otherwise. Every time she looked at him, she could see it hovering like a dark aura. His guilt. The curse he had wrought somehow, so that their family had dissolved into nothing. Now it was just the two of them, living in this silence, moving in their separate orbits.

José Alfredo plunged into work on the house. He broke the trail up the hill and filled it with caliche, so that though it was not paved, it was a true road. He was constantly mending, repairing. Determined that he would finish this house in spite of having nothing to put inside it, except his haunted wife.

One day it was finished. She knew because he told her so. It was the first words they had crossed for weeks.

"Oh," she replied. "That's good."

"Look over it," he said. He was standing in the dark, looking out the bedroom window. He'd not been in their bedroom for a long time. "Tell me what you might need."

"I don't need anything."

"No," he said. "I guess you don't."

The next day José Alfredo was gone. He left for work, so she thought, but he never came back. He wouldn't, she realized. He'd left some money, his bank account passcard, and the deed to the house, all neatly stacked on the kitchen table.

"Do you want to move back to the apartment?" Romi asked her a week later. "It's closer to the bus stop. To everything."

"No, I'm staying here," Pilar said. She was not going to live in the neighborhood, where she'd see everyone whispering about her. She didn't want Romi's pity, could hardly stand her kind brown eyes. "I just want you to go. Just leave me alone."

"All right," Romi said. "I'm here if you need me."

I won't need her, Pilar thought, watching Romi's truck disappear down the caliche road. The next few times Romi came knocking, Pilar didn't answer the door. She was trapped by her terror and fury, by her own body, by the months that would gather until this cursed child came. And what a wretched creature she would be then, in the eyes of the whole world.

After another week, Pilar went down the hill to Caimanes and took the bus to the shoe factory. The foreman told her there was a job if she wanted it.

Chapter Eight

———◇———

Skip-Outs

LULU MUÑOZ, 1994

L ast year when I met Ernie, his band was three guys who needed a singer. The band was called Los Pinche Nacos, the Fucking Low-lifes. Ernie on guitar, Olmec on drums, and Jorge the bassist. They let me in the band because I proved I could sing a passable "Dear Prudence" and scream through "Search and Destroy." Also, because Olmec said having a chick singer was kick-ass, almost as cool as a chick drummer.

Over the summer the band went by the Lucky Losers, and the first week of school, when Jorge thought he got his girlfriend, Ximena, pregnant, he changed our name to Ximena's Demon Baby. It ended up being a false alarm, but she dumped him when she found out.

We've been Pink Vomit for about a month. I came up with it after my friend Danny Flippo barfed Flamin' Hot Cheetos during homeroom. PV might stay our name. The guys said it reflects a punk sensibility. Plus, Jorge is ready to get back together with Ximena. That hasn't happened yet, but Jorge is too stupid to give up.

Marina puts up with Pink Vomit, kind of. Marina likes Spanish rock, pop, country, and Tejano. She gets down with heavy metal too. It's not our band's style she has a problem with. It's that I'm wasting my time. She's mad that I gave up mathletes to practice punk songs in Olmec's garage. This is because the guys are not serious. Actually, she says they aren't artistas. The way Marina says artistas, it counts more. Artista means a genius talent, like Juan Gabriel or Selena.

"Homegirl is putting in the work," Marina said this morning at our lockers.

It was in my mouth to argue that we had been putting in the work. We had just hit a snag, which I was planning to fix by asking Pilar if we could use her garage. But I wasn't sure how to tell Marina that. Especially because she'd be annoyed I didn't take her with me to meet Pilar.

"Selena's always touring. Me and Art saw her three times last summer."

"Don't remind me," I said. I've never seen Selena, even though she regularly tours South Texas. I can't go to concerts, any concerts, because my dad doesn't want me *out running the streets*. Unless I'm with a blood relative, eating at Applebee's after dark is *out running the streets*.

"She's gonna be here again next month. Tell your dad you're sleeping over at my house."

"I don't know." My dad had come home, so I was back at my house again. It was a lot easier to go places when I stayed with Yoli.

"Lulu, how are you in that punk band, how are you punk at all, if you can't even get it together to see Selena?"

"Okay, okay," I said. Unlike Marina, I do not have forty million married girl cousins, so I can't lie and say I'm with my family while they cover for me, like Marina does, when she's secretly on dates with her boyfriend Arturo.

"Well, just saying. If you want something, you gotta put in the work."

Putting in the work is a real thing. But also, Marina just wants me to see Selena with her. She doesn't care about Pink Vomit. She's a lot like my dad. If it doesn't make money, what's the point? I can't argue that my bandmates qualify as artistas, because she's right. They are mostly stupid boys.

Only Ernie is an actual musician. He's a Vega, and the Vega family has had a band for generations. But just because Ernie can play six different instruments does not mean he's not a stupid boy. I feel like he might be the stupidest one.

Marina and I have been best friends since the fifth grade. So instead of arguing with her, I took a position I knew she'd agree with. "I get your point. But for real, nobody can be Selena."

"Truth," she said. And that was that. Because there are two incontrovertible musical intersections in Marina's and my tastes: Metallica and Selena.

I consider myself a heavy metal aficionado, but girly-girl Marina is the most savage Metallica fan alive. She has a Mexican dad just like I do, so she's not allowed to listen to their music. She says missing the Metallica tour with Guns N' Roses this past summer will scar her for life. I believe her.

To prove her loyalty she steals *Circus, Guitar World, Spin, Hit Parader, Rolling Stone*—anything and everything that mentions the band. She has a whole system where she commits the interviews to memory, carefully cuts out photos, stows her cassettes (also stolen) and the photos in her locker, and then throws away the magazines so there's zero evidence. She's so committed to their fandom that, on one academic decathlon trip to Austin, she stole the VHS copy of the 1971 movie *Johnny Got His Gun* from Vulcan Video just because it was a major influence on Metallica's song "One." In the same incident, she also stole Vulcan's copy of *The Last American Virgin* because she's unforgivably into tragic love stories. But she became a klepto for Metallica.

Truth: Metallica is solidly the best thrash metal. More interesting compositions than Megadeth and Slayer, better musicians than Anthrax. Truth: *Ride the Lightning* is their best album. . . . *And Justice for All* is a very close second. Since Marina and I know that's the truth, we never fight because my second-favorite thrash is Pantera and hers is Sepultura.

And then there's Selena. Selena Quintanilla, frontwoman of Selena y Los Dinos.

Selena is not just the truth, she is la pura verdad. I'm not even that into Tejano music, but I worship her. I have all her albums and know them by heart. I've seen her on *The Johnny Canales Show*. Onstage, she was all rhythm and mesmerizing electricity in a black bustier and skintight Rocky Mountain jeans.

It kills me I've never seen Selena live. Instead, I sit in my room with the window open and listen every single time Selena has a gig in town. I live close to the amphitheater. Her voice soars so clear. I can hear her talk to the crowd, tease them, rile them up. I catch every word, every note, her breaths between lyrics.

Her voice is moody and capricious as the ocean. She keeps a note trembling on the edge of tears until I want to weep too. She drags the washing machine cumbia out of me, even though I'm not good at all, devastates me when she sings mariachi with a dusky, full-throated banshee wail that vibratos my soul to pieces.

If she sang in English, people would know her like they know Whitney Houston. Selena's not just an artista, she is a full-on diva. When Selena's sixty, she'll be Aretha Franklin legendary, fat as fuck and don't care, swaggering past all the little newcomers, and everybody bow down to La Reina.

But right now, Selena is a girl with a Mexican dad. He's her manager and he's the boss of everything. She's the queen of Tejano music, racking up Grammys, wearing rhinestone bras like she's Madonna, selling out huge shows in Mexico, and young and old, every man is in love with those traffic-stopping nalgas, but so what? She has a Mexican dad, just like Marina. Just like me.

Selena had to sneak around with her secret guitarist-boyfriend because her dad wouldn't let her date. The scandal almost broke up Los Dinos. Her dad fired her boyfriend from the band and forbade her from ever seeing him again. Selena ended up running away and eloping.

When the story came out, I said it was crazy. Imagine being married when you're only twenty years old. Marina said it was so romantic.

"It's true love," she argued. "They were meant to be. And Chris Pérez is super hot."

"Truth," I said, because I could agree with that. She's the practical one, but Marina does not get it. Selena's pinky nail has more talent than I ever will, but she's the proof that even if you are destined to take the world by storm, a Mexican dad is gonna boss your life. I can't even imagine my dad meeting Ernie, Jorge, and Olmec, let alone being our band manager. I'd probably end up running away too.

But not to get married. A husband is just another man trying to tell you what to do. Trust me, it's the same set of problems.

Ernie stopped me before I went into second period English and gave me a note. He didn't say anything, not even hi. He'd been like that with me for a week, ever since we had sex and I didn't fall in love.

"What's this?" I said. I was so sick of his sulking routine.

He shrugged.

"Just tell me to my face. I don't want to read your stupid note."

"You're the one who stopped talking to me," he started. Then something behind me caught his attention.

I glanced over my shoulder. There was César Allen at the far end of the hallway, coming to get my Physics notes again. He must have just gotten to school because his motorcycle helmet was tucked under one arm, but he wasn't in a hurry. Everybody talks to him.

He waved for me to wait for him, like he did practically every morning.

"That fucking guy," Ernie said, and took off. Ernie absolutely hates César.

I wasn't going to get a tardy because César moved only three feet per hour, so I went to class. My AP English teacher, Miss Williams, was pursing her lips at herself in her compact mirror, making sure her lip gloss was straight. She's the only teacher in the high school who does her makeup during class, like there aren't twenty-five people watching her.

"Was that Ernie?" Marina asked when I slid into my seat at our table. "He didn't come to class this morning."

I shrugged, trying to be casual. I still hadn't told her what happened with Ernie. "Maybe he was out of gas money and had to walk."

"Well, Mr. B said Ernie's almost failing because of excessive absences. He needs to get it together."

Marina draped her boyfriend Arturo's jacket on the back of her chair in jock-girlfriend display—so his last name (Guzman, stitched in cursive across the shoulder line) showed. He was on the track team and a member of the National Honor Society. *It's important*, Marina liked to say, *that your man be college material.*

Ernie's note was short. *Chaparral Disco Rodeo 1:30 p.m., maybe gig.*

Meeting Jorge in the parking lot 4th per. BE THERE. Back by 4:30, the latest. Promise.

I'd never cut class. My dad picked me up at six o'clock every day, right after he got off work. Enough time for school clubs or doing homework in the library. Enough time to go to Mexico and back?

Marina snatched the note out of my hand. "Oh my God, are you going?"

Neither of us had ever been to Chaparral Disco Rodeo, but we knew it was a nightclub across the border. Chaparral Disco Rodeo—or CDR—had dancing *and* live bull riding.

"Shut up, Mari," I whispered. "Tell everybody, why don't you."

She crammed the note in her pocket and whispered, "Are you?"

César stuck his head in the doorway. Miss Williams glanced up from her mirror and said, "You better be out of here by the time I'm done with attendance."

"What'd I miss this morning?" César saluted Miss Williams and sat down across from me. He said it in Spanish, of course; fresas never speak English unless they're talking to white people. Oh, they can. They're just too stuck up to do it.

"We reviewed. There's a quiz on Friday." My dad's always bragging because I'm one of two freshmen in Physics I, but it sucks. There's a reason Mr. Popular César Allen never comes to first period. It's geek paradise.

Marina gave César a big smile. She loves his morning visits. The only thing better than college material is a fresa—a fucking rich Mexican national. Although when I call César a fresa, Marina argues he's not snobby enough to be a real one. She's wrong, though.

On the border there are names for everybody and rules for the names: nacos are lowlifes and you can be a Mexican or a Mexican American and be a naco. Also being a naco is totally punk.

Fresas really means strawberries, but is slang for wealthy Mexican nationals. They dress in designer clothes, constantly jabber away in perfect, upper-class Spanish—absolutely never the vato version like Ernie or, just as bad, rancherito Spanish. They greet their female friends with annoying cheek-kissing hellos.

You can't be a Mexican American fresa. There are poser fresas, but they don't have the family, the money, or the ancestral ranchland to back it up, or they are Mexican American, not actually Mexican. If you're from a wealthy, landowning family on this side of the border, you're a white cowboy.

If you're a rich Mexican American, you still do not have that kind of generational money like fresas or white ranching families. You're well-to-do, so that makes you a Hispanic.

My dad told me that actually, fresas and the real old-school Anglo ranching families on the Texas side are one and the same. They have a history of intermarriage, dual citizenship, own land on both sides of the border. They speak perfect Spanish. I know the perfect Spanish part is true. Colby Halston is from a ranching family, and he's the best Spanish speaker in my AP Spanish class. He learned it from the family nanny.

I know all these things and so does Marina. César is a total fresa. It doesn't matter that he has a white last name. He belongs to the Ruiz family from Mexico.

The Ruizes are like those powerful families on the telenovelas who live on some giant hacienda out on the Sierra Madre, but also, they have a high-rise in Mexico City. They aren't really a family so much as a dynasty. My dad told me one of César's uncles used to be the governor of Coahuila. César's mom owns a lot of trendy stores on the tourist strip across the border. The family has so many ranches. They own a huge swath of land on the Mexican side of the Rio Grande. American industrial companies like ALCOA and GWR have factories on that side of the border because it's cheaper and there's not a lot of environmental regulations. Those companies rent the land their factories are on from the Ruiz family because they can't buy it from them. I can't even imagine how much the rent is on a couple of factories every month. A real dynasty.

Marina should know better. It doesn't matter that César doesn't curl his lip at her because she's from this side and her dad's a truck driver. He's a Ruiz, full stop.

Marina and I are not white or rich Mexican nationals, and we don't have enough money to be Hispanics. Not American to the white ranching kids, who might or might not be nice to our faces, but know they are better than us because they're white and we aren't. Not Mexican enough for the fresas who know they're better than us because they are actually Mexican and we aren't. We're caught in the middle; we're both and neither. We're Tejanas.

My dad has a mountain-sized chip on his shoulder about this. He yearns to be Mexicano, puro Mexicano, whatever he thinks that is, but he's not dumb. I know these things because he sat me down to explain them to me.

Marina is like a lot of people around here. She doesn't see all this because she's inside it. She thinks love conquers all. Or maybe she believes in her own power to cross those lines. Me, I don't believe in fairy tales. I don't trust anybody but Grandma and Marina. César is a good guy, to a point. After that, he is what he is, just like everyone else.

César was in my English class looking for notes and Miss Williams was fine with it. That's a guy who never comes to first period, and you can bet our teacher is not going to fail him for excessive absences. Not César Ruiz Allen.

"Here." I pulled my Physics notebook out and tossed it on the table. "Give it back to me later. You better wake up for the quiz on Friday."

"Thanks, Lulis." He wrote "quiz Fri" on his arm and then tucked his pen behind his ear like it was supposed to make him look smarter. "I got stuck on the bridge again."

"Dude, whatever. I can smell your McDonald's."

César just grinned. Most people would not after they'd just been called out on Egg McMuffin breath, but that's César. You can't piss him off.

"You have any gum?"

I said no, but Marina fished a piece of Dentyne out of her purse. César stuck my notebook in his backpack and winked at us.

Marina waved her fingers at him, but I just said, "L-A-T-E-R."

"Why are you like that?" Marina whispered, when he was gone.

"Like what?"

"Rude."

"Because he's always copying off me."

"If it was me, I would totally pick him over Ernie," Marina said.

"You're dumb."

"I know those guys are about fresa girls and white chicks, but he likes you, Lulu. He does."

Marina's smart about guy stuff. I mean, she's not allowed to date either, but she's had stealth boyfriends since the sixth grade. She knows if someone likes you. Her radar's off, though, with César. She just thinks that because last year, when we were eighth graders and he was a junior, César talked to me at JCPenney.

"He doesn't. Trust me." My dad warned me about fresa guys. They might sleep with me, but they will never date me. I'm just a pocha: bad Spanish, no money, not good enough for girlfriend material. César treats me like a kid sis, but even if he didn't, I won't go there. I never want to see that side of him. I don't want proof. Because then I couldn't be friends with him anymore.

"Well then, why does he come find you?"

"Because he's too freaking lazy to go to class."

Marina rolled her eyes. "Whatever, Loo-lees."

"I've known him since elementary."

She snorted. "Oh yeah. That's why."

"Our parents died the same year," I said. Reminding her made me feel like a jerk. But she shut up like I knew she would. A dead mom is a major buzzkill.

I was in the second grade the year my mom died. César was a fifth grader. His dad was already dead. Six months before my mother, a car accident too.

César used to be chubby. He had big front teeth then and his side ones hadn't grown in yet. He was a fresa, but not all the way fresa yet because he was only ten years old. That year the big boys at St. Augustine's Academy were renaming each other food names, which they thought was super cool. His was "the Caesar Salad." I mean, that's how he introduced himself: *I'm the Caesar Salad. Mucho gusto.*

"Nobody in your class is going to talk to you for a while," he told me. This was just before Thanksgiving. My mom had been dead about a week.

"Why won't they?" I was sitting in the sandbox by myself, but I had wanted to be by myself. I didn't know I was being avoided.

He sat down in the sand. "Because you're scary to them."

"Why?"

"I don't know. But it's just a little while and then they forget."

"How can they forget my mom died?" I demanded.

"They do. I'm telling you."

I cried like the stupid little kid I was. Everything was my mom to me. Her not being there was huge teeth chewing on me all the time. How could anyone not care about that?

"I'll talk to you," he said. "I hated it when no one talked to me."

"You're lying!" I started kicking at him and screaming and throwing sand. "Get away! Get away from me!"

He wouldn't leave, though. I leaped on him, punching and kicking. He curled up like a big roly-poly so I couldn't get at anything but his fat shoulders.

"It's true! It's true!" He sounded like a yipping dog. He wouldn't hit me back, but he kept doing a sweeper move with his arm and knocking me off his back. It made me even madder that I couldn't hurt him.

Sister Agatha dragged us to the office for fighting. Ruiz or no, he got a spanking because he was a boy and older. Me, they sent home. I stayed with Grandma Romi for three more days. When I came back to school again, César played with me every day at recess until the holiday break. He was the only one.

He was right. After Christmas break, the other kids acted like nothing had happened.

That first year my mom was gone, César was my real friend. He played with me even when the other boys made fun of him. I was outraged that everybody else acted like they forgot my mom. Or maybe they really had, which was worse. How dare they?

"They don't get it, Lulis," César said, when I stormed about it one afternoon at recess. We were in the sandbox, our usual spot. "To them, it's like old news."

"That's bullshit," I said. Cursing was new for me. César thought it was hilarious when I spouted off bad words. Except the f-bomb. He forbade me that one because it was not for little girls. Besides, if Sister Agatha heard me, César would get another spanking.

"Yeah, it's bullshit," he said, drawing slow figure eights in the sand with his index finger. "I just want to remember my dad. He was a cool guy."

"Sometimes I can't stop thinking about my mom. And I can't breathe."

It wasn't a blood oath, but we pretty much agreed we'd remember. We'd remember when no one else did. The next year César went off to middle school. I've hardly seen him until now, in high school.

César does not hang out with me. He's a senior and the king of the fresas. I'm just a nobody freshman. Underneath, though, I still know him. That's why I give him my Physics notes. But I was not going to explain all that to Marina.

It didn't matter because she was quiet with me the rest of English class. It's too tacky to say, *Oh, that's right, I forgot about the dead mom thing.* Which was fine. I just waited until the weirdness passed.

When the bell rang, she said, "Bathroom. If you're going to Mex we need to do your makeup."

"I thought you said the band's a waste of my time."

"Not if you could get paid." She looked critically at my hair. "God, I wish you hadn't worn a ponytail today."

Ernie's fourth period is lunch because he never goes to chemistry. He doesn't care. He's got a plan: get a GED and join the marines in December when he turns seventeen. His dad agreed to sign the waiver—that way Ernie'll get a haircut and a real job at the same time.

That's what happens if you're a boy. You do what you want. Go across the border in the middle of Tuesday afternoon? No problem.

"No fucking way," Jorge said, when I came out to the parking lot. "I can't believe she's coming too."

"Fuck off," I said. It was the right answer because he grinned and high-fived me. He didn't even laugh at the red lips and winged eyeliner combo Marina had given me. The wings were dramatic and delicate, and just cool. Marina is a whiz at makeup. I'm always her guinea pig, but only in my room. The liner itched a little. I had to keep reminding myself not to touch my face.

"We're just waiting for Carla," Ernie said. "She's taking us."

Carla's the one Jorge is messing with right now. He's a magnet for crazy. Or like Ernie says, le gusta la mala vida. Before Ximena dumped him, they were the weekly public break-up couple. Ximena is a straight up harpy-screaming, face-slapping, jealous-stalking, tire-slashing, I'm-coming-for-your-ass fiend. Jorge says she's the love of his life. He's hanging with Carla because he knows it will drive Ximena nuts.

Ximena's a maniac, but I have to agree with her on this one: Carla Bowden sucks. She's super skinny-bones and limp, always with fresh cigarette burns on her pasty arms. She and her friends waft through the hallways totally stoned or else curl up in bathroom stalls, pale and shuddering like little sobbing ghosts. Those guys just go to class to take naps.

"Where's Olmec?" I asked. I hadn't seen him at school all week. His name is really Óscar. Everybody calls him Olmec because he has a face just like one of those Olmec colossal heads. Fat jaguar cheeks, a flat nose, thick lips. Small, curving black eyes. He looks exactly like the reincarnation of a Mesoamerican warrior, but with skater hair and Vans.

"That lazy bastard stayed home again," said Jorge. "He said he'd meet us there."

Standing around made me nervous. No rule against going to the parking lot on lunch, but still: I didn't want to be taken for those burnouts who smoke weed in their cars.

"Where's she at already?" asked Ernie, looking annoyed.

"Chicks," Jorge sighed, like he had all the answers to the universe. "Always late."

Carla came out of the science wing just as we were crowding around her red Civic. She gave me this long once-over and then dismissed me. I hate that. I hate that some trashy bitch can make me feel so small.

Still, it was something to watch her move across the parking lot, slow and sullen. She was wearing a faded, paisley pink minidress, an ugly thing that was supposed to be ugly-sexy, which is exactly Carla's look. I can't imagine wearing something like that. Not that short. Not that frumpy, with the white, sewn-on belt and the square pocket over one breast, metallic-green tights and glossy-blue ankle boots.

"Ready?" she asked Jorge, like she couldn't see us all hanging out beside her car. She and Jorge paired off. I followed them, in step with Ernie, but he didn't talk to me.

Jorge took up all the space talking in the car on the way across the border. We had a couple hours to kill. The meeting with the CDR manager was at one thirty. Jorge had given him a tape with some songs.

Being with the three of them made me feel strange. Jorge and Carla, touching each other, flirting. Ernie with me, stiff and silent, like we'd never been friends. The ride was quick; no traffic on the expressway. Jorge paid a dollar at the border toll booth; we crossed the Rio Grande, got in the nothing-to-declare lane, and there we were, in Mexico.

Carla parked behind the big Martinez Curios shop. They sold every kind of tacky thing: baby-rattle maracas; floppy straw sombreros; entire mariachi orquestras made out of taxidermied bullfrogs (all with little brass horns and guitars and suits with neckties); velvet portraits of Elvis, Jesus, and Emiliano Zapata; lots and lots of booze and shot glasses. You got an hour of parking for every three dollars you spent in the store, so we bought a shitload of Chiclets before we hit the main drag.

"Meet us at Chaparral by one thirty," Jorge said. "Olmec said he'd be there."

Ernie gave him a thumbs-up. We headed south, toward the downtown proper. There were lights across the bar fronts, neon switched off, so just the ratty lettering stood out, and I could see how dirty the bulbs were. It probably looked different in the dark, but in the midday sun it was depressing. Stuff like LADIES BAR and POOL was painted all over those places, but I don't know what ladies went in there. All we saw were grim old men.

On the next block, the one with law offices sandwiched between dentists, optometrists, and loads of pharmacies, winter Texans wandered around in little anxious groups. Anybody could tell these turkey necks weren't from around here. Old gringos in La Cienega are true-blue cowboys. They would not be caught dead in Bermuda shorts and Velcro-strap sandals. And they definitely don't carry little tubes of sunscreen in fanny packs. Not even old cowgirls wore Velcro—they'd have been sporting oversized cowhide purses, probably dyed turquoise.

"Let's cross the street," Ernie said. "If they find out we're American, we'll be stuck helping them buy their meds for the next hour."

And just like that we were cool again. I didn't know how it happened, but I was glad.

We cut through the plaza. The guy selling watermelons out of the back of a rusty station wagon was lying on the roof, sleeping. Two flower peddlers sat on the pavilion steps, smoking and talking, their flowers discarded beside them, wilting in the sun. The streets were bursting with music. The shoes and the clothes shops, the hot-pink frutería, and my old favorite: the leather goods store with the life-sized, fully geared plaster horse at the entrance that my dad used to set me on whenever we came down to the plaza—all of them, every one, belted out conjunto jams. There was César's green Kawasaki motorcycle parked outside of Casa Tropical, the furniture store his mom owned. We both saw the motorcycle, and both pretended it wasn't there.

The shopkeepers in the curios shops just watched Ernie and me without saying anything. I guess Ernie and I were nothing to get excited about, because they didn't even try to coax us in, they just seemed bored.

"We must look cheap," I said.

"We're Mexicans with no money. They're not gonna hassle us."

We ended up at Cien Diez. The burgers are crazy—thick slices of fried ham on top of the patty, two kinds of cheese, avocado, mustard, tomatoes, onions, jalapeños, everything stacked high.

Ernie bought me a Sol beer. I tried to drink it but couldn't. "This is gross."

"It's just how beer tastes."

"It's nasty."

"Well, I don't have Don Pedro and Slurpees on me all the time," he said.

I didn't like him bringing up what happened at the lake. But it was sunny out, and the air smelled of frying beef and onions. The light and the hum of the day made it feel easy. I laughed and said I was going to get a Coke.

"I'll get it," he said. "Can you even order one in Spanish?"

"Whatever," I said. But I let him. No way was I gonna tell Ernie I wanted to be just friends. Not now, when he was finally over being mad at me.

"Should we get going?" I asked, after I had had three Cokes.

"We still have like an hour. Let's check out Ninfa's."

"You've eaten there?" Ninfa's is one of the most expensive joints in the city.

"Sometimes my dad's mariachi plays there," he said. "I know the waiters. They'll hook us up. Chaparral is just down the street from there anyway."

I said okay, and we walked a few more blocks south of the zona central to where the main drag splits into a highway leading south to Saltillo. We passed the Gran Mercado, where they sell vegetables and small livestock—chickens mainly—and there was Ninfa's, like an oasis before the no-man's-land of the desert.

The guy at the front looked surprised when we walked up. He had a primpy little mustache and super-slicked-back hair.

"Ernesto," he said, smiling.

"How's it going?" Ernie said.

"It's slow," the guy said, shrugging. "Sit wherever you want, except the party room."

"Thanks," Ernie said. He seemed at ease, even though we were two stupid kids in jean jackets.

A waiter seated us at a small table near the patio. It was nearly empty inside the restaurant: a few winter Texans in the back eating what looked like the Mexican plate, a lone man reading a book in front of a cup of coffee, three women in their forties, drunk and cackling like chickens at the bar. I could see that there had been lots of people recently—the busboys were busy clearing off tables all over the restaurant.

The waiter's name was Rafael. He had tiny black eyes and the sides of his head were shaved. He smirked at us. "You're out early."

"Hey, hook us up with some chocolate flans, man."

"Yeah, all right. But at least order some lemonades. I gotta have a ticket for the table."

"This wimp wants a piña colada," Ernie said. "I'll buy that."

I had just scooped a giant piece of flan into my mouth when like twenty gangsters walked into the restaurant. There were several old grandpa types in plain guayaberas and slacks, talking among themselves. A pudgy dude with a brush of white hair like an elderly javelina was obviously the honcho. Everybody else in the entourage was young. The young guys wore earrings, leather jackets, and western shirts, and all of them were armed. There were a lot of dark sunglasses.

I know this happens. It's just a fact of life on the Mexican side, sometimes mafiosos are around and you just deal with it. Even my dad has stories. But I still spat out my flan. It plopped beside my plate, gooey and gross.

"It's Chivo Mireles," Ernie whispered. "Just eat. They're not gonna bother us."

Ernie looked a little nervous, but that was it. I pushed the glob of flan back onto my plate and set my spoon down. Nope, I could not take another bite.

"Duty calls," said Rafael, and he scurried away without another word to us.

I watched the gangsters from the corner of my eye. One guy with a glossy ponytail and a beard à la Marco Antonio Solís from Los Bukis walked up to the maître d'. Los Bukis patted him on the shoulder and whispered something to him. He moved quickly to seat the group in the party room.

Not all of them went. Los Bukis guy turned to the rest of us. Even the cackling hens at the bar were paying attention. He motioned for two of the guys who'd stayed to guard the front entrance. A couple of others went into the kitchen and out to the patio.

"Please pardon us," Los Bukis said in excessively polite Spanish to the restaurant at large. "We are so sorry to disturb your afternoon. My employer must have absolute security during his meal. He apologizes, but no one will enter or leave the building until after he has finished. He understands this is inconvenient. He will, of course, provide recompense by paying the bill for everyone. So please, enjoy yourselves! Those who will be affected at work, please give us the names of your supervisors. I am sure they will understand when we explain to them. Thank you."

The tourists actually looked excited. The ladies whooped and ordered another round of drinks. One of them called out to Los Bukis to come and have one with her. He answered her in the same cheerful way. He even went over and sipped her fruity drink. Dumb-ass white tourists. They'd go back to Ohio, or wherever, with a wild frontier story to tell.

"I don't know how long we're going to be here," Ernie said. "Wish I hadn't already eaten."

"We're gonna miss the meeting," I said, trying not to seem scared.

"Chivo's a slow eater. I bet Jorge and Carla ditch us for not showing up." Ernie scowled at the tourists. "Fuck, man. Our first gig down the drain. We'll never catch a break!"

"If I'm not back in time, I'm so dead," I mumbled.

"We're fine. They're not gonna mess with a couple of kids. We'll wait and we can take a taxi back across."

"Yeah, and my dad is gonna go ape when he picks me up and I'm not there."

"Get a grip," Ernie said. "If we'd gotten this gig at Chaparral, we'd go on at like one in the morning. How were you gonna explain that if you can't even be late from school?"

"I can get out if he already thinks I'm in," I countered. "This is not the same."

"If you say so," Ernie said. And then, of course, he went there. "Were you avoiding me because you regret it? I'm not gonna blab. I'm not Jorge."

"I don't think you're like Jorge."

"Then what?"

"I don't know." I didn't want to tell him I felt guilty for sneaking out of my grandma's house that night. That maybe I made her die, doing what I did with him. It would sound silly, saying it out loud. "My grandma's dead. Now it's just my dad and me. I'm really fucking sad."

"Of course you are," Ernie said, but he looked relieved. "Shit, I'm stupid."

"Can we talk about something else?"

"You know what," Ernie said. The way he said it, I knew he'd been planning to tell me, maybe even since he gave me the note in the morning. "My dad's mariachi is opening Selena's show next month. We have VIP passes. Come with me."

I had to say yes. How could I not?

We ended up sitting there all afternoon, drinking lemonades and listening to what seemed like every song ever made by Eydie Gormé and Los Panchos. Ernie ordered a couple of appetizers out of sheer boredom, but I couldn't eat anything. By three o'clock, I was fully freaking. We'd no doubt been ditched. In a little while, rush hour traffic was going to make the trip back across the border even trickier.

"I can't wait anymore," I whispered to Ernie. "My dad is coming at six o'clock! Do you think I'm going to give that gangster my dad's name so he can write me an excuse?"

"We can't leave, Lulu."

"What am I going to tell my dad?"

"We'll think of something. Maybe you left to Marina's house. Maybe— I don't know. Just order something else, if you want, what else can we do? At least he's paying."

"I don't want anything else. I have to go back to school."

"Well, we can't."

I couldn't argue that. Most of the men had gone into the party room, but there were still at least six mafiosos pacing around the restaurant. The guy near the front entrance wasn't even bothering to hide his nine millimeter.

"Bummer," Rafael, the waiter, said, as he passed our table. "I'm supposed to be off right now. Pinche suerte."

We sat in silence. The maître d' offered everyone champagne. I tasted it, but it was sour.

"I don't want any more."

"You sure?" asked Ernie.

"Yeah, have it. I gotta go to the ladies," I said. "Be right back."

"Be careful," Ernie said.

I crossed the restaurant with minimal issues. Los Bukis asked me if I needed anything, which I guess was code for, *What are you doing?*

"Um, the bathroom," I said in stumbling Spanish. He waved me by. There was another guard in there, although he hustled out when I walked in. I guess even mafiosos are embarrassed to be caught in the ladies' room by a girl.

"Pardon me," he said in Spanish.

I was finishing up when I heard a sound that was most definitely not part of the restaurant noise. Outside, someone was calling for someone else. Or like when you swear you heard someone say your name right beside you, only when you turn nobody's there. It was like that. And Grandma Romi used to tell me when that happens, pay attention. *That's the way my mother visits me,* she'd say. *When I need help, she shows me the way.*

I turned off the faucet and went to the wall with the near-ceiling window. It was a little half window, a narrow rectangle. If I climbed on the stall door, I could see out. I could get out.

I saw the Gran Mercado across the highway. I clicked open the hasps. It would be tight—a grown-up couldn't do it, even Marina who'd had boobs since fifth grade couldn't do it, but I could get through that window. If I squeezed.

I braced myself against the tile wall of the bathroom and the top of the stall door, even though it just about killed my knees. The narrow top of the metal door left bruises on my kneecaps the rest of the week. I hooked my fingers under the window panel and pulled. It slid open and I wiggled through.

It's not that easy to get through a high window, even if you are small enough to wrench yourself through the space. It's not like in the movies. I scraped the shit out of my belly trying to hold on to the window and not land on my head. Didn't really work. I belly flopped on the asphalt and almost barfed from the pain. I couldn't breathe, it hurt so much. Finally, I managed to pull myself up along the wall and then I ran for the highway, expecting a hail of bullets any minute.

Nothing happened. I crossed the highway and ducked into the Gran Mercado. I watched the Ninfa's parking lot from between two market stalls, where a woman was selling Aztec-themed bean pots and another woman was sitting on a blanket with sets of beaded jewelry laid out in front of her in rows. One of the mafiosos did a lazy stroll behind the restaurant, but he didn't even glance at the window.

I ran hard, clutching my sore belly. I got back to the main drag around four by the clock on the Banco Nacional. César's green Kawasaki was still parked in front of the furniture store. The store was empty, because who the hell is going to buy authentic, hand-carved wooden furniture from Oaxaca in the middle of Tuesday siesta time? César was sitting behind the register, doing his homework.

"Lulu," he said, starting up. "What're you doing here?" He was so surprised he actually spoke to me in English.

"Man, please help me get back to school," I gasped.

"Did somebody hurt you?" he asked sharply. "You've got a cut on your chin."

"No, I fell."

"What happened?"

"I climbed out of a bathroom window at Ninfa's. They locked the place down. Chivo Mireles and his guys."

"I hate when that happens," César said, folding up his homework and sticking it in the register under the cash tray. "Last time Sylvia and I were stuck there for almost three hours."

"Can you take me across? I gotta get back like now."

"Yeah." He looked around the store. "Just let me put up a note for my mom. What are you doing over here anyway?"

"I came with Jorge and Ernie. Only Ernie and I got stuck at the restaurant and Jorge left us."

"Jorge and Ernie. Figures. You're gonna get in trouble hanging out with them."

"You skip all the time."

"I'm helping my mom," he said.

I almost said she could afford to hire someone, but I didn't push it. I needed a favor. Besides, I was starting to feel bad about ditching Ernie. I wondered if he'd figured out I'd escaped. He would be so pissed.

César scribbled his note, then handed me his helmet. "Let's go."

He laughed when I hopped on behind him easily. "All right, toughie. Vámonos."

"I know how to ride," I scoffed. Please. I've been on the back of my dad's bike so many times.

"Yeah, sure. Lean when I lean," he said.

We pulled into the traffic. He weaved between the cars. We turned the corner and passed the plaza headed to the international bridge.

"You okay?" he yelled above the roar of the motorcycle.

"Yes!"

I had gotten the hang of riding with César by the last block before the toll bridge. We were waiting at the light when I saw Pilar coming out of Zapatería Suday. She had a huge department store bag in her hands. Her hair was twisted in a braid around her head, and she wore the same large sunglasses she'd had at my grandma's funeral. She was shopping, so maybe she was staying in town. She'd invited me back. I could take her up on it. If I wanted.

Pilar didn't see me. At least, if she looked my way, she wouldn't have. César's helmet blocked my whole face. I watched her walk to the corner, accidentally clutched César a little when she crossed the street in front of us. He twitched. I could feel his muscles under my hands. Then the light changed.

"Hang on," he said.

I didn't say anything. I just pressed myself against his back, trying to leave enough space to breathe. I moved when he moved, leaned when he leaned, and it was easy to stay with him.

"Good girl," he said, and hit it hard.

And poof—we were out of the main traffic and everything blurred past me. It was different from riding with my dad—this wasn't some heavy Harley, strutting along and growling.

Then we were at the Mexican toll and zipping over the bridge. The officer at the US Customs waved us through—they must have known César's green bike. I wondered how many girls he'd carted around this way, clinging to him, their hair flying back from beneath the helmet. I wanted to say, *That's not me. I just need a ride.* Then we were shooting onto the La Cienega Avenue Expressway, and he really opened the throttle. I pressed my face into his back so the wind wouldn't catch my breath. His detergent was familiar. Tide. That's the one we buy too.

It was almost five forty-five when we got back to school. I leaped off the bike as soon as he parked, shoving the helmet at him.

"Bye," I gasped, and dashed away.

"Hey!" I heard him yell after me, but I was hightailing to the girls' bathroom one more time—to wash my face before my dad came to pick me up.

Chapter Nine

---◇---

Jangly Guitar Rock

When he's in a bad mood my dad favors the Derek and the Dominos version of "Little Wing." It's all raspy voices and full-out wailing guitar punctuated with sweeping classic rock axe-strokes thrum, thrum, thrum, thrum-thrum-thrum. On good days, I might hear a different version—Jimi Hendrix, or lots of times Stevie Ray Vaughan—carry in through the living room windows. Those are the weekends that the doors to his backyard shop are wide open. But since he came back home, he's been locked up tight with the *Layla* album blasting loud enough to shake the shop walls. There's nothing like Clapton for my dad when he's feeling sorry for himself. Except, maybe, Vicente Fernández.

The one thing he loves most in the world lives in his shop. It's a 1970 Harley Davidson XLCH Sportster, the one he had when my mom was alive. He has another Harley now, a 1983 Softail, bigger and heavier, that he rides in nice weather. Sometimes he takes me along if we aren't fighting. That motorcycle is in the garage. It's just a bike.

The Sportster in his shop is a love letter to my mother. It's been eight years since she died in the accident. He rebuilt the whole thing, frame and all. I know the specs just from listening to him order parts on the phone.

But it's never finished. He keeps changing stuff. This month he painted a stampede of curls racing across the tank and down the frame. I don't know how anybody can paint black curls on a black bike, but he did. He did it up with one of those primo low-rider colors, so it shimmers from black to purplish silver wherever the light hits it. It's my mom's hair, her black curls streaming in the wind.

Before he opened his own body shop, when we still lived in the apartment and he was a mechanic at the Ford dealership, we used to go to auto shows all over Texas. We hauled a trailer every time, but if it was a short trip, say to San Antonio or San Angelo, my mother and I would go in the Blazer and he'd ride the motorcycle. I'd press my face to the passenger-side window, watch him. If I shut my eyes, I can still see him easily: his hair slammed back from his forehead, his leather goggles, how he grimaced in the wind, and behind him that wavering slice of pale, hewn rock where the highway had been cut through the hillside.

If my mother was driving, we'd listen to Donna Summer the whole way there. If it was my dad, we'd listen to Cream or the Doors. My mom would drop my dad off at the show so he could clean up the bike and she and I would drive to Kmart. Kmarts only, never gas stations; that way she could pick up sodas, baby wipes, peanut butter crackers, even emergency lipstick if she needed it. Then she'd do some serious glamming in the ladies' bathroom. I remember being too little to reach the sink.

Some people can't imagine their parents as sexy. I have a distinct memory of my mother's butt in a pair of cropped white satin shorts.

"Check me," she'd say, arching to look over her shoulder while I inspected for snags or smudges. In the early eighties, when everybody was getting a Pat Benatar boy cut, my mother still had that seventies miles of hair. When she moved, it swayed back and forth in the small of her back, just above where the shorts started. Once she had the shorts on, it was like she was inside a force field. Nothing, and I mean nothing, could touch her. Her hands darted out to smooth my ringlet pigtails around one lacquered fingernail. No touching back.

I'd be in my regular auto show uniform too—a play shirt and a pair of overalls with the Harley Davidson eagle iron-on patch. She'd get me Pop Rocks and I'd tuck them into the top pocket of my overalls. My dad would pretend he was going to spank her and she'd pretend-glare at him and say, *Don't you dare get grease on me, Jules Muñoz.*

She was small. He'd tinkered and tinkered with the motorcycle so it was light enough that she could maneuver it. He says that's why it was completely destroyed when the Yellow Freight truck hit them. I saw it when my dad got it back from the police impound. It looked like a charred pretzel.

Before the accident, it was glittery red with orange flames. My mom would motor around the auto show parking lot, slow and lazy, like a strutting fireball. Pretty soon dudes would come over to where she parked, right in front of our truck, and start talking to my dad about custom body work.

When we headed home, he'd stick the motorcycle in the trailer. He'd drive home with his arm crooked around her shoulders and they'd put on sappy Spanish music that bored me to sleep.

That was the happy part of our life. My mother was alive and she was beautiful. I know everybody says that about their mother, but you can't believe how they started out before they had you and had a mortgage and stuff. I'm not exaggerating. She was beautiful. Of course she was. She was only twenty-four when she died. Her name was Nayeli.

To prep for the long weekend ahead, I decided to make two mixtapes: *Jangly Guitar Rock* and *Originals & Covers*. That would take up the day while I did laundry and basically waited for my dad to come up for air. Or if he didn't, at least making the tapes would keep me busy until it was late enough to use the phone without him noticing.

I'd barely started doing the jeans when Marina called. I always started with jeans because our dryer gives out by the fourth or fifth load, so I try to get the heavy stuff out of the way first. My dad says it wouldn't happen if I didn't wait until everything was dirty to do laundry, but I don't see him helping out, so whatever.

"What are you doing?"

"Nothing. Laundry."

"I'm coming over. My dad just got home."

Marina's dad is a truck driver. When Mr. Salazar gets home after a long run, the first day all he wants to do is eat his favorite red enchiladas for dinner and then sleep for ten hours. The house better be goddamn silent. No TV, phone unplugged, sign on the doorbell that says DO NOT RING. Her mom won't even wash the dishes until after he wakes up so he won't hear the kitchen tap running.

"When?"

"Maybe thirty minutes. After he finishes eating my mom is taking everyone to my buela's." She sighed dramatically. I could totally tell she was rolling her eyes. "They're going to spend the day making tortillas and watching dumb novelas on the little TV in the kitchen. That's why I'm spending the night with you."

I saw my chance. "Will your mom take me to the grocery store?"

"Sure," Marina said

"Okay. I'll tell my dad."

I had to bang on the shed door for almost five minutes before the volume finally cut off and the door opened. My dad came out to the yard, blinking like a mole, unshaven and red-eyed. I don't think he even went to bed last night.

"Everything okay?" he asked. That's him. Something has to be wrong for him to be interested.

"Can Marina spend the night?"

"I guess. Do we need to pick her up?"

I could probably have sleepovers at my house every weekend if I wanted and he wouldn't turn a hair. As long as he approves of the girls I invite, I mean. He likes Marina because he thinks she's a girly girl, or what he calls *feminine*. This, because Marina never leaves the house without earrings.

"No, her mom's bringing her in a little while. We're going to the store first, though."

"Oh, good." He fumbled in his wallet and handed me his credit card. "Just bring whatever you want and don't forget the receipt. Oh, and get me some peaches."

"Okay."

Marina's mom left us to wander the grocery store aisles together, pulling stuff we wanted for our sleepover: marshmallows, ice cream, the works for spaghetti, which Marina said she would teach me to make, aerosol cheese, gummy bears, Hershey bars, microwave popcorn, strawberry Pop-Tarts, plain, because I hate the kind with icing, and my dad's stupid peaches.

When she saw my cart she told Marina in Spanish we were going to get stomachaches and have indigestion-induced nightmares and not to call her in the night complaining. She doesn't speak English and she thinks since I speak it all the time that I can't understand her.

"That's why they named her Dolores," Marina whispered, exaggerating every *o* in the name. She always says that when her mom is being a pain.

Marina thinks it's wild that my dad just hands over his credit card like that. My dad is a Mexican dad like hers—he would want red enchilada dinners like Mr. Salazar if there was someone to make them for him. He waits for me in the parking lot with the truck running if he has to take me shopping; makes trips to the outlet stores near San Marcos every August for my new school clothes; is always on my ass about being a good girl. But he's been in a free fall for a while now. Home or out, he's drunk all the time. His life doesn't have a linchpin, or if it does, it isn't me.

Nobody's really at the wheel. He does his own thing and I do what I have to do. So it's either we starve or he sends me to the store with someone, usually our neighbor, Mrs. Flippo, and I pick up whatever I want. I've been forging his signature for a couple of years now.

My dad doesn't know how to cook and neither do I. My dad is a snacks guy. He'd rather eat chips all day than take time for regular meals. We mostly eat out or eat at Grandma's—except now there's only eating out. Yoli is *not* about cooking family dinners for us.

"Well, what's the deal with your quince?" Marina asked once we'd put away the groceries and headed upstairs to my bedroom, where the plaintive chords of Eric Clapton plowing through "Bell Bottom Blues" for the umpteenth time in a row were at least far away enough to become background noise.

"Still happening, he says." I flopped onto my bed morosely. "Sucks."

"You need to just get over it. I don't know what your problem is anyway. Mine was awesome."

"Yeah," I muttered. "For you."

"Damn," she commented, glancing out my window to the shed in the backyard. "How many times is he going to play that record?"

"All day. He's in a bad mood. That's his thing."

"Wow."

"At least we don't have to put up with that," I said. I slammed my *Jangly Guitar Rock* mixtape into the deck and turned up the volume. Marina made it through a couple of Smiths songs, but stopped the tape when "The Killing Moon" came on.

"Nope, nope. That's enough sad-ass white guy music."

"Shut up, that is a great fucking tape."

"I'm so constantly sick of Echo & the Bunnymen." She pursed her mouth and sob-sang, "Evvvery day is like Sundaaaay. Evvvvery day is silent and graaaay. Whine, whine, whine."

"That's Morrissey, stupid."

"But it's on there, right?"

"So? It's good."

"If you want to commit suicide. Seriously, Lulu, no wonder you're such a mope."

"You have bad taste. Just admit it."

She flipped open the shoe box where I kept my mixtapes. "I want something dancy. Where's *Wedding 76*?"

Of all my mixes, *Wedding 76* is Marina's favorite. I made it last summer after I found the stash of my mom's things in the attic. It's all from her albums, mostly disco.

"I'll copy it for you," I offered. Again.

"No way! This is your mom's homage tape. You shouldn't give it to anyone." She popped it into the cassette player.

"Dancing Queen" came on. Marina started shimmying around the room, her arms outstretched. She sashayed across the bedroom, pirouetting slowly.

"You are the dancing queen! Young and sweet! Only fii-iif-TEEN!" she

187

sang, changing the lyrics to fit my quince. She jabbed both her index fingers at me like a gunslinger. "You can dance! You can jive! Having the time of your life!"

"Oh my God, shut up!"

She danced through the whole song and the next. She was so nimble it didn't matter that she didn't actually know the steps to the hustle. Thelma Houston started begging for someone not to leave her this way.

"What about a seventies theme for your quince?" she asked, twirling and stepping. "We could do a tribute to your mom, with all her records."

"I dunno. Maybe."

"It has to be 'Dancing Queen'! It's perfect!" Marina flopped down next to me, panting. "It's me and maybe four other girls for damas. And see if your dad will let Art be my chambelán."

I could practically see her little brain whirring a million miles an hour. She has about forty thousand cousins, so there wasn't a chance for me to be in her quince court. Thank God too, because she had "Vogue" by Madonna as their choreographed dance.

"I can't even think of who to ask," I said glumly.

"If you don't pick, your dad will pick for you. That's the way it is."

"I know."

"Rewind the tape," she ordered.

There's no getting away from the quinceañera. It's been looming like a train wreck on the horizon for me. First it was the older daughters of my dad's compadres, my grandma's friends' and neighbors' granddaughters; Jesus, it seems like at some point in their lives everybody in town has a fifteen-year-old daughter.

Maybe I'm stupid, but I used to go to these with my dad and not connect them with me. Yes, I'm a girl. Yes, I'm turning fifteen in February. But seriously, when you're a nine-year-old dozing at a table after you've eaten four bowls of pink and green mints in the center of the table and your dad is still not ready to go home because he's about fourteen beers in and telling jokes you won't understand for another three years, and the smooth bass thump of polka after polka is never ending, you don't actually think, This is going to happen to me. You just find a place to curl up and fall asleep.

When you're older, like twelve or thirteen, you spend the time feeling angry because you're still stuck at that round table with the bland pink tablecloth, and you're still eating the mints, but you don't feel sleepy. All the other kids are wandering around like it's a party for them too, talking in groups, some of them actually dancing, some of them walking outside to the parking lot to listen to real music on their parents' car stereos instead of the ever-fucking polkas the old fat married people are addicted to. And your dad is still getting dead-ass drunk, only now he thinks you ought to go out and dance with him once or twice. Not on his fucking life though. For one thing, you won't dance to polkas, ever.

And no, you're not going to dance with your stupid, beery dad, who is drunk and acting like an idiot. Because you're not five and you're not nine, you're already thirteen and smart, and you can see how when he's drunk he turns into a mean, teasing guy, looking and looking for something to fight about. You can see it turn his eyes little and red and ugly and squinty.

Your momma loved dancing, he sneers. *Guess you're not much like her, are you? She was pretty too.*

He whips that at you, watching to see you flinch, but you don't. Not anymore you don't. And his stupid drunk friends grin, but their grins kind of falter a bit, because it's not funny.

Ah, screw it, he says sometimes. And you've got to stay at the table until he comes back, which sometimes is an hour or more, while he dances and dances with all these different women. They always seem to say yes.

Or if he insists, if he orders, then it's worse, because you get up and dance and the music is thumping and the crowd is pressing on you, warm and glittery with the gala outfits people wear to these things, and maybe you feel the brush of some satin gown as one of the damas of the quince court swishes past, but mostly you are so fucking angry, so furious, because you didn't want to do it and he's making you. So you set your feet as clumsily as you can, dance as limply and half-heartedly as possible, so it's painful, painful to watch you. The most sulky dancing you can possibly do, until he practically has to walk beside you as you feign your way through the cumbia circle, face stiff and scowling.

And then he's really mad. Really, really mad, because anybody, everybody, can see that you don't want to dance with him.

That isn't bad though. Because after a bit, he gets so disgusted with you that he takes you back to the stupid table, now empty of mints, and you sit there alone for the rest of the night, while he goes off to drink by the beer booth with his friends. And you wonder why it is that he's allowed to wander around the party, just like the teenagers, but you have to sit in your chair like you're a baby.

It stays that way, just this inevitable fight time, until the next year when you're fourteen. Your dad is gone every night. He still goes to work, yeah, every day, but Uncle Zero's holding it down at the body shop more and more; he'll never not cover for your dad. You're practically living with your grandmother and the thin stale smell of beer is unraveling your life, but you're supposed to *be happy*, because pretty soon you'll become a young lady. Your dad will give you permission to grow up; in spite of your own body, it's his decision. This frilly spectacle is a sham, awash in your dad's sentimental smarm, but everybody thinks it's great: your grandma, your tía, your best friend. Everyone. Nobody sees that you're on the periphery because it's your name on the cake, you're stuck in the role of daddy's prettiest doll, and after your party, with yes, all those tables full of mints, he'll set you back on the shelf and disappear into the darkness where he lives all the time now.

All of a sudden you see it before you: it dawns like a horrible bad dream. Girls you actually know are dancing the father daughter dance; they wander around in the satin dama gowns, their hair coiffed and set with little jewels, their makeup, their earrings, the fancy heels. No longer sophomores, but debutantes. The horror of it, the mints and the stupid doll he'll give you—when you don't even like dolls and never have! The endless practices at the park with the quinceañera court, and the choreography and, most awful of it all, dancing with your father in front of everyone, when you hate hate hate hate dancing with him like nothing else.

Marina doesn't get it, though. Her dad's cranky, but he's not an asshole. Also, it's agreed around school that she had the most kick-ass quinceañera this year, all the girls in Jean Harlow white satin dresses just like in the "Vogue" video. She got away with it because her parents never watch anything but Univision and Telemundo. They don't even know who Madonna is. They'd have a conniption if they'd ever gotten a load of her dancing around in that giant cone bra.

It's because Marina's parents are real from-the-ranch Mexicans. Marina says her mom doesn't even know who the Beatles are.

"Where did she grow up?" I asked her. "Under a rock?"

"Kind of. It was Rosita." She laughed. "The guys there ride donkeys in the streets."

"So, what do you think?" Marina asked later. I had gone back to folding the laundry and she was expertly ironing the collars of my dad's work shirts. It freaks me out a little, how good she is at everything. Also, that she's personally compelled to iron shirts at all. Wrinkled collars drive her insane. If I want something unwrinkled I just throw it back in the dryer on high.

"It's a good idea," I said, "but I don't know any moves."

"Please, girl. *I'm* planning your dance routine." She pressed the iron across a shirt collar in one smooth motion and of course it flattened perfectly. Tomorrow my dad will want to know if she can teach me to iron. Barf.

Our plan for the night was for Marina to teach me how to make spaghetti while she taped the *MTV Top 20 Video Countdown*. Later, around nine o'clock, we'd switch over to channel three for the Saturday night Frightober Fest double feature: *The Wolf Man* and *Night of the Living Dead*. After that, if my dad was still hiding out in his backyard cave, we'd watch *Headbangers Ball*. It was foolproof: from the dark living room, we'd be sure to notice the shaft of light when he opened the shed with plenty of time to change the channel.

No, it does not make any kind of sense that I can watch zombies chow down on screaming victims all night long, but I'm not allowed to see even one measly Slayer video. Nobody ever accused Jules Muñoz of making sense. He thinks all rock these days is satanic. I don't know where he got that, maybe from Grandma. She was a fan of *The 700 Club*. It might just be him though. He never goes to church, but he's weirdo about religious stuff, won't even watch *The Exorcist*. He's scared of the devil like nobody else I know.

Seriously, though, devil worship is so eighties. That stuff went out with glam rock. Besides, if we're getting technical, he's a total hypocrite for liking Black Sabbath. He doesn't know shit about new music—he thinks Prince is joto and resents the fact that his hero Eric Clapton now dresses like Arsenio Hall. He's in some kind of denial, I guess. But what else can you expect from someone who stopped buying records after Van Halen's *1984*? It's like he decided all the good music was over. At least I can say he's right about one thing: Van Halen should have ended after that album. Sammy Hagar sucks.

I was trying to remember how to preset the VCR to tape *Headbangers Ball* so it wouldn't matter what time he came inside. I'd already decided I'd watch after school on Monday while I did my homework, when my dad walked into the kitchen.

It was only six thirty. Odd, but I figured he'd run out of beer. He sat there watching us—really just waiting for us to leave so we wouldn't see him scrounging for the emergency beer can he leaves in the vegetable drawer.

"Cooking, huh? Smells good."

"Marina's cooking."

Browning, is what she called it. Browning, not cooking, because, she said, it was only the first part. It would get cooked some more once she threw it in with the sauce.

"Are you watching?" she asked me.

"Sure," I said. I said that a lot while she was showing me how to cook or how to iron shirt collars so they're sharp and stiff on the hanger. It's not that I don't appreciate Marina's attempts to arm me with what she calls real woman skills. It's that the more she shows me, the more I know I never want to be a wife. What a fucking drag. About the only thing I'd picked up from her was how to make killer rice pudding, and that's only because I like to eat it.

"You're not listening," Marina said.

"I'm listening. You said browning was only part of the cooking process."

"You're just repeating what I said."

"So?"

"So what are you going to do when you get married?" She actually had her hands on her hips, wooden sauce spoon and all.

"Hah!" my dad said, snagging a piece of garlic bread from the baking tray. "Whoever marries Lulu is gonna starve to death."

"Whatever." It's true though. Whoever marries me should like all the stuff I like or too bad for him.

Marina shook her head. "Well, there's always takeout, right?"

"Or he could learn to cook."

"Órale, that's right!" My dad laughed and hugged me. He smelled like Bud Light and was at least halfway drunk. "You get a good one, mija. Un hombre educado who treats you right. None of this macho shit for you! I didn't have a daughter so she could be some pinche pelado's maid."

That's my dad drunk: he can flip-flop from teasing to sentimentality without batting an eye. He's got to be the most ridiculous person in the world.

"I'm never getting married, Dad."

The phone rang and he dropped his arm from my shoulders. I mean he almost leaped at the kitchen wall.

"Hello?" He sat there for a minute, then shrugged and hung up. "Nobody there."

But I noticed he didn't look at me. He rooted at the back of the fridge for that 911 beer.

"Hey, grown-up ladies," he said, popping the cap on his beer and twinkling at us. He's really good at that. "You two are old enough to look out for yourselves for a couple of hours, right? I've been cooped up all day. I'm gonna go shoot some pool with Zero."

I stared at him. He'd never left me by myself before. But there was no one for him to dump me with. Yoli told him when he came back that that was his one freebie. She wasn't going to babysit me whenever, like Grandma always did.

"You wanted to be treated like an adult, right? So, prove it. Be good while I'm out."

"Okay," I said.

He headed for his bedroom, singing. "Hello cowgirl in the sand, is this place at your command?"

"Is he high?" Marina asked.

"No. He's just done sulking."

Around eight thirty he came out of his bedroom showered, cologned, and all slicked out in fancy western wear.

"Whoa, your dad," Marina said after he went off to find his black cowboy hat. "He's like the Urban Cowboy or what?"

"Yeah," I lied. There was no way he'd get that dressed up, stinking up the kitchen with Drakkar Noir, just to go hang out at Clicks with Uncle Zero. This is Texas, but please. I mean, NASA is here too, but you don't see people wearing space suits when they go clubbing.

Zero might have been at Clicks, but no way was my dad going there in his eighty-dollar Wranglers. The only place I know of to go country dancing is The Purple Sage, which is just off the highway coming into town. I've heard my dad say it's the kind of place where the fight always happens in the middle of the highway, so if you're driving by real late and aren't careful you could end up plowing into a huge melee because the whole crowd goes out to watch the fellas duke it out.

"I'll call you at ten o'clock to check on y'all," he said. "You better pick up."

"I will."

"All right," he said. "Be good. Call Yoli if you need anything."

"Bye Dad."

Marina's eyes were wide. Freedom. Sort of.

She waited about twenty minutes, then called her boyfriend, Art. I ended up lying in the middle of the living room floor, watching most of *The Wolf Man* by myself, which was okay because instead of talking through the movie, like she always does, she stayed in the kitchen to keep an eye on the spaghetti. Another thing I didn't want to learn about.

"You're not watching me," she yelled a couple of times. And then finally, "Lulu, get in here!"

"I can see you," I yelled back. No way did I want to sit through listening to whatever she and Art were talking about. Mostly it was Marina talking about not wanting to babysit her little sisters again.

"No, I'm staying at Lulu's house tonight," she was saying. "Watching movies." Pause. "Lulu, what are we watching?"

"*Wolf Man*. Hey, if the phone beeps, you better click over."

"No, I'm not even watching it," she said, walking back into the living room to sprinkle a handful of peanut M&M's on my head. She made a face at me. "Because Lulu won't get off her lazy butt so I'm stuck making dinner by myself." Pause.

"Yeah, it's just us. What?" Marina stopped making faces and hurried back into the kitchen. I still heard her, even though she was whispering. "She's dead, you know that." Pause. "No, that was her *grandmother*. Her mom died like in first grade, stupid." Pause. "Well, I know I told you. Maybe you weren't listening."

An hour later Marina was pissed because Art was going to a block party without her—not his fault she couldn't go, but still. *Night of the Living Dead* was on, but neither of us were interested.

"Fucking Art," Marina growled. She threw one of the couch cushions on the floor. "He could have come over here. He just didn't want to."

I almost spit out a mouthful of Dr Pepper. "Are you nuts? My neighbor would totally narc on me if guys come over."

"She doesn't know your dad's gone," Marina said. "Maybe he's having friends over. She doesn't know Art's truck."

"Nobody's coming over," I said.

"I know. I asked him and he said he was going to that thing."

"I can't believe you did that without telling me."

"Anyways, he's not coming."

And then an extra stupid thing happened. My dad called from some loud honky-tonk. I swear I heard that same fucking married lady in the background.

"Are you kidding me with this?" I yelled. "Where's her husband tonight, out killing another dog?"

"Don't start with me, Lulu."

"You really don't care that Gonzo got shot, do you?"

"No more sleepover! I'm calling your aunt to pick you up." He hung up on me.

This was the stupid thing that happened: when I hung up, Marina was sitting on the couch hugging a cushion, staring at me. "Oh my God, someone shot Gonzo?"

"Yeah," I said. What else could I tell her? "Some guy shot him because my dad is screwing around with the wife."

"Oh my God," she said again.

"I don't want to talk about it. Just forget it."

She nodded. "Sorry."

The phone rang again. My tía, irritated as hell. "Your dad says he and Zero are driving out to the casino. He wants me to go get you right now because you're grounded. What the hell is going on?"

"I don't know. I guess he doesn't want to come home tonight."

"I'm not driving thirty minutes across town just because your father is having a tantrum."

"He's gonna be mad," I said.

"He's a grown man. If he doesn't want you home alone, he should stay home. Are you okay?"

"Yeah. We're fine."

"I have the cordless right here by the bed if you need me. Just remember to set the house alarm."

"I will."

"Don't let it bother you, mija. The sooner you learn not to put up with some man's BS, the better off you'll be. That includes your father."

"Yeah."

"I'll come over in the morning. We'll go get pancakes."

"Okay. Good night, Tía."

Five minutes later the phone rang *again*. I picked up, thinking it would be my dad calling to bitch me out some more. It was Art.

"Hey Lulu," he said. "Mari said she doesn't want to talk to me, but can you tell her that I won't go to that party? Just tell her."

Marina heard him and yelled, "Liar!"

"Change of plans," I said. Yoli wasn't putting up with my dad. It hit me with wild triumph that I didn't have to either. "We're coming."

"Órale, badass! See y'all there," Art said, lightning fast. I hung up.

"Call him back," Marina said. "We need a ride. It's all the way out by the jail."

"Whatever. We're taking the fucking Harley in my dad's shop." The Softail would be too heavy for me, and besides, why *not* take his prize?

"Oh shit," Marina said, unfazed. This is the best thing about her. "Let's go put on our faces."

Kick-start or don't ride, my dad likes to say. Push button starters are for pussies. You have to know your hog. How many times has he gone through the ritual with me? How many times has he shown off to his friends? *Even my baby girl can do it. C'mon Lulu, show 'em how.* Put the key in, open the petcock, open the carburetor valve, pump the kick-starter til it gets stiff, twist the throttle, one, two, three times, turn the ignition on and then mash the kick-starter, mash it down with all your weight, because it's that hard, the throttle held open light, and then that deep staccato growl when she comes to life: tucka TAK tucka TAK tucka TAK.

Oh, that sound put a song in my heart. I remembered, I felt, how much I loved it. Kick-starting was still a good show too, because Marina said, "Oh my God. You are a badass."

We had raided the back of my dad's closet. Pack rat that he was, everything he and my mother ever owned was still in there. I wore my dad's leather jacket and my Converse because I thought they were the safest to ride in, even though Marina said that with the motorcycle, the guys were going to think I was a total butch.

"I'm driving," I said. "Did you not see how hard it is to start this thing?"

"You're right, you're right," Marina said. She was wearing jeans because I said she had to, but she'd dug a halter top and a pair of my mom's old high-heeled clogs out of the same closet. "But seriously, your mom's wardrobe rocks.

"Lucky she was small," Marina reflected. "My mom is like the *Titanic*."

"Aw, that's mean." But I laughed.

We walked the motorcycle to the end of the street just in case the noise made Mrs. Flippo look out her window. Marina said she wouldn't recognize us with the helmets, but why take the chance?

"Get on," I said. "Put your feet on the pegs and remember, lean when I lean."

"Got it."

"Hold on to me," I said. She clamped onto my jacket. "Are you scared?"

"No," she said, muffled. "Let's go!"

"Put your visor down. Unless you want bugs all in your face."

"Oh right, thanks."

I lowered my visor too and we set out. It wasn't a bit like riding César's green Kawasaki, which is low-slung and moves like a bullet. The Sportster has a high gas tank and my dad had put in ape hangers, so it was like lying back in a recliner going fifty miles an hour while balancing a five-hundred-pound egg filled with gasoline on my lap. I had to talk to myself the whole time. *Left clutch, right throttle, gearshift at my left foot, ease into the shifts and the brakes, be easy, be easy, be easy.* I stalled out at two red lights, but by the time we got to the highway going out to the jail it was fine sailing. I almost wished my dad could see me ride. I really believe if he wasn't busy being such an asshole he would have been proud of me.

There was a moment right when we got to the party, as I swung my leg off the motorcycle, when everything seemed so perfect, so freaking magical, that I actually thought, holy shit, I'm cool. Me.

For one thing, I managed to park like a twenty-year veteran of the Hells Angels. I pulled into the weedy lot across the street from the party, rolled to a stop between the rows of parked cars and set my foot in the dirt. I kept the engine running while Marina hopped off, revved it once just for fun.

It was a block party, everything outside, and somebody was making a toast to a guy named Lico, so it was quiet enough that everybody turned around when one of the dudes yelled, "Ah-wooo! Look at those sexy mujeres! God damn, y'all, that's a fine chopper!"

Right after that I took off my helmet and realized the yeller was a fat, old drunk. Old. Like probably forty.

"Oh gross," said Marina, beside me. "I think that's one of Art's uncles. Sick!"

"I thought this was like a party party," I said, frowning at the house across the street. There were little kids running around the yard.

Marina shrugged. "Art said it was a block party. But looks like a family thing."

And just like you'd expect at a party on the outskirts of town thrown for a guy named Lico by a bunch of rancherito types, someone yelled in Spanish at the speechmaker "Ya córtale already" and the music cranked up loud—accordion conjunto where the band starts the song by throwing crazy gritos, something like a pack of wailing coyotes. People in the crowd went wild, throwing back their own gritos amid the thumping bass and cowbell.

"Yeah!" said Marina, nodding. "At least the music's good. Let's go find Art."

She grabbed me by the hand and pulled me into the mix. We dodged the old perv uncle, who yelled at us again when we passed by.

Art was at a keg filling a plastic cup. He wore a straw cowboy hat and Red Wing boots, totally rancherito-style. I guess since it was his family, it wasn't weird for him. But I felt like he was a whole new person.

"Oh wow," he said, when he saw Marina. "You look fantastic. Hey, Lulu," he said, turning to me. "You want a beer?"

"No thanks," I said. "I'm driving." I hate beer. Besides, there was no way I was going to drink anything and then try to drive home. If anything happened to the motorcycle I'd be dead.

Marina gulped down a whole red cup of beer in one go and they went off to dance. I recognized a few faces from school, but they were no one I knew and the most that happened was a smile or a nod as they went by.

It was lame and I wanted to go home. I couldn't deal with the thought of having to go back into that crush of people to find Marina, to be the whiner who wanted to drag her home when she was having such a great time with Art. Why couldn't I be like her—loving the party, having a guy to dance with, just happy to be here? I couldn't though. I kept thinking about how I was going to have to do all that concentrating on the gears again on the way home, and maybe a cop would stop me, or worse, I'd crash the motorcycle.

At midnight they served menudo. That and the little kids running around everywhere basically confirmed that this party was some family thing. I got in the serving line, thinking at least if I ate something, I could be doing something. Somebody poked me in the back. It was Jorge.

"Hey, what are you doing here?" He had a paper bowl of nachos in his hand and was chewing fast, cheeks absolutely stuffed. What he said came out *eh woo doo hee?*

"Art invited Marina and me. What about you?"

He swallowed hard. "My cousin Lico just got out of prison. It's his party. We're all over there by the cars. Olmec brought some Jack."

"Cool," I said, not bothering to tell him I wasn't drinking. I followed him back to where all the cars were parked. Ernie's car was parked in the farthest part of the lot, all the way in the dark. Ernie and Olmec were out there, leaning against the hood. Both doors were open and Black Flag was spilling out, softer than the party music, but still recognizable. Ernie pretended not to see me, but he did, I could tell by the way he turned his face away.

I took a deep breath, squared my shoulders. When you fuck up as bad as I did you just have to lump it and apologize. I didn't mean to be shitty to him, but still. I cringed, thinking about how long he probably waited for me. He didn't deserve that.

"Here comes Houdini," Olmec said, grinning. He had thick streaks of black eyeliner along his lower lash lines. He loves makeup maybe even more than Marina. "Lose her one place, she pops up somewhere else. I dunno, bro, this one's gonna run you in circles."

"Nah," said Ernie. He was plenty sore at me, that was obvious. "Not me."

Ximena appeared just then. She was wearing black jeans and a tight red top that showed half her boobs, but she was too grumpy to be hot. She always looks pissed. I've never seen her smile.

"I went and got my own nachos," she told Jorge. "Where'd you go?"

"To get you nachos," said Jorge.

"And you ate them all too."

"Well, I couldn't find you," Jorge said.

"Your tía's looking for you," she countered. She gave me the suspicious eye big-time. "Come on, let's go."

Jorge sighed. "Duty calls. Later guys."

Olmec kicked a rock, sending it skittering across the dirt. "Man, we're never gonna get this band together. You're never around, and Jorge is just begging to get murdered in a crime of passion."

"You're the one who said we can't use your garage anymore," I reminded him.

"My mom says we trigger her migraines," Olmec said. "It's a real condition."

"Okay, sorry." I watched him pour himself another slug of Jack Daniels. I shouldn't have said anything. Olmec's mom is cool with him being himself. She doesn't care that he likes makeup, or that he dates both girls and boys. Shit, he told us how one time in seventh grade some guys were heckling him after school, calling him a dick smoker and that stuff. His mom chased them with her car for like twenty minutes, yelling that they were a bunch of little pussies. *She made them cry*, Olmec told us. *My mom's a fucking chola.*

She sounded as crazy as my dad, but in a good way. I wish I could tell him, *Look, I'm in this band. This is what I want to do, okay?* And my dad would say, *Sure, good deal.*

"I have your puppy money," Ernie said. "I would have brought it if I knew you were coming."

"Puppy money?" Olmec repeated. "What?"

"She sold a dog to a dude I know," Ernie said, offhand. He might be mad at me, but he wasn't going to tell about our night at the lake. Thank God, but it made me feel like an even bigger jerk for leaving him at the restaurant. "He paid two hundred."

"Rock on," Olmec said. "That Epiphone is still at Cheve's, Lulu. Calling your name."

"You think Cheve has a layaway plan?" I asked.

Olmec shrugged. "He'd hold it for me if I gave him half the money up-front and I get a discount. Want me to ask?"

"Oh my God, yes," I said, super pumped. I had no idea where I'd stash the guitar once I got it, but so what.

"Cool, cool," Olmec said, sipping from his plastic cup. "I'm going for menudo. Y'all coming?"

"Gross," Ernie said, shaking his head. I made a gagging noise.

As soon as Olmec left I told Ernie I was sorry for ditching him. I squeezed his hand. "I know that sucked. I just had to get back. My dad would go psycho if he couldn't find me. I'm sorry I left you there."

"You didn't even say anything. You just disappeared."

"I freaked! And you just kept telling me we *had* to wait it out." I pulled him to me, and he let me. Sort of. "Sorry. Sorry. Sorry."

"I can't believe you jumped out a bathroom window," he said, definitely friendlier. He turned my palm up, tapped my fingertips lightly. "You're gonna get calluses like mine when you get that Epiphone."

"Good," I said. I leaned against the car too, right under his arm. He didn't let go of me.

"You want some of this?" Ernie asked, tipping his cup at me.

"Nah," I said. "I'm probably going home soon. If Marina's ready to go."

"C'mere," he said, pulling me closer.

"What?" Oh, I knew what.

He sat me on top of the hood of the car. He's so fucking skinny. It's weird how easy it is for him to pick me up. But yeah, I like it. I let my feet brush his legs.

"Stay a little," he whispered, his forehead pressed to mine.

"Okay."

We kissed and kissed and kissed. I don't even know how long. My face was numb from rubbing against his. He touched me through my jeans. I felt shivery, my whole body, until I couldn't even hold myself up. He popped his hip against my thigh, balanced me against the car. Touched me and touched me while I clung to him. This is how he pulls music out of his guitar, I thought, this is how he does it, and a giant, trembling wave shuddered through me.

"Wanna listen to music?" he murmured into my hair. I don't think he'll ever be able to just ask me, *Want to have sex?*

"Do you have condoms?"

"Yes."

I followed him into the car. He put on My Bloody Valentine and we had sex. Twice.

"Hey," I said after we'd untangled ourselves and were kicking back, actually listening to the music. "I want to get back to practicing after school. I know a place, maybe. We have to go there and ask."

"Yeah?" asked Ernie. "Badass. Okay, Monday."

"Okay, but I have to be back at school by six. Like I cannot be late."

"Yeah, sure, no problem."

"I wonder if they still have nachos," Ernie said. "You want any?"

"No. I should find Marina. I need to get home."

"I'll find her," Ernie said. "Gonna get nachos anyway."

It wasn't long before Ernie was back, telling me that Marina promised on her mom that her boyfriend would have her back before daybreak. I knew she would too. Marina's the queen of riding it right up to the line and never crossing it.

"That's cool," I said. "I better go."

"How'd you even get here?"

"Come see."

Ernie walked with me back to the motorcycle, frowning when he saw it sitting there gleaming spangled purple black under the streetlight. "What's going on with you, Lulu? This is like, I don't know."

I wanted to tell him, but I couldn't tell him. It was too stupid to say, *Oh, I got real mad because my dad is a big asshole so I stole his precious Harley for the night.* I'd sound like such a fucking baby. Maybe I was one.

"I saw an opportunity and I seized it," I said, hoping he'd laugh.

"That thing is dangerous."

"I got here, didn't I? I know how to ride it."

"Yeah, okay," he said. "Look, just page me when you get home. I just want to know you got there, okay? It's far to your house and it's already almost two."

Wow, what a load of double standard bullshit. He wasn't going home yet. Who even knew if he was going home at all? "Yeah, sure, Dad. I'll check in."

"Shit. I'm glad I'm not your dad." He stalked off, back to the party, or to his car, somewhere. I couldn't see him in the dark.

"Don't forget about Monday!" I yelled.

What did Ernie know anyway? I thrummed down the highway, all the way back into town, no problem. I took the river road past my grandma's street, just to do it, just to be there, where my mother was last.

Then I did what I really wanted to do. I drove by Clicks, my Uncle Zero's favorite pool lounge. He and my dad went there a lot, true. But tonight, it would be just Zero's old green Ford in the parking lot. He loved staying out late with my dad, but he wouldn't have gone to Lawton to the casino. Not out of town with no notice. Uncle Zero's married.

The Clicks parking lot was mostly empty, but I was right. There was Uncle Zero's old bomber, right under the big neon sign. Just looking at that truck made me furious. My dad lied about everything.

I rode home, the motorcycle roaring in the dark, my party mood gone. Instead, I was filled with loneliness I couldn't outrun, a feeling so heavy, but clear: nobody sees me. Nobody ever sees me.

Chapter Ten

—◇—

Young Coyotes

PILAR AGUIRRE, 1994

I t doesn't make financial sense to keep it," Pilar told Wicho as she
lifted stray pecans out of the grass with the metal gatherer. It was autumn and the trees dropped them constantly. "It never has."

Wicho, dozing on the porch, twitched his ears. He had no opinion. She
sighed. She could sell the house. She should sell it. And yet.

She was still spry enough to clear the yard of pecans. She could lift
seventy-pound Wicho into the truck if he needed a boost. Even so, the fact
of the matter was she was in her late sixties. The eight-hour drive from
Dallas to La Cienega was getting harder. How much longer could she really make this trip?

She'd have to sell the house to move Joselito. Pilar shut her eyes as the
wind lifted her hair. Moving him was the right thing. And then it would
be done. She couldn't afford to otherwise, and she was his mother. She
wasn't leaving him here, unremembered and alone. She'd bought the
two burial plots already, one for him and one for herself. They'd been

expensive, and it would cost even more for the exhumation and reburial. But her bones would rest beside Joselito's bones as long as the earth remained.

She had an ordered life in the Dallas suburb of Mesquite. She had retired from her job as a court interpreter, where she had translated incident after incident of human grotesquery from Spanish to English, transcribing these messy histories into neatly typed narratives. She had her own home, which was set exactly to her taste: books, records, framed movie posters from the Golden Age of Mexican Cinema, a collection of beautiful and easily maintained cacti varietals. She ran three miles every morning, a habit she'd acquired a few years into becoming a city person. She watched telenovelas in the evenings, especially *Marimar* with Thalía. Once a week, there were the fellow crafters she had cultivated friendly, impersonal relationships with through knit and wine evenings. A series of large dogs, four since 1968, the year she'd left La Cienega.

She had balked at clearing out the Loma Negra house for so long. The objects collected in those brief years, todo lo de antes, still hers. Joselito's toys. His clothing. José Alfredo's horse tack and lariats. His collection of work tools. Her photographs of that life. She couldn't take any of it to Mesquite, a place thoroughly disconnected from those precious six years. Where would she keep these things? Not in her condo.

She wasn't ready, not yet, to give up her yearly pilgrimage for Joselito's birthday. Every year, she spent a three-day weekend, the one nearest his birthday, in the Loma Negra house. She would visit his grave and clean it, though she paid Jacinto Gonzalez to have the grave maintained, along with her house and yard. For that long weekend, she inhabited the life she'd had. Pored over it. Gave way to it.

Joselito would have been forty-eight this year. A family man, probably, and she a grandmother to how many? On his fiftieth birthday, she has promised herself, she will sell the house. Nearly a half century had slipped by, fleeting as a cloud shadow. She wasn't sure it would be enough.

Now she was here when it was not Joselito's weekend. Romi Muñoz had passed. The handyman Jacinto had called to tell her. *It was in the paper today,* he'd said, in that odd, warbly voice. *The funeral is this coming Saturday.* Pilar had returned to say her goodbyes to Romi, the only person Pilar could honestly say she still loved. She was not exactly sad for Romi, not really. Romi had reached a good age. She'd had a family.

Pilar dropped a scoopful of nuts into a basket on the porch. This was the most time she'd spent in La Cienega since she'd left all those years ago. The rutted cow paths had become badly paved streets. The factories had all shut down and moved across the border. But the wind through the pecan trees in the yard, the very same trees, their enduring susurrus, had not changed.

She could admit it to herself. She was lingering because of the girl. Was, in fact, collecting these pecans for the girl to play with Wicho. She'd said she'd return today or tomorrow afternoon.

Lulu. The sound of a mother clucking her baby to sleep. Lu-lu-lu, Lu-lu-lu.

Wicho loped to the edge of the yard, where he stood, growling and stiff-tailed. A car was coming. Now she too could hear the tires crunching the caliche road. It stopped out of sight, and for a moment she thought someone must have taken a wrong turn.

"Chssst," Pilar hissed at the dog. "Come back!"

The slope below had grown over with catclaw and mesquite trees, but she could see a black shape approaching. The girl was making her way through the bramble. The black thing was her sloppy, oversized sweater. She was looking down, stepping carefully amid the thorns and loose caliche, and Pilar could see the crown of her head, a topknot of brown curls.

Wicho launched himself at her, barking his fool head off as if he'd never met her. The girl was quite small, not much over five feet tall. Easy enough for seventy-pound Wicho to send flying. She wasn't intimidated in the least.

"Hey buddy," she said, in a low voice, catching Wicho's face in her hands. "What's this? You know me, dummy."

She looked up, locked eyes with Pilar as if to target her. Pilar found herself, again, seized by a desire so strong it frightened her. Oh, the wildness of her heart! It galloped to bursting! There was her own lost beauty, fresh as an apricot—there, that girl standing in the tall weeds. Pilar wanted to lock herself inside the house, draw down the shades and stay in the dark forever. Anything to blot out this serious little face, offered like a valentine in the softening light.

Then a boy walked out of the brush. The dog barked again and ran past the girl. The boy's voice—abrupt, masculine. "Oh shit!"

"Don't move and don't look at him. Let him smell you," the girl said, over her shoulder.

"Wicho!" Pilar called in her sternest voice.

He ignored Pilar and went back to the girl, who he seemed to like much better than the boy.

"I told you," Lulu said to the boy, triumphant. She rubbed Wicho's broad head. "You're just a big puppy, aren't ya?"

"If you say so," the boy replied, unconvinced. He was a lanky sort. Not handsome exactly, though his face carried a pair of dark, heavy-lashed eyes. Pilar could see by the way he settled himself beside the girl, watchful and serious, that he'd take a dog bite for her. And the girl, so frank and unafraid. That was the faith between them, shining and unbearable.

"It's you," Pilar said, trying to sound indifferent. "Again."

"Hey," the girl said, crouching to cuddle Wicho. She tilted her head at Pilar, the boy just a thought hovering behind her. His manner reminded Pilar so strongly of the way Chuy had waited on Romi. Always in her wake.

"You said I could come by."

"Yes," Pilar agreed. She'd found Romi's note two years ago, slipped beneath the door of the old house. *Make your peace with Julio when I'm gone.* How had Romi managed the hill on her own, at her age? Perhaps she still drove. Neither seemed likely for a woman in her eighties, but it was Romi's handwriting.

Pilar had not acknowledged the note. But she had paid Jacinto to let her know if Romi was well. If she was not. If anything happened. Now that something had, Pilar didn't believe she'd honor Romi's final wishes. The last time Pilar had seen the boy, Julio, he had spat his contempt at her feet.

"This is my friend Ernie," the girl said. Behind her the boy gave a brief nod. "Ernie, this is, uh, an old friend of my grandma Romi."

"Pili," Pilar said. "Just call me Pili."

"Hey." Ernie was uneasy, that much was obvious.

"We've come with a business deal," Lulu said. "We'd like to rent your garage."

"If it has electricity," Ernie added.

"I don't understand you," Pilar said. She'd known Lulu wanted something, or the girl wouldn't have come back. But this was bewildering. "Why do you need a storage space?"

"Not for that," the boy suddenly broke in. "Well, kind of. We've got a band. We need a place to practice. If we give you a hundred dollars, will you let us practice in your shed?"

"And leave our equipment, if we need to?" Lulu asked. "I might need to leave my stuff here."

"You want to make music here?" Pilar asked. She could not take her eyes off her. Lulu was short, with a warm complexion that Pilar would have called *aperlada*. She wore, along with the shapeless pullover, grass-stained jeans and muddy sneakers. Her eyes were covered in smudgy black makeup. Romi had written the note knowing this girl was here. Knowing her and loving her.

"It's far away from everything," the girl said swiftly. "And we wouldn't bother you."

"Making a racket in my garage wouldn't bother me?"

"That's why we'd pay you," Lulu said. "For the space and inconvenience."

"What kind of music?"

"Does it matter?" the girl asked. She was pert, Pilar decided, looking at the uptilted chin. Used to getting her way. "It's rock. But do you really care? I didn't think you would."

"I don't," Pilar said, exasperated. "But I have a right to know if you're asking to use my garage."

"We play a variety," the boy said smoothly.

"What if instead of paying money you clean out my garage," Pilar said, considering. Here was an opportunity to see this child and to solidify her own plans for Loma Negra. "It's full of stuff. You'd have to sort and pack up everything. Clean out the whole thing."

"We can do that," Lulu said. "There's four of us, so it shouldn't be hard to get it done."

"I'd need to meet the rest of your band," Pilar said. "I can't agree unless I do."

"I mean, can we take a look first?" the boy asked. "I don't know how much work that is."

"It's no problem," Lulu said, giving Ernie a pointed look. The boy rolled his eyes at her, but he didn't keep arguing.

"You can only use the garage while I'm here," Pilar said. Romi had wanted her to know this girl, a link between them, a granddaughter. "And you'll have to tell me your schedule in advance. You cannot show up at all hours."

"I understand," Lulu said.

"Four to six on weekday afternoons, except Friday," the boy said. "That's worth cleaning out your garage. I mean, it's big. And if we're packing stuff, like organizing it too."

"All right," said Pilar. He'd be doing most of the work and he knew it. "It's a deal. For how long?"

"Until January, if we can," Lulu said, almost shyly, as if she expected the answer to be no.

"I'll be here. I'm renovating the place," Pilar heard herself say, undone by the girl's clear yearning to be taken in, to be welcomed by her. A frightful desire clutched Pilar, but she willed herself to be still, to show nothing. So what if the girl only wanted the old shed? She could stay that long. After all, the home renovations needed to be done, if she was to be ready to sell by Joselito's fiftieth. That was true. I don't have to stay either, Pilar reminded herself. I can change my mind. I can leave whenever I want.

"Cool, cool," Lulu said. Then she made a face. "After that, probably not for a while. I'll have quince practices."

Pilar had a vision of this grubby child transformed by a gown of satin and tulle. What a picture that would make. Behind that thought, another, slender as a hair. I could stay for that, too. I could stay for Lulu's quince. Of course, she couldn't attend. But she could hear all about it from Lulu.

"You need time to plan it," Pilar agreed. "There will be a lot for your mother to organize."

"Grandma Romi was doing it," Lulu said. "My mom's dead."

"Oh, I'm sorry," Pilar said. She could see it now: Lulu's total self-collectedness, her bold manner. A child raising herself, only an aged Romi to serve as her rudder. She wanted to say, *I understand.* She did not. She wouldn't say such a thing in front of that boy.

"That's okay," Lulu said, with the practiced efficiency of someone used to rebuffing sympathy. "It happened a long time ago."

"Do you need help with it?"

"It's my dad's idea," Lulu said in a decided tone. "He can deal with all that."

Her father. In the church that day, Pilar had not looked at him, even once. He was a negative space inside of her. *Make your peace with Julio when I'm gone.* If she helped this odd girl, maybe that would count. And who did Lulu have now, with Romi gone?

"All right, then," Pilar replied. "Just the garage space then."

"Thanks," Lulu said. They turned back toward the trail, but Lulu hesitated. The boy gestured for her to follow him. She refused. Motioned for him to go on ahead. She returned to Pilar.

"Will you tell me?" she asked. "In the church. What you said to my grandma?"

"That's none of your business," Pilar said. Romi and I are square, she reminded herself. This girl doesn't belong to me. Yet here she was, right in her path.

"But you were friends," Lulu said, scrutinizing Pilar.

"When I was first married, yes."

First married. What a thing to say, as if her life were still defined by that time. But wasn't it? Isn't that why she had returned to this long-ago place, now, to say goodbye to Romi? Lulu, fierce little witch, pulled these things out of her, somehow.

"Lulu, let's go," the boy insisted.

"Yeah, okay." Lulu turned to follow him. "See you later . . ."

"Pili," Pilar reminded her. "It's just Pili."

The girl nodded, mouth pulled down, dissatisfied. She followed the boy down the gravelly path. They melted into the brush like a pair of young coyotes. Pilar could hear their voices, poorly hushed, quarreling, down the slope. The boy, perhaps telling her to quit asking questions. Men never liked when you asked questions. A girl like that, though, she'd never stop asking. She'd never stop wanting it her own way. Pilar recognized that arrogance, and it was not Romi's.

Ay, muñequita, Pilar thought. The tilt of your chin when you looked at me. Tanta bravura in your boy clothes and black eyeliner. You're not afraid of anything. You are young. You think the world is at your feet, and always will be. You do not know what it can take from you.

Chapter Eleven

———◇———

Vandals

LULU MUÑOZ, 1994

I yelled my way through "Wasted" by the Runaways, teeth bared, doing my best Joan Jett bitch face. I whipped my hair in time with Olmec's cymbal smashes. Ernie strummed, flung out hot licks, feet planted wide. Jorge's bass the motor underneath. All of us pulsing like a heartbeat.

My voice raged above the music. I hurled away everything inside of me. I punched the air with my whole body. When I sing, it's not a pretty sound, but it's mine.

The song ended on an abrupt drum clap. Jorge charged into the next one, slapped out the opening bass notes to Fugazi's "Waiting Room." The boys crashed and growled and I was leaping again. We slid into the song, Ernie and me on vocals. He and I volleyed, shouted at each other, shouted together. I didn't fuck up the lyrics even once. Ernie shredded hard and I grooved against him, my back to his. I could feel his sweat through my shirt, his hard back shifting against me, chords just throbbing out of him. Inside this wall of sound, inside this moment, all the way through me, I knew, not that I loved him, but how much. Inside the music I always know it.

"Shit yeah," Jorge said, as soon as the song ended. "We need to open with that one."

"Another guitar would thicken the sound," Olmec said. Of all of us, he was the perfectionist. "Lulu, it's not that hard to learn basic rhythm."

"She's not gonna learn it that fast." Ernie grinned at me. "No offense, Lulu."

"Nah, that's cool," I said. Ernie was being nice about it. He knows how bad I suck. I can almost play "The Man Who Sold the World," but I fumble every chord change. My problem is a lack of dexterity and not a lot of practice. I still can't afford the Epiphone. Ernie says if I can't practice two hours a day, I should play a lot of Nintendo.

I drained my water bottle in one go, mainly to avoid eye contact with him. I played it off like I was tired. It was kind of true. We'd been practicing in Pilar's shed for an hour. Yelling and jumping that much will exhaust anybody. Mostly, I just wanted a little space between Ernie and me. I don't know why when we're playing I feel like, *Yes, yes, it's you forever,* but afterward, all the other things crowd back in. It isn't that he's not the one. It's just I don't want to be someone's girlfriend. I don't want to report where I'm going or do stuff just because he's my boyfriend. Marina and Art are like that. They're always policing each other—where they go, and with who, and even sometimes what they wear.

Nope. I just want to be me.

"That guy who works at the Mini Mart. He could be good," Olmec was saying.

"We don't need to dress it up," Jorge said. "We're punk. This is our sound."

Nothing kills the vibe between us faster than Olmec and Jorge arguing about our sound. Jorge thinks we're fine sticking to punk covers. Olmec says Jorge just doesn't want to learn anything new.

"I mean, if that's your whole range," Olmec countered.

Ernie wandered off to mess with Wicho, who was napping in a sunny patch of grass a little way off. He never takes sides when they argue.

"It's not a range," Jorge said. He thrust his fingers into his maroon hair and tied it up in a short topknot. "It's an ethos."

"I'm taking a break," I said, tired of listening to them.

"Yeah, we're done," Jorge said. He always got sulky when people disagreed with him. "I'm going home."

"Hey," Pilar said, walking into the yard. "Don't leave yet. You need to bring those saddles up to the house." She pointed to a far corner at the back of the garage, where there were boxes and boxes of stuff, and yes, a couple of saddles.

"Yeah, all right," Jorge agreed, though he looked annoyed. "Ernie, come help me."

I watched him wade into the dark, cobwebby back of the shed. Pili's house had lost all its supernatural mystique. It was just like any other home in the Caimanes neighborhood: in need of renovations and full of things to sell at the flea market.

The garage was a great setup. It was big—bigger than a normal two-car garage. There was a lot of space for Olmec's kit and we could be as loud as we wanted. The downside was how long it was taking to clear it out. Pilar was not kidding. We'd cleared it halfway, enough to have our practice space. But it was still full of junk, most of which she made us box up so she could take it to the dump, or sell it, or store in the larger of the two bedrooms in her house.

She must have been a recovering pack rat. Old toys, a baby crib, ancient-looking hand tools, clothes, and, well, horsey stuff. Those saddles she wanted moved: two heavy-ass Mexican saddles, the kind with a wide round saddle horn, big as a wheel of cheese. Several pairs of brown leather chaps, real ones, scarred up like someone had done some serious ranch work. A couple of sombreros, woven straw and felt, not the tacky fiesta ones. Bridles, boots, horse brushes, a couple of ancient, crusty bottles of Absorbine. That garage was a cross between a tack room and someone's attic.

"Pili," Jorge said, lugging one of those big Mexican saddles to the house. It was dirty, covered in cobwebs. Jorge set the saddle on the porch railing. "Were you a rodeo star or what?"

"It's a man's saddle," Pilar said witheringly. She started rubbing oil into the saddle with a rag.

"There's another box of shoes here," Ernie called from the shed entrance. "You want it in the house?"

"No," Pilar said. "Put it in the bed of my truck. I'm making a trip to the dump later."

I sat down on the front steps near Pilar. "What are you gonna do with that?"

"Sell it," she said. "If I can get it into better shape. The leather hasn't cracked, but it's so dry."

I nodded. I'd only known her a few weeks, but it was clear Pilar was not like any old lady I'd ever met. In my experience a lot of old people just love to talk about the past. *Oh, things were different back then. Oh, when I was a kid.* Not Pilar. If you asked her a lot of questions, she'd get an attitude. But that was okay because she didn't ask many questions either.

The neatsfoot oil left dark streaks in the leather. She rubbed it until the whole thing was saturated. Then she carefully lifted each saddle string, glazing them individually so they hung sodden and greasy against the porch railing. It was going to take her at least a week or two before the saddle got pliant. She'd have to rub oil into it every day.

I knew a little about these things. Until about a year ago, Grandma Romi still had Grandpa Chuy's old saddles. Usually my dad, or my cousin Carlos, when he visited, helped her keep them oiled. I did it a couple of times, but she said I made too much of a mess. When Carlos left for college, she decided to give the saddles away. Some neighbor had a grandson who'd just gotten hired as a river rider. Grandma Romi was happy because that's what my grandpa had done too.

She'd always tell me about Grandpa Chuy, how he'd come up from South Texas, somewhere near Laredo, from a family of vaqueros on one of the big ranches down there. That he'd been one of the first Hispanic tick riders, mounted cattle inspectors for the federal government. He patrolled miles and miles of border, inspecting cattle for fever tick, keeping an eye out for strays from across the border. Oh yeah. Grandma knew all about the vaquero life.

It wasn't like that made me an expert. But watching Pilar oil that saddle made me so lonesome for Grandma Romi, and even, somehow, for Grandpa Chuy. I'd probably never hear another cowboy story about him again.

"My grandma used to make cowboy bread," I said, thinking that when I got back to my grandma's house, I'd ask Yoli if she knew how to make it.

"Pan de campo," Pilar said. "It's supposed to be cooked outside, over an open fire."

Even watching her oil the saddle like a pro, I could not see Pilar as a cowgirl at all. There's a lot of cowgirls in La Cienega. A bunch at my school, of course—barrel racing is popular with 4-H white girls, but some of the Latinas do it too, or they do escaramuza, which is this elaborate drill team on horseback, only since it's Mexican and they're girls, they've got to wear big poufy dresses like they're in a quinceañera. Yeah, while performing on horseback. You can never not be super femme if you're a Mexican girl.

But on or off the horse, those girls wear boots a lot. Western shirts. Rocky Mountain jeans. Even the moms who used to be barrel racers or escaramuzas. In English, it's western chic. In Spanish, it's ropa vaquera. If you're any kind of horsey girl, it's like a badge of honor to go clomping around everywhere.

Pilar only wore jeweled sandals or, sometimes, a pair of bright-red Reeboks. She was kind of . . . pop trendy for her age. She wore her hair long, middle-of-her-back long, a thick braid down one shoulder. She wore a lot of makeup for someone just hanging around at home. Plus, what old lady wore button-fly Calvin Klein jeans? I only know the brand because Marina desperately wants a pair, and tries them on every time we go to the mall. They're too damned expensive for Marina. Well, Pilar wears them.

She had a lot of fashion stuff. Ernie and I had seen her closet once, when we were loading boxes in the house. We weren't trying to poke around, but there were only two bedrooms, and we put boxes in the wrong one. For some reason, Pilar was using the smaller bedroom, not the big one. That little room had a daybed instead of a regular one, and faded wallpaper with a pattern of cartoon trains on it.

Pilar caught us in there and told us to get out. We did, but not before I saw that the closet was full of scarves and dresses—stuff a much younger person would wear—designer brands, and so many high heels. The child's bureau covered with dainty bottles and jars. Pilar seemed like she never got over being a teenager. Marina would have gone wild with that woman's stuff. But here was another mystifying thing: how a super feminine woman like Pilar knew anything about cowboy bread, enough to call it by its real name.

"I wish I knew how to make it," I said. I was really missing my grandma.

"It's not hard," Pilar said. "Romi and I used to argue over whose was better. She said Chuy's was the best."

"My grandpa taught her?" I asked. I don't know why. Maybe because I could finally see a way my grandma and this woman could have been friends.

"Pan de campo is about the only thing a man teaches a woman to cook. Vaqueros used to make it when they were out on a corrida, bringing in the cattle from the range."

"Did my grandpa Chuy teach you too?"

"No, not him," Pilar said, suddenly annoyed. She got up and walked off.

I felt stupid. It was obvious. The cowboy who'd taught her to make pan de campo, this was his saddle.

One thing different since my grandma died is that I could walk around her neighborhood pretty much at will. Tía Yoli wasn't like my dad, obsessed with deciding things for me. She wasn't like my grandma, trying to feed me and double-check that I'd done my homework, a sharp eye on everything I did. Yoli was into her own things. I said I'd catch a ride from school with Marina, that I'd be doing homework at her house until dinner. As long as I kept track of the time and watched out for emergency pages from Marina, it was fine.

"If someone calls I'll say you're in the bathroom," Marina told me when

I said we'd be practicing at Pilar's place after school. "I'll page you. You haul ass back to your grandma's."

It's actually Ernie's pager. He says we are all the worst and he regrets giving any of us his number, because he gets more pages for us than for himself. Which was true, especially when Jorge was breaking up with Ximena. Marina's pager code is 1118, Kirk Hammett's birthday. Mine is 0416, Selena's birthday. Olmec uses 666. Jorge's code is 80085, which is how you spell BOOBS with numbers.

But nobody ever checked on me. The only thing Yoli said was she'd stay through my birthday and help me plan my quinceañera. Whatever. I knew she wasn't staying for me, even if she did want my help sorting out Grandma's closets.

"Why?" I demanded. It was Sunday afternoon. The three of us were sitting at Grandma's kitchen table eating fried chicken from my tía's favorite chicken place, Chucho's. "Are you already trying to sell the house?"

Yoli bunched her eyebrows at me. "I don't know what I'm going to do with it," she said, "but I can't get anything done with it looking like this."

"Settle down, Lulu," my dad said in an autopilot voice. He was hungover and in a mood. He kept staring out the screen door, barely saying anything.

"God, I think I'd rather plan three quinces than deal with this house," Yoli sighed. "There's at least sixty years' worth of junk to sort through."

"You're gonna help, Lulu," my dad said. "She's planning your party."

My quince? Since when was this ever my idea? But I kept my mouth shut. Before my grandma died, that comment would have sent me into immediate fight mode. But my anger was different now. It was bigger; it waited.

The phone rang and rang. We all knew it was Uncle Charlie, but Yoli had forbidden us to answer it. He was a cheater. That's why he hadn't shown his face at Grandma's funeral. Yoli wasn't talking to him.

At least, that's what she told us when she came back from Houston. She was only there a day, to pick up some of her things. Since she came back he called *a lot.*

"You didn't let him come to Mom's funeral because he was unfaithful?" my dad asked. "Look, that's shitty, but it's Mom's funeral. That's a huge falta de respeto. You're saying you did that?"

"No," Yoli said. "I'm saying he has a girlfriend. He abandoned his family."

Except like everything else with my family, what they said was happening wasn't really what was happening. Yoli, eating fried chicken and pretending like the telephone wasn't ringing every twenty minutes, black murder in her eyes. My dad, not eating anything, slumped across his chair and trying to fake that he wasn't a burned-out zombie from boozing the night before. All of us here, in Grandma's house, and she wasn't here, but her smell was still here. Everywhere, all over the house, everything Grandma-smelling.

I miss my grandma so much it's exhausting. I can pretend when I'm out, at school or with Marina, and especially during jam sessions with the band. I can push it away. But when I'm around my family there's no space from it. I have no energy. My body feels heavy, slow. Moving around takes effort. The brutal truth is that she's never coming back. It's a gut punch that never ends.

Being in her house was why I couldn't eat anything, even Chucho's fried chicken. It's awful, but I don't like being at my grandma's anymore. It's too weird without her. I didn't know how my dad and Yoli could stand it. But there they were, talking like they didn't notice.

"If I didn't have Carlos, I'd file for divorce right now," Yoli said. "But I'm not doing anything while he's in college."

My dad said nothing. I could tell he had opinions though, just by the way he didn't answer her, the way he spent a long time looking in the bucket of chicken for the piece he wanted.

I squeezed a whole packet of honey sauce onto my biscuit just to crush something. It's not that I think anyone should put up with a cheater, but I really couldn't picture Tía Yoli leaving Uncle Charlie. Would she really be willing to lose her five-bedroom house, her country-club lifestyle? Or maybe she'd get to keep everything.

The phone rang seven times. I counted them. My dad clapped his hands over his face. The sound must have been killing his head. Good.

"Christ," he said. "Does he have it on a timer?"

"Yeah, I'm pretty sure he sets the alarm on his watch," Yoli said. "He does that for everything."

"If you're not gonna pick up, at least take it off the hook. It's driving me nuts."

"And give him the satisfaction? Hell no. Let him talk to his sucia."

"I call bullshit," my dad snorted. His eyes were red and watery, but keen. "If he's always calling you when does he have time to screw his girl-friend?"

"Shut up!" Yoli fired a piece of chicken at him right out of the bucket. It bounced off the wall near his head.

This is my family. Tantrums and yelling. No wonder my cousin Carlos decided to go to college three states away.

"You're still side-arming," my dad said, and walked out before Tía Yoli could throw anything else. Yoli throws a lot of stuff at him. She always misses. I sucked the inside of my cheek to cut off a spasm of laughter. My dad is the heavyweight champ of sick burns.

That is also my family: the fights that tremble on the edge of violence, sometimes spill over, but also everything is hilarious. Because we know it's stupid. We know it's absurd. But we do it anyway, all of us. This is like what my English teacher means by a fatal flaw. When you know but you do it anyway. The way we deal with it is by laughing. Later on, maybe tomorrow, he'll call Yoli on the phone, say, *Órale, ¿Nolan Ryan o qué?*, and she'll laugh. I'll laugh. We will all still be mad, but that's how it will end. This time.

But then I heard his truck start. I bolted out the door after him. He was already driving out of the yard.

"Hey! Hey!" I yelled.

He pumped his brakes and the electric passenger window came down, but he didn't park. Steppenwolf came blaring out of the cab. He didn't lower the volume.

"When are you coming back? I have school tomorrow."

"I'll pick you up tomorrow before school. Just tell your tía."

"My backpack's at home. With all my homework," I said. Man, I wished I had a chicken leg to throw at him. It was so obvious he hadn't even thought about me.

"I'll bring it. Don't worry, mija," he said, his voice a little ragged. Normally, my dad is a good-looking dude. The Officer Frank Poncherello type. But in the strong afternoon light, he looked ill, unlike himself. His nut-brown skin had come over all yellowish. His face had cracked into puckers and lines, and there were dark circles under the eyes. Plus, it was probably fifty degrees outside, but he was sweating. A lot.

"Dad, are you okay?"

"I'm fine. What?" He gave me a look like I was crazy. This is what he does. Just acts like nothing is wrong, especially when it's something. I pushed anyway.

"Where are you going?"

"I just have stuff to do," he snapped. "Go inside, Lucha."

"Don't forget my backpack," I said. Not to remind him, just to stall him a little longer. He was absolutely itching for beer, and I was keeping him from it.

He smacked his lips at me. The window went up. He drove away before I got back in the house.

"I guess I'm staying the night," I said when I came inside. My tía shrugged.

The phone rang again. Yoli kept right on chewing, hard, like it was the piece of chicken that had crossed her. I could almost feel her gigantic will not to answer the phone filling up the room.

I watched her angry-eat, those fat jowls pistoning over the chicken. She used to look like Julie Newmar. A face like a lady puma: jutted cheekbones, a pair of slanted lightning bolts for eyes. Big and brown as Grandma Romi, but with a body. A siren and a bare-knuckle brawler. *Damn,* Marina said when she saw the pictures of Yoli and Uncle Charlie's honeymoon in Hawaii, the ones where Uncle Charlie is all freckles and sunburned shoulders and Yoli is in her white bikini, *they shoulda picked her to play Wonder Woman, not that gabacha Lynda Carter.* No wonder he fell in love with her. No wonder.

Only now, he's tired of her because she's old and fat. She says. But the phone keeps ringing.

Here's the thing: I can tell who's the boss between two people. Like with Marina and her boyfriend Art, it's her. She's pretty, but it isn't her looks. If I had to say what it is, it's some kind of built-in demand. Like she comes in with some expectation, and he better do it or get lost. With Ximena and Jorge, they both want to be the boss, and that's why they're always fighting.

With Yoli and Uncle Charlie, it's always been Yoli. Yeah, now she's fat. Yeah, she's bossy. But Uncle Charlie worships her. He's white and a man, a petroleum engineer who makes a shitload of money, but she's the one running the show. Yoli could leave a guy flat, and he'd still love her, want to be with her, want to fight with her. I bet she never even thought about it. My dad says it's just the way she is.

So, no. I do not buy it that Uncle Charlie is a cheater. Even hungover like my dad was, he knew a load of bull when he heard it. Me too. If you're sick of somebody, if you think they're too old and too fat, you don't let them yell at you on the phone. You don't keep calling back for more.

Right now, Uncle Charlie was probably in their spacious kitchen, in the Woodlands suburb of Houston where they lived, dialing and dialing to this little house on the border, trying to find his wife.

"He's really having an affair?" I asked. Uncle Charlie was somewhere eating his heart out. That much was obvious.

"Go start sorting out the closets. A lot of those clothes are yours, aren't they?"

I didn't talk back. Not when she was in that mood. I put my dishes in the sink and went to the bedroom.

I turned on the radio and flopped on the bed. *American Top 40* was on. Boring, but at least it drowned out the ringing phone. Where had my dad gone? When would he be back? I was tired of wondering.

Pretty soon I figured out Yoli wanted me in the back of the house because she wanted to answer the phone. I heard her saying she'd never go back. Calling Uncle Charlie a piece of shit. They fought for at least an hour. Seems like he could dig for a thousand years and he'd never reach the bottom of her anger.

I guess she thought if I was wading through half a century of Grandma's old coats and shoes, I wouldn't hear her. Wrong. Uncle Charlie wasn't cheating. She was yelling, but about my cousin Carlos. "I don't care. I'm his mother. I'll choose him every time. Every goddamn time."

I've known since I was a little kid. One time, when the family visited from Houston for Thanksgiving, Yoli and Uncle Charlie went to the casino in Lawton with my dad. Carlos stayed home to babysit me. He was fifteen and I was about nine, I guess. I woke up in the night and caught him in the living room with another boy.

His friend spotted me standing in the hallway. But only after a good five minutes. Long enough for me to see the flush on the boy's face, how it stained his cheeks, hear his little ragged gasps. Carlos was kneeling in front of the boy. I couldn't see his face, so what I really remember about that moment was his hands. How they knuckled in the guy's denim, holding him down. The wet sound of his mouth.

"Oh my God," the boy said, and shifted right out of Carlos's mouth. His cock was fat and pink, shiny with spittle. He stuffed it into his pants and rolled off the couch in the same movement. Carlos scrambled up, flipped his hair back.

"Hey," he said in an almost normal voice. "Did you have a nightmare? Do you need a glass of water?"

"No. But can I stay up and watch TV?"

He slitted his eyes at me. "Are you gonna tell?"

"No."

"Okay then."

He and his friend went out to the backyard. I stayed up watching a rerun of *Airwolf*.

I cringe at myself now, but I didn't know I shouldn't be watching him. I didn't know it was rude. I mean, I didn't know anything about anything. Now I wish I'd just gone back to bed, left them alone. I wouldn't want anyone watching Ernie and me.

I don't know why Carlos would decide to tell his parents now, maybe because it's safer since he's away at college. But it's the only thing that makes sense. He must have told them, and Uncle Charlie is being an asshole about it. And Yoli is lying to us so we won't know Carlos is gay.

Besides.

Besides, something happened a few months before Grandma died. It was the summer, and I was used to staying up late. I think it was five or six in the morning, because I'd only been asleep for a little while.

I had stayed up listening to the *Bleach* album, trying to learn it enough to talk about it with Ernie. Ernie worships Nirvana. He was devastated when Kurt Cobain killed himself. He might never get over it. *Bleach* was pretty great, especially since Ernie had told me it'd only cost six hundred dollars to cut. I'd gone to sleep after deciding that what I'd say to Ernie was, of all the songs, "About a Girl" was the real weirdo, an early Beatles pop homage tucked in the middle of a hardcore grunge album. Because with Ernie it's not about whether you think the music is good or not. It's what you can say about the music, because what you say actually says something about you. It's one of the first things he said when we met—somebody had really schooled me on music. Well yeah. The only person who thinks about music the way Ernie does is my dad.

I heard Gonzy putting his face between the slats of the mini-blinds in my bedroom. They made a weird crinkly noise. He was always breaking them, and Dad would get so mad about it. I told him to cut it out, sort of, because I wasn't all the way awake.

What I'm saying is I was groggy, real groggy, because that's what happens when you only get two hours of sleep. Gonzy wouldn't listen, so I finally sat up in bed. He stood there, his head plunged between the plastic slats of the blinds, body all alert and tail wagging in that way that meant someone he knew was outside. Then I heard my dad.

My dad was talking real low and growly, in a way I didn't recognize—and I've heard him mad plenty.

I got off my bed and peeked with Gonzy. It was foggy out, but I could see an unfamiliar car parked along the curb. A big green thing, maybe a

Buick. Someone was standing outside my line of sight. I could see my dad's back, his posture. The fists low and cocked, like he was about to spring.

"Don't you go bothering your grandmother either," he said, so I knew he had to be talking to Carlos. Something happened, I thought. An emergency. But why not call? Why not tell Grandma?

"She knows already. She loves me." It was Carlos. Defiant, but just barely.

"You sick little scumbag. I'll cut your fucking nuts off if you go near her again."

Someone in the car said, "Carlos, let's go."

My dad let loose his ugly laugh. The one he uses when he's sneering, when he wants to grind you down even more. I hate that laugh.

"Listen to your joto friend," he said. "Get the fuck out of here."

I saw Carlos then, because he walked around to the passenger side of the car. He was wearing an orange tank and cutoffs. His hair was tied back in a ponytail.

"I'm still your family, Tío," he said.

My dad didn't answer. Carlos got in the car and whoever was driving pulled onto the street.

Now I wondered whether Tía Yoli knew about my dad threatening Carlos. I bet she didn't, or she'd have thrown more than a chicken leg at him. If Grandma was alive, she'd have stood up for Carlos, I know it.

I lay on the bed in the back bedroom for a solid hour, the *Top 40* blaring and Casey Kasem providing trivia for nearly every song. Finally, Tía Yoli came in to say she was going out to dinner with her comadres. She didn't notice I hadn't done one thing with the closets.

"Can I go to Marina's house?" I asked. There was no way I was going to spend the rest of the day by myself at my grandma's. Just thinking about it made me feel like I was suffocating.

"Yeah," Yoli said. "Just be back home by eight. Get her mom to drop you off if it's dark."

"No problem."

"I don't know if I'll be home by then," Yoli said. "But you have a key to the house, right?"

"Yeah," I said, staring at the ceiling. "Don't worry. I'll be fine."

There are only certain people I can be around when I'm in a bad mood. Actually, only Marina. She does not tell me to be happier or ask me what I have to be upset about. She never says I need to talk about it. If I want to talk, I can. If I want to sit around and mope, that's fine too. My moods don't faze her. I wasn't sure I wanted to talk about my primo Carlos, but I knew I could. Or I could sit in the Salazar kitchen and listen to Mrs. Salazar gossip with her sister on the phone. I could help Marina make flour tortillas, flattening out the dough with quick, hard thrusts of the rolling pin. Marina says it's the only thing I'm good at in the kitchen. Pressing out dough is a great mood reliever.

It was my tough luck that her dad's truck was parked in the driveway. But of course it was Sunday. I should have remembered. Anyway, I was not going to ring the doorbell when Mr. Salazar was home. Technically, I wasn't out without permission, but my dad didn't know that. I didn't want to get noticed by another dad who might mention it to mine next time they ran into each other. Nope.

I decided to go to Pilar's house. I'd been over a lot lately, sometimes even without the guys. She was always cool about it. Maybe I could mess around on Olmec's kit. I really felt like banging on something.

I saw her brown truck parked along the side of the house. She was home. I knocked, then stood around on the porch for a while. Pilar didn't come to the door. Through a window, I could see her sitting at a Formica kitchen table, wearing giant headphones. There was a big boom box and an electric typewriter on the table. Pilar was typing. I guess she was pretty good because she didn't hesitate and it didn't look like she had to stop for mistakes. Her dog was nowhere to be seen.

I rapped hard on the window glass. Pilar finally looked up. She clicked off the boom box and put up a hand for me to wait. She gathered up her pages and put them in a folder. She came out a few minutes later, tucking a strand of dyed black hair behind her ear.

"So," Pilar said. "You're here. Where are your bandmates?"

"It's just me today. Can I use the shed for a while?"

"I have to pick up Wicho from the groomer."

"Oh," I said. I was totally striking out with everything. "Yeah, okay, no problem."

"You could come with me," she said. "It's just downtown. When we get back you can be in the garage as much as you want. I don't have more appointments."

Pilar was funny. She didn't try to be friends the way some women do: fake friendly voice, but they're just trying to pump you for information, maybe they want the gossip or they're looking to get you in trouble. She wasn't like my tía Yoli, no nonsense and taking charge. With her it was a peculiar blankness, a kind of silence all around her, that she carried with her, all the time.

"Yeah, okay," I said, not wanting to disagree even though I didn't want to run errands with her. "If we're going downtown, can we stop at Cheve's?"

"The music store? Sure, if you want."

"Sounds good," I said.

We got in her truck. She drove without speaking and I did the same. It didn't feel hard to sit there with her and follow my own mind. I made sure to slouch, in case anyone might spot me in her car. I felt a twinge of guilt. I'd started out wanting to meet her just to get back at my dad, but the more we hung out, the more I liked her. I knew I was being a jerk. To her, not him.

She hummed along with the radio, an AM station playing rancheras, keeping time on the steering wheel with her long red fingernails. In the flood of afternoon light I could see the textured quality of her skin beneath the powder and rouge. It was a strong face too—the bold slash of red lipstick, the prow of her nose, straight, prominent, and with her white sunglasses, almost arrogant. She was beautiful, the way an eagle might be beautiful, not like an old woman at all. My dad had called her a terrible person and I still didn't know why.

"Pili, why doesn't my dad like you?"

To my surprise, she didn't get mad. Probably knew I'd ask eventually. "I've never met your father."

"You don't know him?"

"Just by sight," she said, not taking her eyes off the road. "But I don't blame him. Your grandmother and I . . . there was something we didn't agree about. We couldn't find our way back from it."

No way Grandma Romi was to blame. I couldn't keep the skepticism out of my voice. "My grandma did something to you?"

"No. Ella era puro corazón," Pili said. "I am not good at loving people. That's why her children hold a grudge."

She must have seen on my face that I had a million more questions. "I don't want to talk about it anymore."

"All right," I agreed. For now.

It wasn't a long trip: just two blocks to the San Jose church, then take a left, another two blocks past the crumbly old Lucky Bar, another left, then three blocks and there's the downtown. Just the one street. Main Street. Most of the popular shopping is at the mall, on the opposite side of town. The La Cienega downtown is more like the high street in a western movie, just a long street with small, forgotten shops. Cheve's Music is on the corner after the pawnshop and a fabric store.

We'd just turned onto Main Street when I saw the little Honda CRX with that Mean People Suck bumper sticker. It was parked in front of Toni's Café, across from the dog groomer.

"Oh shit," I said, forgetting myself. It was that freaking chick, the one who got my Gonzy killed.

"What's the matter?" Pilar asked.

"Nothing. I thought I saw someone I know. Never mind."

She looked at me a beat longer. But, true to form, she didn't ask me anything more. "I'll be back in a few minutes."

"Yeah, okay."

Once she went inside I crossed the street at an angle. I didn't want to seem like I was going to the café. I stopped in front of the adjacent store, Flores de Mimi, which apparently specialized in silk and plastic flower arrangements. I tilted my head at a bouquet of white silk lilies, like I was trying to decide whether to buy them, but really, I was looking into the glass front of Toni's Café.

Toni's was a lunch counter joint. There weren't that many tables and it was a slow Sunday. It was easy to spot the likeliest Margarita. She was sitting with a man who was, thankfully, not my dad. Maybe it was her husband. Maybe that guy was the one who'd killed Gonzy. If so, he was a cliché city-cowboy type, in a western shirt and what were probably Wranglers. He had set his straw cowboy hat on the empty chair between them. I couldn't see his face because his back was to me. I could see hers though.

I wanted her to be beautiful. Maybe if she'd been beautiful, then my dad couldn't help it, like he was just overcome, blinded with love, blinded by some spectacular beauty. But she wasn't. She didn't even have red hair, not really. She was a middle-aged Mexican American woman, light-skinned enough to get away with putting red streaks in her hair. She'd probably started getting it chunked once the gray had come in. She was eating a club sandwich.

I hated her. I felt it all the way through me, hot and pulsing, how much I hated her. I wanted to puke from hating her. I couldn't breathe from the sheer suffocating weight of my hatred. This bitch. This nothing-special bitch got my dog killed. I couldn't even pretend I was checking out fake flowers anymore. But she never looked my way.

"Hey, we're ready." It was Pilar's voice, from across the street. I swallowed everything back as best I could. She was standing beside her truck with Wicho. I guess it sent me over the edge, the sight of him all fuzzed out like he'd just come out of the dryer. I'm not a cryer, almost ever. But all of a sudden I was angry-weeping right there on the sidewalk. I couldn't stop. It was so embarrassing.

"What's the matter? What happened?" Pilar demanded. Under her sharp black eyes, I couldn't lie. I didn't even want to.

"The woman who owns that car right there." I jabbed my finger at the CRX, not caring if that bitch Margarita saw me pointing. "Her husband killed my dog."

Pilar nodded, slow and deliberate. She took a long look at the car. She said, "Because of your father."

"Yes! Yes, because of him!" I spat the word. Finally. Someone who would tell the truth and not flinch. "How'd you know?"

"I know what betrayal looks like," she said.

"Well, he was my dog, not my dad's. He was my good boy. He didn't deserve it."

"Of course. Dogs aren't like men and women. They are innocents," Pilar said. She thrust her fingers into Wicho's thick scruff, still watching the car. "Get in the truck. We're going down to the plaza."

"I'm not leaving," I snapped. "Go if you want to."

"Trust me," Pilar said. Her eyes were flat and shiny. Her face was more vivid than I'd ever seen it. It was a little scary, but that's what made me listen. "I have a plan for them."

I got in the truck. The plaza was just up the block, a small park where Main Street ended and residential streets kicked in. I didn't know why she'd rather drive than just walk there. Wicho hopped onto the bench, between us. I couldn't help but take hold of him.

"What was your dog's name?" she asked as she cranked the engine.

"Gonzy. Doctor Gonzo." It was easier talking about Gonzy when I held on to Wicho. "Everybody thought he was named after Gonzo from *The Muppet Show*, but he wasn't. My dad named him Doctor Gonzo after the Samoan lawyer in *Fear and Loathing in Las Vegas*."

"You loved him so much," Pilar said. It wasn't a question.

"My mom gave him to me the year she died, so he was pretty old. But still." I hesitated. Wicho was not like Gonzy, but there was the same big dog bulk. You wrap your arms around it and somehow it anchors you. That's a thing I always loved about Gonzy. That's a thing I felt with Wicho. "That man shot him in the head. Blew his brains out. That's how I found Gonzy. Just one day, it happened."

Pilar made a guttural grunt, almost a growl. She parked the truck and got out, taking Wicho with her. "Can you see the car from here?"

"Yes."

"Okay, keep watching it."

She walked Wicho around the grass until he pooped. Then she took a small plastic bag out of her pocket and actually started picking up the poop. I gagged.

She rolled her eyes. "You have to clean up after your dog. You can't just leave caca wherever. That's dirty. In the city you can even get a ticket."

"Maybe." I wasn't convinced. I didn't care if it made me look like a country bumpkin. Picking up dog poop was too gross, even with a bag. Wicho was a big dog, so it was a full load.

Pilar tied the bag and set it carefully on the dashboard. "Watch the car."

"What the fuck. At least throw it in the trash."

"I have a better place for it," she said. We drove around the block and then parked down the street a little way, still in view of the café. We sat through three ranchera songs, the truck idling, Wicho between us, panting softly. I didn't ask her anything. I didn't feel fidgety. I didn't care how long it would take.

They came out of the café. It seemed like that cowboy actually was her husband. He got in the driver's side of the car.

"That's them," I said.

"Figures."

Pilar waited until they got to the light. Then she followed. She knew how to hang back. She knew when to keep steady. They drove to a residential neighborhood. It was the neighborhood by the public library, the one with a few historic monstrosities and lots of old, snobby white people, the kind with family name recognition. They passed the library, turned right a couple streets down. Gardenia. That was the name of the street. All the street names were flowers here.

Pilar didn't turn after them. She drove past Gardenia. Circled back. We pulled into the library parking lot. Waited a few more minutes in the parking lot. She was letting them get home.

We finally drove down Gardenia. Slow, but not too slow. The car was parked next to a Chevy Silverado, in the driveway of a Spanish colonial–style house. It wasn't one of the overgrown historic mansions, just a regular-sized house. There was a big oak in the front yard. Rose bushes under the front windows. We drove past, not slow, not fast. I knew where she lived now. I had found her, finally. Pilar had found her for me.

"Maybe they need to be reminded of Gonzo," Pilar said when we turned back onto Gardenia. "What do you think?"

I looked at that fat bag of dog shit. My heart thumped hard inside me. "Yeah."

"Do it and run," she said. "Don't look back."

She pulled off a house down from theirs. I palmed the bag, cringing at the feeling of cold, soft shit wrapped in thin plastic. I cupped it gingerly.

Nobody outside. Nobody on the street at all. I ran at the front door, fast as I could. Flung out an arm and let the bag fly. It hit loud against the door and exploded. Dark-brown dog shit all over the door, all over the welcome mat. A voice somewhere inside, alarmed. Maybe her. I hoped it was. Somehow, I hated her more than him.

The door jerked open. There she was, perfectly ordinary Margarita, shock caving in her face.

"Yeah! Fuck you! Fuck you!" I screamed. Which was stupid, but I wasn't sorry. I wanted her to know it was me. *I did this to you, bitch. I did it.* I wished I had ten more bags of dog shit. I settled for spitting at her. The way she flinched! She was afraid of me. I wanted to punch her in the face. Tear out those stupid red highlights. I flipped her double birds.

"Margie, what's going on?" The man's voice. He came outside and I gasped. He'd taken off his cowboy hat, so I could see him clearly. He was disfigured, the left side of his face scarred from temple to chin, as if it had been burned. He'd lost part of his left arm too. He wore a prosthetic arm, the kind with a metal hook hand.

"I'm calling the cops," he said, looking me square in the eye.

"Call them. You sick motherfucker. You came to my house and killed my dog." He flinched when I said it, so I knew it was true. He was the one.

I let out a wild scream. "Come on! Let's call them right now! I bet they can match your gun to the bullet in my dog's head."

"You little psycho," the man said. He pulled his wife back inside and they slammed the door.

I ran like hell for Pilar's truck. "Go, go!"

Pilar had Wicho by the collar so he wouldn't jump out. She was laughing so hard. I'd never seen her have any reaction to anything. She gunned the engine and we sped away, Wicho excited and stepping all over me. She let out a grito, a big-throated hay-hay-hayyyyyy, both wild laughter and a cry of triumph.

"Yeah!" I yelled, punching my fists in the air. "I got them! I fucking got them!"

"You did," she said. "You really did. Good for you."

I must have impressed her because when we got to the intersection just before Main Street, she asked me if I wanted to drive.

"I don't know how," I said.

"I'll teach you," she said. "Come on, trade places with me."

down by the river

Obstinate seed, I cast you out, but you sprouted in a crack of the road to spite me. You thrive, you live—you live!—in my sight and out of reach. How bitter, this remorse that clings and clings, and hungers for you still. I am a knot of blood that cannot weep or heal.

Before you came I was already a field sown with salt, cursed and forsaken. My children were dead. My husband, vanished to some other life. People shuddered and whispered, and gave me the wide, lonely berth of their fear. All of that is still mine, but now I wield it for myself.

You, the last bit of your father. I did not want you. I did not love you. I remember that: When you came, I looked into your face, lashless and wrinkled, fresh from my womb, and could not feel you in my arms. It seemed I had no arms, no heart, no mother's savage tenderness. You and I were both just spirits expelled from my body. I felt nothing, save a glimmer of grief.

What a thing, to watch you grow hardy when you are lost to me. You play stickball barefoot and brown in the sun. You brawl in the street and shout your victories with a bloody mouth. My radiant perdition, it is good that you are fierce. When you are old enough, they will pluck you from these streets and pack you off to Vietnam.

Let other women wail and tear their faces. My wrath has knit itself into your bones, into the fist of your heart, and it charms your life. I have seen your fate in your eyes. Death will not have you as long as that fury stirs within. Mala hierba nunca muere, and so it is with you. Little weed that never dies, you cannot be rooted out.

Still, I do my penance in the sucking, black mud along the river. I mark you with my rosary, lock your name inside prayers. Julio, Julio, bead by bead, ten times five, in the deepest hour of the night, when the lioness coughs in the dark and tusked wild pigs rustle the sweeping river cane.

I am not afraid. I know my way to the water's edge.

Chapter Twelve

Black Cats

PILAR AGUIRRE, 1968

Julio was handsome and full of pranks. He roamed the Caimanes barrio day and night, like a stray dog. He ran with reckless boys, thieves who sickened themselves on stolen watermelons, then lay groaning in the grass, who raided Aurora Ramirez's corn crib and ran away laughing when she stung their backs with rock salt pellets. Father Isidro had banned them, one and all, from church for the entire school year after they'd gotten drunk on Communion wine and set fire to a closet of altar boys' robes.

In the summer and fall, they hired out as day laborers, gathering alfalfa at outlying ranches, grape-picking at Mr. Lee's vineyard. They pooled their money for a down payment on an old Bel Air at Pete's Body Shop. The word was they would have it by Christmastime and the old folks in the neighborhood wagered that they would kill themselves, wrap it around a tree or a light post, just watch.

Yes, the sight of Julio marauding all over the neighborhood was as inescapable as her own heartbeat, but Pilar tried never to look his way. He was enough like, and unlike, Joselito that setting eyes on him, especially as he got older and became a kind of blueprint for the man her lost son might have been, was simply unbearable. And yet, sometimes, she could not help herself.

She would not have seen him, would not have been home at all between shifts—nightly half shifts on top of the regular day shifts at the factory had become mandatory in the past month—but the skies were threatening and her sheets were on the clothesline. She had walked the two miles home intending to collect her linens and march straight back to work.

One more week of this, Pilar thought as she reached the foot of Loma Negra and stopped at her mailbox. One more week and no more extra shifts. The supporters of school board candidate Juan Cardenas, women with their tidy coifs and low-heeled Sunday shoes, were gathered like hens at Pilar's side of the street, the dead end above the irrigation canal. One of the women, Mrs. Aureliano Sanchez, wife of the neighborhood butcher, glanced at Pilar and whispered something to her comadres. A stiffness, a resolution of backs, and they began to make their way back in the opposite direction. Pilar tucked her mail into her purse, indifferent. Yes, they shunned her, but so what? She was glad not to speak to them.

A sudden burst of cold wind crossed her, and then the sound of voices shouting blotted everything. Ahí viene por quien lloras, as the old saying went. Here he comes, the one you cry for.

Julio leaped over the canal like a bird erupting into flight. He scrambled up the rocky embankment to the street above, tumbling loose white stones into the arroyo, but never losing his footing. The canvassing wives let out little squeals of fear as he bowled into their midst, knocking himself and one of the women flat in the dust. Pilar saw that it was Mrs. Sanchez, who sat up with no grace, legs splayed and showing the stockings rolled beneath her knees.

The boy burst into laughter. He scrambled to his feet, didn't offer to help the woman, who cursed him. Pilar held her breath. She had almost never been this near him. He loped past her without a glance, racing to the home at the far end of the street, the one on the corner. Romi's. Pilar watched him reach the driveway, lope past Chuy's truck into the house, still laughing.

His pursuer was a weepy teenage girl with a butcher knife clutched in her fist. Pilar could see the blade winking silvery white in the dusk. One of those girls with loose black hair and heavy eye makeup, but no lipstick and no bra. Her breasts bounced furiously as she pelted toward the arroyo. A long, flowered skirt hampered her so that she fell more than once climbing out of the muddy arroyo. By the time she climbed her way to the street, bedraggled and sobbing in a way that Pilar knew meant he would never turn his eyes to her again, Julio had escaped into his house.

"Julio! Julio, come out here!" the girl screamed, standing on the street in front of his house. But there was no real fire in her. She sobbed more than she shouted, and the knife dangled, useless and muddy, at her side.

The girls were slow to learn, thought Pilar. Girls always were. This one was making a fool of herself before the eyes of every neighbor on the block. No doubt he would be sitting down to his dinner or playing his records in his bedroom. It was Romi who came out to the porch.

"Go home," Romi said to the girl. "Or I'll take that knife and cut your eyes out. Then you won't have to cry anymore."

The girl slunk away, still sobbing. Romi stood on her front steps and waited for her to go.

To Pilar's surprise, Romi looked her way, met her eyes instead of pretending, as she always did, that Pilar was invisible. It was unsettling and

Pilar glanced away first, noting again that Chuy's truck was in the drive-way. Strange that he should be home during the week, but she supposed he was here to vote in the school board election.

She turned away, annoyed at herself for paying attention to things she knew would only give her a sleepless night. She still had to walk up the hill and collect her sheets, then it was a two-mile walk back to the industrial park for the next shift. One more week, she reminded herself, more to banish unwanted thoughts than anything else. One more week. After the election everyone could get back to their own lives.

For years, the school board had proposed the consolidation of the high schools. Separate but equal had been outlawed, but the ruling went unen-forced in La Cienega. Until Vietnam. Amid so many evils: national assas-sinations, the boys called up to the draft lottery, and the stream of them returning, especially after Tet, dead, or maimed, or with their minds per-manently warped, it seemed that this year the board would finally carry the measure. North Cienega, where the Anglos attended, and South Cienega, the barrio school for Mexican and black students, as well as the few Kickapoo living within the city limits, were to be consolidated into a modern, centralized high school: Davy Crockett High. A bigger school, 5A Division 1, meant more opportunities for sports scholarships. Parents all over town were suddenly ready for change, if it meant their sons could go to college and avoid the draft.

Not everyone in the Caimanes barrio agreed. Half a dozen women were canvassing the neighborhood. Pilar saw them knocking on doors, carrying tracts as though they were Jehovah's Witnesses. The wives, carry-ing out their husbands' wills. They were the older generation, against consolidation on principle—like should be with like, and besides, who wanted their children suffering at the hands of white classmates? The pro-consolidation side seemed to be all young people and families with teen sons, whose support for the Division 1 designation had managed this business in the first place.

Not that it matters to me, Pilar thought as she made her way up the winding road, long overgrown with weeds. Neither side ever knocked on her door.

Though there was nothing personally relevant to her, Pilar followed the local contention with interest and then, as the time for the school board elections drew nearer, with increasing irritation. Both the Spanish and English newspapers were full of opinions. Anticonsolidation Mexican Americans supported Juan Cardenas, who lectured parents in the supermarket and after church that it was bad enough their sons were already clashing with white boys, but what about their daughters, excluded from glee club and the homecoming court, and worse, subject to uncouth Anglo boys who would not respect them?

Local ranchers' wives wrote scathing editorials in the newspaper: Were their Anglo children to endure not only inferior classmates, but in all likelihood, the Mexican and Negro teachers who would surely be employed at the new high school? It was a moral outrage. The spread of corruption was already infecting La Cienega: two Mexicans actually running for seats on the school board.

In the Mexican newspapers, the retort came swiftly. Allí está el detalle, the snarled hair of history: Treaty of Guadalupe Hidalgo in 1848, the entrance of Texas into the Union of these United States granted, in this narrow way, that Texas Mexicans, Tejanos, were white citizens. They could be prohibited at stores, hotels, social clubs, and other privately owned entities, but nothing governed by the state. Including school board elections.

Yes, two Mexican Americans were running for school board election. Juan Cardenas was loud, but had no financial support and only his cronies to canvas for him. Felix "El Gato" Gutierrez was trouble.

Felix was a skinny young longhair with eyesight bad enough to keep him out of Vietnam, but a gift for public speaking. His supporters put on lively parodies of the community and shouted things like "¡Justicia!" and "¡La Causa!" Impudent radio DJs, with aliases like Zero, Muy Romeo, or ContraIndio, aired the comments of angry anticonsolidation callers set to the sound of braying donkeys. El Gato riled up Mexicans—*Chicanos*, these new radicals called themselves—inspired young Anglos too, and especially mobilized young teenagers, who, because they could not vote, relieved their feelings by spray-painting black cats all over town.

Pilar had seen black cats graffitied on sidewalks, on the side of Rufino's grocery store, had even heard they were found on the hood of the mayor's own Oldsmobile. With all that ruckus, it was Pilar's opinion that El Gato would not have had a chance, but for Tet and what it meant for his cousin, Margarita Gutierrez.

Margarita was nineteen and beautiful. She had been a popular girl in school, engaged at seventeen to Simon Avila, a solid young man of past athletic reputation. When Simon was drafted in the middle of her senior year, she had not faltered. She went to the prom with a group of girls whose boyfriends had also been packed off to Vietnam, the Stagg-ettes, as they fashioned themselves, and danced with the recklessness and aplomb of dread. Margarita graduated and went to work part-time as the secretary for San Jose Parish and part-time at the Sizzler steak house.

She had waited for Simon Avila for two and a half years. He was home, finally, because a grenade had mutilated him. He had lost an arm to the elbow and an eye (and, it was whispered, his manhood), but he was alive and recuperating at Fort Sam Houston in San Antonio. Margarita was going to marry him.

Now she gathered the people like so many sheaves of wheat, this shining example of womanhood: patient, abiding, faithful. When, at El Gato's rallies, Margarita took the stage and said in her quiet, sweet voice, that it was God's own grace that brought her Simon back to her, every listener felt chastened and full of tears. Simon had been the best pitcher in the league, but the scouts only went to the big schools, to the white ones. If Simon had played in D1, Margarita said, he would have gotten a baseball scholarship to college.

It's not right for our boys not to have a chance, she said, with the elegant seriousness she had developed since Simon had gone to war. The crowd felt the truth of her.

Even Pilar, in her caustic way, felt the pull. There was nothing so inspiring as a faithful woman. Especially if she was as pretty as Margarita, Pilar reflected. The war had returned her beloved to her in pieces, but she had not folded. Surely Margarita was afraid sometimes, wasn't she? Surely she realized the difficulties. But she seemed radiant. They would marry at Christmas, when Simon was released from the army hospital, and the following summer they were moving. He was going to the University of Texas on the GI Bill as a prelaw student. Perhaps in a year or two, Margarita would begin classes at the community college in Austin. *It depends*, she would say, flushing, and everyone knew she meant babies.

Because of Margarita, the ranchers and factory owners had resorted to traditional carrot-and-stick methods: Ranchers threw lavish public fiestas in the barrios and gave gifts of livestock. The factory owners—the shoe factory, the bottling plant, nearly all the manufacturers in the industrial park—instituted mandatory overtime until after the election to suppress meetings and block voting. The lone exception was the automobile upholstery plant, owned by Mr. Ira Rosen, who refused to throw in with other white big wheels because, he said, this was America, not goddamn Nazi Germany, and even the dogcatcher had a right to vote his conscience. Gossip held that he was actually revenging himself on the La Cienega Country

Club for the insult of denying his daughter, Shoshanna, privileges to its pristine blue swimming pool.

Whatever his reasons, it was known that Mr. Rosen was El Gato's chief financial backer. With Rosen's money and Margarita's charisma, El Gato was probably going to win himself a seat on the board. A consolidated Davy Crockett High was on the horizon.

Chuy was sitting on Pilar's front steps smoking a cigarette, which he hastily stubbed out as she came into the yard. He tucked the cigarette into his coat pocket and stood up. He was rail-thin as ever, and must be, Pilar decided, now truly old. His eyebrows had gone shaggy and gray.

"They called us from the sheriff's office in Fort Worth," he said before she could speak. "I just came to give you the message."

Once, she might have been surprised that he'd come instead of Romi. Not now. Romi didn't want to know Pilar anymore. Something must be very wrong for Chuy to come, but it did not change that fact. Nerves darted through her: the truck in the driveway, during the week. Romi looking her way.

"Is it José Alfredo?" she asked. Chuy had climbed the hill on foot, not driven up in his truck where the neighborhood might see him and wonder. "Did something happen to him?"

"I don't know exactly," Chuy said. He fixed his eyes above her head, looking past her at the pecan tree. "They just asked that you return the call. I brought you the telephone number."

Chuy handed her a folded slip of paper, careful not to let his fingers touch her hand. He didn't want to be here, probably didn't want to know what news there might be about her husband, if José Alfredo was still her husband. If he had ever been her husband. Or perhaps Chuy was afraid there might be belated questions about the boy. She couldn't let herself consider that.

"Why would they call you?"

"They said our number was the one they had for you. Maybe José Alfredo didn't know you had a phone."

Pilar let out a short laugh. "We didn't have one when he left. Why would he know I have one now?"

"They want you to call them," Chuy repeated, shuffling toward the road back to Caimanes. "Let me not take any more of your time. Good night."

⌐——·⬥·——⌐

It was Friday before she worked up the nerve to call the Tarrant County Sheriff's Office.

José Alfredo was dead. Forty-eight years old. Massive heart attack. A widowmaker, the deputy on the line called it. José Alfredo had collapsed at the Union Pacific train yard where he worked as a crewman. The Anglo deputy said he was sorry for her loss.

"It was over pretty fast," the deputy said. "He didn't suffer."

He gave her the number to the Union Pacific office, where another Anglo told her there was a life insurance policy to claim. A bank account. Probably a truck. She only had to present his death certificate, which she could get at the county clerk's office. He too said he was sorry for her loss.

"You'll need it for the funeral arrangements too," the man said.

"Yes," Pilar said. "Yes, I am aware of that. Thank you."

She hung up, then sank down at the kitchen table. Contrary to popular dicho, gone was not gone, at least not when it came to men leaving. Surely there ought to have been some proverb dedicated to the penumbratic limbo endured by the women they left. Strange that it was finally over, after nearly seventeen years. He'd been in Fort Worth all this time.

Perhaps José Alfredo had gotten the job a few months after he had left her. Yes, and he had written down the name of his wife as his beneficiary. It made her furious to consider that he might have had it in his mind to return some day, that it was a far-off notion, the act of forgiveness suspended, put away on a shelf like some discarded trinket, while he devoted himself to other pursuits.

And what then? What would she have told him? She went into her bedroom and opened the small top drawer of her dresser. There, pressed among the rough work socks and cotton panties, was the envelope she had received more than a year after he had gone. Plain white envelope, with the address clearly printed. No letter, just the pair of earrings she'd sold for Joselito's burial. It was how she had known he was in north Texas. The neatly printed, clear address.

She had clutched the earrings tight in her fist, feeling a hard plunge of anger. This was how he had won her, so many years ago. With his action. With his trinkets.

He had come to her village the Sunday after that first charreada, and he had come every Sunday for weeks afterward. He had not walked with the other young men at the plaza, shouting piropos at windows, chased away by dogs.

He had had a smooth dark face with a mustache thin as a penciled line, so that he looked like Pedro Infante, except for his complexion, which was velvety dark. Those Sundays he wore a dark jacket and bowtie that managed to be somber. He never spoke to anyone, but sat smoking, on a bench beside the fountain in the middle of the square. Pilar remembered sitting in the plaza with three classmates when he walked across the square and paid the acoustic trio to play "Ramito de Azahar."

José Alfredo had waited for her to see him do it. He sent the musicians to the opposite side of the plaza, not near the girls, which would have been too forward, but across the street from them, so that they might maintain their demureness by pretending that they did not notice the song. The musicians stood on the sidewalk in front of the market vendors that surrounded the square and played for her. Half a dozen heads peered out of the second-story windows, but Pilar sat with her face intent on her hands, pretending she did not hear, and so everyone knew it was for her.

Later that week, a girl in her catechism class told her there was a letter waiting for her at the post office. A stranger had said so, she did not know who. Pilar went and the postmaster said no, that there was nothing for Pilar. But her classmate insisted, and finally Pilar asked if there was anything for Orange Blossom.

"Yes," said the postmaster, smiling slyly. "This is for an Orange Blossom."

It was a piece of amber wrapped in paper. Every week José Alfredo gave her something small, something that could be easily tucked away or explained. A piece of chocolate. A card with a picture of an angel. Blue glass beads, unstrung.

He was not unlettered, but rough lettered. Un peón del rancho. Still, he must have known he could raise his eyes to her, she with her convent education and pretty clothes. It wasn't really such a leap. Someone would have told him she was una hija de la tierra. Illegitimate. It was only now, so many decades later, as she traced the whorls on the ancient Formica kitchen table, that she realized he'd sent these sweet things, cariñitos, because he couldn't write a love letter.

And after their children were dead, after he had left her, after he had been gone more than a year, when he had been gone so long that she had become this fettered, sickened thing, so long that she had left the last child he had given her abandoned in the bulrushes along the river so that José Alfredo, wherever he was, might feel the blow somehow, he had sent her this pair of earrings. His last remaining debt to her.

Pilar remembered the horrid, tormenting fury. He had given them back to her. She had thrown his son away. Yes, and as much pain as she had suffered, at that moment, she had not been sorry. Not one bit sorry, holding the earrings in her palm, with her pride and fury beating inside of her, discarded but not without dignity, she had thought then. Discarded, but not without dignity. I have returned something too, José Alfredo, though you do not know it. How bitter! How bitter, how savage. She had not been sorry. She had not.

The envelope, perhaps that was the real truth. The earrings were something to send, something to give weight to the paper, a thing, an excuse.

She held the envelope to the light. Yes, there it was, that terrible, silent truth. Those clear, bold letters of the return address—large, carefully printed letters. He had not been good at writing, any more than he'd been a good reader. He'd labored to write this return address.

That was the thing he had sent. The way for her to find him.

She saw this now, so clearly. He had entreated and she had not responded. He had never come back, but he had not forgotten her. She was his wife. Had always been, always would be. She was certain, finally.

She looked out the window at the sky. The stars were bright and cold between the bare branches of the pecan trees. José Alfredo had not known about the thing Pilar had done. Whatever place he had gone to, he knew it now.

"You didn't think you would die first, did you? You didn't see that," she murmured. Why was it easy to speak to him only when he was gone?

Pilar pulled on her coat. Whatever else, it was nearly time for the night shift at the shoe factory. She decided to walk back to the industrial park through the marshes at the edge of the river. It was messy, but faster than by the street. Here on the river, the world was full of the sounds of sundown. Animals were coming to drink at the river; she heard them creeping in the reeds around her, though she could not see them. Deer, probably.

There were cattails along the water's edge, huge and full of shadows, blotting out the sky above her as she walked among them. It was colder here, and the scent of muddy green water pressed heavy and dark in her throat, as strong as if she had eaten it. She made out her path—the narrow deer trail through the cane and the marsh.

She had come by this path to purge herself, for the silence, to pray for her dead husband. But now that she was here, she found herself unwilling—unable, really, to pray. What were the words? She did not remember them. She had not prayed since Joselito's novena and even then, she had said the words and not meant them. Her heart had been full of rage and suspicion. Her heart was full of sullen anger, still. She felt it, hard and unyielding, all the way through her. Who could pray? Who could ask for forgiveness? Not she.

I have wronged the boy, she reminded herself. I should be sorry. But when she tried to bring her mind to the wrong she had done, she found only the image of her husband as she had last seen him: his shadowy profile as he stood looking out the window from the darkness of their bedroom. Him saying, *Tell me what you might need* while he was thinking of leaving her.

The old knot of anger resurfaced. After all, the boy hadn't died. He was there, before her eyes, at all times. What other penance was there for her?

That night so long ago she had come to the crook in the river, where the cattails gave way to the sandy lip of the riverbank. There was a shallow crossing here, if one knew where to look. It was narrow, but men and women slipped back and forth across the border, shoes in hand, and hardly more than wet trouser cuffs to show for it. That had been the spot she had started from on that night. She had walked for hours into the darkness, picking her way along the river, with the moonrise tracking alongside her, until she got so far away from the town lights that it was only the bright silvery moonlight that allowed her to see where she set her feet. The mosquitoes had attacked viciously. She had stopped to smear her arms and face with mud.

She had then unwound him from the blue blanket and smeared the crown of his head with mud. She remembered how foul the mud was, dank and stinking, how she had plastered the fine black hair with her dirty fingers. He had not made a sound, only looked at her with large dark eyes that glittered in the moonlight like the surface of the river itself. And then she had dropped the corner of the blanket over his face, replaced him in the bundle on her back, and kept walking.

Long into the night, far into the ranchland outside of La Cienega, she had carried this boy. There had been a spot where the river swelled and became rough. She had heard its white noise long before she arrived. She had taken him in her arms and waded out into the middle of the river.

Deep enough to plant herself, deep enough to freeze her breasts, deep enough so that she hadn't known whether she would get out again. That had not bothered her. That had seemed a reasonable price to pay to have her way.

She had lifted the blanket once more but had not been able to cast him into the water. She lurched out of the river, arms raised high, cold to her bones, trembling not with the chill but with the wild fear of having nearly stepped off a cliffside. She left the baby nestled in the bulrushes on the riverbank. Even now, a horrible self-loathing thundered through her. A coward, leaving the little mite for the animals in the brush. Better that she had flung herself into the river. But she had been too weak, too full of darkness.

A week afterward Pilar overheard two women talking in the produce aisle of the Piggly Wiggly, about the baby Chuy Muñoz had plucked out of the river.

"River riding for stray cows," one woman said, "and finding a baby!"

"Oh, they find people all the time," said the other.

"Not alive," said the first. "But this one. Why, they say he hasn't stopped screeching."

"Well, why not," said her friend. "I'd be mad too." They both laughed.

It wasn't true. Chuy had not found the boy. It had been Romi, of course.

Good-hearted, stubborn, metiche Romi, who kept coming by, even when Pilar said go away over and over. Who kept asking, *What will you do?* Who was troubled, not by the fact that Pilar got a job at the shoe factory, but that she'd withdrawn so completely from everyone and everything in Caimanes, would not come off Loma Negra except for work, and even then, would only take the route through the marshes. Away from the eyes of the neighborhood.

Romi, who'd gotten so angry she'd yelled and yelled when Pilar would not go to the doctor. *It's not a baby*, Pilar had said through the locked screen door. *It's cancer. I'm dying. Go away.* Romi, on the other side of the door, staring and silent for a full minute. *Diosito mío, Pilar. You are out of your mind.*

Romi, who kept coming back for months, when no one else in Caimanes cared anymore, when Pilar no longer answered her knock.

Romi, so good at spying and following, even on foot. That night she must have trailed Pilar for hours. She burst out of the thicket of bamboo, running flat out, understanding, finally, what was happening.

"What have you done?" she panted. "What have you done?"

"Nothing," Pilar gasped. "He's there. He's there on the ground. I didn't do anything."

At the sound of her voice the baby let out a furious wail. Romi pushed past her, rough and unheeding.

"¡Asesina!" Romi hissed, shoving her hard. She was strong. She was so strong, always. Pilar fell heavily to the ground. "Get away from the child!"

Romi had kept Pilar's secret, but she never spoke to Pilar again. Never so much as looked her way. She took the boy for herself. The preposterous story, Chuy finding the child on a river-riding expedition, that was stuff and nonsense. Whispers went around about possible unwed mothers. Whispers went around about Pilar, whose husband had so abruptly left her. Whispers, because she and Romi were suddenly not friends. Whispers and conjecture, forever following Pilar.

What was true, everybody in the barrio knew it, was that old Doctor Mireles had filled out a birth certificate for a home birth. Julio Muñoz, son of Jesús and Romelia Muñoz. Citizen of the United States.

Even now, Pilar could only think on the edges of him: the baby with a head full of mud, the blue blanket's soft, rustling weight. That unnamed baby might have been hers. But the boy, Julio, was not and could never be.

Now she stood in the darkness, in the marshes, finding there was nothing of herself that she could offer up for her own deliverance. José Alfredo had never returned. She could see, now, that he had done his own penance. Her bold charro had condemned himself to railyard work the rest of his life. He'd probably never touched a horse again. And their last boy had grown up another woman's son. She was not sorry that José Alfredo had not come home. What if he had? She would not have told him any of it, never, though he might have lain beside her every night until God took him.

She broke out in a light, sour perspiration, all over her body. There it was, there, within the deep well of terror and of relief, finally, her prayer. Thank you, Jesus, for his absence. Thank you, Jesus. Because I couldn't have told him. I couldn't have. Thank you for taking that cup from my lips. I am humbled, my Lord. I am humbled.

She gathered up her rosary beads, the first prayer on her lips, and swiftly, another thought came to her. Could she pray to the Son, when she could not even ask the Mother to intercede for her? Could she ask the mercy of the Son when she had had none for her own son? Could she ask the Father, when she had betrayed her own husband, though he did not know? No, she could not.

I have damned myself, she thought. Why didn't I know it before? Why only now?

There was a heavy boom in the distance, followed by sirens. That was to do with the voting, she was sure. The election was tonight.

A few minutes later, she heard wild crashing within the wall of giant cane surrounding her. Men running, by the ragged breathing. She stood stock-still, uncertain where they would burst out. But they didn't appear— instead, there was a desperate thrashing and the snapping of broken cane. A voice cried out in pain. She could tell that he was young and afraid.

"C'mon, vato, get up! Move your ass!" a hoarse voice gasped, equally young and scared.

"Pinche Zero, I'm stuck! C'mon man, help me!"

She heard them grunt and struggle. The one must have gotten caught up in the marsh mud. She was surprised they hadn't both gotten stuck sooner, the way they'd charged through the cane. There were headlights now, glowing in the distance. Other voices, distant, but approaching.

"My shoe's stuck in the mud!" said the first voice.

"Leave it!" hissed the other. "We gotta get the fuck outta here!"

They crashed through the bamboo into the sand. There were two of them, both scratched and bleeding: a big boy, stout and brown, with a mop of black hair thick as tentacles across his dirty face, and a smaller one, whip-thin, his pants slathered with fresh mud. It was Julio. He limped along, held up by the bigger boy.

"You can't put weight on it?" the big one asked him.

Julio grimaced. "I'm trying."

"Oh shit!" said the big boy, seeing Pilar. They both scrambled toward the cane.

"Don't go back," she said. "You hear them, don't you?"

"Madre santísima," whispered the big one, staring at her. He knew the stories about her. He feared her.

Julio said nothing. She could see his face, under the mud, drawn with pain. The smell of the mud on him, familiar and horrible. Wet and green. She could feel it again, cold slime on her fingers.

Pilar fixed her eyes on the big one. "I know where it's shallow. You can carry him over it."

"We don't need your help," Julio hissed, eyes slitted in pain. "I don't want anything from you."

Someone had told him. It wouldn't have been Romi. Maybe Chuy. Chuy who could not look at her, even when delivering the news about José

Alfredo. *You don't know all of it,* she almost said, nearly opened her mouth to plead with him. *You don't know what happened.*

He spat at her. Though it didn't touch her, it was enough.

She trembled, feeling the power of his hatred. Ever after, the memory of Julio's dirty, scornful face in the moonlight, oh, it was José Alfredo's finger pressed to her heart. *Did you forgive me all those years? No. You did not. Recoges lo que siembras, mi amor.*

"Listen to me, please. Please," she said, stepping back, giving him space. He must get away. That was the only thing she could do for him. She pointed at the spot in the river. "That's the foot crossing, just past the bend."

"Bullshit," Julio said to the other boy. "We can hide in the cane."

Shouts carried across the air. There were lights flickering in the distance, flashlights.

"Vato, we gotta go," Zero said. He snatched up Julio and bounded toward the bend of the riverbank, clattering stones into the water. Pilar marveled at how very strong he must be.

It was not hard to find the trail the boys had made. They had smashed their way through in a panic. Pilar followed it down to the place where Zero had hauled Julio out of the mud. There was the dark dimple, oozing wet, already filling over. If the shoe were there, no one would find it. But she looked, carefully, patiently, ignoring the staccato light of flashlights in the cane.

She found the shoe by stepping on it. A canvas sneaker, black with mud. She slipped it beneath her blouse and ducked onto one of the deer trails. It was another twenty minutes before she came across a police officer. By that time, she was out of the cane, on the dirt path to the factory. It was blocked, but the officer merely waved her away. She was nothing. Just a middle-aged woman in the coveralls of a factory worker.

"Go on home," the officer said. "The factories are closed tonight."

He said nothing more and Pilar did not press him. At home, she examined the shoe. Beneath the mud it was a red canvas sneaker. On one side etched in permanent marker, a black cat face, like the ones drawn all over town. Romi's son was a Black Cat. One of those agitators that spray-painted buildings and smashed car windows.

In the morning Pilar found out the shoe factory was closed, by police order. Felix "El Gato" Gutierrez had been killed in the parking lot. Killed by arsonists, or at least, killed by the instigation of the arsonists. No one was quite clear on the facts.

Fights had broken out in the parking lot of the shoe factory just before the night shift. El Gato's supporters had gathered in the parking lot to convince—or harass, depending on the version of accounts—the laborers to leave work and vote; police and factory security entered the fray, citing the fact that the parking lot was the private property of the shoe company. The shouting became violence. Then the explosions happened.

Someone had firebombed a car and the first floor of the factory itself. Here again, the stories swirled into rumors. The car had exploded and El Gato had been caught in the head by a piece of metal, or someone had clubbed him with a piece of metal. Or he had been killed by the police. There had been twenty arrests, and six people hospitalized, but no one knew whether El Gato had been killed accidentally or murdered. What was known was this: something had struck him full in the face, hard enough to cave in his forehead and one eye. His Coke bottle glasses were found in pieces around him.

"He wasn't even supposed to be there," said the factory foreman, shaking his head. "He came out at the last minute just to rile them up. I'm sorry, but it's the truth."

People argued conspiracies for both sides. It could have been the vandalizing Black Cats, setting fires to prevent the factory from forcing the night shift. But why would they firebomb El Gato? On the other hand, could it have been staged by the factory owners themselves? After all, who else would benefit from fire insurance? An opportunity to get rid of El Gato was probably too good to pass up.

The next few days, things changed rapidly. The shoe factory closed, permanently. The high schools were officially consolidated. Pilar wondered if Julio had been discovered, if indeed he was involved, as she assumed he must be. She hid his shoe in José Alfredo's old garage and then regretted going in there. Somehow, she could not bear to look at José Alfredo's long-abandoned things now that she knew he was dead.

The last surprise was Romi. She appeared a few nights later, long after dark. She came on foot, by the hillside path, which had the advantage of being the most inconspicuous, but was rocky caliche and steep enough to have been a feat for most women pushing sixty. Romi's strength was undiminished. She did not even appear to be breathing hard as she stood on the porch waiting for Pilar to answer her knock.

"Don't turn on the porch light," she said when Pilar came to the screen door.

"What is it?"

"I came to thank you," Romi said. "For showing him the way across."

"I'm surprised he told you."

"Eliseo did. He had to say something, bringing Julio home like that. He said they were just coming home from the movies, taking a shortcut through the marsh. That's how Julio got stuck."

Pilar did not ask about the boy's leg and Romi did not offer details. What Romi said was, "They're blaming the Black Cats for what happened at the factory. I'm afraid of where Julio was."

"I couldn't tell you," Pilar said. She didn't mention the red sneaker in her garage. That would ruin Romi's life. Her conscience might make her turn in her own son for the crime, and she'd have to live with having betrayed him, or she would not turn him in and live with the knowledge that he, or someone in that gang of Black Cats, had accidentally killed Felix Gutierrez. This way, it was only a suspicion. Only a rumor. Rumors weren't real.

"My Chuy is a stay-at-home man," Romi said, when it was clear Pilar was not going to speak about it. She shook her head, stepping off the porch into the yard. "But it didn't rub off, I guess."

Again, Pilar said nothing. What did Romi expect? After all, José Alfredo had turned out to be a wanderer. They were silent a long time.

"My husband is dead," Pilar said. It felt strange, after seventeen years, that they could still discuss their men, still keep each other's secrets.

"Well, the wait is over, then," said Romi, in the blunt way Pilar remembered. "Where was he?"

"Fort Worth. He was a railroad man."

"Did he remember you?"

"Yes, he did," said Pilar. It was hard to say, but she said it. "He left me everything he had. I'm going north in a few days to arrange things."

"Do you not think," Romi said finally, "that you should find another place to live now? You have the means."

Pilar said nothing. Romi, for all her directness, would not look at her. After a moment she said, "One day, make your peace with my son. Do it after I'm dead."

"I don't think so."

"Don't give yourself more regrets, Pili. Haven't you learned anything?" Romi stalked unhesitatingly into the brush. Pilar knew the darkness did not bother her in the least. Romi had always been one who was sure-footed in the light and the dark both.

Chapter Thirteen

Gritonazo

LULU MUÑOZ, 1994

After Thanksgiving, there was no getting around it: my quinceañera was on the horizon. February.

Tía Yoli wanted to do a Disney theme. She liked *Aladdin*, especially for the song "A Whole New World." She had come over to my house one Friday night. She had a party supply catalogue with her, showing all the themed sets of napkins and decorations. Where do you even find a catalogue like that? Seriously barf.

"She's not wearing a crop top and harem pants," my dad said, frowning at the Jasmine section of the catalogue. I didn't know how many my dad had already had, but he had the slow, drowsy expression I recognized as Dad's Hard Buzz Face.

"What about *Beauty and the Beast?*"

"If I still had Gonzy, maybe," I said. Gonzo would have made a great Beast. He'd been one of those thick-furred shepherds with dark-red markings. I didn't care if my dad got mad. I wasn't pretending not to miss my dog. Not for him. Not for anybody. "Maybe all the escorts can be dogs."

"Lulu, be serious," Tía Yoli said.

"Disney is generic. How many people pick Belle? That's why it's in a catalogue."

"What about a western theme?" my dad said. "It'll be easy to get cowboy hats and boots."

"No," my tía and I said at the same time.

My dad let out an exaggerated sigh. "Everybody's so picky."

"Julio, it's a debutante party," Tía Yoli said. "It's supposed to be special. Do you even want to do this?"

"I'm okay with not doing it," I said quickly. "Really, it's fine."

His eyes went flat. "Goddammit, Lucha. We already talked about this. You're having a quince. How's it going to look if I don't have one for you? What am I going to tell everyone, that you're too cool?"

"I didn't say I was too cool." I stared at the kitchen counter, trying to focus on the grainy pattern, trying to keep my mouth shut. I don't like talking to him when he's drinking. He wasn't slurring, though, or acting overtly weird, so I guess that's why my tía didn't notice. Maybe she did and just didn't care.

"Lulu, will you please work with me?" my tía asked, rubbing her temples. She pushed the catalogue across the table at me. "We need to pick something so we can order all the stuff from one place. It's easier."

I flipped the pages, hating everything. So many princesses and fairy-tale types. Cinderella. Snow White. The Little Mermaid. Even Rapunzel, with hair-related accoutrements. Wait, there was something that didn't make me want to hurl. Masquerade theme. The masks were vivid and beautiful. A blue one covered in peacock plumes. A jeweled red one in the shape of cat eyes. Black satin masks, long and swooping, to cover half the face. Marina would love this theme. It was expensive too.

"This one," I said, tapping my finger on masquerade. "I like this one."

"How many damas are you planning to have?" my dad asked, really sour. But hey, this was his idea, so fuck him.

Before my tía could open her mouth, I said two, because it was the lowest number I could get away with. Two damas, each with an escort. Including me and my escort, that was already six people.

"Okay," my dad agreed. I'm sure he was realizing how much the masks and dresses would cost, maybe even what a giant pain in the ass getting a half dozen kids to practice choreography for a few weeks was going to be. "Who?"

"Marina," I said. "For sure."

"And Zero's daughter," my dad said. Rosalie was only twelve. I tried not to make a face.

"Julio," Tía Yoli said, frowning. She didn't look irritable anymore. No, there was concern on her face. It was weird to see that expression. "Let her choose her friends."

I shrugged. "Marina's my friend."

I didn't really know people I'd feel good asking. I wasn't going to ask Carla or Ximena, because I didn't even like them much. No way would I ask Ernie. My dad would want to know how I knew him, and Ernie couldn't fake being a mathlete or some other nerd type. He was one hundred percent barrio Mexican. Ernie could dress in polo shirts and stupid khakis all day long (not that he ever would) and my dad would still recognize his own. Jorge was absolutely out of the question. Olmec was maybe okay, but he'd never say yes unless Jorge and Ernie were in it too.

"What about Carlos?" I asked. If my cousin said yes, I could ask Marina to ask her boyfriend Art to escort her. Then we'd only need someone for Rosalie. "He could learn the dance over Christmas break and just come down the weekend of the quince."

"That's a good idea," Yoli said. "I'll ask him."

"No," my dad said. "Pick someone else."

This time it was my tía who bridled up. "What's your problem?"

"I'm not having a queer in my daughter's quince," my dad said. "No way."

Sometimes, it's just too much. The hypocrisy. The lying. The fucking double standards, all the time. There he was, actually drunk, passing judgment on someone who was probably a better person every day than my dad ever had been. I couldn't keep my mouth shut.

"You run around with married women and drink all the time. It's okay for me to be around that, but oh, my gay primo, he can't be in the quinceañera? I'd rather dance with him than you, anytime."

My dad popped out of the chair. "I'm your father! You don't talk to me like that!"

"She's just telling the truth," Yoli said in an even voice. "Sorry if you don't want to hear it."

"The truth," my dad sneered. He wasn't one to take anything. "Charlie isn't cheating. You'd rather lie about him than tell people your son is a joto. Charlie isn't putting up with it. Good for him. I'm not either."

"You know what," my tía said, getting up. Her voice was deadly cold. "Find someone else to plan your daughter's quince."

My dad let out a barky laugh, like that was totally hilarious. I hate that laugh so much. I hated him for it. He couldn't ever just stop. Never.

"Lulu," Tía Yoli said to me. The stillness in her voice was terrible. "I'm staying through the new year to take care of Mom's house. You can still come over after school. But I can't plan your quinceañera. I'm sorry."

"I understand," I said, my lips feeling unaccountably trembly. She was going to stand by her kid. I got that. I respected the hell out of it. It still hurt. Even though I didn't want a quince at all, it hurt. Nobody was on my side, ever. It was just me, on my own. Like always.

"Keep the catalogue."

"Yeah, thanks," I said. I didn't know how this quince was going to happen without Yoli. I didn't know anything about planning an event like this, but even her dropping out, that wasn't going to stop my dad from absolutely demanding that we still go ahead. What a nightmare. My brain was like, nope, nope, nope, not going there right now.

Tía Yoli picked up her purse and walked out of the house. My dad stared after her. I guess after years of Grandma taking up the slack all the time, it was hard for him to believe someone would tell him no.

"Just pick whatever from that catalogue," he said, slapping his credit card on the kitchen counter. "I'm gonna be in my workshop. Go ahead and order a pizza."

Well, fuck my dad, and fuck Yoli too. I waited until I could hear the music going in his workshop. Then I called Pilar and asked her if she could help me plan my quince. She said yes.

As usual, Pilar asked no questions when I showed up at her house on Monday, an hour earlier than usual. She was wearing navy-blue sweatpants and a T-shirt, no makeup. But only because she was doing lunges from one side of the front yard to the other. I watched her do two full back-and-forths before she stopped.

"Man, I couldn't make it one time across the yard," I said. She was impressive.

"Yes, you could. You're young." She brushed my face with her fingers, surprising me. "But you won't be fourteen forever. Remember that."

"That's why I'm here. Quince plans." I held up the catalogue my tía had left with me.

"Of course. So the main things are the dresses, the place, and the food," she panted, settling herself onto the grass and stretching. "There's a list on the kitchen table. I want you to take it home with you. Mark off when you complete something on it."

"Cool." I brought back the piece of yellow lined notepaper, scanning it. *What is your budget?* in big letters at the top of the page. A list in her small, precise handwriting. Information for a seamstress, caterer, music, venue. Each had suggestions and phone numbers.

"I would say Villa Verde is the nicest venue in town. If that's the one you want you need to call by the end of the week," Pilar said. "Reserve it with a credit card. Do you know how to do that?"

"Yeah, I use my dad's card all the time. No problem."

"And you picked your theme from that?" she asked, pointing at the catalogue.

"There's one that's okay."

"Bring it. I have some fabric samples to show you too."

I followed her into the kitchen. I'd only asked her maybe three days ago. This was a lot of work. She must have spent the whole weekend on planning.

"Let's see the dress styles and pick a fabric."

"Yeah, okay," I sighed. I sat down across from her at the table, opened the catalogue to the masquerade pages. "This one."

"Oh yes, beautiful," Pilar murmured, running her finger down the glossy page. "And you're going to require masks of all the guests?"

"I can't make people wear them. But the escorts and girls, for sure."

"You can have some, complimentary for the guests. They can pick one up when they sign the registry as they come in."

"I guess," I said. "It seems like a bigger expense. The theme is just supposed to include the kids in the quince, right?"

"Oh Lulu, we can order some plainer masks in bulk, probably get a discount." Her face was awake, a little like when we'd thrown shit at Margarita's house. She spread her hands out, her light eyes glowing. "This way it'll be more fun. More interesting. A real masquerade ball. Nobody else in this boring town would do it."

"That's true," I said. "Marina did Old Hollywood, but mostly around here it's princess or western themes."

"So tacky," Pilar said. "Yours should be unique. Unforgettable."

"Okay," I said. It did sound cool. Besides, at least I knew I could trust her taste.

"What about these samples?" She laid several fabric swatches on the table. I immediately rejected the pearly pink, because no way. Marina would hate the emerald green on her complexion, so not that either. I slid it aside. That left a glossy black satin, a deep red, and two metallic ones, silver and gold.

"The silver, I think," I said, rubbing it between my thumb and forefinger. "I'd like the black, but my dad would never say yes. Same for the red. He says some colors are *too adult*."

Pilar fixed me with the oddest expression. Ernie was right. She really did have crazy eyes. "If you could have the red or black, which would you prefer?"

"I mean, if I could? Red, but not this red. A red velvet, just like Armand wore in that new vampire movie." The funny thing was, I'd never have admitted that to anyone else, not even Marina. It was dorky, wanting something that goth. Pilar wouldn't judge me though. "One of those sweeping gowns, you know?"

"Oh yes," she said, nodding. "There were good costumes in that movie."

"You saw it?"

"You said it was good," Pilar replied. "So I went."

She pulled her hair out of her exercise ponytail, shook it out so it fanned across her shoulders. She turned back to the catalogue, brows drawn down, carefully marking the item numbers for the different mask styles. I imagined her alone in the darkened theater, watching the silver screen with the same intensity. Because I liked the movie and it mattered to her. "Anyways, I can't show up in crushed red velvet," I said. "That would be crazy expensive. Besides, where would we even find that?"

"Well, what about gold?"

"I like the silver better."

"Okay," Pilar said, tapping a French-manicured nail against her chin. "You want silver, so the other girls wear a light jewel tone. Maybe blue? An azure."

"I like that," I said.

"I thought you would," she said, smiling. "We have similar tastes."

"Yeah? What did you wear at your quince?"

"I didn't have one," she said, a chill falling over her like a veil. She swept all the fabric swatches into a pile and dumped them back in the paper sack.

"Maybe you could help me about the seamstress," I said, pretending not to notice she was angry. She had those silent flashes of anger a lot. I knew that by now. I also knew whatever she was mad about had nothing to do with me. She wasn't going to explain it, ever. "I've never gone to one."

"Don't worry about the dress," she said, quick as a wink excited again. "I'll do that. There's a woman across the border. I know just what you want."

It sounds crazy, but Pilar was the only person I'd have trusted about the dress. Yoli wouldn't have cared enough. Marina would have wanted something that was her own taste. Even Grandma Romi, much as I loved her, hadn't had Pilar's keen eye or creativity. Pilar only cared about beauty. She had a talent for it. If she was in charge of my dress, it would be absolutely gorgeous and my style without me having to do any work.

"Come to my bedroom," Pilar said, looking me over with frank eagerness. "Let me take your measurements."

Organizing the party wasn't the half of it. The quince was turning out to be grounds for all kinds of drama. Marina had asked Art to be her escort and he had said yes. That left me with one boy to ask for Rosalie and a fill-in-the-blank for me. I did what seemed like a good idea at the time, but turned out to be the dumbest thing ever: I asked César Allen if he'd be in my quinceañera court.

"I'm going to Mazatlán for Christmas," he objected in Spanish.

"It's not until February."

He heaved this huge, exaggerated sigh. "I was in like a hundred of them when I was fifteen and I'm sick of it. I did my time all sophomore year."

"Come on, man," I said. "How many stupid homework assignments have I let you copy? You owe me."

"You're signing up for Physics II next semester, right? Because you're doing my homework for the rest of the year."

I agreed. Then I made the mistake of telling Marina that César was willing to be one of the escorts. Geez. Marina told Art that my dad said he couldn't be in my quince. She'd been dating Art since the end of last year, but she'd much rather have César as her escort. So then Art was mad at me. When Ernie found out César was in the quince, he was mad too. Only he didn't say he was mad. He just stopped talking to me about anything except for band stuff.

"Why did you do that?" I asked Marina. She and I were at lunch, having terrible cafeteria pizza. I was pissed. I couldn't believe she had made such a huge mess.

"You said you don't like César that way," she said, making her eyes round and innocent, the way she does when she pretends she doesn't understand some pervy joke or that no one smells her fart. "I mean, you don't, right?"

"You know I don't. That's not the point. Ernie thinks I'm a snob because I didn't ask him, but I asked Mr. Fresa. Now I have to find another dude since Art won't be in it."

"Well, why *don't* you ask Ernie?" Marina said. "He'd say yes, even if he's mad right now. Duh."

"This is totally crappy, Mari," I said. "Everybody's pissed at me."

"Hey, I've been having your back all month when y'all are at Pilar's house practicing. I just want a chance with César."

"You could have told me before you did it."

"I didn't know you were going to ask César until after I asked Art. Sorry."

Olmec walked up, stoned. He swigged a Dr Pepper, his little eyes all curled up and squinty from smoking weed.

"What's up," he said, settling at our table. "Are your bandmates even invited to your fifteen, or are you too good for us?"

"Shut up. I can't believe Ernie's mad. It's not even my fault."

"She's right," Marina said. "I'm the one to blame."

"I don't really care," Olmec snorted. "Jorge and I will crash it anyways."

"Yeah, but now I 911 need some guys for the court. Would you do it?"

"And Ernie?" Olmec said slyly. "I've seen y'all mugging down. Why didn't you ask him?"

"Fuck off," I said. No way I was going to let him make me feel like a sucia.

"Girl, calm down," Olmec said. "I'm just saying you should ask him since you're already with him. He told me he's taking you to Selena."

"Oh wow. In your quince *and* taking you to Selena," Marina said, clicking her tongue. "That's serious relationship stuff."

"Oh my God," I snapped. "I don't even have all the court yet. I don't have a date yet. I basically haven't done anything."

"Hey, don't stress," Olmec said. "I will totally be an escort. Ask Ernie too."

"I mean, if you're in it I kind of have to," I said glumly. If César and Olmec were in the quince and I didn't ask Ernie, he'd stop being my friend. I was just going to have to find some pretext for how I knew him. At least Olmec was in advanced classes with me. Maybe I could say he and Ernie were relatives.

"Anyways," Olmec said, "I have news."

The guy from Chaparral Disco Rodeo had agreed to let us play. The gig was December 17, the weekend before school let out for break. We were going on last and we'd have to play at least two norteñitas.

"Jorge agreed to that?" Marina scoffed. "Isn't he punk or die?"

"He just wants to get onstage. He doesn't care."

"We don't have an accordion player," I objected. "And it's Chaparral."

Chaparral Disco Rodeo is a hardcore norteño bar. There was no way we could go onstage without an accordion player. The crowd would eat us alive. That's like playing a rock show without a guitarist.

"Trust me," Olmec said. "I know a guy."

"Are we gonna dress kicker and everything? I don't own a pair of cowboy boots."

"I got that," Marina said. "My red ones will fit you. But what's her cut of the gig?"

"The money's bad. It doesn't matter." Olmec scooped the limp pizza square off my tray and bit into it. "Just start practicing some gritos."

"Are you serious?"

"Don't tell me you can't do it. Are you a Mexican or not?"

"Can you?" I demanded.

Olmec crammed what was left of my pizza into his mouth. He gulped, washed it down with his mostly full can of Dr Pepper. Belched hard.

He threw back his head and let out a piercing cry that cut through the lunchroom. It was a thing that erupted from his open mouth like the peal of an ambulance siren. It went on for at least fifteen seconds. A primal scream from the basement of his soul. It even had the warbling "ha-ha-hayyyy" kicks as he wound down. It was a real Mexican grito.

"No mames." Marina goggled. "I can't believe you had that in you."

All over the cafeteria, people were cheering and throwing their own gritos. You can't send up a grito in a crowd of Mexicans, because hearing a badass grito is like seeing someone yawn and then you have to yawn. Pretty soon gritos were flying everywhere. The rancheritos and the fresas actually got into a contest of intense vocal acrobatics, throwing gritos at each other's tables until the lunch-duty teachers shushed everyone.

"Let's go, Mr. Tovar," one of them said to Olmec. "This is not your lunch period. Office. Now."

Olmec grinned at me. "See y'all later. But seriously, practice."

"He thinks he's so suave," Marina said, watching Olmec swagger along to the principal's office. "Wait til he finds out his quince partner is a twelve-year-old."

Olmec is right. I cannot throw a real grito. But my dad has schooled me on Mexican music forever. That has to count for something.

"Everybody knows Ritchie Valens," he tells me when he's playing early Chicano rock 'n' roll. "But what about the Royal Jesters? What about Sir Douglas Quintet? And look at Domingo Samudio! Vato had to wear a turban and go by Sam the Sham."

Even if no one else cared, my dad cared. He's the reason I know Freddy Fender's real name is Baldemar Huerta.

That evening, I went into my dad's record collection to do some research. It seemed ridiculous that Pink Vomit was suddenly going conjunto. Would we be known as El Vómito Rosado del Norte? Actually, El Vómito sounded totally kick-ass. But something I know from Ernie is that versatility is critical for any musician. It's stupid to be like Jorge and only like a certain kind of music, because you can't grow as a musician that way. You'll stay stuck, limiting yourself.

Ernie plays for his family's band, Conjunto Vega. That doesn't mean he can't thrash with the best of them. He's the best guitarist in school. This is a fact—he is. Because he comes from a family of musicians. But he doesn't only play guitar. He can play trombone, trumpet, bass, piano, and drums. He plays all styles, and that makes him such a good musician. Because he just knows so many different things. It's all skill sets.

Besides, my favorite bands, the thing they have in common is that they're mutable. Selena is Tejano, but she isn't really, she's more than that. That's what makes her amazing. She has an entire career singing in Spanish when she doesn't even speak the language. She does disco, she does pop, she does total ranchera. She does everything.

So no, I did not turn my nose up at norteño—but could Pink Vomit really be a crossover band, actually bicultural? Luckily, dad had stacks and stacks of albums. His range is blues, soul, lots and lots of rock, from the early fifties up to the mid-eighties, country music so old it's properly country and western, and Mexican music. So much Mexican music.

My dad's music collection has a specific kind of order, more about his format choices than anything else. Everything from the fifties to the mid-eighties is on vinyl. The records are in the closet, with the ones he doesn't listen to a lot way in the back. He has some trash 8-tracks on the top shelves from that brief time period in the seventies when he thought he was the coolest cat with the 8-track player in his truck. Cassettes everywhere, not just in the closet. Shoe boxes full of them, all over the bedroom. Cassette tapes are what he still listens to even though lately, he's been getting into CDs.

The CDs are by his stereo. That stereo is a monster with a record player, two tape decks, and a CD player. The speakers are each four feet tall. My plan was to listen to records all evening and decide which songs I could probably learn, and then start making tapes during the weekend. I planned to make another tape of just songs with good gritos, so I could study them. That could be anything, even mariachi, which always has at least one or two members whose job it is to perform some wildly herculean grito soaring over the sound of the entire ensemble.

My dad came in around eight and found me rummaging around. I knew he would. I'm always fiddling with his music. This is one thing we never fight about: my dad loves when I listen to his music, because he loves to talk to me about the bands. He taught me how not to leave smudges and handle the records carefully when I was a little kid. I love to handle them—so shiny, even the old ones. My dad keeps them in good condition.

"Los Relámpagos del Norte," he said when he heard the music. "Are you sick or something?"

"Marina says I need to give it a chance," I lied.

"She likes these guys?"

"Yeah," I blurted. Los Relámpagos del Norte are one of the greatest norteño bands of all time. But I wanted to kick myself. There was no way my dad would buy that some ninth-grade girl was into a Mexican band that broke up in the seventies. I should have said Marina's dad liked them. But why would she want me to listen to her dad's music?

"Good choice," my dad said, in this thoughtful serious way. He wasn't listening to me. He was mulling. "I have Ramón Ayala's album from right after they broke up too. Somewhere."

He went into the back of the closet. I could hear him, muffled, still talking.

"I have both Cornelio's and Ramón's first solo albums," he said. "You know they went on to have careers after they broke up."

"Yes," I said. I have heard this story from him so often. How Ramón and Cornelio were the dynamic duo—Cornelio singing and playing bajo sexto and Ramón shredding on the accordion. But then Ramón stole

Cornelio's wife. Ramón Ayala started his own band, Los Bravos del Norte, and Cornelio went on to have a solo career.

My dad could not resist repeating that Cornelio released the smash hit "Tu Traición" right after it happened. I smothered the urge to say, yeah, yeah, you told me already. Because then I might get booted from his room.

He emerged from the closet with two records. "I still can't believe you're listening to this."

But I was ready for that. "Today in the cafeteria some guys were being stupid, throwing gritos. Like a lot. I said they sounded dumb, but Marina said it was dumb that I didn't know how to do it."

"Oh," my dad said. "Oh, okay. So you want to know how to do it."

"Maybe," I said, waiting for him to laugh at me. But he didn't.

"We used to do that in high school," he said, grinning. "The gringos hated it de amadre. But you know it was right when the high school got desegregated."

"Segregation ended in the fifties, Dad. *Brown v. Board of Education*."

He grunted. "Not in La Cienega. It ended when they consolidated the high school in 1970. I was a senior."

"That's insane."

"We used to throw gritos all the time, just to stick it to them. Principal Thompson hated me," he said. Then he frowned. "But you better not be doing it and getting in trouble."

"I won't," I said. "I'm not in a fight for civil rights."

"We already fought for you," he said in that lecturing tone he always used whenever he talks about The Movement. "That's why you go to school and those gringo pelados don't give you shit. You don't know how it was."

"Yeah, thanks, Dad," I said. I couldn't help rolling my eyes. "You're a hero."

"Do you want to learn this, or not?" he demanded.

"Yes."

"Then stop mouthing off," he said. "And put that record away."

I took off the Relámpagos album. He went back into the closet for some other records. I heard him say güerca malcriada, which pissed me off. No, I am not spoiled. But also, if I am a malcriada, then he's the one to blame, because who raised me? He did.

I wanted to learn gritos, so I shut my mouth. But I did not say sorry.

He came out of the closet again, still looking testy. This time he had albums by Mariachi Vargas de Tecalitlán, *Canciones de Mi Padre*, by Linda Ronstadt, and one by Vicente Fernández. He set them on the stereo.

"Okay," he said. "Before we put anything on, let's practice. There's three basic types."

"Okay," I said.

"There's your rolling r grito," he said. He made a trilling sound that flickered quick as a whiplash. "Rrrrrrrrrr—ah!"

"That one is easy," I said. I mimicked him several times.

"Okay, okay, good. Just remember the note has to go high at the end. Exploding out, but high."

I did it again. He nodded in approval. "Yeah, that's good. I don't know why you can't speak Spanish, your rolling r's are perfect."

"What's the next one?" I asked, ignoring him. This is another of his rants: he can't understand why his own daughter isn't perfectly fluent in Spanish. Whatever.

"The classic ay-ay-ay," he said. "The number of ays depends on the song, but your ay should be deep. And that one, you have to sing it."

He put on the Mariachi Vargas album, set it so "Cielito Lindo" came blaring out of the speakers, then lifted the needle. "Okay so we're gonna warm up by singing along with them."

"I don't know the words," I said. This was not an admission I would have made to anyone else. "Cielito Lindo" is the cliché Mexican song. It's the number one mariachi request from tourists at Mexican restaurants.

My dad pursed his lips. "Well, still, you can chime in at the chorus. It's ay-ay-ay-ay. Or just watch me a couple of times."

"Okay," I said.

My dad set the needle back on the record. Mariachi is beautiful and operatic. Not just anyone can sing it. I can't say my dad was amazing, but he wasn't bad. I already knew he had a goodish tenor. I've heard him sing lots of times when he's drinking. But I don't know, watching him do it so I could learn something, it felt different.

He shut his eyes. That's how you know when someone is not goofing off, like they are really feeling that feeling. And when he got to the ay-ay-ay-ay part, every ay was stretched out, wide and soaring, and just fearless. He didn't care who was listening, only me, but he sang it like it would not have mattered who was in the room. It was just him and that song, and his bold voice trying to match the record and honestly, almost getting there.

I went weepy and angry, because he was making me remember how much I miss him and it hurt. It hurt like an old bruise you thought was gone, but someone touches it and you're wrecked. I watched the muscles in his throat work, the round O of his mouth, the song leaping out. Any minute this bubble was going to pop, but right now, singing, he was more my dad than he'd been in so long. I remembered all those times he sang to me, how he carried me and danced me around. I want to tell him, *I sing too. I sing too, Daddy.* I want to tell him all about my band, how we're going Mexican punk. He would totally dig us, too. I wish so hard I could say it.

But I didn't. I blinked a lot so he wouldn't see my misty eyes. At least he was here with me now, however long it lasted.

"Wow," I said, when he stopped.

"Your old man knows a thing or two." He grinned.

"I could probably do that," I said. "But I'd have to practice a lot with the record."

"You're not going to try it?"

"Not right now."

"Don't be a chicken."

"I'm not. I don't know the song."

"You don't need to learn the whole song. Just do the ay-ay-ay-ay part."

"I can't just by itself," I said. "You already know that song. It's different. Besides, that's not even the grito I wanted to learn."

"You should learn all of them." He put on "Cielito Lindo" again, but I didn't try to sing along. "Come on."

"No, Dad."

"Fine," he said. "But I don't know how you're gonna learn the third one when you won't even do the ay-ay-ay-ay. It's harder."

"Just explain it."

"Fine." He switched to the CD player, some norteño band. It was all accordion and horns over thick oompah-oompah polka bass.

"Okay, here's the real gritonazo," my dad said. "The base of it is wah-ha-ha, like a laugh."

"Wah ha ha," I said.

He shook his head. "Wait."

In the pause before the accordion player went into a serious rager of a solo, there were a series of, well, gritos. Short, high-pitched yips. My dad yipped along. "Ha-ha-ha-iiiiiii!

"Watch me," my dad said. He let one go that could have matched Olmec's for sure. It was not a heartbreakingly beautiful series of notes, like the ay-ay-ay-ay. A gritonazo was an eagle's hunting cry, savage and clear in its triumphant dive. The scream of a thousand Mexican men, drunk and on the edge of tears, puro coraje y sentimiento. Even more than that, it was the scream of my teenage dad. A tenderness for him stole over me. I had never considered my dad at my age, but suddenly, I could, and I loved him for it. I imagined so clearly the boy he'd been, his convictions, his fierce heart. A teenager, full of light and fury, righteous indignation, and miles of style. Him and Zero in their bell-bottoms, their flopping hair and brown skin, throwing their gritos at the white kids, at their teachers, voices lifted in sheer defiance and revolution. Because yes, the gritonazo is a war cry.

"That's the one," I said. "That's it. You really did that at the principal?"

"Yeah," he said. "Pinche vato hated me so much. He was gonna kick me out of school, but I guess since I was a senior, he thought he'd rather just get me out and not have me back."

"Just for throwing gritos?"

"I did it a lot," my dad said, but I knew he wasn't telling me all of it. You don't just get kicked out for yelling. "And I wasn't the only one. Me and my friends got all the Mexicans voting for 'La Chiva Flaca' for the senior song. Man, all the gringos were mad! They didn't let us have it."

"Oh my God," I laughed. "That was 1970. You guys could have picked anything good—what about Zeppelin or the Beatles? That goat song is so dumb!"

"The Beatles. No mames." He smacked his lips at me. "'La Chiva Flaca' is Mexican as hell. We wanted it, just to show it was our school!"

"Sucks they didn't let you have it."

"But we knew we won. That's the point."

"I mean they probably wouldn't let us pick a norteño song even now," I said. Which was a weird thing for me to realize, but it was true. Lots of people liked conjunto, but no one admitted it except the rancheritos or someone like Ernie, who unblushingly listened to all styles of music.

It dawned on me how fucked up my own ideas were. Why should Ernie hide it? Why were so many of us ashamed of our own music? My dad's fight for justice didn't feel so remote anymore.

"I bet we get stuck with some lame-ass Amy Grant or something," I said. Probably our class would be some lame white contempo, but oh my God, I was fired up. Pink Vomit was *so* going to play Mexican music. Hell yeah we were.

"We had to settle for the stupid 'Love Theme from Romeo and Juliet,'" my dad said. "Nobody liked it. The administration picked it after Los Relámpagos won."

"That's crap," I said. I was impressed though. How punk to get everyone voting for that corny-ass Mexican song. My dad had been way cooler than me, by a lot. But then, he'd been a senior. And a boy. I bet Grandma Romi never told him anything about him getting in trouble, or staying out late. Or cared who his friends were.

"So you gonna try it or what?" my dad said. "But you can't half-ass it. The gritonazo needs full commitment. You can't be scared."

"I'm not scared," I said. I blurted out some little kicky cries, like high-pitched laughter, ha-ha-ha-iiiiiii. My dad nodded at me, waved for me to keep going.

I took a deep breath, imagined myself doing something really daring, really, really over the top. Yelling at school, like my dad. Yelling at the teachers. Yelling at the stupid preppy kids. Yelling at my dad, everything I was so angry about. I felt the black glossy thing inside me, the way it was always thickened up and hard, but also ready to erupt. I felt it coming up. I opened my mouth and screeched, a huge shining wail of fury, so much fury. But paced fury, because I wanted it to last and last. It was something I breathed through and kept pushing out of my body. A wall of sound. It was shrill and vibrating. I wound down by throwing in those coyote cackles.

"Órale," my dad said. "¡Eso es!"

"I told you I could do it," I said.

"I never doubted you."

We spent another ten minutes throwing gritonazos at each other, until my dad said we had to stop or neither of us would have voices the next day. We went into the kitchen for Cokes to soothe our throats. Well, I had a Coke. He cracked a beer. I sat on a barstool at the kitchen counter, sipping while he talked. Apparently the gritos had jogged loose memories for him.

"I don't know if I told you," he said. "I was a DJ for a little while in high school. We used to throw gritos on the air and everything."

"I thought you worked at the bottling plant."

"That was when I was younger. Your age. But when I was sixteen, seventeen, my friends and I had a radio show."

"Of what?"

He laughed, remembering. This was so my dad. He could be terrible— he *was* terrible—but also, sometimes, and I never knew when, he would be real with me. Not my dad, but his real self. Just Jules.

"It was dumb. We were telling all about the town and social issues. We thought we were real activists. And we'd play music. Zeppelin or Cream, that stuff. And conjunto too. We even had DJ names so nobody knew who we really were."

I laughed. "What was your DJ name?"

"El Perro," he said. "Just my barrio name. Because I was always running around the streets like a stray dog."

"Pffft, it's not," I laughed. "Grandma told me it was Romeo. *Muy* Romeo."

"Whatever," he said. "It was a long time ago."

I let that one slide. "I can't believe KTBD let you guys have a show."

There were two radio stations in La Cienega. Country-only KLTX and KTBD, which on weekdays from midnight to six p.m. aired *American Top*

40 and from six p.m. to midnight switched to Spanish music. Mostly conjunto, but also Latin contempo crap like Luis Miguel. Weekends were all English.

"Not in La Cienega," my dad scoffed. "We had a show on Estéreo Bravo across the border."

"Oh wow," I said, slurping my Coke even though my dad said it was bad manners. "You got hired as a DJ in Mex?"

"Well, Zero did. But since he was on graveyard shift, they didn't care what he did. So we had a show called *Cuéntame* at two a.m. All the kids at school would listen in. We had a huge following."

My dad is like a piñata full of stories, good ones, that I want to hear but they come out in bits and pieces. He was always telling me about music, about the bands that mattered and why, about El Movimiento, but hardly ever anything about himself. He is full, full, full of secrets. All the time.

My dad was basically admitting what I already knew: that he'd lived his life doing whatever the fuck he wanted. Across the border at two in the morning? Sixteen years old? Meanwhile I'm supposed to be some super obedient kid. We were getting along for the first time in months, and I was so inspired by our talk, by him coaching me, but underneath, the part of me that was tired of him lying was starting to wake up.

All of this flashed through me as I listened. I knew better than to point it out. He'd say, it's different. But the difference is I'm a girl. The only thing girls are doing at two in the morning is sleeping in their beds. Otherwise they're being sluts.

"Nobody does anything cool like a radio show. All I ever hear are people calling in with dedications."

"Well," he said, totally unsuspecting, "it was a different time. Mija, you don't know how it was."

"Like what?"

He finished the beer. Opened another one. I pretended I didn't notice it.

"They weren't playing Mexican music on the radio on this side of the border. But it wasn't just about that. Man, when I was a junior there were still separate high schools. One for brown and black kids, and one for the whites. And that was just one part of it. I mean, other places, yeah, desegregation had happened. But not here in La Cienega. They weren't letting us have a say in anything."

"But you were a kid."

"I mean all the Mexicanos, Chicanos. None of us. So yeah. We spoke out about it. And the way we could do that was on the Mexican radio, where nobody could stop us."

"That's pretty cool," I admitted.

"Yeah, we were vocal. At school. On the show." He drank his beer. I waited.

"None of it probably would have happened except there was a guy. He ran for school board. He was a real mover."

"One of your friends ran for school board?" I laughed. "No way."

"No, no. He was a young guy, but older than us. Twenty-six. Felix. We called him El Gato."

"Oh yeah," I said. I knew the name from seventh grade: Felix Gutierrez Memorial Middle School. "He died in some accident."

"Yeah," my dad said, staring into his beer. "But that's the past."

"You stopped being a DJ because he died?"

"Yeah," he said. "After what happened I wasn't into it anymore."

"Why? Did you know him?"

"No," he said. "I didn't know him like that. It's just he was the main guy. He had stirred everybody up."

"But it didn't end when he died," I said. "I mean, the high school got consolidated somehow. And you just got bored of it all? I don't believe that. You're always talking about the fight for justice."

I thought for sure he was going to shut me down. Stomp off like he always did when he didn't feel like dealing with me. No, he kept staring into his beer. He must have had quite a few before he came home, of course he had. Those two wouldn't have put a dent in him, not the way he drank. That's my guess. Otherwise he wouldn't have answered me. Not sober.

"Mija, you can love something. You can be passionate about it. And it can be the right thing too. What we were doing, it was for the good," he said, still not meeting my eyes. "I mean, you're there in that school and it's just normal for you. So I know we were right.

"But it's true what they say, the road to hell is paved with good intentions." He swigged more beer. "I was born under a bad sign. Cursed. Whatever I do, it comes out wrong."

"Dad, give me a break," I said, trying to keep from sounding annoyed. He's always saying he was born cursed, that he's a bad luck charm. It's just him feeling sorry for himself. "Bad luck isn't real."

"Well, maybe you're right," he said, but he was getting moody, I could see it. "I just wanted to change things. But I got with the wrong crowd. I guess."

"What do you mean?" It didn't make sense to me at all. "Sounds like you were doing awesome things."

"Yeah, but some of the group . . ." He trailed off, for so long. I stayed as still as I could, trying not to knock him out of this moment. "I don't know. They were too intense. They took it too far."

"What did they do?"

"I love you so much, mija," he said, putting his hand over mine. He seemed close to tears. "You're getting older, so I need to tell you. Be careful. You can do something, even for the right reasons, and it's the wrong thing. And you can't ever undo it. Never."

"Are you talking about when mom died?" I asked, confused. "That wasn't your fault. You know that."

"Not that. When I was just a little older than you, I was involved with those friends, that crowd. Something happened that I wish I could take back. I wish it all the time." He got up, pulled another beer out of the fridge. "That's why I know I bring bad luck."

"Daddy, stop it," I said. He was so miserable all the time. We were miserable all the time. "Just because you feel guilty doesn't mean you're bad luck. Don't say that."

He cracked that stupid beer and took a long swallow. Storytime was over. "Anyway, what about those gritos? You gonna show Marina how it's done?"

"I guess." I wanted to ask him what he'd done that was so bad, but no way would he tell me. Hard to believe he'd even said as much as he had.

"It would be cool if we did some gritos together for the father daughter dance at the quince. I want that one to be a conjunto anyway." He smiled at me. I felt a sluggish stir of affection. I couldn't remember when we'd talked so long without fighting.

"Okay, I'll practice," I said. "And speaking of, I finally got the guys for quince court settled."

"Oh yeah? Who are they?"

"César Allen," I said.

"That's your escort?" my dad demanded, eyebrows raised.

"No, he's Marina's escort."

"Okay," my dad said, twisting his face in surprise. "Well, she's real pretty, but I didn't think he'd go out with her."

"He's escorting her, not dating her," I said.

"Yeah, okay. Sure." My dad rolled his eyes. I was glad César wasn't escorting me after all. He probably wouldn't believe I'd agreed to do César's homework for the rest of the year. "Who else?"

"Óscar Tovar. He's in my English and Biology classes. We're both in NHS." My dad nodded. I had hit the right notes. I ticked the third name off my finger. "And his cousin Ernie."

"Ernie?"

"Ernesto Vega. He's in jazz band with Óscar."

It was so scary how my dad didn't say anything for a long moment. Finally, he said, "Is he related to those musicians? Conjunto Vega?"

"I don't know," I said, trying to sound uncertain. "I think he's in the jazz band at school."

"He played with the Vegas at your grandma's funeral," my dad said. "He's a tall kid."

I shrugged, pretending my heart wasn't hammering in my chest. Luckily, he was losing interest. Or maybe he was just ready to start the weekend. He said, "Well, we can have a meeting with the kids in a few weeks, just to set up practices."

"All right," I said.

"I'm gonna meet Zero for a beer," my dad said. "Practice your gritos."

"Yeah," I said, completely truthful. "I will."

After my dad left I called Ernie. I wanted to show him the gritos I'd learned.

He interrupted right away. "Did you ask César to be your chambelán?"

"What? No," I said. "He's Marina's escort. My cousin was supposed to escort me, but that fell through. Can you do me a solid? It's lame, but will you do it?"

"I mean, I guess," Ernie said, a real cool cat.

Then it was fine. It was perfect. We threw gritos at each other over the phone for an hour, until Ernie's mom yelled at him, "Ave María Purísima, shut up already!" I had a giggle attack and had to muffle my face with my pillow, imagining his pissed-off mom.

"We're gonna kill it at Chaparral Disco Rodeo," he said.

"Yes," I said. "I'll be ready."

Chapter Fourteen

Gato Negro

A week before the gig at Chaparral, I found my dad snoring in the front yard. His truck was running, and the driver's door hung open. The stereo was blasting George Jones.

He'd puked a lot. There was vomit smeared across his shirt and in the grass near where he lay, like maybe he'd rolled over. He smelled sour, like old cottage cheese. It was pretty heinous.

"Dad," I said, prodding him with my foot. "Dad, get up. C'mon."

"What?" he mumbled.

"Get up. You need to go inside."

Instead, he swiped a hand in the air, just once, I guess to wave me away. He was still drunk. I turned off the truck. Slammed the driver's side door as hard as I could. At least he'd somehow managed to park it, or he'd have gone straight through the garage. Or maybe he'd have run himself over.

Sometimes, like right now, I hate being a kid. I hate it so bad. Yeah, it was embarrassing, him sleeping it off right there where he fell, in the front yard. Sloppy-ass drunk. It was scary too, though. I didn't have my grandma anymore and I'd lost my mom so long ago that it sometimes felt like I'd always been without her. Gonzy was dead too. What did I have except this stupid, drunk dad? It all made me feel like kicking him, but I didn't.

Lying in the grass, he looked small. Not a bit like the wild tornado I knew. He looked sick too. His brush of black hair fanned against his cheek, thick as ever. That was the only normal thing.

"Daddy," I said, cringing, but I couldn't help myself. The more he drinks, the more it scares me. Look how many rock legends die in their own puke. "Daddy, get up."

"Whatsamatter?"

"You're in the front yard," I said. "You need to go to bed."

He opened his eyes. They were bloodshot and pouchy, but so aware, all at once. He sat up.

"Go inside," he barked.

"What?"

"Just go inside," he said. "I'll be right there."

"Okay, okay," I said, annoyed. It wasn't my fault he'd slept in the yard all night. Why take it out on me?

I went in the kitchen to make myself some cereal. There's a window over the sink that faces the front yard. So yeah, I heard him yak again and it left me with zero appetite. He didn't look at me at all when he came in, just headed straight for the backyard, to his precious workshop.

"When are you getting up? I need to work on a history project with Marina today."

"Call Yoli to get you." He shut the sliding glass door. He couldn't stand that I'd found him that way, that's why he was mad at me.

No, I wasn't going to call Yoli. I'd walk to the mall and goof off for a while, then call Ernie to pick me up and we'd head over to Pilar's house to practice with the new accordion player. My dad wasn't going to check on me, first off because he'd be asleep all freaking day, I had no doubt, but he and my tía were in a standoff to see who'd blink first. They weren't talking at all. I didn't talk to her either if I could help it.

I rinsed out my bowl in the sink. I could do more than goof off at the mall. I went into his bedroom, which was dark and smelled bad. Dirty clothes wadded up beside the bed. Closet door wide open. I crawled under the bed, all the way to the back. There it was: an oversized Bible, white leather binding, the front cover set with a picture of Jesus showing the flaming sacred heart on his chest. My parents' wedding Bible. It's where my dad keeps his emergency stash. He tapes money to the pages.

I took two hundred sixty dollars, all the twenties he had, and shoved the Bible back under the bed. Maybe he'd realize it was me. Maybe he'd chalk it up to another blotto night. More likely he'd never notice.

An hour later, I forwarded our phone line to the public library and left. It was a pretty day out, brisk but sunny, the kind of winter weather I like. I couldn't help smiling as I walked through the neighborhood, headed to the mall. The guys met me there.

We had a band meeting right there at Orlando's Grill, over chili dogs. They wanted to go onstage as Gato Negro. The idea actually came from Jorge, who said Pink Vomit *sounded* cool, but what if we wanted to have T-shirts? What was our band logo gonna be, puke on the floor? A guy puking? That was too boring.

Gato Negro was a great name. Simple, but hip. I was still annoyed though, because our old name had been my idea, and of course, Jorge had to change it.

"What was our logo going to be when we were Ximena's Demon Baby?" I argued. "A picture of you?"

"A demon baby is way cooler than just puke," Jorge said.

"Anyways," Olmec cut in, "we need to make our banner for the show. The logo Jorge found is freaking awesome."

"It's pretty good," Ernie agreed, sipping his Coke. "And actually, you're the reason we got it."

"What?"

"When we were cleaning out the shed for Pilar," Jorge said. He opened his backpack and pulled out a battered Chuck Taylor. It was a high-top, faded red. Old and mud stained. "I found it in that box of shoes she wanted me to throw out. Look at this."

He tilted the shoe at me. In thick, permanent black marker, someone had drawn an image of a black cat on the side canvas. It was a cartoon cat face, the head oversized and shaped almost like a human skull. One ear filled in solid black, the other just outlined. The eyes were huge double-banded circles, so big they looked sort of like tunnels, or maybe, that the cat was wearing glasses. Behind the cat face was the tail, a thin line swirling up the ankle. Black Cats was scribbled along the bottom of the shoe in block letters, just above the rubber sole. It made me think of El Gato, Felix Gutierrez. The guy who died fighting injustice, my dad's hero. That's what made a kick-ass name, even if the guys didn't know it. We would be Gato Negro, Mexi-punks bringing the brown sound.

"It's perfect," I said.

"If you hadn't picked our practice spot we wouldn't have found it," Ernie said, squeezing my arm. Next to him, Olmec sighed and bit his chili dog.

I found myself feeling uneasy about Jorge swiping Pilar's stuff. She was awfully particular, and unlike my dad, she'd be the type to notice. "Did you tell Pilar you took it?"

Jorge rolled his eyes. "God, you're such a Girl Scout. She won't care about an old shoe. It wasn't even a pair. I looked for the other one. Besides, she said she was throwing that whole box away."

"You were gonna wear them," Olmec laughed. "Gnarly old shoes."

"Vintage Chucks with our band logo," Jorge said. "Shit yeah."

"She was throwing it away, for real," Ernie said to me. "So dibs."

"Well, it is fucking cool," I admitted.

"¡Gato Negro!" Olmec said, doing finger guns at me. "Just like Black Flag, but a cat. And Mexican."

"Nerd," Jorge said. He grinned at Olmec. I knew he loved it. Me too.

"Hey," I said, mainly to Ernie. "Somebody take me by Cheve's. I'm ready to get that guitar today."

"Fuck yeah!" Olmec said. "Let's go."

The accordionist met us that afternoon at Pilar's house. His name was Antonio. He was older, mid-twenties maybe, and went by Toño rather than Tony. Toño wore glasses and was impossibly skinny, with a mane of black hair tied up in a ponytail down his back. Olmec jogged over to him before Toño even had a chance to talk to us. The way that guy smiled at Olmec, a little shy, but so happy to see him, I knew something was up.

"Is that your man?" I whispered at Olmec while Toño was getting his gear out of his car.

"What, you're the only one who can screw members of the band?" He laughed and dodged my kick.

Pilar was not home, but she'd left the shed unlocked for us. I guess she got tired of having to be home if we were there. How was she going to take it that we had a brand-new band member at her place without her meeting him? I didn't know where she was or when she'd be back. But I wasn't going to hold up practice being a little *Girl Scout*. So when Ernie said we should show Toño what we had so far, I threw myself into it.

"Honestly, that's a lot of punk for Chaparral," he said, after listening to a couple of songs. "But the crowd will put up with anything if you throw in some Ramón Ayala."

"That's old," I said. I knew his most popular songs, of course. My dad loves that guy.

"Yeah, but it's easy," Jorge told me. "Sorry, Lulu, but no Selena. That's like being the singer in a Journey cover band. You gotta have an incredible voice if you're trying to sound like Steve Perry. Same thing with her."

"Duh," I scoffed. "I wasn't suggesting Selena." No way was I going to strut around singing "Bidi Bidi Bom Bom" with my string bean body. I'd get laughed off the stage. Besides, Jorge was right. Ramón Ayala would be so much easier. He has a plaintive, raspy voice that is fairly undistinguished. Basically, he's a phenomenal accordion player who happens to sing.

The guys wanted to hash out our set list, but I refused to wait through another argument between Olmec and Jorge. I got my Epiphone out of the car.

"¡Qué chulada!" Toño whistled. I duckwalked across the yard.

"Give it here," Ernie said. "I'll tune it for you."

I gave it to him, wishing I could do it myself. He'd be a lot faster though. He fiddled with the chords, playing little riffs. "This is fantastic," he kept saying. "It's gorgeous."

"I love it for real. You heard Cheve, right? I can get lessons with him."

Ernie snorted. "*I'll* teach you. I'm better than Cheve."

"I know, but he's a cool guy."

"We're gonna be able to play so many more things once you get the hang of it," Ernie said. "Never mind Jorge and his stupid punk *ethos*."

"Nobody's committed," Jorge said, mock-sad. "Just a bunch of sellouts."

We finally decided on our list: Runaways and the Stooges for me, Black Flag and Suicidal Tendencies for Olmec, Fugazi and Primus for Jorge. Ernie wanted to show off his solo skills with Slayer's "Seasons in the Abyss" somewhere mid-list and then close the show with "Sleep Walk" by Santo & Johnny.

We decided we'd switch to conjunto near the end of the set. Three songs. Two by Freddy Fender, bilingual Tejano tunes with enough old rock 'n' roll sound to carry us over from English covers to the nitty-gritty norteño stuff: Ramón Ayala's well-known hit "Rinconcito en el Cielo." Toño already knew how to play all the songs. They were slow polkas dominated by heavy accordion, so all I had to do was give Toño space to shred the squeeze-box and basically sing around him.

"Okay, okay, this is how we're gonna do it," Olmec said. "We'll move to funny punk in the middle, right? Let's do 'Detachable Penis' and then 'Punk Rock Girl' because it's funny *and* has accordion. That's our transition to Freddy Fender's 'Hey Baby Que Paso.'"

"Oh yeah," Toño said. "That'll work. I love the Dead Milkmen."

Pilar drove up just then, Wicho standing up in the truck bed. He jumped out and made a beeline for me as soon as she parked.

"Hey buddy," I said, scrunching his ears. I was getting really fond of him, even if he did have a five-second attention span. Sure enough, a moment later, he ran across the yard after a squirrel.

"You're changing styles?" Pilar asked. She had a garment bag in her arms, like she'd gone to pick up dry cleaning.

"We're switching things up," Olmec said, grinning. "This is Antonio. He'll be joining us for practice too."

"Mucho gusto," Toño said. Pilar nodded, obviously not in the least interested in him.

"I almost have the first half of the song down," I said. "Stay and listen."

"Let me take this inside first."

I knew she would. Now that Grandma was gone, Pilar was the only grown-up in my life who'd always listen to me. I didn't know why. But it was true. She came right back, settled herself on a box in the garage.

We took it from the top. The thing I most needed to get used to was singing slow and letting the vowels carry on every line. It wasn't a bit like punk, fast and yelling and discordant. "Rinconcito," like a lot of conjunto norteño, has a formal and symmetrical structure, like blues. So while it isn't hard to learn the lyrics at all, for me it's a little boring.

Pilar could tell too. "So, you're not a bad singer. But I don't think that one goes with you."

"I mean, yeah," Jorge said. "It sounds okay, but you don't really get into it."

"What's to get into? It's about finding a little piece of heaven with your boyfriend," I said, feeling annoyed. "It's sappy."

"What about Paquita la del Barrio?" Pilar asked. "I think you'd like her better."

Toño laughed. "Anything by her would work. You'd like it. I can tell."

"'Tres Veces Te Engañé,'" Pilar said. "That's a good one."

"It's a popular one," Ernie said, nodding. "Especially with women."

"I don't know it," I said. I'd never even heard of Paquita la del Barrio. My dad didn't have anything by her. I realized suddenly he didn't have any records by Mexican women. What the hell?

"I have a tape," Pilar said.

We listened to the song. It was about a woman who was finally sick of some jerk. She tells him to his face how she betrayed him three times. The first out of rage, the second on a whim, and the third time because she started liking to cheat. Jorge cackled when she said in the middle of the song, *You hear me, stupid?*

"Oh my God, that's the one," I laughed. The guys agreed. Ernie and Toño knew who Paquita was, no surprise, but the fact that Olmec did too made me feel really dumb. I hated being right there with Jorge.

"I can play it," Toño said. I wondered if there were any old conjunto songs he did not know. He must have had a real repertoire.

"Yeah, cool," Jorge said. It was almost four o'clock now. "Let's try it tomorrow. I gotta go. I'm having dinner with Ximena."

"Be careful dude," Olmec said solemnly.

Olmec and Toño took off together, probably going to Olmec's house. Ernie asked me if I wanted a ride home.

"I'll take her," Pilar said. "I need to talk to her about some things for her quince."

"Oh right," Ernie said, looking at me in a funny way. "Well, come get your jacket, Lulu."

"What's the matter?" I asked when Pilar had gone back to the house.

"She's helping you?"

"Who else do I have? My tía ditched me because my dad's a freaking homophobe."

"Yeah, but *her?*" He made a face. Yeah, he called her Crazy Eyes behind her back, but I hadn't realized until that moment how much Ernie didn't like her. "Can't you ask Marina and her mom?"

"And what am I supposed to say for a reason? Do I tell Marina's mom all the dirt going on in my family?"

"I'm just saying that chick is weird. She's weird, Lulu."

"Maybe I'm weird."

"Not like that," he said. "You're not."

"Like what?"

"I don't know," he said finally. "She's . . . she doesn't care about anything. She's blank."

"She's just shy," I said, which was a flat-out lie. "Look, I'm going to get a ride from her, okay? It's fine."

Pilar peered out the screen door. "Are you coming?"

"Yeah," I said.

"Call me when you get home," Ernie said.

I agreed so he'd leave. I don't want to have to call someone to check in. Geez, he wasn't even my boyfriend yet, but it was already starting.

The garment bag had my quinceañera dress. Tulle and satin, with a V-neck and butterflies embossed along the collar and down the bodice. The tulle was all in the skirt, frothy, almost ballerina. It was like a silver cloud, but one you could wear. Pilar had somehow gotten the seamstress to do it fast, fast, fast.

"What, did you pay her double?" I asked, shocked. "It's only been three weeks."

Pilar shrugged. "But what do you think?"

"I love it," I said, lifting the layers of filmy tulle. "How did you know to go short?"

"Because your dad probably wanted you in a full-length gown," she said. "So of course, you'd want a short one."

"You're right," I laughed.

"Try it on!"

"Okay, okay," I said, feeling excited about the quince for the first time ever. It was *so* pretty. I ran to her bedroom to change. Sure enough, it fit exactly right and hit just above the knee. I twirled into the living room just to make the skirt flare.

"Oh yes," Pilar said. "This is very good. Very good."

She looked, possibly, the happiest I had ever seen her. Not smiling, not that. But like, proud. Beaming even. She took my hands in hers and opened my arms, just taking in the whole outfit.

"Pili, thank you," I said, feeling so crappy all at once. Crappy and embarrassed. "I appreciate this dress so much, but you can't. I mean, I can't . . ."

"I know I'm not invited." Pilar shrugged. "Don't worry about it. Just be sure to get a picture for me."

"Of course. And seriously, how much was this dress? I can get the money for it from my dad's card."

"It's your birthday gift from me," she said, waving her hand. "It's yours. Go change so I can take you home."

"Do you want to come to the show this weekend?" I asked. At least I could invite her to that. "It's at Chaparral Disco Rodeo. We go on at one thirty a.m."

"Guácala, that's so late," Pilar said, making a gag face. "And I don't know where that is. But I'll be there."

Then Pilar said the most grown-uppy thing I'd ever heard come out of her mouth. She sounded just like Grandma Romi. "Listen, you hang that dress up as soon as you get home. I don't want it getting wrinkled. In fact, don't take it out of the garment bag again until your quince."

"Yeah, yeah, I promise."

The night of Chaparral, Marina and I cut across the alley behind my house, keeping a casual stride as we passed rows of chain-link-fenced backyards. We didn't want to look guilty.

It was a cold, clear night, mid-thirties and starry. My ears and neck were cold. Marina had slicked my hair into two buns on the top of my head. With thick winged eyeliner, a hematite choker, and the Revlon Blackberry lipstick she'd stolen for me, I looked skater chola. It was perfect.

Ernie was meeting us at the intersection up the street at ten o'clock. We'd cross the border with him, then meet up with the rest of the band. Gato Negro wasn't going on until one thirty in the morning, so there would be plenty of time to wander before the show.

"If the truck is there when we get back . . ." Marina said, flicking a last look at my house over her shoulder. She'd given herself magnificent, glittery smoky eyes and her whole face seemed to shimmer in the moonlight. We'd never partied in "Mex," as a lot of our classmates called it, when they went on weekends. She wasn't worried, just reconfirming our backup plan, in case my dad was back before we were.

"I unlocked my bathroom window," I said. "He'll never hear us. It's across the house from his room."

We'd absolutely be home before he was, but I didn't say so. Just like usual lately, my dad already was gone. *To the casino with Zero*, he said. I guess he was recycling his lies. I'd find him at seven in the morning, sleeping in the fresh dew again, or maybe, like last time Marina stayed over, he wouldn't get home until noon the next day, and if I didn't ask him, he wouldn't mention it. We didn't need an elaborate plan to sneak out.

"I'll take them to rent movies and pick up a pizza," he'd told Marina's mom when she'd checked in with him about Marina staying over. He didn't say he wasn't going to stay home with us. She just assumed that he'd be there because she's a normal boring grown-up and that's what normal boring grown-ups do.

Which was fine. After he left, I went into his closet and took his leather motorcycle jacket. Why not rock it onstage?

"I see Ernie," Marina said, picking up the pace. There was his old Chevelle, headlights off, idling near the intersection, just beyond the throw of streetlight.

"What's up?" Ernie said as we hopped in the car. Marina took the back seat. I sat up front, next to Ernie. He blinked at me. "Oh wow. You look awesome."

"Thanks."

"She's ready to rock," Marina said, leaning into the space between the bucket seats to check her lipstick in the rearview mirror.

"Hell yeah," I agreed, staring out the passenger window as Ernie pulled onto the street. My neighborhood looked so quiet, just a bunch of similar houses, rows of living room lights on. Prime time for television. Then, so quick, we're at the highway juncture, headed across the border.

I used to be gone so many weekends on school trips: Physics Club, Mathletes, Debate, swim team. I'd call my dad at eight o'clock at night on the dot. We'd talk for ten minutes, maybe. He'd want to know if I won, what happened, who else got what. My dad had shoved me into as many extracurricular activities as I could fit into a week's worth of afternoons ever since I hit middle school. I never had to remind him which schools we were up against, what the scores were. He said he was proud of me.

But it was a trick, see. If I called him again, at ten thirty, just before lights-out, the phone would just ring and ring. One time I let it ring so long the sound of it wasn't a sound anymore, just a pulse in my ear. He never picked up. That's how I knew he was just sticking me somewhere for safe-keeping.

I never told him I knew—that I knew my life was always just edging toward this blankness. Now that my grandma is gone, so is the pretense. He doesn't ask much about my clubs and teams anymore. I told him I dropped a few because I wanted to focus on doing good in my AP classes and planning my quince. He told me that was a good idea, that I had a good head on my shoulders. I think what having a quince really means is that I'm old enough to be on my own.

Marina poked me in the back. "Why you so quiet? Man, you guys are gonna kill it tonight!"

"We are," Ernie said, grinning. He'd put new silver hoops in his ears and his hair was shiny and loose, falling over one eye. Maybe I was on my own, but I wasn't alone. I leaned in to kiss the side of his mouth. He turned and caught my lips. Kissing him while he drove down the highway was surprisingly intense. I grabbed the collar of his T-shirt. He kept kissing me even though I was getting lipstick all over him.

"Oh my God y'all," Marina laughed. "We're gonna wreck."

"No mames," Ernie said, breaking our kiss. "I can drive with one eye."

"It's true," I said, and the three of us laughed as Ernie drove us across the international bridge.

Downtown Ciudad Bravo was hectic with light and sound, thronged with vehicles. We moved parade-slow past closed curios shops and dental offices, bumper to bumper with other cars full of would-be partiers headed for the nightclub strip. Suddenly it bloomed before us, blocks of bars and dance halls, all of them with blaring neon signs hanging over both sides of the street, like an archway: Club Meneo, Aldo's, El Charro Bar, Las Palmas Bar, El Carnaval, Club Paco-Paco, El Koko Loco, Amigos Bar, El Palenque, and so many more.

There were people everywhere on the street, sexy people. Girls in minidresses and tight jeans, glossy lipstick and heels, the guys in starched collared shirts, brand-new jeans and their best roper boots. There were huge planters with manicured shrubs set at intervals along the sidewalks, something I had never seen in La Cienega, where the downtown was shabby and full of faltering shops. Here, people were sitting on the planters like benches, smoking, talking, reapplying lipstick, waving away the roving street vendors: mariachis and flower peddlers and guys selling packets of gum.

We passed a club with a hugely fat man in a guayabera outside yelling, "Dollar shots! Dollar shots until midnight!" over and over into the street. On another corner, a man made eye contact with me, yelled, "Parking, five dollars the whole night! Five dollars, come in!"

"It's the best we're gonna get," Ernie said, and swerved into the narrow entrance. The guy waved for us to follow him. The cars were crammed in the lot like sardines in a can, barely enough space to open doors. He pointed us to a tiny space between two big-ass trucks.

"Right there," he said in Spanish. "You'll fit."

"It's gonna be hell getting out at the end of the night," I said as Ernie paid the attendant.

"By the time our gig is over, this lot will be mostly empty," Ernie said. "We're going on so late."

"I'm leaving my jacket in the car," Marina said. "The bars will be hot."

She was gorgeous in a pair of tight Rocky Mountain jeans and a spaghetti-strap white cami. Her dark curly hair was swept over one bare shoulder, showing off her glowing brown skin, her big gold hoop earrings. I saw her in this outfit in my bathroom, but it was different in the gravelly lot, with the thumping bass of ten different clubs just a few steps away. Just looking at her made me want to leave my jacket on all night.

"I'm keeping mine," I said, shutting the car door.

"Your jacket is part of the ensemble," Marina said as we made our way to the street. "But I'm not wearing my fucking *hoodie* in the club."

"You're gonna be freezing," Ernie said, shaking his head. Honestly, it's wild to me that he doesn't see how beautiful Marina is. I mean, what is wrong with him? But he treats her like a kid sister.

"I'm tough," she said, flinging her hair back. "Let's go."

The guys would meet us at Paco-Paco by eleven o'clock, Ernie said, and from there we'd make our way to Chaparral. He walked on the outside of the sidewalk, keeping himself between the vendors on the street and us girls. Marina smirked at me. I rolled my eyes at her, but I felt good Ernie was looking out for us.

"I knew it!" Marina screeched, just as we walked up to Paco-Paco. She stopped dead in her tracks, eyes narrowed to slits. "Arturo, you fucking liar!"

She bounded across the street, weaving between the cars, which were luckily not moving, everyone stuck in the traffic.

"Aw fuck," Ernie said under his breath, but he followed me when I bolted after her. Art stood with a few other guys from the track team, in line at a place called Tragos, which I realized was just a take-out window where people were buying tiny paper cups of booze.

"Mari, what are you doing here?" Art demanded, giving her a furious once-over. "What are you wearing?"

"What are *you* doing here? How many times have you been here behind my back?"

"How many times have you?" he yelled back. "You didn't tell me you were going out."

"Lulu's band has a show at Chaparral tonight," Marina snapped, not giving an inch. "I told you that. You're the one who left me home like a fucking pendeja while you're out here drinking with the guys."

"So what if I didn't tell you?" Art smacked his lips at her. "I don't have to tell you anything. Go keep tabs on your fresa boyfriend."

"Oh my God," I said. "You're that jealous about my quinceañera? Wow, dude."

"Oooooh," his friends hooted, and Art said in a hard, deadly voice, "Shut the fuck up, Lulu."

"Man, don't talk to her like that," Ernie said, stepping in front of me. The track dudes shifted a little, drawing together. I grabbed Ernie's jacket, out of reflex. Even though stupid-motherfucker Art thought he could just do that to me, I was scared for Ernie. There were four of them and they'd been drinking. I was angry all the way through *because* I was scared.

Marina wasn't though. Not at all. She looked Art dead in the eye. She spread her palms wide, fingers splayed in the air. "You know what, you're not even worth it. Do what you want, Art. We're done."

She turned to us. "Let's go. We need to get ready for your show."

I don't know if something else might have happened, but right then I heard Jorge's voice on the sidewalk behind me. "Hey, where y'all been?"

There he was with Ximena. Olmec, Toño, and a couple of guys I didn't recognize were right behind him. Toño's friends, I guess. I've never been so happy to see my bandmates in my life. Art and his track buddies decided to ignore us. They left.

"What the hell'd we walk into?" Olmec asked.

Ernie pointed at Marina. "Talk to her. I don't know."

"Oh my God, Marina," I said. "You knew he was here?"

"I've fucking suspected him for a while now," she said. "Whatever. Good riddance."

"Drama already," Jorge laughed. "It's gonna be a good night."

We went into Paco-Paco, which was dark with a strobe light on the dance floor. The DJ was playing Latin pop. We crowded around a big table by the window overlooking the street and a waiter came up almost immediately. Olmec ordered everyone kamikazes. I told Jorge he could have mine. I'm never drinking alcohol.

The whole situation was making me feel nervous and strange. I decided to take a breather. Marina was right, it was hot in the club. I peeled off my dad's leather jacket and gave it to Ernie. "Hold on to this for me. I'm gonna go order a Coke."

"Damn," Jorge said when I stood up. "You finally look like a real punk. Good job."

"Why you looking?" Ximena said, pushing him. Jorge pushed her back. They were always like that with each other.

"Passable," Olmec said, looking me over. "One thumb up."

"Shut up," I laughed. I'd bought a pair of black wide-legged JNCO jeans. Pilar had hemmed them for me, so they weren't too long, but they still billowed out over my Vans. I'd lashed them to my hips with a wide white belt. But it was really my top that did it. I had on a tight yellow net tank top over a black sports bra. That was Marina's contribution. I wasn't curvy, she decided, but I could be skater-girl cool. So I stood there, pretending that showing my whole belly was a normal thing for me.

Ernie crooked two fingers through my belt loop, tugged me a little closer. It made me feel all crinkly, almost like kissing him on the highway. "Hey, get me a Dos Equis?"

"Yeah," I said. He slipped me some money, enough to pay for three drinks.

"I'm coming with," Marina said, jumping up. We weaved our way through the crowd, seeing a lot of familiar school faces. This is a regular Saturday night for them, I thought, as Marina and I got to the bar.

"Can you imagine how much money they spend every weekend?" Marina asked. "This is ridiculous."

"For real," I said.

"Lulu? What are you wearing?"

"Speaking of people who spend money every weekend," I said. "Hey César."

There he was, standing beside me at the bar in all his fresa glory. Tall and tanned in a salmon-pink button shirt neatly tucked into dark jeans. His braided brown belt. His leather loafers with actual shiny new pennies in them.

"Your dad let you come out?" César asked, incredulous. He was staring at my hair buns like they were devil horns.

"My band is playing at Chaparral tonight," I said. "I'm leaving right after these drinks."

"Are you serious?"

"They're really good," Marina said. "You should come see her. She's the lead singer."

César tilted his head at Marina. She was standing by the bar subtly dancing in place, grooving to whatever Latin pop blared over the speakers. She played it perfect, not even looking at César, craning her face over the bar to see if she could catch the bartender's eye. César took her in, just like so many boys did. She was Coca-Cola bottle curvy, bronze skin glowing in the blue bar light, the masses of her hair swaying with her hips. Oh yeah. César noticed her.

"Let's dance," he said as "La Negra Tomasa" by Caifanes came on.

"Sure," she said, easy, indifferent, like she hadn't been angling after him for months.

"Have fun," I said, grabbing my Coke and the Dos Equis. I whispered into her hair, "Be careful with him."

"I know what I'm doing. Anyway, now he'll show up to your gig."

"Maybe," I said. No. Just because he asked Marina for one dance, fresa César wasn't going to show up at some rancherito bar an hour before closing just to see me scream punk songs at a bunch of vaquero types. That was absurd. But why crush Marina's fantasy tonight?

It turned out Chaparral Disco Rodeo was packed at one thirty in the morning, couples swirling around in a huge circuit on the dance floor. The music was a mix: Spanish rock, norteñas, country. Pop music. I hoped that meant they'd like punk too.

The whole nightclub was outdoors, apparently converted from an actual lienzo charro, complete with arena and stables. The dance floor was a huge pavilion with a bandstand right in the center. Judging by the hooting and hollering coming from the nearby arena, the rumors of amateur bull riding were true.

"I'm so doing that after the show," Jorge blurted, wide-eyed, watching the riders.

"You're not," Ximena said, sipping her Corona. "You'll kill yourself."

"Think about it later," Olmec broke in. He, Ernie, and Toño had just come from setting up the equipment. "We're on next. Get your butts on the stage."

"Wait," Marina said. She whipped out the Blackberry lipstick, gave my bottom lip a fresh coat. "Okay, good luck. You're gonna be awesome."

I nodded and had to duck my face away. I just tried to breathe, followed my bandmates to the bandstand. There was just one moment, when I looked out into that mass of people, their stares curious and impatient, and I thought, what the hell am I doing? This is not going to work.

"Somos Gato Negro," I said into the mic, hating how my voice wobbled. Someone yelled, "Here, kitty kitty!" and there was a ripple of laughter.

Somehow, it's always Ernie that saves me. He strummed out the opening chords to "Search and Destroy," sent me charging across the stage, bolts of lightning crackling through me. That hard thing inside me opened up and I found my voice, big and bold and so ready. I crouched and stomped. I windmilled. I bounded to the edge and sang right at a guy in the front, a fat dude with a gold tooth and a black cowboy hat. Everybody was gonna see me. Nobody could look away. I'm here. I'm here. I'm here.

"¡Dale, dale, chiquita!" he yelled, laughing, and I was gone, flinging myself to the other side of the stage. There was Ximena sloshing her beer at us, Marina screaming next to her.

The song ended. I threw back my head and let out a piercing gritonazo, long and keening, furious, super chingona Mexicana. Olmec sent one up with me, our voices like pack howls in the night. The audience roared. They threw gritos right back at us as we dived into "Wasted" by the Runaways.

It was Olmec, punctuating my voice with kicky little cries. It was Jorge yelling "¡Vamos!" every time a new song started. It was Ernie, charging across the stage behind me, like a crazy game of tag. It was all of us throbbing through song after song, knowing them like muscle memory, trusting each other, full of joy and fury.

We had them completely by the time we got to Freddy Fender. They were dancing again, Toño's accordion wail sending them swirling around the bandstand. I did an impromptu polka around Ernie while he soloed.

We didn't play long. Maybe forty minutes total. We burned through our whole set list and Ernie was sending them off with that Santo & Johnny honey-hold-me-close instrumental. He was right. It was the perfect way to close the show. This crowd wanted to be in love.

I swayed along with the music, feeling the sweat drying on my body. I was glad Marina had kept my jacket when we went onstage. I'd have sweated all in it and my dad would've noticed. Or not, I thought, as I stared out into a crowd mesmerized by Ernie's dreamy chords.

In between the crush of dancers I caught a glimpse of ruby shimmer under the strobe lights. It was Pilar. She was wearing a sparkly red headscarf tied under her chin. She'd done her eyeliner cat-style, all heavy and swooping, painted her mouth in a crimson cupid bow. In the darkened club, at this distance, she didn't look her age at all. She could almost have been the star of some sixties Italian movie, a girl in a top-down convertible. All she was missing were her white sunglasses.

She was sitting by herself. Not feeling the music, just watching us intently. She saw me looking and raised her drink at me. I waved back, glad she was here, even if it was weird to see her at a bar in the middle of the night.

After we left the stage, I made my way over to Pilar's table. "I'm supposed to help put up the equipment. I just wanted to say thanks for coming."

"Of course," Pilar replied. "If you're going to practice in my shed for months, I want to see how it goes."

"Yeah," I said. "Thanks for that too."

She sipped her drink. It was something clear. Maybe a gin and tonic. "So, you're okay to get home?"

"Yeah, think so. I'm with Ernie and Marina. Here she comes," I said, recognizing Marina's thick mane of hair even backlit by dance floor lights. A guy was with her, so I guessed she'd found a dance partner all right.

"That was wild," César said, grinning at me as they walked up. "I didn't know you could sing like that."

"Yeah, I told you about my band," I said. What surprised me was his casual arm across Marina's shoulders. I made up my mind to tell her point-blank this was not a good idea. She probably wouldn't listen, but still. That's my job.

"This is César Allen," I said, not wanting to be rude, but not sure I should tell César who Pilar was. "César, this is Pili. She's been letting us practice at her place."

"Un placer," César said, in his impeccably polite way.

"Hello," Pilar said, her voice flat. She stared at him, then around the nightclub. "This place belongs to you?"

"To my family," César said, smiling. "It used to be a lienzo for char-readas, but my mother turned it into this." He gestured at the dancers, the bar. "It's more profitable."

"Oh yes," Pilar said very softly. Something was happening with her, but I couldn't understand what. She got to her feet, straightening her coat. "So, I have to go now. You get home safe, okay?"

"Okay, good night," I said, but she was already moving swiftly through the crowd. She was gone in a blink.

"I better go too," César said ruefully. "I was supposed to be home two hours ago."

He hugged me goodbye, then turned to Marina. He didn't hug her, but definitely gave her the flirty eye. "I'll see you later."

"Bye," she said, all breezy.

"Oh my God," I said, fatigue crashing over me all at once. "Let's find Ernie and get out of here. I'm exhausted."

"You probably burned a thousand calories jumping around on the stage," Marina laughed. "Vámonos."

We got home close to four in the morning. My dad was still out. Somewhere.

Chapter Fifteen

Fallaste Corazón

I just wanted to come thank you. For letting us use your place so long. And to give you this," I said, digging inside my backpack. "Merry Christmas, a little early."

It was a few days after the show. I'd bought Pilar a Selena T-shirt identical to one I had, white with the image of Selena on the *Amor Prohibido* album cover. I knew I needed to do it before the holidays because I wouldn't have a chance to sneak away otherwise.

"Thank you," Pilar said, unfolding it and looking it over. She didn't smile, but I could tell she liked it. Or maybe, she liked that I'd given her a Christmas gift.

"It's a small," I said. "I think we're the same size."

"Just about," Pilar said. "I took your dress measurements, remember?"

I nodded. We probably could have shared clothes. I'd never met any woman her age so dedicated to staying trim, but Pilar really was. I bet she could do more push-ups than me.

"And you booked the venue? The Villa Verde?"

"Yeah, but you know what sucks? My quince is the same night as

Selena. I was supposed to go to the concert with Ernie, but the eleventh was the only Saturday they had available in February."

"That's your birthday," Pilar said. "It's good luck the party is on the actual day."

"I'd rather go to Selena," I groused.

"That's too bad, but you can see her next time," Pilar said.

"I guess," I said. Pilar did not get it. At least she was an old lady and had an excuse. Ernie didn't get it either. It depressed me how much Ernie didn't care that we weren't going to Selena. He was just as happy to be my quinceañera escort. Maybe happier, even.

Since *Amor Prohibido* came out, Selena wasn't hitting the small towns as much as before. She was playing big places: Miami, Chicago, all over Mexico and even Puerto Rico. She still had a few small shows in Texas, but she was getting super popular. I saw her on *Sábado Gigante*, being interviewed about her career blowing up. She was playing the Houston Astrodome at the end of February. Why would she ever come back to La Cienega after that?

"Who's your escort?" Pilar asked, one-track mind on the quince. "Not that boy I met at the nightclub."

"No. He's Marina's escort."

"He shouldn't be in it at all," Pilar said, her uncanny temper showing itself. "He's bad news."

"He's all right," I retorted. "Marina kind of likes him."

"Hmmphf. Well, she better be careful. I know his family. That pile of rich people think they're better than anyone else," she said in Spanish.

It was pretty much what I'd told Marina myself, but somehow it sounded worse coming from Pilar. I didn't *dislike* César. But Pilar sounded like she had a major grudge against his whole family.

"He's just a guy. What's your problem?"

She frowned at the shirt in her lap. "I'll tell you because you need to be careful. You especially."

"Careful is my middle name," I said, trying to shake her out of this odd mood.

"There are people who are bad luck," she said. "They bring misfortune to others."

I felt little prickles on my arms. She sounded like my dad. "Are you telling me César is bad luck? Because I don't believe in that."

She refolded the shirt and put it back in the gift bag before she answered me.

"I want to show you something," she said. She went into her bedroom.

I followed her. She pulled a big black trunk out from under her dresser and flopped it open. It was full of keepsakes: a dirty cowboy hat, badly flattened; ribboned flowers pressed in tissue; tiny, old-fashioned baby booties; and a large photo album, which she pulled out and spread open on the bed. I sat down on the bed across from her.

It was the kind of album where the paper is heavy and black, and the photographs were placed, just one or two to a page, arranged intentionally, with symmetry and thought behind the placement, not crammed in four to a sheet and covered with clear plastic like the ones at my house. She didn't let me touch it. She flipped to the middle.

"Look," she said in Spanish, tapping the picture with her fingernail. "Look here."

It was a black-and-white photograph, the kind with a white scalloped border. There was a little black-haired boy standing on a sidewalk in front of a house. He was probably four or five years old. He wore a white cowboy shirt and a neckerchief. He had a little cowboy hat in his hand, like he was waving it at the photographer. He was laughing. I could see his milk teeth, the happy, squinty eyes.

"My son," Pilar said in a heavy voice. "He died there, at that place where you sang. He died because of your friend's father, the doctor."

"Your son?" How horrible that that laughing baby was dead. Had been dead, for so long. I looked into Pilar's face. She was dry-eyed, calm as always, just that glitter, like the shine of water at the bottom of a well. Oh, this is what it is, I thought. Pilar with her odd passions, her crackling silences. Pilar, who barely said a word about my grandma, or anyone else, ever. She was a person who had ended a long time ago, probably when this boy died.

"What was his name?" A dart of pity flashed through me. This was the child, the one everybody said haunted Loma Negra. How she was to blame. How could they say that about her? Anyone could see how much she'd loved him.

"Joselito," she said. "After his father."

Looking at the photo, I realized something else. I knew the screen door. It was black, the middle set with a curling aluminum filigree. There wasn't a banana tree in front of the house anymore, that's why I hadn't recognized it at first.

"That's my grandma's house."

"Yes," she said. "We rented the apartment in the back before we moved here."

"There's no apartment in the back," I said. I thought of the building behind Grandma's. A storage building, but with a kitchen and bathroom.

"I think Chuy turned it into a garage," Pilar said, like she was reading my mind.

"I'm sorry about your son," I said, trying to be kind. "But, César's dad wasn't a doctor. He died when we were kids. I think he was some kind of businessman, like an exporter."

"No," Pilar said. "A doctor. From Boston."

"That's César's grandpa," I said.

Pilar glared at me. "It doesn't matter. He hired my husband to teach him to ride like a charro. He wanted to be a fine, fine jinete just to impress those rich Ruizes. And my son died out there, on that ranch."

"That's why you had those saddles," I said slowly, remembering how she'd oiled them so expertly.

"My husband was the best rider," Pilar said smugly. "The best charro. So talented in the arena. Everybody knew it."

She flipped the page again, spread the album for me to see. It was a picture of a young man sat astride a dark horse. He was brown, very brown, with thick black curls that were smoothed back from his forehead in waves. He wore a charro suit, a short jacket and pants combo that looked kind of like the suit Ernie wore for his mariachi gigs, but less ornamental. The young man held his sombrero under his arm like a disc. He faced the camera, but as if someone had called his name and he'd turned just as they snapped the photo. It was someone he knew, because it looked like he was about to smile; it was already in the eyes, bright and expectant, like a laugh waiting around the corner. He's beautiful, I thought. Beautiful.

My brain caught up and the world seemed to fall out from under me. My stomach did a slow unpleasant roll. I saw plain as anything that this guy in the picture, if he'd had seventies-style muttonchops and if you swapped the horse for a Harley, he could have been my pre-Lulu dad sitting there in black and white. The only difference was the guy had curly hair and my dad's is crow-wing straight.

Pilar was smiling, a creaky, wrinkled smile, full of pride in a handsome charro husband. It was the first time I'd ever wanted to punch an old lady right in the face.

"Don't show me this!" I whispered, pushing the album away.

"Lulu—" she began.

"No!" I was scuttling away so fast I fell off the bed and landed hard on my tailbone. Everything was coming together, all the bits I'd joked away or ignored. *Money or betrayal*, Marina had said. She was right, only it was me, betrayed. Yoli, my dad, and Grandma Romi, everybody knew but me.

The truth had been there all the time, waiting for me to see it, and now it was swallowing me whole. It was real, all of a sudden it was real all the way, not a bunch of magic stories. Not the silly yarn Grandma Romi always told about my dad, the miracle baby brought home in a horse blanket, and not the stupid rumors about a house haunted, or Pilar murdering her own child, or even the thing Zero had told once when he was real drunk, about meeting her out by the river when he and my dad were kids.

My family wasn't my family. And Pili, oh my God. Pili, who'd drawn me to her like a flower charms a bee, Pili that I had defended time and again, who, yes, loved me, and it was sickening, sickening because I loved her too. She was a monster.

"You threw my daddy away! You threw him away!" I jumped to my feet and ran out of the room.

Pilar ran after me. "Come back! Lulu!"

"I'm not coming back!" I banged open the screen door. "How can you think I want to see that? I know what you did!"

She wasn't a witch. She just sucked. She was a selfish old thing who couldn't think about anything except bragging by showing me that picture. How could she have abandoned him? And the man on the horse—the stranger with my dad's face. What happened to him? A man I didn't know, a whole grandfather missing. All these lives cut off like a limb. And she thought she could, what, come back and be my fairy godmother?

"I hope that man left you!" I yelled from the yard. "I hope he found out what a fucking scumbag you are and dumped your ass!"

Pili wailed and wailed. It was the most terrible sound I had ever heard. Long, wild, shuddery sobs like somebody was taking a horsewhip to her, like the sound was clawing its way out, the photonegative of a grito, all jagged edges and black horror. She came out of the house, her face wet and streaked with red scratches. I stood at the edge of the yard, rooted to the spot, as she clutched her own face again. Pili the stoic, the stylish, was gone. Now there was only this insane banshee.

"I tried to take it back!" she screamed. "I tried! I did! But Romi wouldn't give me my baby! She wouldn't give him back to me! She kept him and I didn't have anything! I didn't have anything! And it's my turn now, it's my turn! I'm the one that's here!"

"You're not my family!" I screamed back, thinking of my father, the terrible darkness he lived in. He wasn't the bad luck. It was her. It had always been her.

"Don't say that!" she screeched. "Don't you say that to me!"

I ran like hell out of the yard. Down the hill, fast as I could go, right through the brush, not the road, never mind how the thorns tore my jeans, the prickers that filled my shoes. I didn't care. I was terrified she'd come after me in her truck. I ran all the way to my grandma's, through the alleyways, to avoid being seen.

"Lulu, what happened?" Tía Yoli cried when I burst into the living room. She was sorting some of Grandma's clothes into piles on the carpet. "Are you okay?"

I couldn't stand to look at her. Knowing the truth now, it made her seem like a stranger to me. Or maybe I was the stranger. Just say anything, I decided. Anything to get past her, so I could get to the bedroom I stay in at Grandma's and shut everybody out.

I'm just like all of them. I never run out of lies.

I didn't tell anyone in the band what happened. Instead, I said Pilar told me her son died at Chaparral Disco Rodeo, a long time ago when it was just a ranch. That she blamed the whole thing on César's grandfather, and she'd flipped out on me because César was in my quince.

"You think she'll trash our equipment?" Ernie asked. I'd paged him as soon as I got to my grandma's house. He and Olmec called me from a pay phone at the Sonic. "I told you something was off about her."

"We need to get our stuff," Olmec said in the background. "Right now."

"She's crazy," I agreed. I felt a guilty little twinge and smothered it. What the hell, Pilar *was* crazy. I wasn't lying about that.

I should have known she'd get me back, but good. Ernie called me later to say she wasn't there when they arrived, but they'd gotten our stuff out of the garage. Almost all of it.

"Lulu, I'm sorry," Ernie said. The line crackled. "She took your guitar."

A few days later, Marina called to talk about the quince choreography, and I told her basically the same thing I told the guys. She was more sympathetic. "I can't believe her kid died at Chaparral. How awful. No wonder she flipped out after the show. I mean, why would she even go there?"

"I think she didn't realize it was the same place until she met César."

"Why would she keep your guitar and not the other stuff though?" Marina paused, and then like the bloodhound she is, asked, "Is she mad at you?"

"Not that I know of," I lied. "Unless she's mad about César."

"Wow," Marina said. "Are you going back to get it?"

"I think she left town," I said. That was the part I couldn't stand. I didn't know where she'd gone. I'd never get my guitar back.

"Fuck, that sucks. But on another topic, what are the song choices for the quince court dance? We're gonna need to start practice right after New Year's."

Geez, was everyone obsessed with this quince? "I don't know. I don't care. I can't think of anything except my fucking guitar."

"Yeah, but we can't do anything about that right now," Marina said. "What about 'Bidi Bidi Bom Bom'? It's happy. Plus, it'll be easy to come up with cumbia moves. Don't argue. You love Selena."

Of course, "Bidi Bidi Bom Bom" was the one. I wasn't a great cumbianera, but Marina would drill me into shape. "Yeah, fine."

"What about for you and your dad? Have you picked anything?"

"No." I didn't want to dance with my dad on general principle, but now it was even worse. I felt weird and self-conscious around him and Yoli. Besides, he'd probably pick the song himself, never mind what I thought about it. "I'm trying not to think about the father daughter dance."

When we hung up, I felt blank and restless. It wasn't just my guitar. I wished I could tell her, tell anyone, how shook up I was now that I knew about Pili, about my whole family. That I was living in a kind of genetic penumbra. Pili with her secret furies. My dad existing in the shadow of some past sin. And wasn't I living in my own darkness too?

That evening my dad asked me to go shopping with him. "Come help me pick out gifts for your tía and your cousin."

I stared at him. He and my tía had not so much as been in the same room since Thanksgiving. Now he was acting like nothing ever happened.

"Your tía wants to have Christmas at your grandma's house, like we always do," my dad said, not meeting my eyes. "Your primo is coming too."

"That's cool." I didn't ask when they'd patched it up. I knew there was something else. There had to be.

"She said she'll help organize your quince practices. And the rest of it." He was casual, like he thought he could fool me. Or maybe he really didn't care. "Right after Christmas if you want."

"Okay," I said, just as casual. "I'll talk to her about it."

My tía had won the standoff, probably because my dad needed her help. I wondered if my dad was even sorry for what he said about Carlos. He wouldn't admit it, even if he was. He'd never say it. My dad doesn't apologize, period. Probably he did the same thing with my tía as he was doing with me, just started talking to her like nothing ever happened. Maybe my tía had played along too, just like me. I guess anything is better than ruining Christmas.

When we got to the mall, I made my dad come with me to the Macy's makeup counter. I decided on a bottle of perfume for Yoli—Carolina Herrera, a winter scent, bold and musky.

"It's nice," my dad said. "Is there one for men?"

"Yes," said the woman behind the counter. She smiled at him, probably hoping to sell another fifty-dollar bottle of cologne. "Would you like to try it?"

"Dad, we're not buying them matching gifts. I don't think Carlos wants cologne."

"What does he want then? I don't know what kind of stuff he likes."

"I mean, a couple of sweaters is probably fine," I said, trying not to sound annoyed, but it was hard. *Jesus*, I wanted to say, *just because he's gay doesn't mean you can't figure out a Christmas gift for him.* What about the eighteen Christmases before this one?

"The men's section is to the left," the counter woman said. "I'll hold the perfume for you."

We were halfway to the men's section when Margarita appeared in front of us. Right there in the store, with stupid Christmas jingles playing overhead—it was "White Christmas." She stepped out from behind a display of male mannequins in puffy jackets, surrounded by cotton swaths of fake snow. She was wearing jeans and a red pullover sweater with "Feliz Navidad from Felix Gutierrez Memorial Middle School" in block letters above a smiling cartoon reindeer.

"Jules," she said, and the way she looked at us, I knew she'd been following us. No doubt for payback. "I need to talk to you."

My dad was furious, that was plain. His face flushed, eyes hard and sparkly. That's how fast he loses his temper. But he said in a flat voice, "No, I don't think so."

"Yeah, we do." She pointed a finger at me. "Your daughter vandalized my house."

I opened my mouth to say something. *I don't know you. No, I didn't. Yeah, and I'd do it again!* But before I could decide how to answer, my dad said, "Lulu, go wait for me at Sam Goody."

"No, you need to hear this," Margarita said, looking right at me.

"Don't talk to my daughter. Ever." My dad sounded the way I'd heard him only once before, those early hours in the summer, the way he'd talked to Carlos. "Go on, Lulu."

I left, but no way did I go to the record store. I hung around the Macy's entrance, trying to see them. Her voice was too low for me to make anything out. She kept jabbing her finger in my direction. I had no doubt she was telling him all about how I threw dog shit at her, what I said. Maybe even who I was with, if she knew Pili.

Could she know Pili? I didn't think so.

My dad just let her talk. He had the expression I knew so well. That little smirk. Like he's trying to show he's not really listening to you, because you're not even worth it.

It was pissing her off too. She said, really loud, "What are you going to do about it?"

"We've been done three months," my dad said in an even bigger voice. No one was gonna yell at Jules Muñoz, especially not in public. "I don't care what pathetic shit you say about me, but don't you ever talk about my daughter. Don't speak to her. Don't look at her. Stay the fuck away."

"You're such an asshole, Jules."

"So just pretend I'm dead. We'll both be happier," my dad shot back. He actually went to the makeup counter and paid for my tía's perfume while everyone stood there gawking. Holy shit. Sometimes I hate my dad, but damn. That was cold. And hilarious. I ran to Sam Goody before he could spot me outside Macy's.

"Everything okay?" I asked, heart thumping, when he came to find me. It wasn't hard to look nervous. I was.

"Have you ever seen that woman before?"

"No," I lied stoutly, figuring he wouldn't bring up Grandma's funeral. Then he'd have to say how *he* knew her. "Who was she?"

He gave me a long, long look, then he shrugged. "Just some crazy chick, probably off her meds. Don't worry about it."

A crazy chick. Just like I'd told everyone about Pili. My dad and me lying our asses off. Merry Christmas, I guess.

We went to Abercrombie & Fitch because my dad said they had

sweaters more Carlos's style. I almost said, *Oh, I thought you had no idea what he likes anymore.* But I didn't.

My dad defended me in front of a whole store full of people. He didn't believe anything stupid Margarita had to say about me. He wouldn't hear a word against me, not from her. I hugged him on the way to Abercrombie.

"What about you? What are you gonna want for Christmas?" he asked, pulling my ponytail.

"Nothing," I said. "There's nothing I want."

It was like the fight with Margarita put my dad in a good mood. He hugged me again. "You know what, I'll surprise you."

***

Christmas Eve was ridiculous. Before we left for dinner with Yoli my dad gave me my Christmas gift: a necklace with a Virgin Mary pendant. A real piece of jewelry, 14 karat gold, complete with a black velvet box.

"Oh, it's pretty," I said, trying to hide my lack of enthusiasm. I'm sure it was expensive, but heavy religious stuff? We hardly go to church. I'd never wear it either. I could almost hear Jorge asking me when I was joining the convent.

"For your quince," my dad said. He hugged me. I tried not to mind that he already smelled a little like beer. "It's tradition to wear a symbol of the Virgin, since you're becoming a woman."

Unbelievable. I was allowed to become a woman, but only if I hung a chastity sign around my neck. Sorry, that ship sailed a while ago. "Thanks."

"Merry Christmas, mija."

Dinner was similarly awkward. My tía and my dad were trying to get over their fight, I guess because they were both missing Grandma. My tía gave my dad a warning stink eye when she met us at the door, but he behaved himself. Uncle Charlie had not been invited.

"Merry Christmas, Lulu," Carlos said when we arrived. He was wearing a black sweater with reindeer pattern on it, which made me think of my dad's jilted lover, Margarita. What was she doing tonight? Probably plotting against my dad. I would be if I were her.

"Hey, Carlos," I said, hugging him. I was happy to see him, but so many things had gone wrong since he'd been away.

"Short stack," he said, squeezing me. "Hey, I can't make it to your quince. It's in the middle of the semester, you know? But I'll send you something."

"That's okay. I get it," I said, fake cheerful, so I wouldn't seem upset. Of course he wants to stay away. Only now that Grandma's gone, he's my favorite person. At least, he's the only one who doesn't lie to me. That I know of.

"Merry Christmas," my dad said, and shook hands with Carlos. Carlos pumped his hand, but didn't say anything. It didn't take me long to figure out he wasn't talking to my dad or Yoli.

We ate dinner and opened presents, the TV blaring some musical variety show on Univision. My dad got a new pair of cowboy boots. Yoli got her perfume and a gorgeous pashmina. I got a bright-red telephone shaped like a giant pair of lips and some ridiculous candy cane–striped pajamas. Carlos got a sweater, tickets to Janet Jackson, and a new Visa card. Yoli was pulling out all the stops.

"Thanks, Mom," he said, biting off the words.

"Merry Christmas, mijo." She tried to hug him, but he pulled away. I thought she'd get mad, but she tried to act like she didn't notice.

"Is it though?" Carlos said. "Not to me."

"Hey, she's doing the best she can," my dad snapped. "It's hard with Grandma gone."

"You know what, Tío?" Carlos said, looking my dad dead in the eye. Man, that took guts. "At least you told me to my face you hate me. My mom has been telling everyone in this town that my dad is cheating on her because she doesn't want anyone to know about me."

"I'm supporting you!" Yoli cried, her face getting pink. "I won't let your dad cut you off. You're my son!"

"Mom, you're ashamed of me," Carlos said, his voice soft. "You are."

"Can you blame her?" my dad retorted.

"Dad, stop it already," I said. He can never just shut the hell up.

It didn't matter. Carlos locked himself in a bedroom and stayed there, wouldn't even answer me when I knocked to say good night.

I spent the rest of the visit on the couch, trying not to think about how it was Christmas, when you're supposed to be with family, but Carlos and Yoli weren't even related to me. I tried to tell myself it didn't matter because Grandma Romi loved my dad and me just the same as her real family, but then I cried because I wasn't her real family.

"Don't complain about getting a Guadalupe necklace. At least it's jewelry," Ernie said when I talked to him on the phone that night. "I got socks and a ten-dollar gift certificate to Wal-Mart."

"Lame," I laughed, glad to talk to him. Glad to make fun of corny presents. I just wanted to forget all the other things for a while.

"Hey, I have something for you."

"No! I didn't get you anything. Don't give me a gift." I wasn't trying to have a boyfriendy girlfriendy Christmas.

"It's not a present," Ernie scoffed. "Everybody in the band got one. Meet me at the end of the street tonight. Two a.m."

We'd been seeing each other two or three times a week since the gig at Chaparral. He'd drive up to the end of my block and I'd sneak out of my house to meet him. He'd drive us out to the Fina gas station, just a mile away, and park behind the building. We'd listen to music and have sex. Afterward, we'd talk about what songs we should learn for the next show until we were almost falling asleep. Then he'd bring me back home.

It wasn't hard to see Ernie. My dad was *trying* to stay home more since the mall, but that didn't change much. Instead of going out and getting drunk, he stayed in and got blitzed. Sometimes I'd get back from being with Ernie, change into my pj's and still go to the living room to throw away all my dad's empties. I hated waking up to the thin, sour smell of cheap beer. I hated it so much.

Tonight, I went out in one of my retired Selena shirts, from her *Dulce Amor* album, and my new candy cane pajama bottoms.

"Where's Waldo?" Ernie asked, laughing, when I walked up to the car.

"Shut up."

We parked behind the gas station. The Cure played softly in the darkness of the car, the radio dials making a dim radiance. It was good. The best part of the night by far.

He'd brought me a T-shirt, gunmetal blue, with *Gato Negro* across the chest in cursive, over the image of the grinning cat skull. "Olmec only made four, so take care of it."

336

"Badass!"

"Right?" He settled back into his seat, propping his feet on the dash. "Merry Christmas to us."

⌐——•——⌐

In January my quince court started choreography practice a few times a week. Since my dad was staying home more, my tía had thawed enough that she'd drop me off at practices. She'd mellowed with me too. As for me, what I discovered was that even if you find out telenovela-level family scandals, nothing actually changes in real life. Which, honestly, is comforting.

"You got the venue and your dress already," she said, looking impressed. "Good work."

"Yeah," I said, like it wasn't a big deal. I wanted to take a pair of scissors to that fucking dress ever since Pili stole my guitar. But Marina said we didn't have time to get a new dress made and we needed it to pattern hers and Rosalie's. I knew she was right and that made me even madder.

After school, my friends and I practiced our dance opening at the little park downtown, the one where Pili and I had conspired to throw dog shit at Margarita's house.

César came to at least one practice a week. He said he would absolutely have the routine down, no problem. A couple of times he and Marina even showed up together, though all Mari would say about it was they were "just talking." Little Rosalie, Zero's sixth-grade daughter, was there every time. It could have been worse: she wasn't a brat. She obviously thought we were really cool.

Everyone liked my Selena choice, basically because all of them could at least cumbia a little bit. I refused to have a "surprise" dance in the middle, and Marina knew better than to assign us ridiculous moves ripped from the drill team manual. So mostly, it was learning when and where to turn, and Marina coaching Ernie and me through spins.

She and César were amazing together. They spun and twirled, feinted, kicked, Marina's hips swaying like an ocean tide. César already knew how to spin her, how to guide her so she'd revolve like a top around him.

"I wish you two could be the lead dancers," I sighed, watching them. The quince was two weeks away and I still wasn't good.

"Well, we can't," César said, in Spanish. "Get up there. Ernie, you too."

Jorge, who wasn't in the quince, but still came out to watch us practice, thought the whole thing was hilarious. "Lulu, sorry but you suck."

"Maybe we should wear eyeliner," Olmec said. "Like, all the guys. Just to still be us."

"Everyone will be wearing a mask," Marina said. "Duh."

Jorge laughed. "Do it anyway! Then you can do your surprise dance to Type O Negative." He sang out, in a fake deep voice, "She's got a date at midnight with Nos-fer-a-tu. Oh baby, Lily Munster ain't got nothing on you!"

"No surprise dance," I said. "One is enough."

My dad drove up in his truck, Black Sabbath radiating from the cab. I walked over with Marina. He was wearing gold mirrored sunglasses, aviator-style. There was a Coors in the fork of his crotch. "Hey, y'all want some hamburgers?"

"Sure," I said. "I think we're wrapping up anyway."

"What is that?" he demanded suddenly, shutting off the truck engine. "What the hell is that?"

Marina and I looked at each other. I turned back to him, for once, completely mystified. "What's what?"

"That shirt. Where did you get that?"

It was my Gato Negro shirt. I didn't see what the problem was. It's not like he knew it was our band, or even that it was a band. But he was out of the truck now, a hand on my arm. It was scary.

"It's a T-shirt, Dad," I said, pulling away from him. "Let go."

"Where'd you get it?" he demanded. "Who gave it to you?"

Everyone was dead silent. I wondered if he'd haul me off in the truck in front of all of them, and I was so angry. God, always embarrassing me. Treating me like a kid. "It's from the thrift store."

Maybe he would have believed me, but then he looked around. Jorge was also wearing our band shirt. Goddammit.

"That pinche pelado is wearing the same one," my dad said. He snatched Jorge's collar in his fist. "Who the hell are you, vato?"

"Jorge Acosta," Jorge stammered. He was all bug-eyed. I don't think he'd ever feared any parent as much as he feared Jules Muñoz in that moment.

"Why are you wearing the same shirt as her? Huh? You went on a thrift-shopping date? Answer me, chavo."

"It's just a band, man," Jorge squeaked. Even César looked anxious, which was a total first.

"It's a band?" he asked, like he didn't believe it. "No it's not. Where'd you get it? Who gave it to you?"

"Dad, calm down! What's wrong with you?"

He seemed to register that everyone was watching him wolf out. He let go of Jorge and kind of shoved him away. "Everybody go home. Practice is over."

They all scattered. César took Marina and Rosalie. Olmec and Jorge left together. Ernie hesitated, but I shook my head. They were gone so fast. It was just my dad and me.

"What the hell, Dad? You're being crazy."

"You're lying," he said. "That's not a band."

I just didn't give a fuck anymore. He'd embarrassed me so bad. "It's *my* band, Dad."

"Your band?"

"Yeah. I'm in a band." I tapped my own chest. "We're Gato Negro."

"That little punk is your boyfriend?" he demanded.

"No," I scoffed. "He's the bassist."

"Which one is your novio?"

"I'm in the band because I'm a musician," I said. "Not to get a boyfriend. Give me a break."

"Oh, you're an *artist*," he jeered, in exactly the same tone he'd used on Margarita at the mall. "Excuse me."

"Yuck it up," I said. I hated him, just hated him, but also, he was so small to me in that moment. I could see him for what he actually was, just a bully. I kept my voice totally normal, like it wasn't anything. "I'm not like Margarita. I don't care what you think. You're just the guy who got my Gonzo killed. You're a loser."

He sucked in his breath like I'd slapped him. "Shut up! I would cancel your quince right now if I wasn't gonna lose the deposit on the venue."

"Cancel it. Good. Then I don't have to dance with you." I laughed at him, just as ugly as he ever did. "You're nothing but a pathetic drunk. I hate you!"

He popped me one across the cheek. Not as hard as he could, it was more surprising than painful. But yeah. He slapped me. Then he punched a bunch of dents in his truck. I guess so he wouldn't punch me.

——◇——

Chapter Sixteen

Selena Forever

Predictably, my dad kicked Olmec and Ernie out of the quince. He took my Gato Negro shirt, my stereo, my new lips phone. He even threw out the portable phone in the living room, so there was only the one in the kitchen, and of course, in his bedroom. He nailed my bedroom windows shut, which I secretly thought was hilarious since I'd never once used them to get out. That was about the only funny thing, though.

He kept on at me—where did I get this shirt? Who told me about the Black Cats? The more confused I got, the madder he was. I didn't tell him about the Converse sneaker. Then I'd have to say where we found it.

Tía Yoli backed my dad against me. Probably he didn't tell her about the slap. Or maybe he did and she didn't care? "I'm really disappointed in you. If you want people to take you seriously, you need to act responsibly."

"Did you know I balance my dad's checkbook?" I asked. "I'm on the honor roll too. What do you want from me?"

"Lose the attitude," Yoli said tartly. "And just be honest with us."

Be honest. I almost choked. Okay, I couldn't say, *I found out we're not related* without implicating myself. They didn't know about me hanging out with Pili, and I was going to keep it that way. But there were enough other things.

"Oh, like you were honest when you said Uncle Charlie was cheating? Or like him"—I pointed my chin toward my dad's workshop—"acting like he has *no idea why* someone killed Gonzo."

"Jesus Christ," she said, grabbing her own forehead. "Let's just get through this damned quince, okay?"

"Is that true?" I heard Yoli ask my dad later. They were out back, I guess thinking I wouldn't hear them. "Did your sancha's husband kill Lulu's dog?"

"I paid him back. Threw the carcass in his truck. Left him a note to come find me. That pussy never did."

"Do you even hear yourself?" Yoli demanded. "What is wrong with you? No wonder your kid needs therapy."

There was a long silence. Then my dad said, "Did you tell her about the Black Cats?"

"Why would I do that?"

"I don't know. Somebody did." I pressed my ear to the window hard.

"Look, Julio," my tía said. "I'll stay through the quince. After that, I'm going home. If you want me to take her with me, I will. Maybe she needs a change of scene for a while."

"So you're finally taking Charlie back, huh?"

"I said I'd come home if he stopped being an asshole to Carlos."

I heard my dad's grating, ugly laugh. "Guess you miss his bank account."

"Síguele," my tía said, in her most chingona tone. "But I'm telling you right now, Mom's gone. You're not anybody's consentido anymore. I can take Lulu with me, or you can deal with her yourself. But I am not rushing down here every time you make a mess. You better believe that's over."

"Fine, take her. It's better anyway," my dad snapped. He does not like being told *anything*. Still, I couldn't believe he gave me away so easy. My cheek felt hot against the window glass. I guess if you grew up knowing your own mom threw you away, why care what happens to your daughter? Yoli was acting like Grandma Romi, bringing home strays. Only this time, I was the stray.

"She can transfer after spring break," Yoli said. "That'll be a good time."

You know how much grown-ups suck? They didn't say anything to me about it. Nope. A little while later, my tía came into my bedroom to say her comadre Elida had offered her twins to be escorts in the quince. We could practice in Grandma's backyard from now on.

"Bummer," Jorge said when I told him and Olmec at school.

"At least there's a real music scene in H-town," Olmec offered. "Better than here."

It went completely sideways with Ernie though. We were sitting in his car at the lake. We'd skipped our last two classes. He told me it was going to be okay, not to worry. He said that *a lot*.

"We're gonna be fine," he said, squeezing my hand in his. "I bet it's just until the end of the year. I can drive to see you like once a month. More in the summer."

"Ernie, that's not the point. They just *decided this* without me. They haven't even told me to my face."

"I know. I'm just saying it doesn't mean we have to break up."

I was mean. I know that. But I did not have any bandwidth left to deal with Ernie being heartbroken and planning trips to Houston when my entire life was disintegrating. I was so incredibly aggravated that I said, "We can't break up. I'm not your girlfriend."

It was a long, awkward car ride back to school.

The only one who was right there with me was Marina. I didn't tell her until that evening because she'd skipped out of school to hang with César.

"Oh my God!" she said, voice trembling on the other end of the line. She's the kind that cries when she's really mad. "This is fucking bullshit!"

"I know," I said.

"And we can't even have any sleepovers because you're grounded. God-dammit."

"I know," I said again.

"You know what?" she said. "Fuck them. Fuck all of them."

I'm ready.

Today, I spent two hours at the Origins counter at Macy's for a full face of natural-looking makeup, and then another two hours at the salon. My hair is coiffed in one big, loose braid, artfully plaited sideways, so all my curls spill over one shoulder, a chain of gold and silver flowers woven through. My brows are sculpted. I've got fake French tips. I'm wearing the gold Virgin Mary pendant necklace. Tiny diamond studs in my ears. Real ones. They were my mother's. My dad is letting me wear them for my quince. They'll be mine someday.

I've done the official quinceañera photo shoot. My portrait is at Villa Verde right now, on an easel next to the guest registry.

All I need to do is put on my dress. I sit on my bed. I wait.

"The limo's going to be here in an hour," my dad yells from the living room. "I'm gonna take a shower."

"Okay," I call back. I sound pliant. I sound like any dutiful daughter, just before her quinceañera. I'm ready.

I hear his boots in the living room, clock, clock, clock, swift, but not rushed. The door of his bedroom shuts. My face is hot under the base and powder. I resist the urge to scratch it, even though it's so itchy.

There's my dress, hanging on my closet door in a plastic garment bag, like a body awaiting an autopsy. I unzip the bag, fling the dress on the bed. This stupid, hateful dress: silver and twinkling, with all that ballerina tulle. But okay. I slip it on and stand in front of my mirror.

Here I am. Fifteen. Today is my birthday. This is the woman. According to everybody, this is who I've been waiting to be. I don't feel it. I'm just a skinny girl in crispy, hair-sprayed curls and an overbright made-up face.

I go back into the closet, pull my sneakers out from the old dress bag at the very back, the one with my mother's wedding dress. I keep it behind my old jackets and that terrible, ugly shoe tree I took from Grandma Romi's house, the one that still has a bunch of my grandma's old sandals in it.

I set my shoes down lightly and reach into the dress bag again. There's the envelope I pinned to the bodice of my mother's wedding dress. All the money I have left. I set it on my dresser.

I slip out of the silver dress, let it fall in a silken heap in the middle of the floor. Right where my dad will find it.

I put on my tightest black jeans and my *Amor Prohibido* T-shirt. I'm kind of digging the hairdo after all, so I leave the metallic flowers and braid. The last thing I pull out of my closet is my dad's leather jacket. I've had it since the gig at Chaparral. He hasn't noticed it's gone. Maybe he thinks he left it at some bar or other, wherever he goes those nights he's away. I wonder just then how many things my dad has lost and never bothered to look for.

Well, this jacket's mine now. I love the smell of the leather, its weight. The way it creaks and jingles. Even the scuff marks. I pull it on, zip it up. Pad out of my room in my socks, shoes in hand, careful not to make noise. I walk out of the house, into the backyard, headed for my dad's workshop.

He'll notice I'm missing tonight. Even if it's only because I spoiled his party. I don't care. There's nothing else he can do to me.

It's not like there won't be good things about Houston. Marina will visit and we'll go to The Galleria and the IMAX. I'll hang the portrait of Gonzo, the one Ernie drew, right on my bedroom wall and nobody will yell at me for having it. I'll even get it framed. I'll go to school with rich white kids. It'll be just as obnoxious as that show, *My So-Called Life*.

In the yard everything is bright, the grass on my dad's new sod squares extra green, luscious. Fake. It's shining and cold, the desert winter, which is all light and no heat.

The workshop is unlocked. I stand for a moment, looking into the darkness, my socked feet squashing the grass on the cold sod squares. There's the shadow inside the shed. There it is, toward the back. The motorcycle, shining and black, glimmering in a mock repose, as though its nature was silent and not the hazy thunder of its movement, its restlessness.

Quietly, I let myself in, breathe the musty, oily air. My daddy's special motorcycle, with its shimmering black hair painted on the black gas tank, the eye of the woman barely visible. Watching. Waiting. It seems like she meets my eyes.

I see you. I see you too.

I slip inside and put on my sneakers in the dark. I go out the back of the shed, to the long gate at the back of the yard, the one my dad uses to drive in the truck, like when he brought home the sod. I open it enough to let the motorcycle slip through, but not enough for anyone glancing out the window to notice it's open.

I steady the bike, knock the kickstand away with my foot, begin to push it out the back of the shed. I can hear the gasoline in the tank slosh a little.

I wish I could keep it, this bike he's rebuilt a thousand times. It's the best of what he does. Tallish, but with the correct angulations for a small woman to ride, strutting the engine, strutting herself, lightweight and sparkling. It was my mom's. It should be mine, more than these diamond earrings.

The tires crunch the gravel, but quietly. Once I had it moving, a slow, thick roll as of a heavy thing coming to life, it was easy to maneuver it out of the shed. The grass is harder to push through, but even that was not so much. Then I'm through the gate and in the alley behind the house. There's caliche and dust, the pale whitish yellow of afternoon dirt dry from weeks without rain, puffing up around my feet. But the going is easier, even with the rocks.

I fix my eyes on the far end of the alley. Beyond it is the brush, the undeveloped part of the neighborhood. I'll be gone before they clear it. I push the motorcycle through the brush, come out on the other side, next to the highway. I throw my leg over.

"Push starts are for pussies," I murmur. Then I'm roaring down the highway, the wind snatching stars out of my hair.

"You're wearing your dress?" I laugh as I pull into the 7-Eleven parking lot. Marina is waiting, full-on glam in her ice-blue dress and a white faux rabbit-fur jacket.

"I look fantastic," she says. "And we paid money to have it made. I'm gonna wear it."

She's ditched the nude pumps my tía made all of us get for a pair of hot-pink slouch boots. With the flared tulle skirt and the furry jacket, she looks almost punk. At least Cyndi Lauper new-wave.

"And those boots?"

"They're my prima's. Who do you think dropped me off here? She thinks I'm going to your quince with a secret date."

"You're missing out on César escorting you," I tease.

"He's gross. He wanted me to go down on him and when I said no, he said he doesn't date freshmen anyway."

"What a douchebag," I say. Marina has a haughty lift to her chin. Pride, and something else. Maybe she didn't say no. Maybe something worse happened. Pilar's words flash in me: *He's bad news.* But do I believe that? I don't know.

"Wish I could see his face when he figures out I ditched him," she laughs. She climbs on the bike behind me. "Let's get out of here."

At a red light just before the turn onto the highway, a man my dad's age calls at us from his truck window. "Hey chulas! Where y'all going?"

"Selena!" Marina and I scream as the light turns green. "Selena!"

I rev the engine ear-bleedingly loud, blotting out whatever pura mamada is about to come out of his mouth. We hurtle away, the Harley growling beneath us, our wild laughter snatched up by the wind.

Tickets at the door are forty dollars apiece. Near the fairground entrance there are vendor stalls everywhere: for beer, for food, for band merchandise, everything swarmed by concertgoers. Marina and I buy a couple of water bottles and head toward the music.

We're late enough that the opening band, Ernie's family group, Conjunto Vega, has already played. He's probably here somewhere, but I don't see him. There's another band onstage, one I'm not familiar with, Bronco or maybe Pesado. Marina would know. Whoever they are, the whole group wears skintight red satin western outfits, enormous gold belt buckles, and black hats. The accordion player is grinding out brokenhearted polka strains on a twinkling gold accordion.

It's an outdoor theater. There's a half circle of tiered rows sloping down toward an open grassy area right in front of the stage. Through the swirl of red and blue lights, I see a lot of available seats, though that could be because so many couples are dancing in the grass.

"Is he singing 'I hope you die'?" I ask as we make our way toward the grassy area.

"It's about getting dumped. He's bitter," Marina says, and then blurts out, "Oh, hey."

"What's up?" It's Ernie, appearing out of the crowd. Marina immediately leaves, saying she's going to stake out a place by the stage. That traitor.

Ernie's in all ropa vaquera: black Stetson hat, super tight Wrangler jeans, boots, and even a western blazer with rhinestone designs, just like a real Tejano musician. He looks taller, older too, like he could actually go on tour with some hot new Tejano band. He could do it. He's the most talented guy I know.

"You look good," I say. It's the truth and it hurts.

"I opened for Selena," he says, a little cocky. He's got a big yellow VIP pass on a lanyard hanging in the middle of his chest. "Why aren't you at your quince?"

"My dad's getting rid of me. Might as well do what I want."

"You always do," Ernie says. He's got a massive scowl under the cowboy hat. But I don't want to fight.

"Sorry I missed your show," I say, even though I'm not. I'm so glad Marina and I were late. Watching him onstage would tear my heart to bits. "Did you get to meet Selena?"

"Yeah." Even though he's so mad, he breaks out a giant grin. How could he not? "She's fucking awesome. For real."

"Oh my God," I say. I want to ask a million questions, but someone yells his name from the food area—"Ernesto!" His dad or maybe an uncle. He waves at them to wait, but when he turns back to me, I can tell he's got to scram. I bite back my questions.

"They're looking for you," I say, trying to sound casual. "Don't let me keep you."

"Yeah, I gotta go," he says. I can't see his face so well, not under the black brim of his hat, the flickering lights of the concert. But he swoops down so suddenly, pulls me close, kisses me high on the cheek. "Happy birthday, Lulu."

It takes everything I have not to clutch him to me. Oh my God, it's so hard. If I do it, if I just squeeze my fingers on his arms, he'll stay. But I can't be a selfish jerk every waking moment. So I just say, "Thanks, Ernie."

"I'll see you," he says. He goes. All I see is his black cowboy hat as he leaves, gets sucked into the crowd. I swallow hard and walk away.

Marina is right up front, just a little left of center, one arm across the metal guardrail, saving my spot. She waves wildly, like I am not looking right at her.

"And?" she demands.

"We're good. I think."

"Long distance was never gonna work," Marina says. "Amor de lejos."

"Amor de pendejos," I agree.

Marina puts an arm around my waist, bumps her hip against me, dancing a cumbia in place.

"Don't worry," she yells over the sound of the band. "You still got me."

"Always," I say. She moves me like a river current and I bend with her.

The band plays for another half hour, belting out polkas and cumbias. A few times guys ask Marina to dance, but she says no, she doesn't want to lose her place. They're not even mad about it.

I zip up my jacket, glad I wore it. Even under the lights and at the edge of the crowd of dancers, it's cold. I am not out of place in my leather motorcycle jacket. Most of the crowd is dressed vaquero, cowboy hats and Wranglers, women in Rocky Mountain jeans, but there are plenty of dudes in heavy metal T-shirts, even girls in black baby doll dresses and heavy goth makeup. Everybody loves Selena.

It's past eight o'clock. Yoli is probably in the big event room at Villa Verde, flanked by her comadres Renata and Elida. Their families settling themselves in their places, every table covered with white linen, and in the center, a tiny candy bowl filled with mints. Zero and his wife, their daughter Rosalie in her floofy dress. Snobby César, standing around looking confused and ridiculous. Every person my dad and tía invited, every one of them signing the guest registry and grabbing a glitter mask from the party favor table, just to keep with the masquerade theme. Restless guests probably finishing the mints, waiting for the quince court to make their entrance. The DJ playing song after song. The pounds and pounds of catered brisket barbeque, the iced tea. That enormous pink frosting quinceañera cake.

What would my dad say to them? Would he feed them anyway, give everyone an obligatory slice of cake? Would he leave it all to Yoli to figure out? Maybe they'd make up a cover story—I'd twisted my ankle, come down with the flu. I could totally see my dad making up some insane lie about me, right on the spot too. I feel a little bad about the waste, the whole waste of it, but only a little.

I push that feeling away fast. Selena's band is onstage. There's her siblings, Suzette and A.B., and the guitarist with the glasses and ponytail, that's Selena's husband, Chris. There are other band members onstage, backup singers, a keyboardist, another guitarist, but those are the only ones I care about. Everyone wears satin burgundy shirts and black jeans.

They jump into the opening of "Como la Flor." The crowd around me goes absolutely nuts, everyone screaming and rushing to the front. Marina and I clutch the metal bar, buffeted by so many bodies, but we don't give ground.

Marina squeals in my ear. "Here she comes!"

Selena saunters onto the stage, smiling at everyone, waving, asking how we're doing out there, saying how glad she is to see us all. Her hair is long and loose down her back, bangs curled and slightly lifted away from her brow. She wears a burgundy crop top, if you can even call it a top. It's teeny tiny, basically a bra, except that, somehow, it has off-the-shoulder sleeves. Enormous, billowing black and burgundy flamenco ruffle sleeves, like she's in a Cuban swing band. She wears high-waisted black jeans, a silver conch belt, black ankle boots. Her jeans are insanely tight, clinging to every curve of her thick, thick thighs and that staggering, heart-shaped pompis.

"I'm gonna sing a song for you all. It was a big hit for us, our first big hit," she says, walking leisurely around the stage. "It goes something like this." Everyone just screams and screams.

She walks to the middle of the stage, stands there, one foot slightly ahead of the other, and pointed. She tilts her face toward the sky and lets loose the opening lyrics, husky and soaring, brokenhearted. She half shuts her eyes, pouty lips trembling with every grieving line. Her enormous ruffles shiver up and down as she twists her hands above her head.

And then the funniest thing happens. She pops her eyes open and grins at us, a big, toothy grin. She's goofing on us, making everybody love her more. We are all on tiptoes, hanging on her every breath. She whispers the word "but," in this breathy voice, and the crowd screams "ay-ay-ay" with her, and then the cumbia beat bursts forth and everybody is grooving.

Selena dances across the stage, hips flashing, arms snaking into the air. Marina does her best washing machine. I throw back my head and let out a piercing grito, just as loud as anything Olmec can do.

Beside me, a man in a black Stetson and a salt-and-pepper goatee gives me a one-armed hug and throws a grito too.

Selena takes us through cumbia after cumbia, then switches it up with a Spanish pop song, "Enamorada de Ti." She bounces, actually bounces, in the air, throwing hip-hop moves like she's one of the Fly Girls on *In Living Color*. The Roger Rabbit, the running man, ending with furious crisscrossing footwork. She crosses the stage, singing, still swaying, perfectly on beat the entire time.

The song ends and she stalks the stage like a panther. The band keeps playing, slower, some vibing good beat. She walks right by me, so close I can hear her catching her breath. For a second, I think she looks at me, maybe, but then she's past, headed for the other side of the stage.

"I need a good actor," she says, one hip cocked out. "Any guys out there want to volunteer?"

The crowd roars, dudes are trying to climb over each other to get to the stage. Marina and I grab each other and push against the tide of fans pressing us against the stage barricade.

"Are you okay?" Marina gasps. "Can you breathe?"

"I'm not fucking leaving," I pant.

"Truth," she says.

Somehow, a guy gets fished out of the horde of men. He's a dark-haired fella in his twenties, dressed vaquero in a cowboy shirt and Wranglers, though no hat. Probably he lost it on the way up to the stage. He smooths his hair nervously as Selena approaches him.

"Okay, what's your name?" She points the mic at him.

"Francisco," he says. "Francisco Gomez."

"Tonight, Francisco, you're gonna make your debut in acting." She paces around him, sizing him up, then stands next to him. She turns to face the crowd. "Tonight, you're going to be *my ex-boyfriend.*"

Everyone screams, including me. Francisco says something to her, but nobody can hear him. Selena says, full of sass, "Baby, we ain't got time for that."

She puts her hand out, lightly touches his chest. "Okay, stand over here and behave yourself." She winks at the audience. "Just let me do the talking."

Francisco nods. He's blushing ferociously, but he can't stop smiling. He stands there, just like she said to. If she wanted him to moo like a cow, he would do it.

"Ladies," she says, and Marina and I whoop as loud as we can. "Pay close attention."

Selena walks slowly up to Francisco, gets close enough that their noses are almost touching, her face lifted up to his, just the mic between them, like she is going to kiss him. I think he thinks so too.

"¿Qué Creías?" she whispers into the mic, right in his face.

Beside me, Marina starts bouncing up and down and yelling, "Yes yes yes yes yes!" It's her absolute favorite song by Selena. It's not Tejano or pop, it's straight up classical ranchera with mariachi accompaniment.

On cue, a band of mariachis files onto the stage. Selena pokes Francisco lightly again, singing at him, all scorned ex-girlfriend attitude and throaty growl. *What, you thought I was just here waiting for you?* She throws herself on her knees in front of Francisco. *You thought I'd be thrilled to have you back?* We are all screaming and stamping our feet. Selena arches her back as she sings, holding the note impossibly long. She hops to her feet in one light motion, saunters up to Francisco again. It's like he's made of grins and beet-red blushes. She pretends to brush something off his shirt, and then sings out, full of power and self-respect, *No, it's not that way.* She skips across the stage and acts like she's flinging something out to the crowd. *So you can leave.*

Marina and I are smashed against the stage barricade, having to shove people away just to breathe. My feet keep getting stepped on every few minutes. None of that matters. I can't drag my eyes away from Selena. She owns the stage. She owns the audience. She owns me.

"This is the best night of my life!" Marina screams in my ear. I can barely hear her over the crowd, over Selena's gorgeous siren song, the full complement of mariachi horns. But I'm right there with her. I never want this night to end.

We stop at the Peter Rabbit convenience store because it's after midnight and Peter Rabbit is the only one still open that sells Choco Tacos.

"Dude, you have to go back in and wash your hands," I say. I'm holding her rabbit-fur jacket. "You're gonna mess up your fur with nasty-ass Choco Taco bits."

"I was starved though," Marina says, burping. "Be right back."

My feet are aching from standing so long and from getting stepped on.

I kick-start the bike so I'm ready when Marina comes back out. Just a few feet away, the person at the red light turns at the sound of the Harley coughing to life. It's Renata, Yoli's comadre. Her window is open. Under the streetlight I can see her clear as day. Her makeup is wrecked. Her lips curl back in a snarl so big I can see all her teeth.

"You little shit," she yells at me just as Marina emerges from the store. "You absolute little bitch!"

"Come on!" I holler at Marina. She leaps onto the bike and we tear ass out of the parking lot.

"Oh fuck!" Marina gasps as we speed away. "You're in so much trouble."

"Worth it," I yell into the wind. It is. My dad took everything from me. He can never get this night back. Never. It's totally worth it.

Marina's wrong though. I don't get in trouble. When I arrive, all the lights are on in the house. Someone should be here waiting to give me five and a half pieces of their mind, but nobody's home. Fear engulfs me, cold and black as the lake water I almost drowned in the night my grandma died. I know this silence already, the sound of my own guilt in an empty room. What have I done?

I rush to the kitchen for the phone. There's a note on the kitchen counter. *Come to the hospital. Your dad had a heart attack.*

The story they'll tell about that quinceañera goes like this:

It was like Cinderella's ball, the clock striking midnight, only backward. The party had started, tables filling up, swirling lights on the dance floor, the air filled with perfume and the rustling of beautiful dresses. There were the escorts, standing around in their tuxes. There was the table of gifts, piled high. There was the girl's portrait, on the easel beside the fancy pink cake. There was her father, charging around the kitchens, the bathrooms, even the parking lot. Because nobody could find the quince, no way no how.

An hour went by, and still nothing, only the DJ playing song after song, just to keep people happy. The waiters served dinner. The guests were too embarrassed to eat, but they had to stay because no one would admit the quince wasn't coming. They waited and waited, but her father wouldn't cancel the party.

They say there was a woman. Nobody knew who she was, but that was not strange because it was a masquerade quinceañera, almost everyone was masked. That woman, though, hers was a gorgeous black mask, the eyes outlined in red paste jewels, dyed red plumes rising from the temples. She wore a gown of crushed red velvet, big swinging sleeves. Her hair was long and black, flowing over one shoulder in a thick braid. She was like a little fluttering cardinal the way she ran outside to the courtyard. Because the quince's father had seen her and followed her.

The quince's father yelled at her under the black canopy of sky. "Where is my daughter?"

"I thought she'd be here," the woman said. "I came to see her beautiful party."

"You have no right."

"I have every right. I planned this party for her. No one else would help her. Only me."

"You lie," the quince's father said. "Leave! Get out!"

Oh, then she tilted her head at him. Took off the mask. In the moonlight she could have been any age. Her eyes were huge and dark, shining like an animal's, like the gleam on the surface of a lake. "I'm not a liar. That's something I never was."

They say she said his name, just once. They say the quince's father fell in a thunderclap, a bolt of lightning, in the space of a breath. They say the woman ran away, leaving her plumed mask on the ground beside him.

That's what the story will be tomorrow, and the day after, in ten years or thirty, when no one remembers whose quince it was or when it happened. They'll remember the strange woman in a gorgeous dress. How just by saying his name, she struck the man down.

—◇—

Chapter Seventeen

Mala Yerba Nunca Muere

Jules Muñoz, survivor of attempted infanticide, car accidents and bar fights, vengeful husbands, and, somehow, his own insane drinking. My dad's walked away from it all. Like Grandma Romi used to say, *Mala yerba nunca muere.* Weeds never die. Only this time he didn't walk away unscathed.

A few days after the quince that didn't happen, he was still in the hospital. Recovering. Drying out too. Shaking and sweating, mad as a dog shitting tacks, contradicting the doctors and their lab results. No, he didn't have a drinking problem. No, he wasn't going through withdrawal. No no no no. Absolutely not.

My dad's pendejadas nearly drove Yoli to fits. I found them comforting. He still had his fighting spirit. He'd make it through this.

I wasn't allowed to visit. Yoli said the sight of me would probably rile him right into another infarction. I couldn't fault her thinking. But still, I wore his leather jacket every day to keep a piece of him with me. Maybe that's even why I'd worn it, all those times I snuck away.

But he wanted to talk to me. So Yoli had finally agreed, and we were going to call his room at seven o'clock, after his dinner. She bristled with warnings.

"I don't give a shit what he says to you," she said before dialing, the telephone receiver clutched in her fist like a weapon. "You *cannot* fight with him right now. He could die. Do you understand that? Don't. Argue. With. Him."

I nodded. Since it happened, I constantly caught the rough side of her tongue. I was staying at Grandma's house with her, so mostly, I kept my mouth shut. Truth was, I didn't remotely want to fight. Not now. I just wanted him to be okay.

I almost went to pieces when I heard his voice. He sounded alert, but smaller, like the attack had eaten a part of him. "Mija?"

"Daddy," I said, my eyes and throat burning. There would always be a five-year-old inside me, anxious and wanting him. "When are you coming home?"

"Maybe a week," he said. "If the food doesn't kill me. I keep telling your tía to smuggle me some Chucho's, but she never does."

"Yeah, I'm so sure she's gonna bring fried chicken."

"How about you? You okay?"

"Yeah," I said. "Just here at Grandma's. I got a ninety-five on my math test today."

He laughed, a surprising sound, bubbling clear and liquid into my ear. "I got the only delinquent kid on the honor roll."

"Is that why you're sending me to live with Yoli in Houston? Because I'm a delinquent?"

"Goddammit," Yoli hissed. She stalked out of the room, fed up with the both of us.

"Ay, Lucha," my dad said. I heard the telephone clicking like he was shifting around. "It's me, okay? I'm fucking it up. I've *been* fucking up. You need to go with your tía because of me. Look where I'm at. You didn't put me here. Neither did that pinche vieja loca."

"I didn't know she was gonna show up. Seriously, I had no idea."

"Yeah, she was mad you weren't there."

I said nothing. Jesus, I was dense. Of course, Pili had planned to come to my quince. That's why she'd wanted masks for the guests. It didn't matter that we'd fallen out either. She was still going to come to the party.

"She's the one who told you, right?" my dad asked suddenly. "About the Black Cats.

"I want you to know it was an accident. We were trying to shut down the factory so people could vote for Felix," he said. "Maybe it was me and Zero. Maybe it wasn't. There were a bunch of us there that night."

"Felix." Hadn't I thought of him, seeing the graffiti cat? I should have known.

"He was El Gato. The Black Cats, we were his supporters. We were doing it for him and look what happened." His breath sounded labored. I couldn't tell if he was crying or having chest pain. "That's why I try to tell you, be careful who you run with."

"Are you okay?" I asked, alarmed. "Hey, are you okay?"

"I'm bad for you," he said. "That's why you gotta go. You gotta go before I mess up your life like I messed up mine. Don't be like me, mija."

"You aren't bad, Daddy," I said, out of reflex. I felt sick to my stomach. "Anyway, why would Pilar know that?"

"She saved me that night."

"She didn't tell me that," I said. Pili had never said a word about that to me, not the whole time I knew her.

"I think she did it for your grandma. Because your grandma did something for her. A big thing. Your grandma told Yolanda that and Yolanda told me, a long time ago."

"What was it?" I thought of those photographs. The little cowboy. The charro on the horse. The horse blanket story about my dad, which was . . . true? Suddenly, I realized I didn't know anything about Pili and Grandma Romi, together, being comadres. I didn't know anything about them at all. I never would.

"Your grandma didn't tell Yoli what it was." The way he said it, I could tell my dad knew that I was aware of who Pili was to him, to us. He just couldn't speak the words out loud.

"No te digo," Renata said, pausing to inhale a load of smoke. "When I saw her at the Peter Rabbit on that motorcycle! Lord, quería agarrarla de las puras greñas. ¡Meterle unas buenas! But she and that other one, n'ombre! They took off so fast."

Renata and Yoli were sitting out on Grandma's front steps, smoking cigarettes and drinking wine in the dark. I could see them through the translucent blue curtain of the living room window. It was only about eight thirty. They'd probably stay out there for at least another hour.

"Girl, I let her drive the motorcycle home from the ER," Yoli replied. "I tried to get Zero to do it, but the kick start was too tricky for him. Little Evel Knievel Jr started it, no problem."

"Sounds like Julio has the daughter he deserves," Renata said. "Who else taught her that?"

They giggled together, just the way Marina and I do. Comadres just getting started on a good plática.

"Seriously," Yoli said, her tone a little lower, her laughter gone. "When I found out Lulu was spending time with that psycho, I wanted to pull her hair out myself."

"Pilar Aguirre," Renata whispered. "My mother told me that she was very beautiful, I mean, hermosa. Pero qué celosa. All her good looks and she was convinced her husband was married to someone else. She went insane from jealousy. That's why he ended up leaving her."

"Someone told her he had another wife," Yoli said softly. I edged closer to hear her. Yoli was staring into the darkness, toward Loma Negra, the smoke curls from her cigarette floating into the air. "An old, old lady. I was playing outside when it happened. She was there demanding to see Pilar's husband. They got in a fight."

"No me digas," Renata said, eyes wide. "He really had another wife?"

"It wasn't true. I saw the old woman again a few months later, close to my mom's birthday," Yoli said. She ran a hand through her hair. Took a long drag off her cigarette. "Across the border. I was with my dad at Gonzaga bakery. We were buying my mother pan dulce." She paused to smoke again. "That old lady came in while we were there. Yelling that Gonzaga's son was her husband. Armando, the oldest. She knew his name and everything. But he was only seventeen!"

"Who was she?"

"Just some old lady," Yoli replied, stubbing out her cigarette. "Not right in the head. Gonzaga said she did that to a lot of young men. He knew her. He called her brother to pick her up."

"You didn't tell your mom?"

"No," Yoli said. "I was eight years old. That lady scared the shit out of me. I didn't want her to come back to my house."

I stood there listening for the longest time, but Yoli didn't say anything else. Renata asked about my cousin Carlos, if he was still not talking to Yoli. I knew they'd be on that for a while, so it was safe to use the phone.

Pili picked up after just one ring. I guess she knew I'd call eventually. "Is it you?" she asked.

"Yeah."

"You ruined my party."

I heard a light, fast clicking sound. Pili furiously tapping a manicured nail on her kitchen table. She was mad. But I was mad too. "You stole my guitar. I want it back."

"You know where I am." She hung up.

I still had a few minutes before nine o'clock. I called Marina.

"What's up? Any word on your dad?"

"He might come home next week," I said. "Hey, can you meet me tomorrow by Loma Negra, right at four? I'm gonna get my guitar back."

"Let's do it," Marina said.

My quinceañera portrait was in Grandma Romi's storage building. Former apartment, I remembered as I stepped into the dim kitchen after school the next day. Once upon a time Pili had lived here with her family. Because she and Grandma were friends, or was this how they became friends?

Someone, probably Yoli, had set up the easel right beside the kitchen sink. The portrait was on it, though that same person had covered it with an old pillowcase. To protect it or because it was a testament to my family's public humiliation. I didn't remove the pillowcase. I'm sure I saw the photo right before the quince that wasn't, but I couldn't recall it. I didn't want to see it now. Marina was waiting.

"I should go with you," she said when I got to the foot of Loma Negra. She was all business in an oversized hoodie and high-tops, her hair slicked back in a horsetail.

"No, just be lookout. She'll be weird if I bring someone."

"She's already fucking weird."

"I mean more difficult. I just want to get this over with."

"Okay." Marina stuck her fists in her hoodie. "But I'm waiting right there on the trail. If something feels off, I'm coming."

I agreed. We made our way up the hill.

My Epiphone was on the porch, winking blue reflections at me in the sunlight. Pilar was nowhere in sight. I wasn't fooled. As soon as I got close enough, Wicho raced up to me barking his head off.

"Hey good boy." I set the portrait in the grass, out of harm's way, so I could cuddle him. It was true enough I'd missed Wicho, that I would miss him. At least I knew his life was awesome. Pili took particular care of him, as she did with all her things.

I gathered up my package and walked across the yard. The garage we'd used for months stood open, both doors wide. It was completely empty except for the little red truck parked inside. A sign was staked in the grass near the front steps of the house: For Sale. Dominguez Realty.

"Come in," Pili said from behind the screen door. "Talk to me."

She was sitting in her living room on the red chair she'd kept out on the porch. She looked as she always did, small and birdlike, eyes quick, taking in everything. Same thick black plait across one shoulder. She was wearing a fuzzy white pullover and a pair of pink stonewashed jeans. Lip gloss tinted the same color as the jeans. White Reeboks.

"Selling the place, huh?"

"I'm getting old," Pilar said. "I need to bring Joselito to his new resting place, where I live now. So we can be together."

She meant the little cowboy. A shudder went through me. Loving someone, grieving for them so long. God, that's a lot of pain.

"Why did you do it? Why did you ruin the party?" she demanded.

"I was mad at my dad. He's making me move to Houston."

"So you got back at him," she said, more to herself than to me. Revenge always made sense to her. "Where were you?"

"At Selena." We said it at the same time. She'd asked, then answered herself. I almost smiled. She knew me that much.

"So you got to see her after all. But look what happened to your father."

"He had a heart attack. It wasn't because I skipped the quince for a concert."

"My husband died of a heart attack. Years after he left me."

"So it's genetic," I said. "And my dad's alive."

"Of course he's alive," she said, in the calmest voice imaginable. Like she was explaining how gravity worked, or the water cycle. "Nothing can hurt him while I walk this earth. He's my penance."

"What?"

"Come see this." She stood up, headed for her bedroom.

I almost didn't follow her. She was too spooky. Maybe unhinged. I thought of what my dad had told me, that she'd saved him for Grandma Romi. "What are we doing?"

She didn't answer. Reluctantly I moved down the brief hallway. Almost everything was gone from the bedrooms. The larger room was completely empty. The smaller one had furniture: a bed and a big wardrobe with a mirror. The faded wallpaper with cartoon trains was still there. It hit me that this was the little cowboy's room and I stopped on the threshold.

"Pili?"

"I want you to see it," she said, sounding just the way she always did all those afternoons of band practice. She wanted my attention, my opinion. She cared what I thought. "My dress."

She pulled a garment bag out of the wardrobe. She spread a dress across the bed: claret red, satin, with a sweetheart neckline and wide, swooping skirts. The bodice and the bottom of the gown were scalloped with black netting. Elegant, gorgeous. A real gown for a masquerade ball.

"Jesus," I said. "You made this?"

Again, she didn't answer me. She dug in the bottom of the garment bag, pulled out a drawstring bag, the kind Yoli keeps her fancy purses in. Carefully lifted out a plumed mask. She put the mask to her face and turned to me. "I had it special ordered. Isn't it lovely?"

"I bet you had the best costume of anyone there," I said, my heart thumping hard. Her eyes behind the black mask looked even lighter than usual. It made her that much scarier.

"Your grandmother wanted me to make peace with . . . your father. I can't. I can't. It's too hard." Pili fixed the mask in place, evaluating herself in the wardrobe mirror. "But you. I could help you. I did help you. Didn't I?"

"Yes," I said. It was the truth. "But I'm here for my guitar."

"Did you bring me a picture, like you said you would?" she asked, suddenly gruff.

"What do you think's in the pillowcase?"

She pulled the mask off quick as quick. "Show it to me."

"Well, come outside. There's better light on the porch."

Marina was standing at the edge of the yard when Pili and I came out of the house. I motioned for her to wait. I pulled the pillowcase off the portrait, leaned it against the house.

"Here it is," I said.

It's a studio photograph. I'm standing slightly in front of a retro blue velvet divan, everything else shadowed, chiaroscuro. It looks like I'm emanating silver light: the shining trail of butterflies down the bodice, the tulle skirt a metallic cloud floating around my legs. Even my hair, darted with gleaming threads. In my hands is my silver mask, glittery and bejeweled, plumed with ice-blue feathers. I'm lifting it slightly, as if I'm about to put it on.

I looked alien, not really me. Smoothed by makeup and the weird plastic smile the photographer coaxed onto my face. Nonetheless, I could see, a little, what I'd look like when I'm grown.

"It's perfect," Pili said, staring at the portrait. She covered her mouth with both hands, hard little sobs bursting out between her fingers. Not crying, but only just. A tiny old lady who was the strangest person I would ever meet. "This is just what I wanted. This is what I've always wanted."

"It's yours," I said. "I promised."

I slung my Epiphone across my back. "I'm gonna go, okay?"

"Yes, of course. I understand," she said, lifting the portrait, holding it to her body. She gazed at me in that way that only she had, unsmiling and still, and yet unspeakably happy. Maybe you had to know her to see it. But she was. Something was finally right for her.

"Gracias, mija."

I found I couldn't answer. I nodded goodbye and turned away fast. Maybe she watched me go. Maybe not.

MALAS

* * *

It was near dusk when Marina and I got back to the Caimanes barrio. We were at the cross street to my grandma's house when a grito cut across the low hum of traffic. A vato listening to rancheras, grilling meat on a mild winter evening, sentimental as fuck.

I threw a grito too. It shuddered out of me, wild, powerful, like a tidal wave about to break, all the things my head and my heart couldn't hold. Which I guess is the reason we throw gritos, or maybe we'd fly into little bitty pieces. The ranchera music cut off abruptly.

A dad-voice, startled. "Who the fuck is out there?"

"Run!" Marina yelled, pulling me along.

Hand in hand we pelted to my grandmother's house. Scream-laughing so hard we could barely breathe and run. We knocked into each other, staggered, held each other up, choked on our own mirth, our hair in our faces, our whole lives before us.

Acknowledgments

———◇———

For generous support during the writing of this book, many thanks to the Iowa Writers' Workshop, Georgia State University, and the Wisconsin Institute for Creative Writing. Many thanks also to the Macondo Writers Workshop and the good folks I met in these places. Special thanks to Connie Brothers, Deb West, and Jan Zenisek at Iowa, for their invaluable support.

Muchísimas gracias to my family, especially Robert and Sam, my brothers and stalwarts, whose love and confidence has sustained me through the years. To my two wonderful sisters-in-law, Shelley and Angela, the heavy lifters for the family. To my mother, Queta, my tía Alma, Tía Boni, and my grandma Angela, for your strength and wisdom, for your pride in me. Thank you, family. I love you all beyond words.

Mil gracias to my comadres Lety Contreras Moreno, Khaliah Williams, Ann Rushton, and Kecia Lynn, for the heart-to-hearts, the parties, the balcony chats and phone calls, your abiding love. To Vanessa Chan for being a screaming cheerleader and helping me navigate these waters. To

ACKNOWLEDGMENTS

Jason England, for your brilliance and humor, for always looking out. Much love and gratitude to Manuel Muñoz for your advice and mentorship, for giving me ánimo when I needed it, for your good, good heart, for being the tremendous, inspiring talent that you are, for believing in me, siempre.

Many thanks to my first mentor and writing teacher, Mitch Berman. Thank you for teaching me to love revision, and for urging me on all these years.

Big-time gracias to my super-chingona agent, Michelle Brower, for the sing-alongs and stolen wine, and for wholeheartedly championing my book. To Nat Edwards, Allison Malecha, Khalid McCalla, and the entire Trellis team, for your tireless advocacy and your confidence in me.

Special gracias to my editor, Laura Tisdel, for your insight, for unerringly drawing out emotional depth from my characters, for the inspiring chats. Thank you for loving my book. To Brianna Lopez and the whole Viking editorial and production editorial team, for your care and acuity. To Jason Ramirez for my gorgeous book cover. To everyone on the Viking team, thank you.

Thank you to more friends, family, and fellow writers than I can possibly name, for your kindness, guidance, good conversations, encouragement, and friendship over the years. In particular, Eduardo C. Corral, Rigoberto González, Santiago Vaquera-Vásquez, Rolando Hinojosa-Smith, Norma Elia Cantú, Matt Sailor, Jocelyn Heath, Stephanie Devine, Rachel Wright, Kristin Hayter Amberg, Angelique Stevens, Mary Terrier, Jeff Snowbarger, Sterling Holywhitemountain, Derrick Austin, Sarah Fuchs, Desiree Zamorano, Erika T. Wurth, Tisha Marie Reichle-Aguilera, Jamel Brinkley, Marta Evans, Pritha Bhattacharyya, Jemima Wei, Heather Swan, Jon Hickey, Dionne Irving, Denne Michele Norris, Ayşe Papatya Bucak, Laura Spence-Ash, Rubén Degollado, Eileen G'sell, Misha Rai,

ACKNOWLEDGMENTS

Elizabeth McCracken, Edward Carey, Rebecca Makkai, Tiana Clark, Alexander Chee, Lan Samantha Chang, Marilynne Robinson, Josh Russell, Judith Claire Mitchell, Jesse Lee Kercheval, Emily Shelter, Jenny Seidewand, Deborah Taffa, Isaac Zisman, Timothy Bradley, Xochitl Gonzalez, Danielle Evans, Bobby Muñoz, Chris Saldaña, Brian Argabright, Inez Reyna, Lety Ramos, Mari Sandoval, Aaron Martinez, Tony Moreno, Katy Peel Williams, Guillermina Bósquez Gallegos, Susan McBee, Regina Mills, Emily Johansen, and Mikko Tuhkanen.

Deepest gratitude and love to my father, Roberto Fuentes, for being the sun in my sky, for constantly talking in stories, for his lionheartedness, his fabulous style, his wisdom and foolishness, for giving me his love of music and history and justice, for teaching me to dream and dream and dream until it's real. I wouldn't be a writer without him. Dad, I love you with all my heart. I'll see you on the other side, cowboy.